THE COMMAND

"Evvy, Daughters of the Garden can marry. As Principal I can have a wife of my own, unshared."

She swallowed. "I'm sure many women would be honored to be your wife."

"I don't want any woman! I want you. I've wanted you for a very long time. You must have sensed it."

"I sensed something when I was younger. It frightened me then."

"You're not frightened now?"

"No."

"Then come with me."

Evvy clasped her hands together and took a long breath. "I can't. I love another man."

"What other man?" he asked, shocked. He could feel his temper rising like boiling water. He looked at her as if through a fog, trying to understand what she was saying. Then, suddenly, with a certainty that froze him, he knew. The man she loved was Zach.

Also by Kathryn Lance

Pandora's Children

Published by
POPULAR LIBRARY

PANDORA'S GENES

GENES

Kathryn Lance

POPULAR LIBRARY

An Imprint of Warner Books, Inc.

A Warner Communications Company

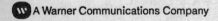

To Nan Schubel,
with love and thanks

PART ONE

Zach

One

He knew they had been expecting him. When Zach rode into the dusty yard, scattering the fowl, a face almost immediately appeared in the small window at the front of the cabin, and another peeked from behind a corner. Slowly, he climbed down and tethered his mount to the wooden rail which ran along one side of the house, then stretched to get the stiffness out of his limbs. It had been a very long ride, and he was not young.

The door opened and a small man stepped out, dressed in leather trousers and a worn cotton tunic. He was followed by a woman, also wearing trousers in the northern fashion. A dirty boy-child clung to her, sucking his thumb.

"Yes, stranger?" said the man.

"Marson and Eugenia?" The little man grunted assent. "I am Zach, delegate of the Principal. You were told to expect me." He showed his seal ring.

"The arrangements have all been made?" The little man looked at once nervous and greedy.

"Yes." The man relaxed and stole a glance at his wife. She looked away. Zach spoke again: "The girl is ready?" The man nodded. The three stood for a moment, not looking directly at one another, then the woman turned to her husband.

"He must be tired and hungry," she said.

The little man grimaced slightly, not hiding his distaste at sharing hospitality with Zach. Clearly this was not a question of thrift—it was obvious the family had barely enough for themselves, but like District people everywhere they would be honor-bound to share with a visitor. This was not the first time

3

Zach had been hated while in service to the Principal, and it would not be the last.

"Come inside." Marson abruptly turned and followed his wife through the door. Zach had to duck his head and, once inside, found he could not stand up quite straight except to one side of the long room. It was large and bare, with fresh rushes spread over the packed-dirt floor. Most of the space was overhung with a loft which dropped perhaps twenty inches from the roof. This appeared to be used by the family for sleeping. Although his head cleared the bottom edge of the loft, Zach could not see anything beyond darkness and heaped bedding. A long table flanked by benches, two rickety stools, a loom, and a straight-backed rocking chair completed the furnishings. At the far end of the room was a large fireplace, with a heavy metal cooking pot set on a rack.

"Sit," said Marson, offering Zach the chair.

"Thank you," said Zach. He settled gingerly onto the wooden seat, which was barely large enough to hold him, while Marson and his wife sat side by side on one of the benches. Now he noticed small pairs of eyes staring at him in curiosity and fear. He counted five children; with the girl, that made six, and from the look of the woman a seventh was on the way. For her sake, he hoped it was not a girl. The silence was surprising: the children seemed spiritless, perhaps from malnutrition.

"If I may impose on your hospitality, I prefer to begin the trip back in the morning," said Zach. "There are at most two hours of light left."

"Yes, of course," said Marson.

"That means we have her one more night," said the woman.

"Be quiet!" said Marson.

The woman looked at him angrily, seemed about to speak, then turned to Zach. "We have no bed to offer you," she said.

"I'm happy to have a roof over my head," said Zach.

"How long a journey is it to the Capital?" asked the oldest boy. He had been working at the loom and looked to be about ten years old.

"Not far if you could get there directly," said Zach. "But the going is slow through bat country. After that, it's best to follow the river south and east. By foot, it would take a very long time. By mount it took me just under ten days, riding hard, to get here."

"How did you find us?"

"The Principal's tax men are preparing maps of the entire District. They have marked every town and cabin in this sector."

"That way they don't miss squeezing anyone," said Marson. "No matter how poor."

"Marson!" hissed the woman.

Zach pretended he had not heard the exchange. He didn't blame the little man; taxes were necessary for building the District and securing it, but the burden seemed to fall most heavily on the very poor.

To cover his embarrassment, Zach opened his leather pouch. "Do you mind if I smoke?" he asked.

"Please," said the woman.

As Zach tamped new-smoke into his pipe, the older boy came closer. His dark blue eyes were enormous as he studied Zach and his trappings. "What's that?" he asked, pointing at the delicate feathers which poked up from Zach's pouch.

"Don't bother him, Daiv," said Marson.

"I don't mind," said Zach. He opened his pouch and pulled out a narrow instrument made of thin, polished pieces of dark red wood. Between the two end pieces were stretched six double strings, their splendidly feathered ends fastened with bone pegs. "This is a feathered lyre," he told the boy. "The strings are made from the tail feathers of a new bird that lives in the south and can't fly. The ends of the feathers are very strong and stretchable, like hair. When I pull on a string, like this, it makes a tone." He demonstrated, and the cabin was suddenly filled with the haunting moan of the feathered lyre. No one spoke as the sound slowly faded.

Zach put the instrument away, then lit his pipe with a glowing piece of kindling from the fire and sat puffing, wishing that he weren't here, wishing that the Principal had not asked this of him. But, of course, Zach was the only man he could trust on this mission. It was strange how two men who were so close could be so different, in the most important ways. Of

course, the Principal had always maintained that they were
more alike than Zach ever cared to admit. Zach's mind drifted
with the new-smoke and was gradually pulled back to the long
room by the aroma of cooking food, and by the bustling of
the woman as she set the table with bread, drinking gourds,
and wooden bowls.

"Will you have brew with dinner?" asked Marson.

Zach hesitated. Clearly brew was something precious to the
man, and just as clearly he did not really want to share it; but
to refuse would be an insult, and besides, after the long, gruel-
ing ride Zach craved the bitter taste and relaxing warmth.

"Yes, please," he said. Marson bowed his head slightly and
disappeared outside.

The boys squirmed themselves onto a long bench which
barely seated all of them. The oldest, Daiv, was the only one
who seemed able to look at Zach for more than a few seconds
at a time. Marson returned with a large stoppered crock and
two pottery tankards, and poured.

"To your health," said Zach, raising his tankard. Marson
lifted his but didn't speak. The brew was surprisingly good,
as fresh as any he had tasted in the Capital. "Did you make
this yourself?"

Marson nodded. "My father was a brewer. I was to follow
in his footsteps, but outlaws took the town and we were burned
out. There's not much market for the stuff here, or much time
for brewing."

"You have the touch," said Zach. "Perhaps someday you'll
be able to put it to use."

"Not likely, living as we do," said Marson. "Good ingre-
dients are too rare, and too expensive. For this batch I used
real corn—we traded last fair day for some beets we'd grown."

"It's excellent," Zach repeated. He now tasted the stew,
which was thin and mealy and seemed to consist largely of
beets and unidentifiable greens, and what might once have
been fowl. "The stew is good too," he said. "Thank you,
mistress."

"We're happy to share," the woman said. Then, leaning
across the table, she whispered to the oldest boy. "Daiv, take
a bowl up to your sister. She's hardly eaten for two days."

Zach watched as the boy disappeared up the rough ladder to the loft.

"I've heard the Principal plans to expand trade," said Marson.

"That's true," said Zach. "The first step is building better roads. Once they've come into this region, it's possible that you could set up a brewery and inn. Such places exist now closer to the Capital."

Marson grunted. "You put all your work into something, try to build it up, and outlaws take over. No, thank you."

"That is what the Principal is trying to prevent," said Zach. "The risk of outlaws goes down as more people move into an area. The Principal hopes to extend civilization to all corners of the District and beyond."

"Civilization," muttered Marson. "That's what got us into the mess we have now."

Zach had no answer. Marson was about to speak again when there was a sudden, piercing, feminine cry of "No!" and a thumping noise, followed by "Deenas take you, Evvy!" There was another thump, and then Daiv descended the ladder, holding the bowl, its contents soaking the front of his tunic.

"She doesn't want to eat," he said and took his place again.

His mother started to say something, then stopped, looking up at the loft. When she returned to her own meal, she kept her face lowered. For a moment nobody spoke, then Marson said gruffly, "Pass over the serving bowl, Daiv."

Zach felt he could not swallow one more bite of this family's food.

"I'm quite full now," he said, pushing himself from the table. "Thank you."

"Welcome," said Marson. Unceremoniously he took Zach's half-empty bowl and poured its contents back into the serving pot.

"I believe I'll take a walk," said Zach. "If you'll excuse me?"

The man and woman didn't bother to hide their relief. "We close the house when the sun goes down," said Marson. "You won't want to be out then, anyway."

Hanging his smoking pouch on his belt, Zach stepped outside, then went to his mount, which had been lapping water from a trough in the side yard. He took his short sword from the saddle, then walked toward the woods. He was too tired to do much walking but wanted to give the brewer's family more time to sort out their troubles. He half expected that when he returned they would announce that they had changed their minds. Of course he could not allow that—the Principal had become obsessed with the project. Zach sat on a boulder and, using his flint and steel, lit his pipe, then he gazed beyond the roof of Marson's wretched hut. The smoke escaping through the chimney-hole seemed to blend with that from Zach's pipe; only by focusing could he keep them separate, just as he was able to separate himself from the general misery of humankind by keeping his own wants and expectations so low that he was seldom disappointed.

Whether it was his reluctance to return to the hut or the reverie inspired by new-smoke, sunset crept up on him. It happened so gradually that there was no one minute when he could say, "This is dusk." Rather, the air changed impercep- tibly, becoming more moist and cool; the color of the sky went from blue to bluer, then indigo. The trees began to vibrate with the sounds of insects, and it was only after he had been startled by the bite of a shiny green fly that Zach realized how late it was. He must get back to the cabin.

His mount had already assumed the immobile position of sleep by the time Zach reached the yard. He started toward her, to retrieve his blanket, when he heard the swishing of wings above him. He threw himself to the ground barely in time to avoid the poison-dripping talons of the bat which had found him out at night, unprotected. He rolled over twice to avoid another attack, then rose to a crouch, his sword out defensively. He began to back up slowly, listening for the flapping wings which were invisible in the near-total darkness. He had nearly reached the door when the eerie swishing sound again approached, and he threw himself against the door, fell into the room, and kicked the door shut. A second later he heard the sound of talons scraping wood, a high-pitched squeal of frustration, and then silence. Zach took a deep breath, then slowly stood. His legs were trembling and he felt foolish as the brewer's family looked at him, the children wide-eyed, Marson and his wife impassive.

"It gets dark quickly here," said Marson.

"Sit down," said the woman. Zach sank into the chair and gratefully accepted the tankard of brew she poured for him.

"You had no trouble with bats on the way here?" she asked.

"I saw none, though I heard one once," said Zach.

"I heard a bat can kill you in ten seconds," said Daiv. "Is that true?"

"Quite likely," said Zach. "The poison is very powerful and fast-working."

"I saw a bat take a sheep down in half a minute," said Marson. "It was years ago, before poison-bats were as common as they are now."

"Enough talk of bats," said the woman. "It will give us all bad dreams." Then she flushed, perhaps remembering that there was already reason for bad dreams. "Daiv, go on up to bed," she said. "Make sure the little ones are settled and see if Evvy wants anything."

With a show of reluctance, Daiv mounted the ladder. Hushed whispers drifted down and Zach hoped there wouldn't be another outburst.

"Does the boy know what has been arranged?" asked Zach in a low voice.

"Only that Evvy's going away to the Capital," said Marson. He snorted. "He wanted to know why he can't go too." The little man looked down at his feet while his wife suddenly busied herself with some mending.

Zach sensed that they would prefer to settle the business tonight, but were hesitant to bring it up. He too would prefer to get it over with, but the Principal had been explicit: he mustn't turn over any metal until he had the girl secure. But what was the harm? They would leave at daybreak, and she couldn't go anywhere before then, not with bats hunting. On the other hand, he hadn't seen her, only heard muffled whispers and some scraping noises. Perhaps it was all a trick. But then Zach remembered the high-pitched "No!" and the hurt and puzzled look on Daiv's face. Those could not have been faked, nor could the pain and embarrassment of the brewer and his wife.

"We'll be getting a very early start tomorrow," Zach said casually. "Perhaps we should settle our business tonight."

"That might be best," Marson agreed.

Zach reached into his pouch and brought out a small cloth bag, heavy with metal. Marson's eyes followed the bag as Zach held it in his hand.

"You both understand that once you take this you cannot change your minds. That you will never see the girl again."

"I understand," muttered Marson.

"And you madame?"

There was a long silence, then she nodded.

"Her other fathers?"

"Her first-father is dead."

"Very well. The Principal wants his citizens to know that he himself observes his laws scrupulously. A few years ago, his men could simply have taken her, whether you agreed or not."

"That's so," said Marson.

"This way, it's a fair exchange. Value for value. I give you this metal and you give your daughter to the Principal, in my care, forever."

"We agree," said Marson.

"Yes," said his wife. "Only, can you tell us what is going to happen to her?"

"She's the Principal's to do with as he wishes," said Marson. "And he's an honest man. He obeys his own laws."

Zach reached for his brew without comment. Yes, the Principal was an honest man, and in most ways a good and kind one. In this one area only he showed a dark side so strong that all of his good intentions and works seemed powerless against it.

"I'll take good care of her on the journey," Zach found himself telling the couple. "I'll care for her as if she were my own daughter. In the Capital, she will be well fed and well clothed." For the time that she remains with the Principal, at least, he thought privately.

The man and woman seemed overwhelmed, and Zach sensed

that they were once again on the point of changing their minds. He spoke: "Why don't we all have a bit of brew, to seal the bargain?"

"Yes," agreed Marson. He hopped up and refilled Zach's tankard, then his own and a drinking gourd for his wife. As she took it, Zach could see that her hands were trembling.

"To our bargain," said Zach. They drank. He rose and handed the moneybag to Marson, who opened it onto the floor in front of him. He and his wife counted through the shiny round coins, twice.

"It's so much," the woman said.

"Value for value," said Zach. "I advise you to hide it in a very safe place. Even in this remote area, it's possible I have been seen and recognized."

"I already know the place," said Marson. "I'll attend to it as soon as you've left in the morning."

"I wish you luck," said Zach.

Marson looked at him, then: "Thank you." He sounded exhausted. He gathered up the metal and replaced it in the bag, then stood and took his wife's hand. "Come on, then," he said. "Let's go to bed."

After they had climbed to the loft, Zach finished his brew, looking at the fire. He thought of his blanket still outside on the mount, then spread his cloak and stretched his long frame out on it, resting his head on his hands. He was so tired that he ached, but it was a long time before he fell asleep; when he did, he dreamed that he was lost in a snowbank, hands and feet turning blue, while needles of ice fell from the sky around him.

Two

Zach was awakened by hands gently shaking him. He sat up quickly, startled, then recognized the face of the brewer's wife.

"Wake up," she said. "The sun's just rising."

Zach stretched, then stood, feeling stiff from head to toe. The fire had burnt down to ashes and the room was cold.

"You can wash outdoors by the shed," said the woman. "In here we keep only enough water for cooking."

Zach pulled his cloak over his shoulders and went out into the yard. Shallow footprints in the lightly dewed ground showed that Marson and his wife had both been out earlier. Zach bent over a barrel filled with rainwater and splashed his face, rubbing the sleep from his eyes, then dried with the edge of his cloak. His mount was whistling softly. He gently stroked her side, then brought her to the front of the cabin in grazing range of some scrub. He stood for a moment gazing at the surrounding woods, orange and yellow in the early morning light, then went back indoors.

The woman was busy at the fire while Daiv and the four young children stood around her, making sleepy sounds.

"Go and wash up, children," she said. "And Daiv, please see to the cut on Josef's cheek."

After a curious glance at Zach, Daiv herded the younger children outside, and presently the door opened again and Marson entered, holding a pail of water and some greens. "It's bitter cold this morning," he remarked. "Looks to be another early winter." He inclined his head toward Zach then. "Good morning."

"Good morning," said Zach.

12

"We have a simple breakfast," said Marson. "Porridge and root tea." His tone was fairly sarcastic.

"That's better than I've had in many days," said Zach. Then, realizing what that might portend for Evvy, he added, "I've been in such a hurry I haven't taken much time for food."

Marson walked over to the fire to warm his hands, then looked into the kettle.

"Hurry that up," he said.

The woman pushed stringy hair off her forehed with the back of her hand, then turned and looked at him. "The water is just boiling, as you can plainly see."

"Leave the tea to me. It's time to prepare Evvy."

She didn't answer. A few minutes later she carried the pot of porridge to the table, then without another word ascended to the loft.

"Will you have tea?" asked Marson. Without waiting for an answer, he ladled hot water into a cup and handed it to Zach. Through the steam Zach could see what looked like dried roots at the bottom. Marson went to the door and called out, "Come in, boys. It's cold."

Almost immediately the five boys entered, Daiv carrying the youngest.

"I think Josef's sick," he said. "He's hot, and he keeps rubbing the scratch on his face."

"Give him to me," said Marson. He took the youngster in his arms, then turned the boy's cheek to the window. "He'll be all right," he announced. He set the baby down, and Zach saw that the wound was red and oozing, with angry little lines beginning to spread from it. He felt a sudden chill and turned to his tea, cupping his hands around it for warmth.

"It might help to clean the wound with soap and water," he said after a moment.

"That's old-fashioned nonsense," said Marson. "Scratches heal or they don't. Sit down, boys. Daiv, give me the bowls."

Zach had become aware of a low, urgent murmuring from the loft, then shuffling sounds. He heard the woman and, he presumed, the girl descending.

"Come along, Evvy," said the woman. She had her arm around a figure who was almost completely hidden by a long blue cloak. Zach looked after them as they went through the narrow door.

"Eat your porridge!" Marson snapped at the boys. The five young faces turned from the door and to Marson. Daiv looked down at his bowl and began to eat. Zach fought the urge to walk out and ride away, as fast as he could, far beyond the borders of the District. He sipped from his cup and nearly choked. The liquid was bitter, heavy, unsavory. He set the cup down. "A strong tea," he murmured.

"I pick the herbs myself," said Marson. "It's not to everyone's taste, but it will wake you up."

Marson drank deeply from his own cup, and Zach gave it another try. The bitter warmth spread through his body, calming him. He began to eat the porridge, surprised how rich it was. The four young children ate greedily and unselfconsciously, while the older boy picked at his breakfast, stealing curious glances at Zach. Marson continued to sip tea, the porridge in front of him untouched.

There was a scream from outside, then the sound of a slap.

"What's the matter with Evvy?" asked one of the younger children. Not receiving an answer, he turned back to his breakfast.

Finally Marson spoke. "You must understand," he said. "We are very poor." Zach tried to think what to say in answer, and then the little man added bitterly, "But I'm sure you've heard that before. The fact remains. Since Evvy's first-father died, we have nothing. Not even enough food for our children. And what we manage to earn is taken away almost as soon as we get it. What choice do we have?" He stopped speaking abruptly, looked down at his cup, then drained it.

"Henny wants more, Pa," said Daiv.

"Give him what's in my bowl, then," said Marson, and he got up from the table and went to the fire, where he began to make more tea. The silence was broken only by the noise of the children eating, and Zach was certain he could bear it no longer when the door opened and the woman came in, her face grim, her eyes red-rimmed. Behind her was Evvy.

Zach had been about to drink the last of his bitter tea, but the cup stopped just at his lips, and he set it down again and stared. In spite of dark circles under eyes which had spent many hours crying, in spite of the too-pale skin and dazed expression, this was the most striking girl he had seen in his life. Her long hair, just drying, was the rich brown of freshly turned earth, mixed with golden strands that reflected the feeble morning sun, and her eyes were as dark as plums. She was thin and tall, and moved with a presence which accentuated and was perhaps the basis for her beauty.

"Come along, Evvy," said the woman. The girl looked up and for a moment her plum-colored eyes met Zach's, and he felt a chill go through him. Then she looked away and sat beside her mother at the end of the table.

"This is Evvy," said the woman. "Evvy, this is Zach, who will take you to the Capital."

Evvy did not answer. A bowl of porridge sat at her place, and she looked down at it but did not pick up a spoon.

No wonder, Zach thought, the Principal had sent him to this far corner of the District. Though the Principal's tax men could not have begun to describe Evvy, they surely had made clear how extraordinary she was. Perhaps, he thought, a wild deena was in the girl.

"Please eat, love," said the woman. "You have a long journey." Evvy didn't move. Zach couldn't take his eyes off her.

"Marson, bring some tea," said the woman.

Marson, who all this time had stood by the fire, approached slowly, like a man sleepwalking, and put his own cup in front of Evvy.

She put both her hands around it and drank. Zach saw her grimace as if she were forcing herself to drink the bitter liquid as a kind of penance. There were red-and-blue bruises on her wrists, and Zach realized with shock that she had been kept tied waiting for him.

As last night, he could no longer bear to sit at the table. "I'll get the mount ready," he said.

In the yard Zach stood with his back to the cabin and took three deep breaths. The forest was now green in the sunlight, and he tried to calculate how far they could ride and where they would stop, but his mind wouldn't cooperate. All he could think of was the girl: the bruises on her wrists, her shining hair, and the plum-colored eyes which had met his once.

He went to his mount and adjusted the saddle, then replaced his things, making room for more bundles. When all was secure, he ducked back into the cabin and announced, "It's time to go."

The children were up from the table now, all but Daiv and Evvy. Daiv looked puzzled and apprehensive. The woman was bent over the table tying a woolen satchel, while Marson again stood by the fire, his back to the room. Evvy sat as before, looking down at her untouched bowl of porridge.

Zach took the bundle from the woman and stepped outside again, grateful that he would never again have to enter that room. When he had tied Evvy's things securely to the mount, he turned and stood, waiting.

After a moment the door opened and the woman came out, followed by Evvy and then Marson.

Marson turned at the door and muttered, "Your sister is going on a trip. Stay here."

Evvy seemed to be in a trance as her mother led her across the yard and almost formally offered her hand to Zach. He felt a physical jolt when his fingers closed around her wrist. He drew her forward.

"Have you ridden a mount before?" he asked.

Suddenly, with surprising strength, Evvy pulled her hand free and ran to the door, but Marson was blocking it.

"Please don't send me away, Father!" She sank to her knees and threw her arms around the little man's legs.

Marson stood, unmoving, his face pale but without expression. The woman was even paler, and she spoke through tears. "Marson," she said. "Perhaps we—"

"No!" said Marson. Then: "Go with him, Evvy."

"No, please." She stood and looked at him. "I can earn money by trapping, Father. I know how to do it already. Daiv will help me." Marson didn't answer, but shook his head, then turned his back to her. Evvy turned to the woman. "Mama, don't make me do it. Please, let me stay!" She was now sobbing her words, and Zach watched helplessly, his heart breaking for all of them.

At last the woman knelt and held Evvy in her arms. "We love you, Evvy. Please believe that."

"Then don't send me away."

"We don't want to. But it's best for everyone. Please try to understand."

"I don't understand!" the girl cried. "You don't love me and I hate you!" She began to run across the yard, but Marson was close behind her. He pulled her, crying and struggling, to Zach. "Take her!" he said. "Tie her if you have to."

"I won't tie her," said Zach. Then, very gently: "Evvy please. I don't want to hurt you."

Marson pushed the girl toward him and Zach reached out, steadying her. Though still sobbing, Evvy was no longer struggling, and he held her a moment in comfort, then lifted her onto the mount. He swung up behind. "Put your leg over," he said. Mechanically she obeyed him, then settled back between his arms, her narrow back nestled snugly against his chest. "You won't fall," he said. "But if you get frightened, you can hold on to the mane."

The girl seemed not to hear him. She sat stiffly, her body shaking with sobs. Zach turned his mount toward the forest and rode quickly out of the yard. He did not look back.

Three

Zach rode mechanically, trying not to think. He was aware of the warmth of the girl between his arms and thighs, and as he urged his mount on to greater speed Evvy's hands reached out and grasped the mane.

I will not do this for him, he thought, but continued to ride steadily, guiding his mount through the hilly woods.

At last the labored breath of the mount and his own hunger forced Zach to recognize that it was time to rest. He reined in to a shady clearing by a shallow stream, then dismounted and reached up to swing the girl down. She didn't resist. When he set her down her knees buckled and he steadied her.

"Come over here, Evvy," he said. "Sit down." He led her to a moss-covered rock which overlooked the stream. She was no longer crying, and she looked at the ground, breathing deeply. Zach took the mount to the stream, where she knelt to drink. Behind him he was aware of the girl, and wondered if she might try to escape. He whirled at a sudden sound, but she sat as before. An overripe fruit had fallen from a tree.

He must try to make her eat. He couldn't bring her sick and emaciated to the Principal; her mother had said that she hadn't eaten in two days, now three.

He still had a bit of hard cheese which he had been saving. He approached the girl and smoothed a place in front of her, then spread a large new-vine leaf as a plate. On this he put a bit of cheese and some of the bread her mother had sent.

Evvy sat like one of the remaining statues in the Capital.

"I'll get you something to drink," Zach muttered. He rinsed his drinking horn in the stream, filled it with cool water. He held it out to Evvy but she seemed not to notice.

He tried not to let his exasperation show. "It's a long journey. We may not have much time to eat or drink later in the day."

After a moment she reached out and accepted the horn. When she had finished, she held it to him for more. He refilled it for her. She had shed many tears and must be thirsty. Evvy drank most of the water in the second horn, then gave it back to Zach. He finished the water, then squatted just to the side of the rock, not facing her.

"Your mother's bread is good," he said conversationally. He bit into a piece of cheese and continued. "If there's time to hunt later, I'll try to get a rabbit. Would you like that?" He paused. She didn't answer. "I don't imagine you've tasted meat

many times in your life, have you?" He waited again, but the
girl remained still. He felt his annoyance growing and turned
to see if she were mocking him. At his sudden movement she
started back, with a small cry.

Zach's anger vanished. "Don't be afraid of me, Evvy. I
won't hurt you."

He pulled off another piece of cheese. He had eaten little
at the brewer's house and was hungry. When he had finished
he leaned against the rock. He could sense the girl's eyes behind
him, staring at his back.

If only she would talk to him. The Principal, of course,
wouldn't care if she talked or not. He might find it more
interesting if she didn't.

After a few minutes Zach rose and walked a short distance
into the trees to relieve himself. His ears were alert for any
sound Evvy might make, any movement to escape, but when
he returned she was sitting where he had left her. He looked
down at her, once again struck by her unusual beauty. Perhaps
he could simply turn his mount around, return the girl to her
home, tell the Principal he had been unable to find her, that
her family had moved from the District or been murdered by
outlaws.

But of course that wouldn't do. The Principal would discover the truth sooner or later, and that would mean the end
of Zach's livelihood, if not his life.

"We must get going," he said at last. "Will you eat?" Evvy
hesitated, then reached for the bread and cheese. Before he
could stop her, she stood and threw them into the water. Her
face was sullen and defiant, and Zach had to suppress his anger
once again. She knew how scarce food was; that was why she
had made the gesture.

"Come on, then," he said and walked toward his mount
without looking back.

He pushed the mount faster than he had that morning, once
using a leather thong when she began to slow. He had lost
time trying to get Evvy to eat and didn't want to spend more
than one night awake tending fire.

The mount began breathing in gasps and Zach slowed,

ashamed. It was no use taking out his anger on the beast or
on Evvy. Neither had any control over her life, not even as
much as Zach had of his own.

The shadows were deep by the time they reached the eastern
slope of the mountain. Zach nodded to himself in satisfaction;
if all went well there should be no difficulty reaching the
foothills by tomorrow afternoon, and then he could relax and
have a good night's sleep.

He had been following a narrow stream and now began to
look for a suitable spot to stay for the night. At last he found
a small clearing, well protected by trees.

"This is our inn for the night, Evvy. How do you like it?"
The girl didn't answer, and Zach swung her off the mount,
then unloaded and tethered the beast by the stream.

While Evvy watched, he set about making the campsite safe
and comfortable. After preparing a shallow pit for a fire, he
smoothed away the stones just in front of a tree and swept a
heap of dried leaves over the ground. This would be a bed for
Evvy. He realized with surprise that he wanted to please the
girl; he had thought all fatherly feelings had died fifteen years
ago.

As Zach worked, Evvy watched him silently, still brooding.
At last he stood up, saying, "Now I have to gather wood for
our protective fire. You may help me if you like."

He thought that she wouldn't respond, but evidently she felt
she had a stake in her own survival or simply wanted to move
about, and she followed him into the woods, stooping as he
did to pick up dried twigs and branches.

"Zach." He stopped in surprise, then turned in the direction
of her voice. It was the first time she had spoken to him.

"What is it?" he asked.

"I've found a large log, but I can't move it."

"Let's have a look at it," said Zach. He went to where she
stood and examined the object. It was thick and dry and would
be ideal for the long-lasting fire he needed, but it was half-
buried in the ground and would take some work to move. "This
is a fine log," he said. "Why don't you take the kindling we've
gathered back to camp while I try to pry it up?"

Without another word she accepted the branches he was holding and turned back to the clearing. Zach dug under the log with his knife and pushed and pried till at last it came free. With some difficulty he hefted it onto his shoulder, then returned to the campsite and placed it to the side of the fire pit he had dug. He sat a moment to get his breath. He was more tired than he had realized; the hours he had spent with the brewer's family had drained him.

"I'm going back for more kindling," Zach told Evvy. "Do you want to come along?" She shrugged, then stood and followed him. In a very short time they had gathered enough for the night, and Zach was about to turn back when he heard a sudden noise in the brush to his right.

A rabbit! Thank the deenas, he thought. Quickly, he unslung his bow and fitted an arrow to it, drew, and let the arrow fly. It caught the rabbit through the throat just as it started to run, and Zach felt unreasonably proud of himself. He was seldom that good a shot and was pleased that Evvy had witnessed it.

It was deep dusk by the time Zach had started a fire and prepared the meat. Evvy hadn't spoken again, but he felt she was relaxing a bit. The smell of roasting rabbit made his mouth water, and he smiled to himself as he caught Evvy taking hungry glances at it. While he waited for it to finish cooking, Zach leaned against a tree and looked at the sky. One by one the stars appeared, twinkling pale blue. Puffing on his pipe, Zach thought how good it would be to live as people had before the Change. In another kind of world he might be sitting like this with a family around him. He thought of Leya, and the brief happiness they had had together, and for a moment his eyes misted. If she had lived, they would have had children, perhaps even a daughter like Evvy. In the firelight Evvy looked like a portrait he had once seen in an ancient book, her features so delicate and soft that they seemed to be lightly sketched in the air. Zach had counted the money paid Evvy's parents, and he knew that had the Principal seen her, he would have offered ten times the amount.

By the time Zach had finished his pipe, the meat was done, and he set it on a flat stone and began to cut. "It's ready,

Evvy," he said. Gravely she came over and knelt by the stone.

"It smells good," she said.

"Too good to throw in the water?"

She gave him a swift glance but said nothing.

They ate in silence, hungrily. This was the first substantial meal Zach had eaten in over a week. There had been no opportunity to hunt on the trip to the brewer's.

After dinner Zach bent over the stream and washed, then drank from his horn. Evvy refused his offer of the horn and instead drank from her cupped hands. He put the remainder of the rabbit in his pouch, and slung it from a tree branch to protect it from fox-cats.

"You'd better get some sleep," Zach said to Evvy. "We have a long ride tomorrow."

Evvy didn't answer. She settled herself on the bed of leaves he had prepared for her and sat with her arms around her knees, her cloak over her shoulders, staring at the fire.

"Do you mind if I play my instrument?" he asked.

"Was that what I heard last night when you came to our . . . to my parents' house?"

"It's called a feathered lyre."

"I never saw one before."

"Not many people have. New plants and animals make new instruments, and new songs to be played on them. Before the Change there were hundreds of different instruments for making music, and thousands of songs."

"Do you know any old songs?" she asked.

"Just the folk tunes that everyone knows. There's no way to ever know the other ones. That's why I make up my own. Would you like to hear one?"

She nodded.

Zach smiled and stroked the strings. Evvy watched him, squinting across the fire. He had won the lyre ten years ago, gambling in the Principal's camp, before the President had been defeated. The lyre usually took years to learn to play well, but he had picked it up right away; the uniquely mournful quality of the lyre's sound had immediately seemed to suit him and his nature.

He started another tune, then happened to glance at Evvy.

Tears were sliding down her cheeks. With a pang of guilt, he stopped playing, then took his time putting the lyre away. "That's enough for tonight," he said. "Time for you to go to bed, young lady."

"I'm not a child," said Evvy. "And I'm not tired." After a moment she lay down on the blanket Zach had spread on her bed of leaves and pulled her cloak over her. Zach wanted to smooth it around her but stayed where he was.

"When will you go to bed?" she asked.

"I have to make sure the fire stays bright to keep bats away."

"But you have to sleep," she said.

"Perhaps I'll doze a little," said Zach. "I'm used to it. Good night, now."

Evvy didn't answer, and Zach shrugged. On the trip to the brewer's house he hadn't needed to keep a fire going the one night he was in open bat country. He had simply constructed a very small leaning shelter using his cloak and some branches, then built a small fire near the open end. The glowing embers gave enough light to keep bats from flying directly at his head, while the lean-to protected his body. This arrangement necessitated staying in the tiny tent from the time the sun went down until it rose again. Though Zach had considered making such a shelter for Evvy, he couldn't be sure that the girl would obey him and remain still all night; besides, he knew it would be uncomfortable and frightening for her.

Zach purposely remained where he was. The ground and the tree he was leaning against were bumpy and slightly damp—uncomfortable enough to keep him awake. For the same reason he did not pull his cloak around himself until his teeth began to chatter.

After a while he got up and stretched, then laid more wood on the fire. It was becoming quite cold, and he extended his legs toward the warmth. It would be tempting to stretch out just for a minute. . . .

Zach was startled by a sound. He leapt up instantly, but the fire was still burning brightly; he hadn't dozed more than a minute or two. On her bed of leaves Evvy was moaning and twisting. Zach relaxed. The girl was having a nightmare, and no wonder. He knelt by her and put a hand on her shoulder.

"Wake up, Evvy," he said.

She started awake, eyes wide and terrified. "No!" she cried.

"Shh," said Zach. "It's only a dream."

She pulled away from him, then seemed to come slowly awake, her plum-colored eyes beginning to focus. Zach watched as memories of the day came back to her, and then she looked up at him, less disoriented. "I was dreaming."

"That's right, it's a dream. Go back to sleep now."

"But it's not a dream that I'm here. It's not a dream what happened."

For a moment Zach couldn't think what to say, but then he spoke in what he hoped was a soothing voice: "You're safe here. Nothing will happen to you. It's all right. Go back to sleep."

He continued to stroke her shoulder and felt her begin to relax. After a moment, she lay back down. One hand brushed her face, then reached out for Zach's hand, which was resting on his knee. Very tightly, like an infant, she gripped the hand, then closed her eyes.

For a long time Zach sat with her, looking down at her face, now again peaceful in sleep.

The Principal had told his tax collectors to look for beautiful young girls just between childhood and womanhood. There was no doubt that in many ways Evvy was indeed a young woman, but at this moment as Zach held her hand and watched her sleep, she seemed very much a child.

The quality of the night began to change, and Zach could see by the movement of the stars that dawn wasn't far. Laying a last load of wood on the fire, and checking that it burned properly, he at last let himself lie down and immediately fell into a dreamless sleep.

When he awoke, full sunlight was shining in his eyes and he knew that he had slept far too long. He sat slowly and saw that Evvy was already up and, from the look of her, had washed. She was sitting by the fire, now ashes, and looking at him gravely.

"Good morning," she said.

"Have you been awake long?" asked Zach.

"I thought you'd want to sleep."

He sighed. He had hoped to get an early start, just so he would be able to sleep through this coming night. He held in his irritation, touched by the girl's concern. "Thank you," he said. "I'm afraid I slept a little too late, though. We'll have to breakfast quickly."

"I already had some of the bread Mother sent."

"Good," said Zach. "Let's get started, then, and we can stop in a few hours and finish the rabbit." He didn't feel like eating now—his stomach was queasy and his head ached, as if he had had too much to drink. The fly bite on his forearm had begun to itch badly.

He quickly loaded the mount, and they set out, riding hard, not talking. At midday they stopped in a shady area, where Evvy ate most of the remaining meat, while Zach drank horn after horn of water. "Aren't you going to eat?" she asked.

"Perhaps later. I'm not hungry now."

She looked concerned. "Do you feel all right?"

"I'm fine," Zach said. "Just a little tired." He smiled at her.

The afternoon sun was hot, and as they rode Zach realized how exhausted he was. He'd had a hard ride of almost two weeks to the brewer's house; this return trip would take even longer with the girl. Zach had to admit to himself that he felt his age, and the many fights he'd been in, and the missions he had undertaken for the Principal.

His knowledge of the area was not exact, but he knew that they were not far from the low foothills, which were pocked with small caves. If they reached the hills before dusk, he could sleep through the night safely. A large fire in the mouth of a cave would still be glowing by morning, and no bat would fly directly across a light, however dim. After a good night's sleep, with an early start, they might even be out of bat country by late tomorrow. The rest of the journey would be far less trying, because they would follow the river east and south, along the Principal's roads.

They continued to ride, and still the foothills did not appear.

Zach's exhaustion had grown worse; the effort of guiding the mount down steep paths, of holding Evvy in front of him, had made his arms feel so heavy that they seemed no longer a part of him. His head throbbed with each step the animal took. For a moment he considered stopping short of the foothills and again sleeping in the open. Perhaps he could manage it, just for this one night. . . .

Zach jerked himself upright; he had been dozing. Something was very wrong with him and he knew it was essential now to reach the caves. Evvy sensed his alarm. She turned and looked up at him.

"Maybe we ought to stop soon," she said, sounding worried.

"We will," he said. "Just a little farther."

Once again he started to fall asleep, and only pulled himself back to consciousness when the mount stumbled on a rock. He was beginning to feel frightened, for himself and Evvy. If the foothills did not appear soon . . .

"What's that?" said Evvy. Zach looked in the direction she was pointing and almost wept with relief. Half-buried by dirt, rocks, and vegetation, he recognized the unnatural angles and reddish brown color of dead machine bodies. There were many such burial grounds scattered throughout the District, and almost always some of the bodies were large enough and well enough preserved to serve as shelters. Indeed, the same plants and animals lived in them as in natural caves. Although Zach wasn't superstitious, he preferred to avoid machines but had used them when necessary.

The bodies were buried just across a shallow stream. Zach dismounted, then walked across the stream, Evvy following him.

"These are dead machines, aren't they?" asked Evvy. She sounded awed.

"Yes," said Zach, "and thank the deenas you found them." He picked up a large bare branch and approached the twisted mass of rock and metal. The first body he came to was large enough, but badly damaged, and in any case it was marred by several large openings, too many to afford protection from bats. The next was suitable but already occupied by snakes, as he discovered when he thrust his branch into it. At last he found a machine body that had only one large, jagged opening. It was also unoccupied, at least for the present.

Zach leaned against the hill that held the machine body for a moment, hoping his strength would return. "Evvy," he said, "Please help me bring firewood up here. I'm too tired to tend fire in the open tonight."

She put her hand to her mouth. "But wild deenas live in machine bodies."

"Nothing lives in machine bodies but snakes and rabbits," said Zach, irritated. "That's just a superstition."

"I'll make the fire tonight," Evvy said. "I'll stay awake."

"We're going to sleep here. Now, help me gather wood." He walked back toward the stream and began selecting branches. Each time he bent over his head felt heavy and his vision blurred. He handed his load of wood to Evvy. "Take this up there and put it inside the machine body."

She accepted the load but began to cry. "Please," she said. "I'm scared of the deenas."

"Do as I say!" he bellowed. "Don't be such a child!"

Evvy looked shocked and began to cry harder, but she took the wood to the machine body and quickly thrust it just inside. Then she returned and once again followed Zach's instructions. The last load he took himself. Now all that remained was to unload his things from the mount and bring them back, then build a fire. He would sleep and by morning be himself again.

Zach stood up and started to walk down toward the stream, but his legs refused to cooperate. He felt his body falling back against the harsh earth and metal wall. As he slid toward the ground he saw Evvy looking at him in alarm.

"Evvy," he said. "There's something wrong." But the sounds that came from his mouth were not words, and he had a moment of panic before everything faded away.

Four

Zach dreamed he was sliding down an endless mountain, his hands unable to get a purchase on rock or limb, his skin scraping from his body bit by bit. At last he came to the bottom and lay there, pebbles and pieces of broken wood sticking into him at throat, belly, and thighs. He tried to roll away from his torment and woke.

At first he didn't know where he was and thought that he was still dreaming. Gradually, his eyes focused and he saw shadows jiggling, purple and gray. He groaned and rose on one elbow. He was inside a very small cave, the mouth of which was guarded by a badly smoking fire. Beyond the fire all was dark; it was night. He tried to sit up and groaned again, then fell back.

Evvy's face, small, pale, and frightened, was above his.

"I thought you were dead," she said.

Now it came back to him, and he realized he must be inside the machine body he had found, with a fire guarding him from bats. Somehow, Evvy had brought him in here and had kindled the campfire. How, he did not know. Why, he could not imagine.

He tried to answer her, but his mouth and throat would not obey his commands.

She understood. "I think you have the fly fever," she said. "It comes from the green flies that live in the woods. We usually get it as children, and then we never get it again. I never saw a grown-up person have it."

Zach understood her and again tried to answer, but all that came out of his mouth was groans.

"You can't talk when you have it," Evvy went on. "It does

something to your mouth and tongue. When you fell before, I thought you were dead, but then I saw you were breathing. I decided to bring you in here, in spite of the wild deenas. You're so big, but I kept pushing and pulling. I'm sorry if I hurt you."

Zach understood that she was talking because of her own fears. He wanted to reassure her but could do no more than look at her, and even that was an effort.

"It took a long time to get you in here," she went on, "and by that time it was getting dark and I was afraid to go back out. So I took your flint and metal and made a fire. I never realized before how hard it is to make one." She sighed. "I think it's nearly dawn now. I've been awake the whole time. I'm . . . glad you're alive."

Zach cursed himself for being unable to answer, to thank her. She had saved his life, a man she could have reason only to hate. He turned his head in humiliation and frustration.

After a moment he felt her cool hand on his forehead.

"I'll bring you water as soon as it's light," she said. "I know you must be thirsty, with the fever." After another moment she went on: "I hope you don't mind my talking to you. I was talking to you even when you couldn't hear me. I kept thinking about the wild deenas, and the bats. I wondered what I'd do if you died. I thought I might take your mount and go home, but I don't know the way, and I don't know how to ride. If you want to go to sleep, blink your eyes three times and I'll be quiet."

Zach turned his head back to her and summoned all the strength he had to keep from blinking.

"I've been thinking all night," Evvy said. "I know that you have to obey the Principal. And I have to obey my mother and father. With my first-father dead there was no other way to get money. But they wouldn't tell me what was going to happen to me in the Capital. And they . . . they tied me up so I wouldn't run away. Why did they do that? Where would I run to? I was so afraid, yesterday. Now that you're awake I feel safer. When you told me not to be afraid, I believed you. You want to go to sleep, don't you?"

Zach fought to keep his eyes from closing, but his eyelids flickered, and once again he slept.

When Zach next awoke the machine body's interior was lit by the reflected sun, revealing strangely shaped, twisted bits of rotten wire and metal embedded in the walls. After a moment he remembered all that had happened. Painfully he turned his head and saw that the little cave was empty. For a moment he felt a stab of fear that Evvy had left him, that he would die here alone and in thirst. Perhaps, he thought, he could drag himself to the stream to drink, and then back. But he knew he didn't have the strength to gather more wood, and in any case, if Evvy was gone, so were his mount, his weapons, and his provisions.

He heard a scraping noise outside and imagined that fox-cats had scented him and come to finish him. Better that, he thought, than a slow, lingering death of paralysis and thirst.

Evvy's face appeared above him.

"You're awake," she said. "I went to sleep right after you did. I think it's about midday. I've been gathering wood for tonight. Your mount is all right, I've seen her eating grass by the stream, but she won't let me get near her."

Zach tried to explain how Evvy could approach the skittish mount, but all that came out was the strange moan of last night.

"I wanted to bring water," said Evvy, "but your horn is still on the mount."

Zach felt tears of despair start to his eyes. His thirst had become a torment, and he knew he would die if he could not drink. Perhaps the girl could help him get to the stream.

"When children get the fever it usually lasts just a day or two," Evvy was saying. "I hope it's the same for you. I know you have to have water, the fever burns it all off!" She took a deep breath, then said, "I'll be right back."

Zach watched her go and tried to rise and follow her, but fell back weakly. After a few minutes she reappeared, an odd expression on her face. She knelt, brought her face close to his. And then Zach felt her soft lips upon his. Her mouth parted and he felt water trickle against his own, and he understood what she was doing. He opened his mouth and let the water drip in. Painfully he swallowed. When Evvy's own mouth was empty she returned to the stream and repeated the process again and again until he nodded that he had had enough.

"I'll bring more water in the afternoon," said Evvy. "Do you feel better?"

Zach tried to convey in his expression how grateful he was, but the paralysis of his tongue and throat seemed to have spread to his face.

For the rest of the day and into the long night Zach lay helpless. Twice more Evvy came and gave him water, though he was still tortured by thirst most of the time. In the few minutes that he was able to think clearly, he wondered how and what she was eating and what would happen to her if he died. She did not know this area; she could not ride his mount. He must stay alive now for her sake.

As suddenly as Zach had fallen ill, he began to recover. When he awoke the next morning, he had little trouble focusing on the walls of the machine-cave, and he realized that the throbbing in his head was gone. He stirred and almost immediately Evvy knelt over him. Before she could speak, he moved his lips and muttered weakly but intelligibly, "Feel better . . ."

Evvy's face relaxed with relief. "Then it is like with the children," she said. "You'll be all right." She went on gravely, almost like a parent lecturing, "You probably won't feel quite right for a few more days."

Zach took a deep breath and felt stronger still. After a moment he spoke again. "Evvy, I owe you my life."

"I couldn't have left you to die," she said.

"I think," he went on, slowly but distinctly, "that if you had not taken care of me both of us would have been lost. I thank you and . . . I swear . . . I will pay you back."

By late that afternoon Zach was so much better that he was able to make his way to the stream and drink his fill. With some embarrassment he cleaned himself and his clothing, then approached the mount and took from her his sword, the remaining food, and his drinking horn. Exhausted, he lay against the wall of the cave and watched while Evvy prepared a fire and food for both of them.

The following morning, Zach felt almost himself again, and though he was still weak, he thought they could travel a few miles. When he suggested moving on, Evvy began to protest that he was not yet well, but he persuaded her that they were better off finding a larger, natural cave; they had been here enough days to have attracted attention from human or animal predators, if such were about.

Besides, he needed to feel action, to stir his brain. For things had changed, irrevocably, and he had to think.

They did not travel far. Zach was much weaker than he had expected, and the exertion of getting on his mount was enough to leave him trembling. Evvy was solicitous, glancing at him from time to time and doing what she could do aid in guiding the mount. In any case, there was little difficult riding to do, as they were soon in the foothills, where the paths were slow and winding, leading down toward the river plain.

At midday, Evvy insisted that they break for lunch. Then she suggested that perhaps they should make their camp here for the night. Zach made only a token protest. They had come upon a large, empty natural cave. It would be easy to protect from bats, and Zach could have a long night's rest to heal his still-weak body. While Zach sat at the mouth of the cave and dug a small pit for the fire, Evvy brought in wood. They worked in silence, companionably, as if they had been traveling together for years.

They ate the last of the food Evvy's mother had given them for dinner. Zach would have to hunt tomorrow, which would slow their journey, but it would also give him more time to think. They were not far from the river, and a decision would have to be made soon.

The food made Zach very sleepy, and he lay down near the back of the cave, his cloak half covering him. Evvy was wide-awake and wanting to chatter, but Zach was too tired to respond in more than grunts. Finally she asked him, "Could I try to play your lyre?"

"Of course."

Gingerly, she pulled the leather case from Zach's large

pouch and slipped out the lyre, which she held in both hands before the fire, looking at the polished wooden frame and the delicate but strong strings, each of which ended in what seemed to be hundreds of iridescent fronds. She plucked one string and almost dropped the instrument as it responded with a melancholy, lingering note.

She sighed aloud and plucked another string, then three together. On her next attempt, one of the strings broke with a whining snap. "Oh, Zach!" her voice was filled with distress.

Zach smiled. "Don't worry, Evvy. It happens all the time. Bring it to me." He reached into the bottom of his pouch, where he always kept one or two feathers coiled for such emergencies. While she watched, he removed the damaged string and replaced it with a whole feather, first scraping the scales from the flexible shaft with his fingernail. While he tightened the bone peg holding the new string, testing its tone as he did, she held the broken one up to the firelight, causing its fronds to move delicately with her breath.

"May I keep this?" she asked.

Zach laughed. "Of course. In fact, let me show you a trick I learned as a boy." Setting the lyre aside, he took the feather and deftly braided its many fronds in and upon themselves, then twisted the whole into a circle, weaving the ends into the braids. "There you are," he said. "A feather bracelet."

Evvy slipped it on her slender wrist, then held out her hand and admired the way the bracelet's many shiny colors gleamed in the light.

"Do you like it?" he asked.

"It's the most beautiful thing I ever saw," said Evvy. "Thank you!"

Zach smiled to himself. He picked up the lyre again and, after a final adjustment, played a chord. "As good as new," he said. He replaced the instrument in its case and yawned.

"When you feel better will you play more songs for me?" Evvy asked.

"I'll write one for you," he said. "Would you like that?"

She nodded, her pupils so wide that her eyes appeared black. The sounds of the lyre seemed still to fill the cave. She ran her fingers over the soft surface of the bracelet, then moved to the side of the cave opposite him and lay down on the blanket, beneath her cloak.

"Good night, Zach," she said.

"Good night, Evvy."

Zach was pulled awake what seemed the next minute.

"Zach," said Evvy, shaking his shoulder. "Wake up. There's something in here with us."

Still groggy, he sat up. "What are you talking about?"

Silently, she pointed upward and to the right. Zach followed the direction of her finger and saw a point of light. He refocused and realized that it was a star, that the top of the cave opened into the air above. The opening was far from the protective fire.

He whispered, "Why do you think something is in here?"

"Because I heard—there it is again!"

Now Zach too heard the whirring of wings above them and the high-pitched squeal of a hunting bat.

"Evvy," he whispered urgently, "Get under my cloak. Cover yourself completely. Now!" he added as she hesitated.

Evvy burrowed under his cloak while Zach moved toward the mouth of the cave. Why had he decided to sleep so far from the fire?

As he moved, trying not to make a sound, he remembered that his sword still lay with his blanket and bundles. Small matter; the only weapon really useful against a bat was light. He had nearly reached the small pile of unburned wood when the bat sensed him and dived at him. He rolled toward the fire quickly, knowing the beast could not follow, and put his hand on the first piece of wood it came to. He cried out—his hand had closed on a burning ember.

"Zach!" It was Evvy, frightened by his cry.

"I'm all right!" he shouted. "Stay covered!"

He heard the enraged bat whirring just beyond the circle of light. Two long branches were burning just at their ends. He took them one in each hand and crouched, steadied himself, then began to move toward the bat. The animal screamed in pain as the glow of the fire reached it, and pounded its wings furiously, trying to get away. Zach beat at it with the branches.

In its panic, the bat veered into the wall and then began flying wildly in circles, reaching out with its long talons. Zach tried to herd it toward the hole at the top of the cave, but the animal was quicker than he, and he retreated toward the fire to give it a chance to calm down.

The bat, however, was in a frenzy, and suddenly it flew directly toward Evvy, still huddled under Zach's cloak.

"Don't move!" he called. "No matter what happens, no matter what you feel, don't move!" Then the bat, in its crazed flight, brushed the edge of the cloak, catching it in its talons. Evvy screamed as she felt the cloak being pulled from her, and the bat thrashed desperately in its struggle to get free.

Instantly Zach crossed the cave and pulled the cloak completely away from the girl. The coarse wool had wrapped itself around the bat's claws. Zach heard a ripping noise as the bat continued to struggle. He laid down the burning branches and picked up a large limb which lay in a corner and began to beat at the trapped animal. The bat made its eerie sound for a moment more, then fell silent, unmoving. To make certain, Zach approached it with a burning branch, holding the fire near the now-staring eyes. There was no reaction.

"It's dead," he said, his voice sounding strange and hollow. "Evvy, did it hurt you?"

The girl threw her arms around him, trembling with sobs.

"It's all right," he said, awkwardly patting her shoulder with his burnt hand. "It's over now. Everything's all right."

He continued to comfort her for a moment. When her sobs had subsided, he gently held her away. "Let's go back to sleep," he said.

"What about the bats?"

"There won't be any more," he said, hoping it was the truth. "This fellow just wandered in by mistake. But to be sure we're safe, I'll put more wood on the fire and we'll sleep next to it."

"What about your cloak?" asked Evvy.

Zach eyed the rough woolen garment and considered. It was torn and bloody, with the dead bat lying twisted in its folds. He didn't want to risk a scratch from the still-poisonous talons.

"I'll clean it tomorrow," he said.

"You can sleep with me under my cloak," said Evvy.

"Thank you. I have my blanket and I'll be warm enough by the fire."

"Please," she added. "I'm so frightened."

Evvy's little cloak was scarcely large enough to cover her, but Zach lay beside her, spreading the wool over both of them. The girl shivered and wriggled closer to him.

"Am I hurting your arm?" she asked.

"It's pinched just a little," said Zach. He moved it and found that it was best to let his arm fall over her, in a protecting, but far more intimate position than he had intended. Well, he thought, let it be. I will hold her as I would hold my own daughter.

Evvy soon fell asleep, breathing deeply, but Zach found that despite his exhaustion he could not relax. He told himself that it was because of the need to stay alert, in case another bat should wander into the cave.

His body told him that it was more; and at last he began to understand why the Principal had risked so much to send him on this mission.

Five

On each succeeding day Zach felt stronger, and each day they traveled farther than the last, though still more slowly than necessary. They were well out of bat country now, approaching the river crossing, and Zach would have to make a decision soon.

Evvy often chattered as they rode, commenting on the scenery, questioning Zach about his life. Although Zach was accustomed to traveling alone, he found that he enjoyed her company.

"Tell me about the Capital," she asked one day.

"Where shall I begin?"

"What is it like to live there?"

Zach mused. There was no way he could possibly convey to Evvy the confusion and bustle that were the Capital, the sense of continuity with the pre-Change past provided by the many old buildings and monuments still standing. To many, as it once had to Zach, the Capital represented a dream of what had been in the past and what was still possible. Lining the broad, decaying pre-Change avenues were shops, taverns, and houses of women or boys for hire; there were literacy centers, encouraged by the Principal, and theaters for entertainments of all sorts. Still standing were many old museums from the past, some holding books; others, repositories of ancient weapons, used now by the Principal's army. Living in and around the vast mall were merchants, technicians, and craftsmen, trying to relearn the simple technologies of the past, as well as poets, dreamers, and scoundrels of every variety. Here too congregated soldiers, farmers, and simple folks like Evvy's family, families with two or more husbands and a wife and children. For those in the Principal's service, the Capital provided a life of such comfort as was still possible, in exchange for loyalty and obedience, and the willingness to share the Principal's own dreams and risk one's life for them.

"Zach?"

Zach thought again how to answer Evvy's question. "Your second-father told me you once lived in a town," he finally said. "What was that like?"

"I was a little child then," said Evvy. She sounded thoughtful. "My first-father was a fur trader. We had a big store. I remember the cabin, and lots of people. Too many people, and bad smells."

Zach smiled. "Well, that's just what the Capital is like, only much bigger. There are people, animals, dirt, and noise everywhere."

"It sounds wonderful."

He laughed.

"Is it true there are old buildings a mile high?"

"Not a mile. Very tall."

"Do people live in them?"

"In the bottom parts, some of them. Some are just ruins, and no one can live there. In the top parts no one lives—at least no one who doesn't have a reason to hide. It takes too long to climb up them."

"Why were they built so tall then?"

"Before the Change, there were machines to carry people to the top."

"How?"

"We can't really know. But there were machines to do nearly everything, Evvy. I'm sure you've heard that."

"Life must have been good in those days," the girl said after a moment.

"They had their problems, just as we have ours," said Zach.

"When I get to the Capital I'm going to climb to the top of the tallest building I can find," Evvy said.

Zach didn't answer. Evvy seemed to have forgotten that she was on this journey against her will.

"Zach?"

"Yes, Evvy?"

"What's the Principal like?"

"He's a man like other men. I've answered enough questions now. Let's ride."

Evvy didn't seem to notice that Zach was keeping each day's journey short; although he felt well he let her think he was still suffering the effects of fly fever. Inevitably, however, the morning of decision came. They had finished breakfasting on the remains of a large snake Zach had caught, and Evvy was gathering their things into bundles to tie on the mount. Zach watched her a moment, then spoke.

"Stop," he said. She turned around, surprised. "We're going to leave some things here."

She started to speak, then fell silent, looking bewildered.

Zach took stock of the things they had on hand. Very little food; they were living off the land. The drinking horn, his large pouch; his smaller personal pouch and drinking skin; two ragged blankets; Evvy's own small bag and the clothes that they were wearing. Not much. His pipe—Well, he could do without that and another would be easy to make. Likewise his leather pouches. As for the feathered lyre, they were so rare and costly that he could never hope to buy another one. Still, if he wanted his plan to succeed, he must make it as convincing as possible.

"Let me see what you have in your bag," he said.

She hesitated, then turned the contents of the bag onto the ground. There were three hard green fruits, a comb made out of carved bone, a necklace of dried seeds colored purple, and a small dilapidated doll made of rags and twine. As soon as he saw them, Zach wanted to tell her to put everything away, but he needed some evidence that she had been here.

"May I have the comb?" he asked after a moment.

Without a word she handed the object over.

"You can put the other things back," he said. "And these with them," he added, handing her his flint and metal.

He took the comb and the pouch containing his pipe and new-smoke, and dropped them by the fire. His larger bag he ripped open, then shoved into the brush.

"What are you doing?" Evvy sounded frightened.

Zach didn't answer. He kicked the still-smoldering campfire, scattering coals and stones. With his knife he gouged the bark of a young tree, then broke off several of its branches. He would keep his sword and bow, of course; all weapons were so valuable that none would be left anywhere for long. He thought for a moment to hunt for a small animal and its blood, but it might take more than a day, and he had become very aware of the time that had passed since his journey began. Even now there might be a search party on his trail.

He stood back and looked around the now-ruined campsite. Although the evidence did not necessarily indicate a struggle, it would appear obvious that something unusual had occurred here. Then, realizing that the manmade objects might be picked up by anyone, he took them one by one and scattered them nearby, each partially hidden by rocks or dried leaves. As a final touch he took his feathered lyre and placed it, in its protective case, just under the overhanging edge of a large rock upstream from the camp. It would not be readily visible to anyone who was not carefully searching the area, and if he were able someday to retrieve it, it would be at least partially protected from the worst weather.

"Come on, let's go," he said. Evvy, looking distressed but not saying anything, followed him to the mount and let herself be lifted onto it. They had ridden a short distance when she spoke:

"We're going back the way we came yesterday."

"That's right," said Zach. "And we'll ride in the water for a while. Get ready for some splashing." He guided the mount down into the shallow edge of the river and turned her upstream.

Now that it had been done, he felt curiously free.

At last the crossing place came into view, and Zach guided his mount out of the water and onto a pre-Change roadway which was now a mixture of weeds, powdered white rock, and occasional brownish clumps of rotting metal.

"Where are we?" asked Evvy, who hadn't spoken in all this time.

"This is known as the Northern Ford," said Zach. "It's an ancient pre-Change bridge made passable by the Principal's men." The ancient stone pilings supported long wooden boards, carefully laid and secured with thick bark rope. "We'll have to get off and walk across. You go first and I'll follow with the mount."

Evvy looked frightened, but didn't protest, and soon she was across. Zach followed her, the mount behind him. On the other side he looked back across the river. *Good-bye, Will,* he thought.

They had ridden in silence for perhaps two hours when Evvy finally spoke again. "Someone's following us. That's why you did that, isn't it?"

"Yes," he said. It was close enough to the truth.

"Are we going to go back for your things?"

"I hope so," said Zach. "But not for a while."

She was silent again. He could see that she was thinking, trying in her mind the various reasons why he might have done such a thing. He knew that she would half guess the truth and knew just as well that he did not want to tell her more; telling even a part would lead to telling all, and he wasn't yet prepared to do that.

They continued to ride, through sunny days and clear nights. It was early autumn, and though the weather grew milder the further south they rode, their blankets and each night's fire provided welcome warmth. Evvy could not know, of course, that the Capital lay to the north and east of them, that they were moving farther from it every day.

Three nights after they had crossed the river, they camped in a grassy clearing. Zach felt drowsy and comfortable; he had managed to catch two fish that afternoon, and he and Evvy had eaten both of them. Crickets and new-insects chirped in the trees; the night air in this part of the District was moist and heavy.

"I miss your lyre," said Evvy.

"So do I," said Zach. He leaned back with his hands behind his neck and watched as the stars appeared.

"Zach?"

"Yes?"

"Why won't you tell me the truth?"

For a beat Zach was silent. He didn't look at the girl but kept his gaze fixed on the dark sky above him. "I haven't lied to you," he said at last.

"It can be a lie to tell only part of the truth," she said.

He looked at her now, sitting cross-legged against a tree. The fire was burning low, and he saw that she was gazing at him calmly and openly. For the first time he realized that she was not, after all, a child, but a nearly mature young woman. He couldn't think what to say to her, and after a moment she spoke again.

"We're not going to the Capital, are we?"

He spoke slowly and with relief. "No, we're not."

"That's why you left your things at the camp all those days ago. You wanted the Principal to think something had happened, so he won't look for us."

"Yes," said Zach, wondering what else to add, how much to tell her, how to explain what he had decided when she was nursing him back to health. But perhaps he had unconsciously made the decision even before that, on the day he had reluctantly agreed to travel to the remote part of the District where Evvy's family lived.

"What will happen if he finds us?" she asked.

"He won't find us," said Zach. "Don't worry."

"Don't say that," she said. "That's all my parents told me the whole week before you came to our house!"

"Ah, Evvy. Let me put it his way, then. I don't intend to be caught. Not by the Principal or anyone. And as long as I'm with you, I promise that I won't let anything happen to you."

"How long will you be with me?"

"Until I know that you are safe and happy."

She didn't speak again for several moments, then: "Will you tell me where we're going?"

"The name of the place wouldn't mean anything to you, but it's where I grew up. I'm very sure that you'll like it and the people there."

"When will we get there?"

"In two or three days at the most."

"What will we do then?"

Again Zach hesitated. "I don't know," he said at last. "I have an idea, but I haven't made up my mind. I'm not lying or hiding anything from you. I just don't know yet." The only thing he did know, for certain, was that he could not stay at the Garden, nor could he ever return to the Capital.

Evvy sighed. "All right," she said, accepting his answers for the moment.

Between them was the knowledge that she had not yet asked the most important question: why.

Now that the decision had been made and uttered, there was no reason to delay, and the next day they rode hard and long. Zach was sure that the girl was as tired as he of constantly living off the land, the daily search for clean water and food, the animals and insects everywhere. Besides, he felt a growing excitement at the thought of returning to the Garden for however short a period, for the first time in nearly twenty years.

The remainder of the journey took just under three days

from the evening Zach had admitted the truth to Evvy. Though they often passed the time in talking as before, Evvy seemed unusually quiet, lost in her thoughts, and not once did she mention the Capital or the Principal.

When they approached the large shallow lake which lay near the Garden, at first Zach didn't recognize it. But as they turned onto the narrow path by the shore, he realized where he was.

"I used to fish in this lake when I was a boy," he said.

Evvy caught his excitement. "When will we get there?"

"I'd say by nightfall, or at the worst, early morning. It's just across, on the far side of the lake." But as they continued to follow the lake south the path abruptly ended, disappearing into a soupy marsh. Either a stream had changed course or, more likely, men or animals had dammed one.

"Looks as if we'll have to take a detour," Zach said, feeling unreasonably disappointed. Now that he was almost there, he didn't want to wait another minute. He turned his mount and began skirting the swampland. It was large and no path was cleared; the area alongside was treacherous and he rode into the woods some way to avoid it.

"Look," said Evvy. She pointed to a low, narrow wooden bridge, which seemed to lead across the swamp. Beyond it was a red-dirt road. Zach turned his mount onto the bridge. Once across he was about to head back toward the lake when a man's voice cried out, "Halt!"

Zach reined in. "Who are you?"

A short, stout man with a ruddy face and graying hair stood by the path. He was dressed in skins, and on his head was a cap made from the fur of a fox-cat. "You've used our bridge," he said. "Now pay the toll."

Zach was disgusted. The man had no right to collect tolls; such things belonged only to the Principal. But in a region of the District as ill-patrolled as this, enterprising men could get away with anything their imaginations devised.

"How much?" he asked, deciding to pay rather than risk confrontation.

"Two pieces of metal for you . . . and two for your rider. Four altogether."

"That's outrageous! I'll pay nothing! Get out of my way!" Zach started to turn the mount past the little man.

"Not so fast!" Now another man, much taller than the first, nearly as big as Zach himself, stepped into the road. He was holding a crossbow, its bolt aimed at Zach. The small man had swiftly pulled out a knife and held it in throwing position. Zach sighed.

"All right," he said. He reached into his boot and removed four metal coins and flung them to the ground. "Take your deena-cursed toll!" he said.

The two men exchanged glances, then the first one shook his head. "Sorry, stranger," he said. "You should have paid when we first asked. The price just went up."

Feeling sick, Zach realized that both men were now staring, not at him as he had first thought, but just in front of him.

"What my brother means," said the tall man, "is that we want the girl."

Six

Zach hesitated. The big man ahead of him was blocking the road, while the other cut off retreat to the bridge. If he had been alone, he would have turned his mount quickly into the woods, but didn't dare take the risk with Evvy vulnerable in front of him.

"Throw down your weapons," said the little man.

"You're making a dangerous mistake," said Zach.

"You'll be making a bigger one if you don't do what I say."

Zach lifted his sword and knife free from his belt and dropped them. Then he spoke again, in a commanding tone: "I am Zach, delegate of the Principal. If anything happens to me or my daughter you'll be very sorry."

The highwaymen exchanged glances, then the smaller one spoke again. "Get off your mount." He had drawn a sword and approached. Zach dismounted, and the little man moved between him and the mount. "Orin," he said, "take the girl."

The large man put down his bow and reached for Evvy, but the mount whistled in alarm and reared, baring her teeth.

"Zach!" cried Evvy, gripping the animal's mane.

"Hold on!" said Zach. Then, to the men: "The mount won't let anyone near her that she doesn't know."

"Evil-tempered beast," muttered Orin, backing off.

"Take her from the mount," the little man told Zach. "Now!"

Reluctantly, Zach swung Evvy down, while the mount continued to whistle in alarm. Zach put a hand on the beast's head and stroked it to calm her, then tethered her loosely to a nearby tree. He did this slowly, trying to think. He knew his best chance was to maintain the bluff he had begun, to establish himself as a man used to commanding authority. He turned back to the highwaymen.

"I am a delegate of the Principal, traveling on official business," he said. He showed his seal ring. There were very few such rings in the District; with the present state of technology they were impossible to counterfeit.

"It looks genuine," admitted the little man. "What sort of business do you have in this remote area?"

Taking a chance, Zach went on. "I'm an emissary to the leaders of the Garden. You may know of it."

"The place across the lake? We trade with them sometimes. But to tell the truth, we're no more afraid of the Garden than we are of the Principal. Laws ain't too important out here."

"Laws are important everywhere," said Zach. "Without them men become beasts."

The small man shrugged. "Even beasts have to make a living."

Zach took a moment to control his anger, then spoke again. "You seem to be sensible men. Take the metal I gave you and let us go on. I won't report this."

The highwayman's eyes narrowed. "Can you give me one good reason why we shouldn't just drown you in the swamp and take the girl?"

Zach sensed he was losing any small advantage he had. "The penalties for girl-stealing—" he began.

"Death by machine. Yes. Neither of us wants to die that way, but you know as well as we do the chances ain't good we'd ever be caught."

"Don't be too sure," said Zach. "A contingent of the Principal's men is riding a few hours behind us."

The brothers again exchanged glances. "I see no reason to believe you or not to believe you, stranger," the small man said.

"Then let us go."

"I don't see how we can do that now. Especially if what you tell us is true."

"If anything happens to me, the Principal himself will track you down and punish you, even if he has to spend the rest of his life doing it." Zach spoke with conviction; this, at least, was the truth.

"Perhaps," said the little man. "But that don't change anything. You see," he went on, "my brother and I have been lonely. A few months ago our wife ran off with the Traders. We've been looking for another, but unattached women ain't so easy to find. And then you come along with this girl, and it seems like a deena-sent gift, if you see what I mean."

Zach felt sick. After everything that had happened, his decision to betray the Principal, his promises to Evvy, he could not allow her to be taken by two such men.

"But lonely as we are," the man continued, "now that we've taken a closer look at you and the girl, other possibilities come to mind. A girl like this would be worth a lot of money to somebody."

"My daughter is not for sale," said Zach.

The man looked closely at Evvy, then at Zach. "She is very beautiful," he said. "But I don't need to tell you that. I also don't have to tell you that she doesn't look anything like you. I don't believe you're her father."

"He's my second-father," Evvy said quickly.

"Then why do you look at him that way? That ain't the kind of look a girl gives to anyone but her lover."

Zach tensed, but there was nothing he could do or say.

"Where did you steal her from?"

"Ermil," said the taller brother, sounding nervous, "let's get on with it."

"Don't worry," said Ermil. "Look at his face. He's lost and he knows it."

"What about his seal ring?"

"Most likely he stole that too, or . . ." The little man stopped talking and thought for a moment. "Maybe you didn't steal her at that," he said to Zach. "If your seal ring is genuine, and you're on business for the Principal . . . Well, we've heard things about the Principal, and I think I know what your business is." He waited a moment, but Zach didn't speak, so he went on. "You're far from the Capital, my friend. Farther, I think, than you are supposed to be. You are one of the Principal's procurers, but when you saw the girl you decided to take her for yourself. Is that right?"

Zach felt dizzy. The little man was very clever, and he could not think of a way of answering without letting Evvy know more than he wanted her to.

"You needn't answer," said Ermil. "Your silence tells me everything I want to know." He paced a few steps, then stopped and approached Zach. Zach hoped for an opening, but the big man, Orin, still held his crossbow trained on him, while Ermil's hand continued to touch lightly the throwing knife at his waist. The little man was looking at him with intensity, and Zach knew that anything he said or did might make matters worse. He waited.

"If I'm right," Ermil said after a moment, "and I see that I am, you are in a great deal of trouble. You can't go back to the Principal, no matter what we do. You mentioned the penalties for girl-stealing. I imagine the penalties for one of the Principal's own men, one who took a girl intended for the Principal himself, would be much worse. Perhaps flogging and castration before a slow death in the machines?" He waited, then went on. "No matter. If, as you say, the Principal's men are behind you, I don't think you'll want to be here when they arrive. And far from arresting us for the minor matter of collecting tolls, they will no doubt reward us for turning over to them a criminal like you. And the girl."

Not for the first time, Zach wished he were quick and clever at lying. Everything the little man said was true, except for the fact of the Principal's men being on the road. At last he spoke. "That is a very good story. But unfortunately for you, none of it is true. The fact is that I am a delegate of the Principal, on an important mission, and Evvy is my daughter."

"I'll say one thing for you, stranger. You don't give up." Ermil seemed relaxed, very sure of himself. "Still, my brother and I are not criminals. We may not be the Principal's most loyal subjects, but we do believe in law, up to a point. I offer you a chance."

"Well?" said Zach, knowing he should not have spoken.

"It is this. We will let you go on your way. As you know, you ain't far from the western border. In return, you will leave us the girl. If you're as clever as you must be, you will have covered your trail long before this, so there's little danger to us. We can make good use of the metal we'll get for this girl after we make some use of her ourselves. I imagine the Principal will pay a great deal to get her back."

Again Zach had to control his anger. He took a deep breath and was about to speak, but Ermil went on. "I ain't saying you have to like it," he said. "But you don't have much choice."

Orin, who had been silent through this exchange, spoke now. "Why don't we just kill him, Ermil. What if—"

"No," said Ermil. "Not unless we have to. He is not what he claims to be, I'm sure of that. I'm beginning to lose patience, stranger."

"Zach—" Evvy gripped his hand.

"Hush," he said. "Let me think." It had all happened so quickly; he wasn't sure what to do. Of course he must fight the men, but he'd have to wait for an opportunity. The important thing was to give Evvy a chance to get away. As for the outcome of a fight, Zach had few illusions. He had never been outstanding with weapons, always relying more on his size and wits than his reflexes. Still, he had this on his side: Ermil seemed reluctant to kill him outright. Orin he was more unsure of, but he seemed stupid and Zach had observed that he moved awkwardly.

"Well?" said Ermil.

Zach let his shoulders sag. "All right," he said. "I accept your terms. As you pointed out, I don't have much choice."

Evvy drew her breath in sharply but said nothing.

Ermil looked pleased. "Good," he said. "My brother will escort you as far as the border, on your mount. Then he will leave you there. Of course, we'll keep the mount and your weapons. If you get any ideas about coming back for the girl, we'll be long gone by then."

Zach nodded. Once again, as when he had crossed the river three days ago, he felt relieved. The decision had been made: he knew what he must do.

"One thing," said Zach. "Let me have a few moments alone with the girl." Ermil raised his eyebrows and Zach added quickly, "Just a few words. We've been together a long time."

"Don't trust them," said Orin.

"What can they do?" said Ermil with a shrug. "He's unarmed and she's a girl. I don't see the harm." He turned to Zach. "My brother and I will be standing right here in case you decide to try anything."

"And don't think we can't stop you," said Orin. "You see the cap Ermil's wearing? He took it from a fox-cat that he stopped with his knife."

Zach was impressed. Fox-cats' reflexes were such that they were said to be able to catch birds taking wing.

"I only want to say good-bye," said Zach.

Ermil and Orin moved a few paces away. Zach squatted in the shade of a tree. His legs were shaking from tension. Evvy sat beside him.

He didn't know where to begin, and she surprised him by speaking first.

"Is it true what he said? About what the Principal would do if he caught you?"

"If he caught me," said Zach. "Evvy—"

"You don't have any choice. I can see that!"

"Be quiet," he said. "We don't have much time." He spoke urgently, keeping his voice as low as possible. A glance showed him that the brothers were watching closely, Orin plainly distrustful.

Evvy was crying now, and he put his arm around her and

awkwardly stroked her shoulder as he had done that first night when she'd had a bad dream. After a moment she calmed, and he took her chin in his hand, turning her face toward him.

"Do you remember what I promised you? That I won't let anything happen to you?"

"As long as you're with me," Evvy said.

"I won't break that promise. I have a plan. But I need your help."

"What do you want me to do?"

"When it comes time for me to go, I'm going to create trouble. I can't be exactly sure how or when, so I want you to promise me something."

"Hurry it up, you two," said Ermil. "It's time to start for the border so Orin can return by dark."

"Another moment," said Zach. "As soon as both men are busy with me, I want you to run into the woods. Then you must go back in the direction of the lake, and follow it north until you come to the Garden. It shouldn't take you more than a few hours to get there."

"But you don't have a weapon!"

He shook his head and went on quickly. "Even if you don't get there tonight, you know how to live outdoors, and you have the flint and steel. I know you can do it."

"But—"

"Promise me, Evvy. Promise you'll do that."

"What about you?"

"I'll try to catch up to you. If I can't, I'll meet you later at the Garden."

"That's not what I mean. What if—" she stopped.

Zach understood her. "I'll be all right. I've fought before. Promise me you'll go there, and not look back."

"If you're so sure you'll be all right, why do you want me to run away?" She sounded angry.

"Come on, that's enough," said Ermil.

Zach sighed. "I can't fight them if I have to worry about protecting you. It's the only chance we have."

She was silent a moment. "Do you promise you'll come there?"

"If I am able, I'll come. If not, at least you'll be safe."

"You said you wouldn't leave me until I was safe and happy. I could never be happy without you." She looked at the ground. He watched as she twirled the bracelet he had made her, round and round her wrist. After a moment she looked up at him. Her face was streaked with tears, her eyes as clouded as a stormy sky. Zach thought that she had never looked so beautiful. "I'll do it," she said.

Zach turned his body so that Ermil could not see his hands. He removed his seal ring and pressed it into Evvy's palm. "Show them this when you get there," he said. "Tell them I sent you."

She nodded, then put her arms around him and squeezed tightly. "Be careful," she said.

Zach returned the hug, then stood. "I'm ready," he said.

Seven

Zach was on his mount, Orin behind him. Ermil, now holding the sword, was directing Orin in tying Zach's hands to the mount's lead.

The big man was awkward and, Zach sensed, afraid of the mount. He must make his move soon, and as Orin struggled with the leather thongs he saw his chance. Shifting his weight, he suddenly lunged back into Orin. The mount reared and the two of them slid off.

"Watch out!" shouted Ermil, but it was too late. The men were on the ground, and while Orin rolled frantically to get away from the mount's kicking feet, Zach rolled with him. Ermil had jumped away from the enraged animal, and now Zach threw his arm around Orin's neck from behind.

Slowly he stood, pulling the big man up with him. Orin's hands had gone to Zach's left forearm, and with his right hand

Zach reached for Orin's knife and jabbed the point of it against the man's lower back.

All this took a very few seconds. Ermil had recovered and was moving toward them.

"Drop that sword or your brother dies," said Zach.

Ermil looked disbelieving, then dropped the sword.

"I should have killed you," he said.

"It would have been safer," Zach agreed. "Now drop the knife and move over by that tree. Now," he added, jabbing the knife point into Orin.

Orin let out a yelp. "I'm sorry, Ermil," he said. "That deena-cursed animal—"

"Shut up," said Ermil.

Zach took a moment to catch his breath. There was no sign of Evvy in the clearing. Thank the deenas, she had escaped. He would stall to give her a few minutes more, then try to get away himself.

"I underestimated you badly," said Ermil. "But I think you underestimate us. You'll never get away."

"That remains to be seen," said Zach. He was working on a plan but was in no hurry. The more lead time Evvy had the better.

For what seemed a very long time the three men stood, Zach with his forearm all but choking Orin, the knife poised above the big man's right kidney, while Ermil watched warily from a few feet away. Zach felt sweat dripping down his neck and imagined he could hear the other men's thoughts, though the only sound was of breathing.

Then there was a rustling in the brush behind him and he saw Ermil's face change.

"Zach."

Zach felt his stomach drop. He didn't turn. "Evvy, you promised to run."

"I did what you told me," she said. "But when I saw what happened, I thought I could help you."

"You didn't do what you promised!" he shouted. He was so angry that Orin grunted and began to struggle as his breath was cut off. Zach relaxed his hold on Orin, then continued, "You promised you'd go to the Garden and not turn back!"

"But—"

"A promise is a promise! I thought you were grown-up enough to understand that!"

"I only wanted to help!"

"Your childish nonsense is likely to get us both killed!" he said. "Now do what I told you and get out of here!"

He heard her intake of breath, but she didn't say anything, and a moment later the sound of running footsteps told him she had gone into the woods. He hoped that she would do as she was told this time, but knew that he would not be able to maintain the standoff much longer. He would now have to try to disable the brothers in some way.

"Your 'daughter' ain't too obedient, is she?" said Ermil.

Zach didn't answer. The safest thing would be to kill both men if he could manage it, but like Ermil he had no taste for cold-blooded murder. In any case, he could no longer continue to hold the struggling Orin; the man was nearly as big as he was and Zach's arms were beginning to quiver from fatigue.

Slowly he backed up to where his sword lay on the ground, and, still covering Orin with the knife, he picked it up, then stepped back. At least this gave him a bit of mobility.

"You can't stop both of us if we decide to rush you," said Ermil.

"I can kill at least one, though, and I don't think you want that."

Ermil shrugged, and Zach turned to Orin. "Orin, take those thongs and tie your brother to the tree."

"What if I don't want to?" said Orin.

"Then I'll run you through," said Zach. "And don't think I won't."

With every minute the brothers were gaining confidence, and Zach knew that his time was running out. If Evvy had obeyed him in the first place he would now be able to break for his mount and try to get away.

Orin was moving very slowly. Zach turned to prod him with the sword, then too late saw Ermil move. The man's aim was deadly. Before he could fend it off a rock struck Zach just behind the ear and he staggered. Orin lunged and knocked him to the ground; the sword fell from his hand. In the other hand he still held the knife, but Orin's fingers closed on his wrist. The man was strong, and Zach had to relax his grip or have his wrist broken.

Orin reached for the sword and stood, holding its tip against Zach's throat. "I've got him, Ermil," he said.

"Go after the girl," said Ermil. "On the mount. I'll take care of our friend here."

"That mount don't like me," said Orin.

"Take the thongs and beat it, then," said Ermil. "Stop wasting time."

Ermil took the sword from Orin. Zach tried to raise himself on one elbow and was hit by a wave of dizziness. Feeling helpless, he watched as the big man cautiously approached the mount. She whistled menacingly, but Zach could see she was tired and confused, and after a brief moment of skittish dancing, she let him climb on. Orin disappeared into the woods.

Zach knew it was over. Even if she had obeyed him this time, Evvy had no chance of outrunning a mounted man.

"Once again things have turned," said Ermil. "You're far too dangerous, my friend. You understand I'll have to kill you now."

The little man had both sword and knife, and it was quite clear by now that he knew how to use them. Zach's only hope was to break and run, but he knew that with Ermil's ability to throw he would not get far.

"There's nothing personal in this," Ermil went on. "I have an idea the Principal lost a good man when you decided to take the girl. But your time has run out." Still the man didn't move, and Zach sensed he was struggling with his reluctance to kill in cold blood. Perhaps he might yet manage to outwit him. . . .

"If you let me go," said Zach, "I will reward you. I—"

"No," said Ermil, almost sadly. "I can't trust you." He was standing above Zach, the sword poised. He pulled it up, ready to thrust, and Zach did the only thing he could: he rolled to the side, into the little man's legs. Ermil's own hesitation was his undoing; Zach had caught him by surprise and he fell. Zach threw himself onto Ermil, grabbed for the sword arm and twisted it. Ermil struggled, but Zach was much larger and stronger, and he quickly retrieved the sword. Now things had once again turned, and Zach forced himself to do what he must. He pulled his arm back, hesitated only a moment, then thrust the blade deep into Ermil's belly. Ermil grunted and his hands went to the wound. He looked up at Zach, his eyes startled and slipping out of focus.

"I'm sorry," said Zach. He pulled the sword out and wiped it on the grass. He felt sick and unclean, and had to breathe deeply several times to clear his head.

He told himself that this had been necessary for Evvy's sake. Now he must find her before Orin did, and take her to the Garden. That was all that mattered.

He put the sword into his belt and stood, unsteadily. Ermil was breathing in shallow gasps, his eyes staring at nothing. Zach turned and walked across the clearing to where the red-dirt road disappeared into the trees. He had nearly reached it when he heard a noise behind him. He turned, and was stunned to see Ermil propped on one elbow, incredibly still alive. He had forgotten about the knife, and by the time he realized what had happened it was too late. Ermil threw before he could move. He felt the knife slip into his chest like a diver into water, and knew that he was a dead man.

He did not fall at once. In slow motion, as if under water, he turned and walked toward the woods. Behind him he thought he heard Ermil laughing. He felt a deep and overpowering anger, not at Ermil, who had killed him, but at himself. Every promise he had made had now been broken, and for nothing. All his life he had considered himself a man of honor, but now he knew that honor was as fragile as the shell of an egg. Whole, it would support a man throughout his life as an egg protects a baby chick. But once a crack appeared, however small, the life inside an egg was doomed; further cracks would radiate from the first as inevitably as one act of dishonor followed another. In both cases the end was the same: contamination and death.

His anger spread from a white-hot point where the knife had gone into him, and moved to his limbs, making them heavy. He could no longer stand and fell to his knees. Even as his legs gave way and he began to cough and spit up blood, he continued to crawl toward the woods where Evvy had gone. He was still trying to follow her when his body stopped moving and he felt his life draining away into the soft, mossy ground.

PART TWO

The Principal

One

Evvy woke cold and stiff, damp leaves pressed into her face and hair. She was huddled in a hollow at the base of an oak tree. The faint light of early dawn showed through pink-and-gray clouds, and a gentle drizzle was falling. She pulled her sodden cloak tightly about herself, then slowly sat up. Automatically she looked around for Zach, then remembered all that had happened yesterday: how she had disobeyed Zach, his anger, and her own headlong flight into the woods.

Long after dark she had fallen, exhausted, at the base of the tree where she now lay. It had been too late to build a fire, and in any case she no longer had Zach's flint—she had lost it one of the many times she had fallen in her despair and panic. Frantically, she had searched her pocket for the seal ring and had fallen asleep with it clutched tightly in her hand. She opened her palm now and looked at it, wondering what to do.

It was too late to go back and try to help Zach now, and she wouldn't want to risk disappointing him again. She thought of simply waiting here for him to find her, but she was cold and hungry, and besides, the rain must by now have obscured any signs of her passage.

Above her and around as far as she could see were thick, leafy branches and wildly growing stalks. She would never find her way out of here—she would starve or be eaten by a wild animal. Each wet rustling of the leaves might be a fox-cat preparing to spring. Her teeth began to chatter, and she squeezed her eyes tightly shut, wanting to cry, to call out for her mother or for Zach.

But her mother had sold her and Zach wasn't here.

"You're acting like a child!" She opened her eyes wide. Zach's words of yesterday echoed inside her head, and she realized she had spoken them, aloud, to herself. The menacing leaves were once again just forest, where she had been for weeks. She would do what she must and prove to Zach that her childishness was in the past.

She took a deep breath and stretched, trying to work out the stiffness of sleeping in the damp. She brushed leaves from her hair and straightened it with her fingers. She would follow Zach's instructions and meet him at the place he had talked about—the Garden. A little flame of fear that he might not have escaped from the highwaymen licked at the edges of her mind. She shook her head. Zach was strong, and good—he could not have been overcome by two such evil men. He was probably at the Garden already, waiting for her.

But where was it? She had become hopelessly turned around yesterday. He had told her to find the lake and follow it to the north, but she had no idea where it was from here, or even which direction she had come from. She felt that she must be east of the bridge where they had met the highwaymen, in which case the lake must lie even further east. But the clouds obscured the sun. She looked through the dark canopy of leaves and finally decided that it was a little lighter in one direction: very well, she would follow the light. She stood and shook out her cloak, preparing for the walk, and then she heard the rhythmic footsteps and faint whistling of a hard-ridden mount.

It was Zach. Somehow, he had tracked her. Her heart began to beat so rapidly that she felt dizzy, and she turned to greet the approaching rider. After a moment Zach's mount broke past the bushes and she cried out to the hooded figure riding it, "Zach!"

"Halt!" cried the rider. A hand snaked out of the cloak and used a short whip on the rearing mount.

Evvy put her hand to her mouth.

"So there you are," said the gruff voice. His hood fell back to reveal the black-bearded face of Orin, the highwayman. "Who would have thought a little girl could run so far in the dark? I would have caught you last night but for this deena-cursed mount. She sat right down at dusk and wouldn't budge no matter how I beat her."

"Where's Zach?" Evvy demanded, her voice quavering.

"Your 'father?' Gone to where he won't cause trouble for anyone else," said Orin.

"What do you mean?"

For an answer the man grinned and slowly pulled a finger across his throat. He began gingerly to dismount while the mount, her shiny tan flanks spotted with dried blood, danced nervously, whistling.

"Hold still, you deena-cursed beast!" cried the highwayman.

Evvy watched in fascination and terror, and only when the man stood on the ground did she think to begin edging into the brush.

"Oh, no, you don't," he said. He dropped the reins and lunged at Evvy, pulling her to the ground.

"No!" she cried, and rolled away. As she did, the seal ring tumbled from her hand, and before she could retrieve it, Orin had picked it up and slipped it on his own finger.

"Give that back!" she cried and grabbed for his hand. Orin deftly grasped her wrist and pulled her toward him.

"It fits me just fine, don't it?" he said, admiring its gleam in the pale light. "I'm just about your papa's size ... most likely all his things would fit me."

The grip of Orin's hand on her wrist seemed to freeze her, the pressure spreading up her arm and through her body. What would Zach do if he were here? Somehow he would try to outwit the big man. Through the panicked jumble in her mind, Evvy said the only thing she could think of, her voice shaking slightly.

"You'd better let me go. I'm not what you think. The truth is I belong to the Principal."

Orin gaped at her, his thick eyebrows meeting quizzically; then suddenly he began to laugh, a loud, full roar from deep within him. "Well, ain't that just what Ermil and me thought?" he said. "The reward's going to be more metal than we can count." Then his face changed. His eyes became narrow and slipped out of focus. "The Principal's going to be real happy to get you back," he murmured. With force, though not roughly, he pushed her down onto the leaves at the base of the tree.

Evvy whimpered and tried to roll away, but she was twisted in her cloak. The highwayman looked down at her and licked his lips.

From a last reservoir of strength she spoke again. "The Principal will kill you if you hurt me."

For a moment Orin looked startled, a hint of fear in his murky eyes, but then he grinned again. His breathing was quick and she could scarcely make out the words as he muttered, "I ain't going to do nothing different than your 'father.' Just relax and pretend I'm him."

His hands had found the ties on her trousers, and she felt the belt loosening, then his hand on her belly, pulling and probing.

Horror and nausea gave Evvy more strength than she thought she could possess. "No!" she screamed, and she managed for a second to escape the probing hands.

"So you want to play rough?" he asked, almost good-naturedly. He leaned forward and pressed her into the ground. His body lay across her legs, and one arm pinned her hands behind her head while the other continued to pull at her trousers. She felt them rip, and then the soft wetness of earth against her bare buttocks. "No," she said. "No, please, no."

Now Orin was fumbling at his own belt, making soft noises to himself. With a last desperate effort Evvy pulled her right arm free and grabbed the first thing her hand came to, which turned out to be a sharp, thick piece of wood. Without thinking, she brought the stick forward into the face of the highwayman and saw it go into his left eye.

For a moment everything stopped—all noise, all movement—then blood began to spurt as Orin let out an inhuman-sounding bellow of pain and surprise. He fell back onto his knees, both hands to his face. Evvy only stared in horror, all will to move suddenly drained from her.

Orin moaned. "Look what you've done!" he cried. The moan changed to an incoherent cry of rage and he pulled out a knife. Once again he lunged at her, foam flecking the corner of his mouth. Evvy quickly moved away from him, but she became tangled in her torn trousers.

"I'll kill you," he was muttering. "I'll kill you."

Evvy began to kick at the trousers, trying to get free. Orin stabbed once, into the ground, missing her by several inches. She realized that he couldn't see what he was doing and rolled clear.

All at once she heard a high-pitched whistle, and then the sound of hooves on stone. She looked up at the same moment as Orin to see the mount rearing, whistling in her own rage.

"No!" cried the highwayman, but it was too late for him to get away, and the sharp hooves of the mount came down with all its weight on his chest. There was a noise like the sound of kindling breaking, and the man screamed. He turned his knife on the mount and she whistled in anguish as he slashed at her, drawing a great fountain of blood. Again she reared and again she came down, her legs buckling as she fell across the screaming man.

Evvy finally managed to break away from the tangled ruin of her trousers, and wearing only her short tunic, began to run as quickly as she could. Her only thought was to get away from the horrible sounds of dying man and beast, each uttering cries of final pain as they killed each other.

She continued to run, tripping over exposed roots, slipping in the mud, each time picking herself up and running further. At last she slowed, her legs trembling so that she could hardly stand, and realized that the only noises were the ordinary ones of the forest. She squatted where she stood and vomited, little coming up but the roots she had chewed the previous evening for dinner.

There were no more tears left in her, and after a moment, shakily, not knowing what else to do, she continued to walk, directionless, her mind as blank as a wall. There was nothing she wanted to think about: all that seemed important was to get as far away from that horrible scene as possible.

She drank from puddles from time to time, though curiously she felt no hunger. At last she decided that she must be dying, and if the ancient religion was right, that meant she would soon be reunited with Zach. But perhaps he wouldn't want to see her, even in the beyond. She had broken her promise to him and now had lost his flint and seal ring. She heard herself whimpering as she continued to walk, stumbling, her soft boots sodden and full of mud, her bare legs scratched and icy with cold. She had found a sort of path and began following it, without aim or thought. Gradually she became aware of a scuffling sound and a faint, high-pitched mewling. Her heart thumped heavily in her chest as she realized that she must have walked in circles back to the scene of death at the base of the tree. She stopped moving and put her hand to her mouth. She bit heavily on her knuckles, certain that she was about to die.

Something moved in the underbrush, and she stood, waiting for whatever it was, even the blinded ghost of Orin. All at once the leaves shook as if they had been suddenly drenched with water, and a small, furry, orange animal leaped out onto the path in front of her. Evvy took a step backward, her legs quaking. She knew from the extraordinarily large, pointed ears that the creature must be a fox-cat, though she had never seen one before.

The creature did not attack, but stood quizzically looking at her, its pale eyes wide, its moist brown nose twitching as it sniffed her from a distance. Then it put its bushy tail straight up in the air and walked up to her. Evvy braced for the attack, but the animal turned and rubbed against her legs. She almost laughed in relief: it was a baby.

"Hello," she said, her voice a nasal croak. It was the first word she had uttered since that morning. She bent down and cautiously put out her hand, half expecting to be bitten, but the fox-cat sniffed her fingers, then again rubbed against her legs, emitting a soft, high-pitched growl.

"Where's your mother, little fox-cat?" she asked, her voice still sounding strange to her. The animal answered with another of its half growls and walked directly away from her toward the underbrush, then stopped and looked back expectantly. Again it uttered its growling noise.

Evvy knew that she should get away before the mother came looking for its baby, but she couldn't take her eyes off the little animal, which stepped cautiously forward, then stopped again. When she still didn't move, it trotted back to her and stretched its paws up against her legs. She stepped back in alarm, but the fox-cat moved between her legs and took the top of her muddied boot in its mouth and began to tug at it. It let go the boot, growled again, then again pulled, this time at the other foot.

Evvy was more perplexed than frightened now. "It's almost as if you want me to go with you," she said. The animal immediately bounded off in the original direction, again stopping at the edge of the underbrush and looking back expectantly.

"Well, why not?" said Evvy. She followed the fox-cat to the edge of a dense, thorny bush, and pushed herself past it. The fox-cat stayed a few paces ahead of her, stopping every few steps to make certain she was following. The ground was becoming marshy, and more than once Evvy's feet sank into mud over her ankles. She followed the fox-cat only because it seemed easier than deciding on her own what to do.

At last the baby animal stopped and began mewling, steadily and without ceasing. Evvy could see ahead of her a shining silvery ribbon edged with green: the lake!

In gratitude she looked back at the baby fox-cat and saw now that it was standing next to a stake-trap in a partially concealed hole. Inside the trap, its once-golden fur matted with dirt and blood, lay the lifeless body of an adult fox-cat, its body pierced with sharpened stakes. The baby continued its pitiful crying, and Evvy realized that the larger animal must be the little one's mother; that the small creature had been asking her to help it.

Pity for the baby's loss welled up in her, and she sank to her knees beside the trap. "It's too late," she said, stroking its short, thick fur. "Poor baby."

She looked at the trap in disgust, wondering what to do. She knew how such traps worked, having watched her first-father set them for small game near her home. A conical pit was set with slim, strong, pointed sticks, often tipped with the poison of the fire-berry. Shorter stakes were then set at an angle pointing downward at the top of the pit. Finally a bait of food was tied with vines to a solid-looking cover of twigs and leaves. Any animal unlucky enough to take the bait would tumble through the false top, becoming trapped at the narrow bottom. Impaled, the animal would exhaust itself struggling and die.

"We can't do anything for her now but bury her," said Evvy. Somehow it seemed important to give the animal a proper burial, as she had seen her mother and second-father do for her first-father. She considered trying to remove the animal from the spikes, but was afraid of the poison that might still be on the wooden tips. Using her hands and a flat piece of wood, she began to fill in the hole from the soft earth around her. The baby fox-cat had stopped crying and now sat on its haunches, watching quietly as she worked.

It seemed to take a very long time to fill the pit completely, and from the corner of her eye Evvy could see that it was beginning to grow dark. But she worked steadily, thinking of nothing but the task at hand, and at last she finished, patting down the sodden earth in a gently curving mound.

She looked at the baby fox-cat, which was now resting on its outstretched limbs but still watching alertly, and sat back.

"In the name of the fathers and mothers," she said, remembering as well as she could the long-ago ceremony, "I put you to rest. God be with you as you are with him." Slowly, she made the sign of the spiral, her hand circling as she touched her forehead, her chin, and then her chest.

The baby fox-cat yawned, then stood and touched its right paw once to the mound as if to dig. It drew back the paw and approached Evvy, rubbing against her knee, then growled and looked up at her as if to say, "What next?"

Two

The dying sunlight grazed the trees and bounced off the lake into the now-thinning clouds, turning lake and sky into a single golden fluid streaked with palest, almost greenish blue. The colors seemed unnaturally vivid to Evvy, as did the dark outlines of the trees, their leaves and branches forming a pattern against the sky like a delicate tangle of hair. Ever since she had buried the mother fox-cat, her vision had been unusually clear. She imagined that she could see everything, even the damp, chilling air in front of her.

She felt as if she had lived longer in this single day than she had in all her life before, that her former life was a dream, only dimly remembered. Zach had been part of that dream, and waking, she would never see him again.

At the thought of Zach an ache spread from her throat throughout her body, filling her with emptiness and longing. If Zach no longer lived, then how could she, or any other creature, be living?

Over and over she remembered how Orin had drawn his finger across his throat, and said that Zach was gone to where he would cause no trouble.

But Orin had not said that Zach was dead.

Quite suddenly Evvy realized that Orin had lied to her, or had not known in truth what had happened to Zach. Perhaps he had escaped after all. If not, then maybe he was a prisoner of the highwayman's brother or, worse, was lying wounded, in need of help, by the bridge.

Zach was alive and needed her. She was certain of it, as certain as of the strange clarity of the air. And she was certain too what she must do. With renewed strength she began to walk along the shore of the lake, following it to the north, her body trembling with cold, her legs soaked and scratched, and with a single thought in her mind: to get to the Garden, the place where Zach had told her to wait for him. She had no idea what the Garden was, but had no doubt that she would find it, and that the people who lived there would return with her to the bridge and to Zach.

From time to time she heard splashing in the water around her, and saw that the baby fox-cat was still following her, apparently confident that she knew where she was going. The little creature was feeding, snapping at insects along the water's edge, its movements quicker than her eyes could follow.

"Why are you staying with me?" she asked it once, and the baby immediately rubbed against her leg and then bounded off. Zach had told her that fox-cats, like many other new creatures, had once been animals that lived with humans, and after the Change had become wild and learned to live on their own. Maybe the baby remembered the earlier times when its ancestors had been friends of men.

True night had nearly fallen, and Evvy became aware how tired she was. She knew that no poison-bats lived so far south, but she began to imagine that every dancing shadow was ready to swoop down on her. The noises of leaves rustling and birds bedding down became human voices, talking to her. Once she was certain that she heard the song of the feathered lyre, and stopped, her heart pounding, but it was only the sound of wind rubbing tree against tree.

Since the light had left, it had become steadily colder, and her skin began to prickle and her teeth to click together. Once she stumbled in the dark and, putting out her hand to steady herself, felt the fur of the fox-cat baby. She lingered a moment to let the warmth of its body move into both her hands, while the baby made a soft buzzing noise and then licked her fingers, its little tongue as rough as the sand on a river bottom.

She kept the lake to her right and continued to walk, her legs responding ever more slowly. She smelled woodsmoke long before she saw anything, and then suddenly a large dark shadow appeared ahead of her, the faint glow of firelight just showing over its edge. She ran toward the structure, which was so large that it was farther than she had first supposed, and put out her hands when she reached it. Her fingers closed on thick prickly vines, and she pulled back, stung by the brambles. She turned away from the lake and began to move around the great vined wall, certain that an opening must appear. From within she could hear faint murmurs and high-pitched, melodious laughing. Her vision had blurred in the dark and she wondered if she were imagining the voices, the woodsmoke, and the wall itself.

The wind had begun blowing, and Evvy realized she was losing feeling in her legs and hands. The urge to lie down and curl up next to the vines grew stronger, but she forced herself to keep walking, for Zach's sake. She reminded herself that every step her reluctant feet took brought her that much closer to him. At last she came to a break in the vines and a massive wooden gate. She pushed and pulled, but it was locked and so heavy that she could not budge it.

"Let me in!" she called, as loudly as she could, but her voice was no more than a croak, and it was taken from her mouth by the roaring of the wind. She beat on the gate, sobbing without tears, calling Zach's name again and again. Without noticing, she sank to her knees and then lay down on her side, curling up tightly. She was no longer cold—she was, in fact, beginning to feel warm and relaxed. She would try again later, when she had rested a little and her voice was stronger. Her whole body throbbed pleasantly, and the events of the day passed through her mind in vivid pictures. Zach's face was in the pictures too, smiling at her.

As she gave herself up to delicious sleep, she became aware of the fox-cat pawing at her, mewling. "Go away," she said crossly, pushing the little animal away and snuggling closer to herself.

After a time the fox-cat gave up, and then Evvy heard a startlingly loud, high-pitched crying and then a scrabbling sound above her on the wall. The crying changed to a continuous howl, and then began to fade. An image of Zach appeared, holding out to her a warm cloak made of white wool. Evvy stretched out her arms and let him enfold her in the soft, warm fabric. Not since the night he had slept with her under her cloak had she felt so safe and so at peace.

The dream of Zach was suddenly replaced by glaring torch-light, and Evvy looked up to see two leather-helmeted warriors standing above her, their bodies grotesquely distorted by shadows. She looked around. Where was Zach? He had been here only a moment ago.

"It's a girl-child," said one of the warriors, sounding surprised.

"She's freezing," said the other, and unhooked a long, heavy cloak. Evvy tried to twist away, hating the cloak and its ugly dark color. Why were they bothering her? The warrior knelt down and placed the cloak around Evvy, then swept her up in strong arms.

"Zach," Evvy tried to say. "Where's Zach?" but her mouth could not form the words correctly and she looked up helplessly. The last thing Evvy saw before she fell asleep again was the strong, clear face of the warrior and the silky golden braids which spilled from beneath her armored hood.

When Evvy awoke, bright sunlight was streaming through a curtained window just behind her head. Astonished, she looked around, thinking at first that she must be in the loft bed in her own home far to the north. Beside her on either side were rows of neat, empty wooden beds, stacked one above the other, like the one she was lying in now.

Quite suddenly she remembered all that had happened yesterday and the day before and felt a clenching in her chest. Where was she? And where was Zach?

She threw off the covers and ran to the massive wooden door. Her legs were scratched and bruised, and her bare feet felt cold against the wooden floor. She realized she was wearing nothing but a very short woolen tunic, much too small for her. Fearing the door might be barred, she pushed against it with all the force she could summon. It swung open easily; and she stumbled, then stopped in confusion. Before her was the largest room she had ever seen. At one end was a stone fireplace, its hearth taking up nearly the entire wall; ahead of her soft light fell through oiled-skin windows; and at the other end of the room four women sat at a long wooden table, working with their hands and talking in low voices. There was no one else in the room.

Her confusion began to turn to panic. Before she could think what to do next, one of the women at the table put down the green wool she had been working with and stood. As she approached, the woman's short red hair stood out from her head like a cloud; below it her plump face was dotted with tan freckles. "Look who's awake," she said, smiling. "How do you feel this morning?"

The woman looked kindly. Evvy hung by the door, embarrassed by her skimpy costume. "Where am I?" she asked.

"You are at a place called the Garden," said the woman.

Evvy felt her heart skip. So she had found the right place! "Is Zach here?" she asked next, unable to keep the excitement out of her voice.

"Who?"

"The man I've been traveling with."

The woman frowned in puzzlement. "You were alone when we found you. Don't you remember?"

"He promised he would meet me here."

"We've seen no one named Zach," the woman said. "Hilda," she continued, speaking to one of the women still at the table, "fetch Katha. Tell her our guest is awake."

Evvy scarcely heard her. Zach was not here. That meant . . . She didn't want to think what it meant. Perhaps he had lied to her, had never intended to come here. Or worse . . . She remembered again the throat-cutting gesture Orin had made, his statement that Zach had gone to where he would cause no more trouble. She must return to the bridge as quickly as possible, and with help.

The woman with red hair took her arm. "My name is Gunda," she said. "We can get acquainted while you eat breakfast."

Evvy felt that she was about to start crying. But this was no time to act like a child. She would not do that again. She put her hand on the lyre-bird bracelet and turned it around her wrist, then took a deep breath and held it until the ache in her throat was gone. She looked directly at the kindly red-haired woman and spoke in as adult a manner as she could manage. "Thank you for letting me sleep here," she said. "But now I have very important business. May I speak to the father in charge?"

"There are no fathers here," said the woman. "No men at all. Only women and children."

Evvy was too shocked to speak. How could women live without fathers and husbands to take care of them? Who hunted for them? Who wove their cloth? And who would be able to help her now? Once again she felt tears pressing behind her eyes, and she looked down at the bracelet, turning it round and round.

"Sit down and eat," said Gunda firmly. "You can't do anything if you're starved. I'll get you some proper clothing. Then you'll see our leader, the Mistress. She has asked to talk to you. I'm sure she'll be able to help with whatever your trouble is."

Evvy felt as if the world she knew had turned inside out. It was true that there were no men here—everything was done by women. The golden-haired warrior she had seen last night, Katha, was a military commander, apparently as competent and deadly as the Principal was said to be. Although Evvy realized that Katha could not be more than a very few years older than Evvy herself, the woman was tall and muscular, and her tanned face was lined and grim-looking, as if she had never been a child. As soon as she had heard Evvy's story, Katha had dispatched two mounted and armed women to the bridge where Evvy had last seen Zach, brushing aside Evvy's urgent demand to accompany them.

"If he's alive, they will find him," she said with cool certainty. "You would only be in the way. Don't worry about it. My soldiers know what they are doing."

How could she not worry? Never in her life, not even on the day she had first left her family home, had Evvy felt so helpless. Her whole being was clenched with the need to find Zach, a need so urgent it felt physical. She could not focus her mind on anything else even for a moment. Every minute her ears strained for the sound of mounts' hooves, though she knew it might be hours, or even the next day, before the women soldiers returned.

Only the little fox-cat, which had led her here and had been waiting for her in the yard, seemed to understand how unhappy she was. She scooped it up in her arms as soon as she saw it, and sympathetically the small animal began to lick her cheek with its rough tongue, then buzzed reassuringly as if to say, "I am with you."

Just now it was indeed with her, helping her to satisfy the curiosity of the leaders of this strange place, while she waited for word of Zach.

She was sitting on a wooden bench in a tiny, dark cabin. Although it was full daylight, the two small windows were shuttered, and the only illumination came from flickering odorous fish-oil lamps. Beside her was Katha, and across from her, in a dark wooden chair on rockers, sat the Mistress, leader of the Garden. The tiny room seemed to be all furniture, with scarcely space to walk. There were chairs, tables, and chests of shiny polished wood, all obviously made before the Change. On a long, high bench at one end of the room were dozens of dark and shiny objects, some glittering with metal, others glass, and all with mysterious shapes. Lining two of the walls from floor to ceiling were row upon row of dusty, colored boxes which Evvy realized with a start must be books.

The Mistress was by far the oldest person Evvy had ever seen. She was dressed in a long dark gown with a short white coat buttoned over it, instead of in the tunic and trousers worn by the other women Evvy had seen, and she was small, shrunken, like an animal or a sick child. Her thin, pale hair was pulled sharply back from her face, but her tiny features did not look severe. When she spoke it was slowly and with some difficulty, as if a part of her mouth no longer worked, and Evvy had to lean forward and concentrate to hear her.

Just now the Mistress and Katha were watching the baby fox-cat as it played on the wooden floor. "Remarkable," said the old woman.

"It saved the girl's life," Katha said. "Its cries appeared to be deliberate, as if to attract our attention. Apparently it has imprinted on her." The fox-cat seemed abruptly to tire of playing and yawned, then trotted over to Evvy, jumping into her lap.

"Remarkable," said the Mistress again. "It's almost as if it understood you." Now she turned her intense blue eyes on Evvy. "Evvy, daughter of Eugenia," she said. "I can see you are impatient. You want to learn what has become of your friend. But I can promise you that Katha's soldiers won't return one minute sooner than they return."

Evvy was astonished; the old woman had scarcely seemed to know that she was in the room. After a moment the Mistress's face twisted in what Evvy finally identified as a smile.

"Now, you can fill this time in worry and imagining. I expect you are very good at that. Or you can make the time pass by telling us how you have come here. The choice is yours."

When Evvy had finished her story it was late afternoon. The Mistress and Katha had both listened with absorption, asking many questions, making her go over some parts. Katha in particular had seemed anxious to discover if Zach had touched her or hurt her in any way; the Mistress had wanted to know what, exactly, Zach had done at each juncture, how he had behaved, and what he had said.

The Mistress asked Evvy once again to describe Zach's appearance, and she did, explaining how frightened she had been at first by his size and power, and how quickly she had come to see his gentle side. As Evvy spoke, the Mistress closed her eyes and nodded her head. For a moment Evvy thought the old woman had fallen asleep, but when she reached the end of her description, the Mistress's eyes snapped open.

"When do you expect the guards to return?" she asked Katha.

"Soon," said the younger woman. "Before sunset, anyway. You're convinced it's he, then?"

"I'm certain of it," said the old woman. "Zach is not a common name, and only one Zach we know of works for the Principal."

"I'd caution against too much hope," said Katha in a matter-of-fact tone. "From what Evvy says, it's not likely he's alive."

Evvy felt her throat tighten, and she was about to protest when the old woman shook her head, looking impatient. "Zach is a remarkable man," she said. "Anything is possible."

"It's true, then?" Evvy blurted. "You know him?"

Again the Mistress made her grotesque attempt at a smile. "Zach spent the first twenty years of his life here," she said. "Katha was a baby when he left, but I knew him well. Very well indeed, though I haven't seen him in nearly as many years as he lived here. He is my son."

Three

The Principal was in a rage. It seemed that nobody around him could be depended on. In the early days, when he had first taken the Capital and was beginning to unify the District, he had been able to see to almost everything himself. But the Capital had long since expanded from a half-settled ruin to a thriving city, and with it had grown the complexities of management, as well as the necessity of training new men to extend this small area of light into the darkness that was the world. He simply didn't have the time or patience for routine anymore, and Zach, who generally attended to such details, was out in the District. Berton, the bumbling fool who was covering a small part of Zach's duties as general factotum, seemed incapable of anything but stammering apologies.

"It wasn't my fault," Berton was saying for the third time. "Nobody knew anything was wrong till it was too late, and they just died."

"They just died?" said the Principal as evenly as he could. "Fourteen of the finest mounts, just died because nobody noticed they were sick?"

"The mount-master has been sick himself these last few days, and we thought he'd see to them when he returned."

"Do you know how much those animals cost?" said the Principal. Before Berton could answer, he went on: "More than you could earn in a hundred years! And it wasn't my metal, it was money I've collected from my people to build a better life for them. I suppose the deena-cursed criminal who sold us the sick mounts is gone too?"

"I . . . don't know, sir," said Berton, trembling.

"Well, find out!" the Principal shouted. And with that he hurled the book he had been reading after his rapidly departing assistant. He stood still and took three slow, deep breaths, then crossed the room to retrieve the book. He sighed. The binding had been split in half. His aides' incompetence had cost him some valuable animals; his own intemperance had damaged an irreplaceable book. If only Zach had been here, none of this would have happened. Zach would have seen to the new mounts, would not have accepted ill animals, would not have waited for the mount-master to recover. If Zach had been here, he himself would not have given in to this childish tantrum.

The Principal ran a hand down the face of the book and set it on his desk. It could be mended. Not so the mounts, but he realized that they were not really the cause of his outburst, or of the unease that had kept him on edge for weeks; rather, it was just that Zach was not here.

The journey that Zach had undertaken was long and perilous to be sure, but Zach was a seasoned traveler, and no matter what sort of difficulties he had encountered, he should have been back at least three weeks ago. For the first week or two that Zach failed to return, the Principal had been impatient because of the prize that Zach was to bring him. The descriptions of the girl had been intriguing and stimulating, even allowing for his tax men's inevitable exaggerations. It was unlikely, but it might even be that this girl was one he would want to make his legal wife. In any case, he had not had a girl in a while now and felt the needs building in him.

As the days had passed, the Principal's thoughts of the young girl had begun to fade, and his concern centered on

Zach himself. What could be delaying him? Had the girl's parents changed their minds? But if so, Zach had orders to take her anyway, and certainly poor farmers and their wife wouldn't be able to prevent him.

The Principal had allowed his mind to rest only briefly on the possibility that Zach had come to harm. In the first place he had utmost faith in Zach's abilities to protect himself from bandits, poison-bats, or other common dangers; in the second he simply could not face such a catastrophe. Perhaps, he finally decided, something had happened to Zach's mount. She was not young, and possibly the journey was too much for her. Very likely Zach was on foot now, with the girl, which would necessitate moving very slowly.

A week ago an armed party had been sent out to meet Zach and the girl. Perhaps even today they would return, and the Capital would once again begin running smoothly. As it was, the Principal was almost dizzied by details. Deenas take Berton! Of course, he would have to be punished, as an example, but the Principal hesitated to act too harshly. A public flogging and a fine, to be taken from his monthly pay until the mounts were at least symbolically paid for, seemed the best solution.

The Principal sighed. He strove always to be, above all, fair, obeying the law to the letter and with the spirit of justice. And nobody followed the laws more closely than he, who made them.

In the ancient books there were stories about men in the Principal's position. The greatest leaders, those who had done the most for the cause of civilization, had been as he was: controlled and controlling, and consequently lonely. If only Zach were here now, he thought, to play his feathered lyre and sing the poems that he made himself. The Principal was the ruler, the head of the District, but Zach was its heart. The Principal realized that he missed Zach with almost a physical longing, and for a moment he wished that he were like other men, that he could be satisfied with a simple living and a shared wife and children. Of course there were not enough women to go around, and though the Principal could choose any woman in the District, he had not found one he could care about, and he had never known a man he could trust but Zach.

It was getting late, and he had a scheduled meeting with his generals about the long-planned campaign to improve communications throughout the District.

For a moment he considered canceling the meeting, then shook his head. He must move, constantly, no matter his personal feelings. This was his destiny, and he had known it since he was a small boy growing up in the Garden.

He sat behind his wooden desk, which, like all remaining manufactured objects, was a link with the past, and ran his hand over its polished surface. On the curved wall across from him hung a painted likeness of Zach, showing the broad head, the fair, almost white hair so different from his own, the full, bushy beard now grizzled at the cheeks. Once again he felt his mind wandering to the route Zach had taken, the steep mountain trails and thick trees which he had not seen since the year when he had taken control of the District from the President. The late afternoon sunlight fell across his face with an almost physical weight, and the Principal let his head fall onto his arms as he began to doze.

He was startled awake by an urgent knock at the door. Robin, his elderly secretary, stuck his head in and announced, "Sir, I'm sorry to disturb you. An advance scout from the party you sent out last week has returned. It is General Ralf."

"Send him in," said the Principal, instantly awake. "And bring refreshment."

He straightened consciously in his seat, aware of the fading sunlight over his shoulder. Soon it would be time to light the fish-oil lamps, and for the generals. Why Ralf and not Zach? As he waited for Ralf to come in, the Principal lit a pipe of new-smoke to calm himself.

Within a few seconds there was another knock and Ralf entered. Ralf was nearing fifty, which for these times was quite old, although the Principal knew that before the Change fifty was considered midlife. Ralf's clothing was worn and dirty, and he looked exhausted, but not injured or starved or abused, and the Principal relaxed. Behind Ralf stood Robin with a tray of steaming mugs and scones.

"Thank you, Robin," said the Principal. "That is all. Welcome home, General Ralf."

"Thank you, sir," said Ralf, ducking his head and approaching the desk. There was something strange in his manner as he held out his hand. On his shoulder was a large leather bag which he did not remove.

"You must be tired. Have some refreshment."

Ralf sat, then reached forward and cupped both hands around a red pottery mug. The Principal, taking the other cup, saw that the old man's hands were shaking.

Hating the formalities, the Principal leaned back and took a deep drink of the warm liquid. As it flowed into his stomach, he became aware of how tired he was, and how on edge. Ralf too seemed to relish his drink, and drank deeply twice before he set the mug on the edge of the desk and began self-consciously to speak.

"I'm afraid I have b-bad news to report," he began.

"Zach—" said the Principal, but Ralf was already continuing.

"We had not gone far before we discovered some refugees— a family of six who had been driven from their home in the southwest. They had crossed the Northern Ford, trying to get to the Capital."

"Refugees? From the west?" The Principal leaned forward.

"They had been burned out. But apparently not by outlaws. They were attacked by followers of a new religion."

The Principal frowned. "I've heard nothing of a religion."

"It started in the far west, beyond our borders," said Ralf. "Or so we pieced together."

The Principal rubbed his nose and thought a moment. A new religion was not unexpected and was not necessarily even an important threat. But that it appeared to be taking hold in the southwest could be very bad news and would have to be investigated immediately.

"Where are these refugees now?" he asked.

"With the rest of our party," said Ralf. "But let me go on, sir. Shortly after we met up with the refugees, we were set on by a pack of outlaws—"

"So close to the Capital?"

"Again, near the Northern Ford. But these were not ordinary outlaws—they were followers of the new religion I told you about. They call themselves the Traders. They were fanatical, sir, like nothing we have ever dealt with. We sustained heavy losses."

"How heavy?" asked the Principal. This was beginning to sound like a bad dream—surely Ralf was exaggerating.

"One dead, two more wounded."

"How many in the attacking party?"

"Five," said Ralf.

The Principal took three deep breaths. When he spoke, his voice shook. "Are you trying to tell me that fewer than a half-dozen ignorant outlaws disabled a party of as many of my trained men?"

Ralf looked directly at the Principal. "I told you, sir, these were more than ordinary outlaws. They used poisoned weapons, and they fought without a care for their own safety. We were lucky to get away at all."

"Did you take prisoners?"

"One—but he hanged himself in the night."

"Deenas take it!" shouted the Principal. He struck the desk with his fist, then turned to look out the window. In a moment he turned back, now calm. "I'm sorry, Ralf," he said. "Of course you're only reporting what happened. When may I speak to the other men?"

"Within two days," said Ralf. "With the invalids and refugees our way was slowed. I rode ahead because we all agreed you should know as soon as possible what had happened."

"Yes, of course. And thank you for doing this. How long have you been without sleep?"

"I'm fine, sir."

"You are exhausted, and you will be rewarded for your service, after you've had a meal and a good night's sleep." The Principal paused, then spoke the words he knew he had to say next. "As for your primary mission, I gather you were not able to continue on the route that Zach followed?"

For a very long moment the old man just looked at him, eyes big and frightened in the exhausted face. "It was on the same day we met the refugees," he said slowly. "We came upon what had once been a campsite, but obviously ruined. There were broken branches, weapon marks, signs of struggle everywhere. We found . . . indications that a man had camped there, and a woman. A bit of torn cloak, a pipe with the new-smoke still tamped into it, and after a little searching we found . . . these."

Looking as if he expected to be struck, Ralf reached into his pouch and pulled out a comb, carved of bone. He put it on the Principal's desk.

"A woman's comb," said the Principal. He picked it up. "Nice workmanship, but nothing unusual. Have you—"

He stopped. Ralf had reached into his pouch again and was holding another object. It was made of two long, curved pieces of polished dark wood, separated by a half-dozen taut strings. At one end, the strings branched into hundreds of brightly colored feather fronds. Ralf laid the object silently on the desk, then stepped back and remained standing.

The Principal sat motionless, looking at the objects, his mind rejecting what his senses told him was the truth. This was a feathered lyre, one of the rarest objects in the District. At one end of one of the pieces of wood was burned in the initial Z. This was Zach's feathered lyre.

Finally he spoke. "You found nothing else."

"Nothing."

"You did not follow the trail."

"There was no trail. Only the signs of struggle—and a ruined camp."

The Principal put the comb on the desk beside the lyre, where it gleamed orange in the fading light. He stared at the objects, not trusting himself to speak. A rage was building in him, a rage he had never known, and he did not want to take it out on the faithful Ralf. He took one deep breath, two, then three, and after letting out the last looked up at the old man, who was terrified to be bringing such dreadful news.

"That will be all, Ralf," he said, not recognizing his own voice as he spoke. "Robin!" he called, "Robin!" Belatedly he remembered the bell at his side and rang it. At last Robin appeared.

"Give Ralf a meal and a good place to sleep. If he wants

one, give him a woman for hire. Bring me more food and a pitcher of brew, then do not disturb me again this evening. Tell the generals I will see them in the morning."

Robin looked startled and opened his mouth to speak, then thought better of it. "Yes, sir," he murmured.

The Principal was aware that Ralf was waiting for a formal dismissal, but he knew he could not speak again. Finally, following the secretary, Ralf muttered, "I'm sorry, sir. Thank you," and followed the older man out the door.

The Principal raised his eyes from his desk now and turned to look out at the layers of sunset which were beginning to build in the sky. The colors spread and began to run together. He blinked, then stood and walked to the fireplace, where, using a flint and steel, he lighted the fire that had been laid for him. It started with difficulty, and he spent a long time at it. When the fire was glowing, he walked back to the desk and poured himself another full cup of brew, then looked down again at the two objects on his desk: the comb and the feathered lyre. At last he picked up the lyre and, his hand trembling, plucked a string. The eerie, melancholy tone reverberated in the room, and he put the instrument down, damping the sound. Then he walked to the window and looked out at the darkening night as stars began to appear.

Four

When the Principal awoke, he was twisted among the cushions on the wooden couch in his office. His head ached badly and there was a foul taste in his mouth. Immediately the thought came to him: *Zach has disappeared.*

The faint light just filtering through the east window showed that it was still very early, before sunrise, and he closed his eyes, thinking to sleep more, but after a moment knew that he could not. The thought of Zach had filled his head, leaving room for no other thought or any rest, and he knew that everything was now changed. For his own life, for his greater plans, this was as profound a change as had occurred two generations before he was born.

He rose to one elbow and shook his head. "He is not dead," he said aloud, as if by his will he could make it true. In any case, whether Zach was dead or not, whether captured by outlaws or by followers of this mysterious new religion, it was clear to the Principal that he must investigate the situation in the southwest as soon as possible, to protect his holdings there. This must be his primary mission. The second, which he knew would become an obsession, was to find Zach alive if possible, and if not, to discover who had been responsible for his death and then to kill the man himself, in the slowest, most painful way he could devise.

He stood, upsetting the pottery pitcher which sat empty beside the couch. Irritably, he kicked it away, then went to his rooms and washed quickly, not bothering to ring for hot water. The icy liquid began to sting his body awake, banishing the headache left by too much drink. Then, while almost everyone in his House still slept, he made his way downstairs to the great kitchen, where he surprised two young cooks who, not expecting anyone so early, were trading stories and passing a pipe of new-smoke while a large kettle of water boiled over on top of the stone oven.

The sweet scent of the new-smoke mingled unpleasantly with ancient cooking odors, and he stepped out into the herb garden off the kitchen to clear his head. When he returned and sat himself at the massive pre-Change table in the center of the room, he found that the cooks, terrified of his famous temper, had made a hasty botch of his breakfast, overcooking the pigeon eggs and failing to crisp the cured pork the way he liked it. After two bites he shoved the food away and shouted for tea, which arrived too weak and so hot that he burned his tongue. He hurled the cup into the fireplace and finally, after a cup of tea was prepared properly, settled down to make notes for his meeting with the generals.

The intended subject of the meeting had been the improvement of long-distance communication throughout the District, preparatory to expansion of the areas firmly under his control. His plan was to establish line-of-sight signaling towers where possible, and more communications stations with mounts and human runners in other areas. Although the homing birds which had sometimes been used to send messages in the past had not survived the Change, he intended to begin working with some species of new-birds to see if they could be trained to home reliably. He reflected that communication might be more important than ever now, especially to the southwest; but his resources were limited and he would have to be very careful how he committed them. Clearly, if this new religion was a genuine threat, he would have to train as many new troops as possible.

He quickly estimated the number of young men recently conscripted and the greatest number that could be trained in the next few months. While he worked on increasing his army, small scouting expeditions could begin to investigate more fully the reported trouble in the southwest. For now, however, the important question was the most efficient use of the trained troops already in the Capital; his generals, he knew, would have sharply opposing ideas, so, as always, he would work out the best solution with Zach before the meeting—

Only Zach was not here.

For a moment the Principal felt cheated and helpless, like a young child who cannot get an answer to an urgent question. In spite of his temper, he was on good terms with all his close aides, but to all of them he was above all the Principal, looked on with respect and awe—to all of them but one.

The meeting with the generals did not go well.

He had opened with the news of Zach's disappearance. The expressions of shock and regret were not faked; Zach was well loved, and all his men knew how greatly the Principal depended on him, but he saw looks of disapproval too. Even though Zach's mission had not been made public, it was common knowledge that on this one occasion the Principal had not trusted his regular procurers but had sent Zach instead.

General Ralf then told of his encounter with the refugees

and the Traders. As the Principal expected, the two youngest generals, Daniel and Eric, scoffed at the idea of any outlaws overcoming trained, professionally led soldiers.

"You haven't seen these Traders," Ralf said angrily, beginning to stutter. "Th-they care nothing for life. It will take all our t-troops and more to subdue them if they have an army."

Daniel, who had been with the Principal since he was a boy, spoke slowly and with the customary self-assurance which sometimes approached arrogance. "Perhaps, then, it's time for the older generals to retire and leave fighting to men who are not afraid of any number of outlaws."

Ralf rose to his feet, his mouth working in rage.

"Sit down, and shut up, both of you!" snapped the Principal. "Whoever these Traders are, they must be stopped. And we won't stop anyone if we're fighting among ourselves!"

Still glaring at each other, the two men sat, Ralf muttering to himself.

Once again the Principal missed Zach and his calming influence. No matter what the dispute, Zach seemed always able to find a solution which satisfied everyone.

In the end it was decided to send two small but well-armed parties under Daniel and Eric; the men under Daniel were to investigate the southwestern border area, while the others would scout around the Northern Ford, then move southwest and join Daniel's contingent. The evidence of the woman's comb indicted that Zach had reached the girl's home, but the Principal wanted to make certain, so he assigned Red, a quiet, reliable man of Zach's age, to lead a third party in retracing Zach's route to the northern mountains. The Principal did not give in to the temptation to order the purchase of the girl if by chance she were still there; that would have to wait until the current difficulties had been resolved.

Ralf and Quentin, his oldest and most experienced generals, and Marcus, who was in charge of peacekeeping troops in the Capital, would remain here and help train new men.

After the meeting, as the Principal began working out the details, he finally started to relax. He found he was able to think for minutes at a time without the thought of Zach's disappearance coming into his consciousness.

One thing further remained to be done, which he had not mentioned in the meeting. It involved a secret contingency plan known only to himself and Zach. He had longed to put it into action for years; the news of the trouble in the southwest might prove at last to be the excuse he had needed.

Telling only Robin that he was leaving, but not why, the Principal would make the short journey himself, to the isolated peninsula just to the south and east of the Capital.

Though the Principal was striking-looking among men, few of his subjects would recognize him. As insurance he would wear a false beard. Most men in the District did not shave; a clean face was another relic of civilization which he affected himself and encouraged among his men. Of his closest advisers, only Zach and Ralf did not follow this custom.

The Principal set out in early morning, on the best mount in his stables, his mind at rest for the first time since he had learned that Zach was missing. He knew that in some ways what he was doing was foolish and even dangerous, that he ought to take at least one or two men with him. But he felt a need for time to think, alone.

Also, though he did not like to admit it to himself, he had felt for some time a restlessness building in him, an irritability which was a sign of the compulsion which overtook him from time to time. The failure of Zach's mission meant that he would not find release soon, but physical action might serve to quiet him. The compulsion was something he had long ago given up hope of controlling, and his position as Principal had made it easy for him to indulge it. He was certain, from his reading, that this was not common in civilized men, and thought that it was perhaps due to a wild deena.

He also knew that any obsession, continued unchecked, could topple an empire no less surely than a revolution or a coup.

He rode hard into the late morning, enjoying the clean air and the moist fragrance of the forest. His face under the false beard itched, but the idea of traveling incognito was exhilarating, as if the responsibilities of his position had disappeared with the recognition of his face. It was easy to let himself slip back in imagination to the days when he had been an outlaw, champion of the people suffering under the President's despotic, chaotic rule. It was during the last days of that struggle, in fact, when he and Zach, fleeing the President's private police, had stumbled through the forest upon the remains of a great old estate hidden by wild and choking vegetation at the tip of a small peninsula outside the Capital. They had rested there for over a week, waiting for their wounds to heal before rejoining Ralf, Red, and the other men in the tunnels leading to the city, preparing for the final assault. In some ways, those days had been the best of his life, when his destiny lay before him and everything still seemed possible.

During that time he and Zach had planned together the structure of the government they would build, setting priorities for establishment of sanitation, security, education. Neither of them had ever doubted (or at least had not admitted to doubt) that they would indeed defeat the much-despised President, a man who had seen the chaos of the world after the Change only as an opportunity to grab personal power. The Principal had always had in his head a grand outline of what he wanted to accomplish; it was Zach, as always, who methodically worked out the details. It was Zach too who had suggested possible future uses for the estate. Several times since, the two men had traveled there, making certain that the buildings remained sealed and that no one had taken up residence.

By early afternoon the Principal had reached his destination and saw that nobody had disturbed anything since his last visit. With satisfaction, he surveyed the ancient house, a solid stone structure of three stories, showing the impeccable, machine-aided workmanship common before the Change. In addition to the great house, there were several smaller outbuildings and a large orchard, much overrun with weeds, but luxurious with healthy, fruit-bearing trees. All the buildings were in disrepair, but still intact, and it would not take a team of builders long to make them habitable again. Surrounding the entire compound was a solid stone wall; again, most of it was of pre-Change workmanship and most of it still stood.

A freshwater stream leading to the bay would provide adequate water; most important of all was the remote location of the compound. There was no sign that it had been visited for more than a short period by anyone in all the years since the Principal had discovered it.

Satisfied, the Principal sat by the stream and had a meal of the dried meat he had brought with him, then began to ride back to the Capital. He had intended to arrive well before nightfall, but his mount's sluggish behavior indicated he had stayed at the estate too long and it was growing late. This was not a well-populated area, but he had seen signs of some dwellings on the trip here, and he began to look for the telltale smoke that would indicate a cabin where he could ask for lodging.

Presently a narrow but well-worn path took him into a large yard, planted lushly with vegetables and fruit trees. Beyond the gardens was a small cabin with smoke just beginning to curl toward the sky. From the looks of it, this would house a typical family: two or more husbands, a wife, and several boy-children. As the Principal rode into the yard, a small figure stepped through the door of the cabin, intent on some errand. The figure suddenly stopped, then straightened and put up a hand for shade, watching him approach ahead of the falling sun.

As the Principal drew near he saw that it was a young girl, with thick, pale hair tied in braids. She was not beautiful, but there was a freshness and openness about her. He felt his stomach clench and kept his voice steady as he spoke:

"Good day. Does your family have room for a lodger for the night?"

"I can't say," she said uncertainly.

"I have metal," said the Principal. "If you'll send your fathers out I'll settle with them."

"They're not here right now," she said, sounding nervous. Quickly she added, "I expect them any minute. They've been out hunting."

She glanced toward the cabin door, and from her manner the Principal suspected that her fathers would not be returning soon. He felt almost dizzy at this realization and told himself to go on quickly, to find another place to lodge, away from the girl. But suddenly she spoke again, her voice surprised.

"You're the Principal."

At first he could think of no reply. He had not expected to be recognized so easily, and certainly not by a child.

After a moment he laughed. "I'm flattered that you think so, but in truth I'm one of his soldiers."

"I know who you are," she said with some intensity. "Last year, my first-father took me to the Capital to hear him—you—speak. I remember your eyes, as black as the bottom of a well. You've grown a beard, but I recognize you."

The Principal felt something growing in him and, remembering how he had been feeling lately, decided to move on immediately. It was not too late to find another dwelling, or if it came to that, he would sleep in the open, under his cloak. "I don't have time to play games," he said. "It's growing late." He turned his mount and was on the point of moving out of the little yard when the girl spoke again:

"Wait!"

He turned his mount and halted.

"I didn't mean you couldn't stay here—it would be an honor."

"Not without your fathers' permission," he said. "They might come back and decide to turn me out."

"They won't be back till tomorrow," she said. "And they would be honored too."

The Principal took a deep breath and considered. Clearly this girl knew him, and she seemed to be infatuated with him. Given that, and that her fathers were gone, and given his own rising compulsion, he knew fully what the outcome would be if he stayed here. But she was willing, although she didn't know what she was getting into, and he was tired, and lonely, and suddenly he knew that he would stay, and the consequences go to the deenas.

"Very well," he said, returning to the doorway. He dismounted. "You are a very observant girl to have recognized me." He pulled off the false beard.

The girl looked at him, blinking, then sank to her knees.

"Great deena, don't do that!" he said. "It's barbaric."

She scrambled to her feet, then looked at the ground.

"What's your name?" he asked.

"Lina," she said.

"How old are you?"

"Thirteen."

"Listen to me, then. I would like nothing more than to stay here tonight. But you don't know me, even though I am the Principal, and it might be dangerous for you. I'm giving you a chance now to send me on my way. You may have heard my reputation, that I am not gentle with girls."

"I only offer you food and lodging," said Lina.

"That will not be enough."

She looked into his face then, her eyes widening with fear and something more. Her lips parted but she didn't speak.

The Principal thought for a moment, then went on. "This has never happened before in this way. At least not since I took over the District. I have a very difficult job, Lina, and I work hard—harder, probably, than any other man in the District. When necessary I fight, and my life is always at risk. I have few friends, and very few forms of relaxation." The girl continued to gaze at him. He could not guess if she was understanding him or not. He continued: "It's known that I do not have a wife, that I do not travel with or keep women. Neither, however, do I keep boys. From time to time . . . I require release. I require girls like yourself, young and unspoiled. . . . You have not had a lover?" he suddenly demanded.

"No," she said in a whisper.

"Well, then. If your fathers were here, I would give them money for you. A fair bargain: value given for value. And tomorrow I would take you to the city, and keep you with me for a time. A day, a week, perhaps a month or more. During that time you would grow to hate me, because I would hurt you, in ways that you can't imagine. When the time was over, I would see that you had a husband, or husbands, or were safely in a house of women for hire, if that is what you wanted. Do you understand what I'm telling you?"

"Yes," she said. Her expression had not changed. The Principal could scarcely breathe. Once again he thought that he must ride away, quickly, before he made a mistake that might jeopardize his mission and perhaps his entire empire.

But he couldn't make himself move and knew that all would depend on what she said next.

She repeated, "My fathers are not here."

"And your mother?"

"She died of the woman sickness last summer. I'm alone."

"Then I offer the bargain to you. Value for value. But Lina—if you agree, there is no turning back, and afterward you will not be the same."

For a very long while she continued to look at him, saying nothing, then spoke, almost inaudibly. "I have dreamed of your eyes," she said. "Stay."

The Principal thought once again of going on and then looked at Lina, young, and vulnerable, and full of invitation. Without a word he followed her into the cabin.

Five

As she skipped across the wet earth, bare legs under her long skirt tickled by the tops of weeds, Evvy reflected that the Garden was truly named. She loved the fresh plant-and-dirt scent in early morning when the sun broke the fog into a shining veil, softening the outlines of the lodge and smaller out-buildings and letting the bright colors of the vines on the wall run together like a tapestry.

Ahead of her on the left were the orchard and gardens, just beginning their new season, and to her right she could hear the animals stirring, beginning to look forward to breakfast. Here and there a brave spring bulb thrust a pointed leaf through the ground, wagering that the last snows were gone.

At the wide back gate Evvy worked the heavy metal bar into its grooves on the side of the wall. Smoke rising from the chimney of the lodge kitchen reminded her to hurry. She pushed the gate open, then, taking two large buckets, stepped onto the crunching stubble of last year's grain fields toward the stream.

She filled both pails in the icy stream and, after carefully replacing the security bar, balanced them on a curved yoke across her shoulders.

Work on the new well should be completed today or tomorrow, according to Gunda. Evvy didn't mind fetching water from the stream. She didn't mind anything she was asked to do here. She was, after all, waiting.

From the third day of her arrival, Evvy had been given her place in the routine of the Garden, rising with the first light of day and helping the youngest children with their toilet, dressing, and folding their bedding. This was no different from her life at home. Sometimes she missed her brothers, especially the thoughtful Daiv, but it never occurred to her to think of going back there.

After breakfast, if she was not on kitchen duty, Evvy helped tend the livestock. She liked being with the animals, even those called "experimental," and sometimes felt closer to them than to the strict and single-minded women of the Garden. In particular she liked the new-goats, which were so misshapen and odorous that they were shunned by most other animals and people, but were loving and gentle when attention was paid to them. Evvy spent most mornings cleaning the pens, feeding the animals, and talking to them, usually accompanied by Jimmy, a solemn, thoughtful boy who reminded her in some ways of her brother Daiv, and by her fox-cat. Through chinks in the flowered wall she would sometimes look outside at the forest and think about her long trip here.

She had grown taller in the months since she had come to the Garden; and her body was starting to change. She had recently begun her monthly bleeding and found that with it came new feelings of impatience, and longing, and daydreams which seemed as real and as changeable as the pictures in her memory.

At night as the children lay sleeping in rows beside her, Evvy would lie with her eyes open, her body aching with fatigue, and remember Zach. This was her favorite time, when she was alone and could think of him. She kept the bracelet he had made her in her pillow to protect it, and only slipped it on at night, as if having it next to her skin made her memories of Zach more real. She sometimes imagined that she could see his face above her: the tangled blond beard, his blue eyes with crinkles at the corners, and the hollow cheeks which always gave him a look of melancholy, even when he was smiling. Although she was always aware of the rustling of bedcovers and soft breathing of the children, she liked to close her eyes and imagine that once again she was sleeping snuggled next to him, feeling his strong arm around her, holding her as he had the night the bat had entered their cave. That night was the warmest and most protected moment of her life. In the days that followed she had longed to sleep beside him again but had never dared to suggest it.

The day afterward he had been awkward and almost formal with her, speaking in short sentences and avoiding her eyes. At first she had thought that he was angry with her, and finally asked him.

"Why, no, Evvy. Why should I be angry?"

"Because I was afraid to sleep alone after the bat got in."

His face had colored then, and he turned his head, then slowly looked back. "I'm sorry," he said. "It has nothing to do with you. I'm . . . a little tired, that's all."

Looking at him, she could see that he wasn't lying to her, but that he wasn't telling the truth either. She didn't want to disturb him, so she never mentioned it again.

Although they had only been together a few weeks, sometimes she felt she knew Zach better than anyone in her life, even her parents. When new animals were born—or a child did something funny, Evvy imagined telling Zach about it, and knowing just what he would say. Sometimes, when the moon was shining, she would creep to the window and pull open a slat on the shutters to look out, wondering if Zach too, wherever he was, was looking at the moon and thinking of her.

Repeated searches of the area surrounding the toll bridge had failed to turn up a trace of Zach, or of the remaining highwayman, Ermil. A further expedition to the cabin where

Ermil and his brother had lived had likewise revealed nothing but the charred remains of a structure, so thoroughly burned that the only sign of former habitation was a heap of stones where the fireplace had been. Carved deeply into the bark of a tree in the yard was a double spiral; nothing further had been found.

The Mistress and Katha both believed that Zach was dead, but Evvy did not listen to them. If he had died, what had happened to his body? *Wait for me at the Garden,* Zach had told her. *If I am able, I will meet you there.* If he was not here now, he was not able. But Evvy believed with all her heart that one day he would come for her.

As the mornings were given to routine housekeeping and farming, the afternoons and evenings were devoted to study: lessons for the children and mysterious work for the adults, called experiments, some of which took place in the long, narrow building with many windows called the "lab," and others involving the new-grain and certain other crops of new-plants.

From the very first week, Evvy was made to sit at lessons, taught by a slender, white-haired woman named Mira. Sometimes they worked alone, but more often Evvy was part of a group of a dozen children, most of them, like Jimmy, a good deal younger than she. Her first-father had taught her the alphabet, but like most children in the District she had never learned to read and write. Literacy was, after all, associated with science and the Change.

At the Garden, nevertheless, all children were expected to be able to read and write and work with numbers.

Evvy shrugged off this peculiarity just as she accepted the odd "experiments." She was certain that these eccentricities had developed as a result of so many women living without men.

Gradually at first, and then more quickly, Evvy learned to read sentences, paragraphs, and then full pages. Mira gave her a book of stories from the very ancient past, and sometimes while Evvy was reading it she forgot that what she was doing was a little dangerous, that it was work, and she began to enjoy it. The book seemed to be a window into another world in the same way that the chinks in the fence around the Garden let her look into the picture-memories in her mind.

The stories she read explained how things came to be the way they were. Evvy learned that spiders weave their webs because the first spider had been a girl named Arachne, who had been transformed by a goddess jealous of her weaving ability; she read about the inevitable punishment of the giant who stole fire from the gods and gave it to men. One of her favorite stories was about a beautiful girl named Pandora, who had been given a golden box along with instructions never to open it. As soon as Evvy began the story, she could see there would be trouble, for what person could possibly resist opening a box, especially when told not to?

Evvy understood that these stories were only one way of looking at the world, and Mira spoke of others, such as religion and history. She gave practical lessons too, on the best ways of growing plants, and the uses of medicinal herbs, and one day an explanation of how men's and women's bodies worked together to create children.

Two or three times a week the Mistress herself, who had been born not long after the Change, came into the classroom to talk about life before the Change. Evvy had heard stories about the world then, of course, but never with the detail supplied by the Mistress. She and the children would sit, rapt, while the old woman talked about a society where illness could be cured, where everyone had plenty to eat, and where there were servant-machines to take care of every need, lighting the dark night, making necessary goods, and even carrying people through the air.

As the old woman's damaged mouth painfully formed words, the schoolroom was as silent as deepest night, and all the children leaned forward, not wanting to miss anything.

As she listened, Evvy would examine the old woman's face, looking for signs of Zach. There was a little of him here, mostly in the blue eyes and the deep lines in the cheeks. At these times she felt closer to Zach than ever.

* * *

For some time now, Hilda had been "borrowing" the baby fox-cat for her mysterious experiments. One day after class the old woman invited Evvy and the fox-cat to come to her cabin.

Evvy was mystified but pleased. She had not spoken with the old woman since the day she had arrived.

She brushed her pet's fur until it shone and, after feeding the new-goats, presented herself at the Mistress's cabin. Hilda and Katha were there, along with Lucille, the chief healer, and her daughter Lucky, a round-faced girl a year or two younger than Evvy, who had shiny black hair and sparkling dark eyes. Lucky was sitting cross-legged on a stool in the corner of the room, reading a book. When she saw Evvy, she looked up and smiled. Evvy smiled back, and the younger girl giggled.

"As we suspected, the fox-cat is extremely intelligent," Lucille began. "We've tried every test we could think of— mazes, tricks, choice experiments—she learns everything at once. She also tires of any game very quickly. The important thing, though, is that we've become convinced that she's truly empathic."

Evvy frowned at Lucille. She had not understood most of the words and wondered if Baby were in trouble.

Hilda caught her look and smiled reassuringly. "It means only that she seems to sense moods, or thoughts. I'd like to try an experiment with you."

Evvy's heart began to race. At last she would find out what an "experiment" was. She hoped that it would not last too long or be uncomfortable.

"Now, Evvy, I want you to sit right there while I hold on to Baby. When I say go, try to imagine the most frightening thing that has ever happened to you. Imagine it very hard. Close your eyes and see a picture of it. *Go.*"

Evvy shut her eyes and went back in imagination to the scene with Orin. It took only a few seconds for her to begin to feel again the terror of that dreadful morning. The terrible expression on his face . . . the fishy smell of his breath, and the way his breathing had changed as he began to tear at her clothes. After a moment she became aware of a strange sound and opened her eyes. Across the room Baby was growling and struggling with Hilda, who let her go. The fox-cat came bounding across the room and jumped into Evvy's lap, peering closely at her face and mewling.

"Remarkable," said the Mistress.

"We must try to capture others," Lucille said. "There's no telling what we might be able to train them to do."

Hilda and Lucille continued talking, their voices excited, but Evvy stopped paying attention. The memories of Orin had been frightening and brought back her longing for Zach. She pressed her face into the sweet-smelling warmth of Baby's fur, while the little animal buzzed reassuringly.

The Mistress seemed to have taken a liking to Evvy and her pet, and from that time on frequently invited them to visit. Lucky too was often there, and the girls began to spend time together in the evenings, talking and doing needlework after all chores and studying were done. Although Jimmy still accompanied Evvy on her rounds with the animals, he became more and more withdrawn, and finally began to avoid her company altogether. She was puzzled and hurt by this behavior, and one evening asked Lucky about it.

"It's just 'cause he's a boy," she said, giggling. Then she added, more seriously, "They can't help it. They can't ever grow up to be like women and learn the things we do. It's just the way it is."

Evvy was still puzzled and the next day made a point of finding Jimmy after lessons. "What's wrong?" she asked him. "Don't you like me anymore?"

"You're one of them now," he said, his dark face solemn. "You go to her cabin every day. They don't care about boys. And I don't care about any of them."

It was true that Evvy now spent most afternoons in the Mistress's cabin, usually with Baby and Lucky. The girls would quietly do lessons or work at the loom while the old woman busied herself with the mysterious objects at her table, or covered flat leaf-papers in tiny tracks of writing made with a bird quill and the ink of new-plants. Baby, who hunted most of the night, usually lay curled and sleeping on one or another lap.

Sometimes the girls would begin talking, discussing something they had read or some event in the Garden that day, Lucky usually giggling infectiously, and after a few moments the old woman would shoo them outside, her face drawn into a fierce frown that both girls knew was not in the least serious.

When she was tired of lessons, Evvy liked to peer into the more difficult books which lined the walls of the old woman's room. For the most part they were much harder to read than her children's lesson books, and she still felt a thrill of the forbidden whenever she opened one of the heavy, dusty volumes and began to look at its crumbling pages. Her favorite was a very large book picturing the world before the Change. Its pages were covered with faded, astonishing images of cities with tall buildings and strange machines, animals, and people of all ages dressed in fantastic costumes. The title of the book was *The Best of Life*. It seemed to Evvy that, indeed, this magical time before the Change must have been the very best that life would ever have to offer. How she wished she had lived then!

One afternoon when Evvy and the Mistress were alone, the old woman startled her at her reading by asking, "Did Zach ever tell you why he brought you here?"

Evvy shook her head. "He told me it was where he grew up, and that I would like it here."

"Do you?"

Evvy stared at the old woman. "Yes, of course."

"Are you happy with your work?"

Evvy shrugged. She couldn't understand why the old woman was asking her these things. It seemed to her the work here was like the work of humans everywhere, hard and necessary: the planting and gathering of crops, the trapping and hunting of animals, the making of soap and candles and collecting of oil for lamps, spinning and weaving and sewing, accumulating and bartering. The only difference was that here in the Garden all these things were done by women.

"There is a great deal more to the Garden than you imagine," the old woman went on. "We are doing important work here— work vital to the survival of the race. It's my feeling that Zach thought you could help us with it. That's why he brought you here."

Evvy frowned, not certain how she should respond. She thought perhaps the old woman's mind was wandering, the way her first-father's had before he died.

"You know there are no boys past late childhood here," said the Mistress. "When they reach that age we send them to the Capital, to work for the Principal. With girls it is different. In their thirteenth year they are given a choice—to stay or to leave. Those who stay are formally dedicated to the Garden and its true purpose.

"Those who come here later, like you, must learn a great deal before taking the decision. Mira and I feel you are almost ready. But before we finish training you, we must know—are you prepared to dedicate your life to the Garden and its purposes?"

Evvy sat motionless, the carved back of the wooden chair pressing into her spine. She was confused and not a little frightened. "I don't know," she finally said.

"You must decide," said the Mistress.

Evvy felt tears at the backs of her eyes. Like so many things in her life, this necessity for a choice was being thrust on her abruptly, with no time to consider. Then she realized what her answer must be. "I can't decide anything until Zach returns," she said.

"Ah, child. You still believe he is alive?"

"I know he is."

The old woman was silent for some moments, her lips smacking together while she thought. At last she sighed. "You may be right," she said. "But if he were to return, it would only be to see that you are safe. He cannot stay here and he would not take you with him."

The hidden tears began to spill. "You don't know that!"

"Evvy, I'm going to tell you something about Zach that you may not wish to hear. When he was a very young man, he did not leave the Garden as most boys do. That is, he left the compound, but he remained nearby, supplying our wood while his wife continued to work here."

His wife. Evvy felt as if her heart had stopped beating. How could she not have known? All this time she had been waiting for him to come back for her, when in reality he would have returned to another woman. She tried to think who, of the older women, it might be. Fat Gunda? Proud Mira? Or perhaps she no longer lived here and was waiting for him in the Capital. Perhaps he was with her even now.

"Is she still here?" Evvy asked, feeling sick and defeated.

"Here? Oh, no," said the Mistress. She seemed suddenly to come to herself and gazed directly at Evvy. "She died many years ago. But she is more of a rival to you than you can imagine."

Evvy just looked at the old woman, embarrassed to be so transparent, and wanting to know more, though she feared to hear it.

"They married very young, Zach and Leya. They were in love—unusual in these times. But Leya soon conceived a girl-child, and less than a year after the marriage gave birth and died of the woman sickness."

Evvy bit at her knuckle, her heart breaking for Zach's loss and her own.

"It was very soon after that Zach left us for good, to join his brother, who had left two years before. He told me before he went that he had taken a vow never again to be with a woman, never to cause that to happen again."

"But men don't have anything to do with the woman sickness," Evvy blurted, wanting even now to talk Zach out of such a dreadful vow.

"They have everything to do with it," said the Mistress. "Zach knew that, and I'm sure he has kept his vow all these years. By keeping it, he has helped to carry on our work."

Once again, Evvy felt the loss of Zach as if it had just happened. Yet still she felt that he was alive, somewhere, and that she would see him again. But she also knew that Zach, once he had made a vow, would let nothing prevent him from keeping it.

"So you see that if Zach lives, he will never be anything but a father to you. Despite your ignorance and impatience, you are a bright girl. We are offering you a rare opportunity. You may join us and stay here, working to save the human race. Or if you choose to leave we will find you suitable husbands. But I can promise you that Zach would have wanted you to stay."

Evvy felt dizzy. Her world had suddenly turned inside out. This final loss of Zach made her ache all over.

Yet another part of her was strangely exhilarated. Whatever the nature of this mysterious work she was being asked to give her life to, it promised to hold more interest than years of poverty with a pair of husbands, waiting to die of the woman sickness. Even more important, the work had been important to Zach.

If he lived, Zach might someday return and be proud of her. If not—she would keep his memory alive. He had given her a new life. In return, she would take a vow of her own. If she could not be with Zach, then never would she be with any man. As Zach had remained true to his dead wife, so she would remain true to his memory.

She approached the Mistress and held out her hands.

"I will stay," she said.

Six

The ceremony was held on the day exactly one year since she had first arrived at the Garden. Once it was known she had chosen, Evvy was treated differently, with a new respect, by Gunda, Hilda, Mira, and the other elder women. The younger girls seemed excited and envious of her, while the boy-children, as always, went about their business silently, as if they moved in shadows.

For the first time Evvy understood what it must be like to

grow up knowing that the most important choices in your life had been made for you. Only last week, Jimmy had been delivered to a neighboring farmer who was to take him to the Capital. Evvy, practicing sword work with Katha in the broad front yard, heard his sobs and pleas and wanted to comfort him. Instead she turned her head and brought all her concentration to the movements she must make.

In the four months since her talk with the Mistress, Evvy had been very busy. Because of increasing outlaw attacks in the area, Katha had initiated daily weapons and self-defense drills for all women and older girls. In addition to weapons work and her regular chores, the Mistress and Mira had greatly increased the reading Evvy was required to do, insisting that she stay up till late at night to finish, if necessary.

Evvy didn't mind, for the things she was learning were fascinating. At first, she was given books and journals about the world just before the Change. These books told her a great deal more than her folk-learning or the classes she had taken here at the Garden. Like every child in the District, Evvy had been told that the Change occurred when the wild deenas ate up the machines' food; she had always assumed that the machines had been animals of some sort, made by men but at least half-alive. Now she learned that they had been constructed of metal and were no more alive than a house. Their food had been a special kind of oil, which came from the ground where it had been formed millions of years ago. Burning this oil gave the machines the power to move and to perform their miraculous work. Other things had been made of oil which was changed in special ways: clothing, machine parts, and even some kinds of furniture.

Evvy learned that the area where she lived had once been just a small part of a vast nation populated from one great ocean to another, and that across those oceans had been other nations just as great and populous. Even more astonishing, she learned that in the days before the Change most women had looked forward to childbearing, which had been nearly without danger, and in some cases could even choose the sex of their child.

She read of these and many other marvels of life before the Change, not understanding how they all fit together. The Mistress promised that it would all become clear at the initiation.

There was a full moon that night, by chance; Evvy took it as a good sign. The moon always make her think of Zach, and she knew he would be pleased and proud if he could know what was happening tonight.

The younger children had been put to bed early. Dark curtains had been drawn across all the windows of the long, low lab building.

Evvy had hoped that she would be allowed to bring Baby to the ceremony; her pet's presence always comforted her. But Baby, who usually waited until after Evvy was asleep to push her way past the window slats to hunt, had, inexplicably, demanded to be let out after the evening meal. Once outside she had begun to set up such a howling that Gunda had gone out and shooed her away from the lodge. The little animal had seemed nervous and excitable all day, once snapping at Evvy in irritation. Evvy wondered if her pet were perhaps in heat, and if it could be dangerous for her to mate with a wild fox-cat; she resolved to discuss the matter with Gunda and Lucille the next day.

Or perhaps, she decided, Baby's unsettled mood was due simply to the presence of the full moon or to her own barely suppressed excitement.

Evvy and Lucky dressed carefully in clean tunics and long, southern-fashioned skirts, then took turns twisting each other's hair into an adult knot at the back of the neck. They had been warned not to discuss the rite and chattered nervously of inconsequential matters, Lucky giggling often, but with an edge of nervousness Evvy had never before heard in her voice. Evvy tried to sound and appear calm, but she found herself continually touching her feathered bracelet, as if it somehow contained Zach's reassuring presence. When they were satisfied with their appearance, the girls sat side by side on benches in the women's quarters, where they would hereafter sleep. There was a knock at the door, and Evvy and Lucky looked at each other, then rose and followed Gunda out across the moonlit yard to the lab.

Evvy had never before been in this adults-only preserve; like the Mistress's cabin, the walls of the lab were lined with row upon row of books, and mysterious metal and glass instruments were neatly arranged on four long, chest-high wooden tables. Gathered solemnly at one end of the room were the senior women of the Garden, each wearing a loose-fitting white jacket over her clothing.

Flickering candles and fish-oil lamps cast a dark glow across the room and the faces of the women in it.

The Mistress was seated on a stool among the other women. Gunda conducted Evvy and Lucky down an aisle between the high narrow tables. Evvy's heart was pounding so hard she was sure it could be heard, and her hands were cold and damp. Although she was aware of the women of the Garden looking on, she felt as if she and the Mistress were the only two people in the entire world.

"Evvy, daughter of Eugenia," the old woman said. "Lucky, daughter of Lucille. You have been called to the Garden. You have been given the choice to leave or to stay. This is your last opportunity to affirm your decision. If you choose to stay, you will devote your entire life to our cause. You will do as our leaders ask, always, instantly, without question. You will do this for the highest good there is—the future of the human race. Do you understand?"

Evvy nodded. "Yes," she said.

"Yes," murmured Lucky. Evvy could feel the younger girl trembling next to her. She reached out and took Lucky's hand. The Mistress gazed at both of them for what seemed a very long time, then spoke again.

"Repeat after me. I am a Daughter of the Garden."

Both girls repeated the phrase in unison.

"I belong to the Garden, and to all humankind. The will of the leaders is my will; and the good of mankind, my goal. I will live my life in service, as a Daughter of the Garden."

When they had finished the vow, Lucky had stopped trembling and Evvy felt exhausted. Now Gunda, Hilda, and a handful of other women approached, carrying handwritten scrolls.

They stood in a semicircle around the Mistress, facing Evvy and Lucky. Then the Mistress began to speak again.

"We tell the story of the Garden whenever we receive new Daughters. We tell it so we will not forget. We tell it so that the good can go on, and the evil that has been done may remain buried. We preserve, we build, and we create, for we are the scientists of the Garden."

Afterward, Evvy could remember only the smoking candles and the sounds of the words, but not the words themselves. A year ago she would have been shocked to learn that the women of the Garden were scientists, whom she had always believed to be the worst kind of criminals, but now the knowledge seemed natural, expected, and comforting. She had read enough of the ancient and near past to know that almost everything she had believed her whole life was superstition and untruth.

As the senior women had related the story of the Change in singsong rhythm, Evvy imagined she had witnessed the events they described. She could visualize the great ships moving the oil needed by machines from countries where it was plentiful to those where it was not. She saw the seas crowded with tankers the size of cities, and watched the waters become dark and foul as there were accidents.

Several women read together, in mournful tones, telling how the sticky, black oil began to accumulate on the waters, spoiling them, choking the seaweed, fishes, and birds. Evvy imagined she could see clots of oil washing onto the beaches, streaking them with dark slime and killing the animals who lived there.

> *"All this while were scientists at work*
> *In labs, in secret, men and women both.*
> *They found the key to life within all creatures;*
> *They used it to unlock forbidden doors.*
> *This deadly secret key was DNA,*
> *So small it can't be seen but only known,*
> *And yet it has the power to make life.*
> *They learned to work with DNA and change it."*

Now Lucille, Lucky's mother, began to read:

> *"And so our fathers thought to change the world,*
> *To help all men with their new secret knowledge.*
> *They changed the DNA inside E. coli;*
> *They gave it appetite to eat spilled oil;*
> *And thus was born the mighty Petrophage.*

In spite of the difficult words, Evvy had no trouble following the story as other women took it up; how the Petrophage bacteria had spread, first to the ships which brought them to fresh oil spills, and then, through men, to all machines on land. Finally, having eaten all the oil, the creatures had changed again and began devouring any products derived from oil.

All the senior women were chanting now, in a wailing singsong. Evvy felt the back of her neck prickle as the voices grew louder and more insistent.

> *"The world they knew began to slow and stop.*
> *And Petrophage had still not done its work.*
> *Petrophage now came into the labs,*
> *Where evil scientists were tampering with life,*
> *Creating fearsome weapons and diseases.*
> *To keep these secret horrors from the world,*
> *Were traps and cages made of special oil.*
> *But everything was food for Petrophage.*
> *Changed DNA was let into the world,*
> *Attacking, changing, humans, plants, and*
>   *beasts.*
> *The death and terror spread from place to*
>   *place,*
> *And mothers died in giving birth to daughters."*

The reading suddenly stopped. Evvy started involuntarily, then Gunda went on, in a quiet tone of voice.

"This was the beginning of the Change," she said.

"And this is the hope of the Change," said Mira.

"The hope of the Change," continued Hilda, "is that terrible weapons can never again be made."

"The hope of the Change," added Lucille, "is that civilization may one day be restored."

"The hope of the Change," said all the women together, "is the hope of the Garden."

There was a long pause, and then the old woman began to speak, conversationally. "You may not have understood everything here tonight, but as you study and grow older, you will understand more. The Garden is one of several enclaves formed by scientists who survived the Change. They were devoted to two causes: first, saving as much knowledge as possible from the past; and second, applying that knowledge in an attempt to undo the damage caused by the Change. They were hunted down in those terrible days, and many of them were killed, but some survived, and continued to work, in secret.

"That is what we do here. We are scholars, preserving past knowledge. And we are scientists, working to alter the legacy of the Change. This is the most important work there is. If we do not succeed, within two or three generations there will be no humans left on the earth."

The old woman had finished speaking, and Evvy saw that her face was wet with tears. She felt profoundly moved, and excited, and still a little frightened. All these feelings, along with her gratitude toward Zach, and her longing for him, were somehow connected in a complicated knot at the base of her spine.

Now Gunda stepped forward, holding white coats for Lucky and for Evvy.

"This is the uniform of the scientist," she said. "Welcome to the Garden, Daughters. And remember that even if someday you should leave the Garden physically, your life remains dedicated to our goals."

The fish-oil lamps had been turned up, and sweets and flower wine were set on the long lab tables. Evvy and Lucky, both dazed and happy, were being congratulated by the women of the Garden, many of them still obviously moved by the ceremony. Evvy was just starting to sip a cup of the fragrant gold-colored wine when there was a heart-stopping cry from outside, then the sound of running footsteps. The outlaw attack had begun.

As she had been painstakingly trained by Katha, Evvy ran with the other women to the shed off the lodge where weapons were stored. Taking up a very light museum-sword and a thick stake, Evvy stationed herself as she was assigned, at the outside entrance to the children's dormitory wing.

Hyper-alert and with every muscle trembling, Evvy realized only when it was over that she was still wearing her white lab coat. The full moon showed her a score of women moving in the yard, their swords clashing with those of the invaders. The outlaws seemed to be few in number, but fierce. It was clear that the Garden women were winning; still, Evvy stood ready, prepared to fight, her heart beating quickly, not knowing how she would react, only that she would never allow any harm to come to the Garden's children.

She jumped as something touched her, and then she realized that it was sweat running down her body under her loose clothing, in spite of the coolness of the night.

Time seemed to have lost its normal flow; Evvy had no idea whether hours had passed since the attack began, or only minutes. She found herself wishing that Zach was with her, and imagined his power and courage flowing into her, giving her strength.

She was startled by a noise close by and turned quickly, then gasped. Staggering toward her through the shadows was a man in tattered dark rags, with a crazed look in his eyes. He held aloft, in both his hands, a heavy ornate sword. He lifted the sword above his head, grinning crazily, clearing intending to bring it down on Evvy, cutting her in two.

For a moment she simply gaped at him, as if he were as unreal as her daydream of Zach. Then her training took over and she stepped back, lifting her sword, prepared to fight. But her back was pressed against the wall of the lodge, and she realized that she had no room to maneuver, to practice the thrusts and counter-thrusts Katha had taught her. Never, in all her weapons practice, had she imagined that she would actually have to use the sword. *I must protect the children,* she told herself, and she held the sword in front of her, resolved to do as much injury as she could before her attacker overcame her. She wondered what it would feel like when his sword cut into her flesh, and felt the strength going out of her arms. Her sword started to tremble in her hands as the grinning man began to bring his weapon down.

At that moment there was a sudden eerie howl, as if something long dead had awakened, and the man looked up, his eyes going wide with terror. Evvy turned her head in time to see Baby leap off the slanted roof of the lodge and land on the man's chest with all four of her paws outstretched, her hooked claws extended. The man screamed and fell backward, dropping the sword as his hands frantically pulled Baby away from his body. Still howling, Baby raked his arms with her claws and bit at his fingers. With a terrified, spastic motion, he at last freed himself and stumbled away as quickly as he could, his sword forgotten.

Evvy realized she should pursue him, but she felt suddenly so weak it was all she could do to remain standing. Baby shook herself all over, then approached and rubbed against Evvy's trembling legs with a reassuring *"Mowr?"*

Evvy knelt and hugged the fox-cat. "Thank you, Baby," she said. "You were watching over me all along, weren't you?"

In answer, the little animal licked her cheek. After a deep, shuddering breath, Evvy resumed her station, holding the sword tightly in both her hands. The fox-cat sat at her feet, her sharp ears pricked alertly, her tail twitching from time to time as she looked about.

Most of the fighting had now moved to the south wall, away from Evvy's view. Despite Baby's presence, she prayed it would not return to the lodge. She heard shouts and one horrible scream, a man's; shrieks; the clash of weapons; curses; the sound of bodies falling heavily; and finally silence. The silence was presently broken by sudden, surprised sobbing.

After a moment Gunda appeared, her short red hair plastered to her wet, dirt-smeared face.

"It's over," she said. "Put away your weapon and come inside."

As Evvy relaxed, she realized that her entire body was tense and shaking. Her tunic was stuck to her sides with sweat, and her throat ached from holding back tears. She had been far more frightened than she had wanted to admit.

Most of the women, except the Mistress, were in the lodge. Hilda was preparing herb tea in the large kettle, while Mira and Lucille bandaged minor cuts and wounds. On a long bench someone lay sleeping, exhausted. Suddenly Evvy realized that the woman, a skinny girl named Joan, was not sleeping but was dead. A dark stain of red covered the upper part of her tunic. Evvy felt suddenly sick and looked into the fireplace. The loudest sound in the room was the sobbing of the woman who had been Joan's lover. Presently Hilda offered the sobbing woman a warm drink and led her outside while Gunda directed that the body be covered and removed.

In spite of the months of drills, in spite of the fact that the women had in fact won this battle, Evvy knew from the silence in the room, and the sorrowful, strained expressions, that such an attack had never really been expected by most of the women, except, perhaps, those few who had been trained as soldiers. Lucky, who, Evvy knew, had been stationed at the other end of the lodge, was pale in a chalky, sick-looking way, and she was clinging to Lucille as if she had become a child again. Suddenly Evvy remembered Zach's struggle with the highwaymen at the bridge, and wondered if he had been frightened then, as she was tonight, and had forced himself to act in spite of fear, simply because it had to be done.

The door opened again and Katha entered, with her deputy, Kim. In front of them were two securely bound and bloody men. Katha herself was wounded, her right arm loosely bandaged and seeping blood, but she seemed not to notice.

She pushed the men into the center of the room, where they fell, groaning. Her face was so twisted with anger that she was almost unrecognizable.

"Three more are dead," she said. "The rest escaped." She turned to the men. Evvy could see now that they were uncommonly dirty, their long hair and beards ungroomed and tangled. One of them was grinning foolishly, and Evvy's heart lurched as she recognized the man who had attacked her earlier. Baby, sitting in her lap, began to growl, and she tightened her arms around her pet, whispering, "Shh."

"Who are you?" Katha asked the men on the floor.

"Poor wanderers," said the grinning man.

"Twelve heavily armed men are not common wanderers," Katha said. "Why did you attack us?"

The man shrugged.

"You'll answer now!" Katha said. She kicked the pointed toe of her boot into the man's groin. With a grunt he doubled up and lay there, wriggling and gasping. Katha turned to the other man. "I can kick you too," she said. "With your stomach wound it might kill you. Will you tell me who you are?"

"Kill me, then," the man said, his eyes taking on a crazed look. "Kill us both. You can't kill the truth."

"What nonsense is this?" asked Katha. She was about to kick the man again when Gunda laid a hand on her shoulder.

"Let it go till morning," said Gunda. "You're wounded."

Katha shook her head. "I'm all right," she said, but Evvy thought she looked pale and sick, and her face was wet.

"Who sent you here?" Katha asked the first man, her voice noticeably weaker. She kicked him again, and Evvy turned her head. She did not know how the man could stand the pain and still not say anything; but the look in his eyes was that of a madman. Perhaps he did not feel anything, not really.

At last Katha gave up, looking disgusted and a little frightened.

"You'll tell us what we want to know tomorrow," she said. She ordered the men locked into the root cellar for the night.

In the morning the prisoners were found dead, both hanging by their belts. On the floor, scratched into the dirt over and over until it made a deep furrow, was the sign of a double spiral.

The next day the Principal arrived with his troops.

Seven

A chilling dawn mist turned the Principal's breath white as he squatted just outside his tent, sipping herb tea. To the east, splinters of light sparkled on the lake; around him the trees and brush were thick with red-and-brown leaves. He had scarcely slept all night, despite fatigue from the week-long journey, despite the exhaustion of setting up camp for more than two hundred men. The clearing was now thickly set with tents and hazy with smoke from early-morning campfires.

It had been fourteen months since Zach's disappearance, and he felt as if he had aged ten years in that time. He stood, his knees creaking, and settled his cloak around his shoulders, then motioned to Daniel, the young general.

"I'll go alone," he said, keeping his voice low. "I don't know how long I'll be. Prepare for action, but do nothing. Come after me only if I don't return by nightfall."

The younger man seemed about to speak, no doubt to urge an armed escort, but simply nodded. Daniel, like all the Principal's men, had learned what came of arguing once the Principal had decided on a course of action.

The Principal started up the familiar, steep trail, his leather boots slipping on the wet yellow leaves. His mouth was as dry as if he had spent the night in drinking, and his breath came heavily by the time he reached the top. He felt a physical jolt when the Garden appeared. Its sheer bulk was still overwhelming, and though the wall seemed shorter and less imposing than he recalled, a rush of memories flooded his mind. He heard that leaders had arisen from among the younger women, yet in his mind's eye he saw the old woman, her white lab coat fluttering behind her, directing everything herself, from the work rosters to the choice of plants and animals to be crossed in breeding experiments. She must be very old by now, he thought, and though he knew he had nothing to fear from her, his stomach clenched when he thought of the inevitable confrontation.

There were two sleepy-looking guards at the gate. The older of them, a black girl of perhaps twenty, opened her mouth in fright when she saw him. Her hand reached for her sword, but she stopped as his voice rang out.

"Tell your mayor that the Principal is here," he said. "Go! I won't enter till you return."

With a frightened glance backward, the second guard, little older than a child, followed the first. He grimaced in disgust. Clearly he had made the right decision. Ill-trained, skittish women could not be trusted to guard this most valuable outpost of his empire.

Presently a tall, strong-looking young woman with thick blond braids, wearing armor of leather, strode toward the gate. Her right arm was in a sling, the left just touched her sword, a museum piece made of polished bronze. Behind her were the two other, smaller women.

"I am Katha, mayor of the Garden," she said. "What do you want?"

"Do you know who I am?" he asked.

"You are the Principal, or so you told the guard. From the look of you, I have no reason to doubt it. I repeat: what do you want?"

Her tone set his teeth on edge, bringing back dark memories. He wanted to strike her down and march in over her body. He took three slow, deep breaths, then said, "We have come to evacuate you. The District is under attack by barbarians from the west."

"We know about the barbarians," said Katha evenly. "And we thank you for your offer, but there is no need. We can defend ourselves."

If all of them were like her, the Principal thought, they no doubt could. "I've picked out a site for you near the Capital," he went on. "If you don't like it, you may choose another. I will give you as many men as you need to help move your things and to rebuild."

"We will not leave," she said.

Again the Principal had to hold in his anger. "Unless this place has greatly changed," he said, "this is not something that you can decide yourself. Call a council together and let me speak."

The woman gazed at him a moment, her hazel eyes showing a flicker of what might be fear. She nodded. "Very well. It will be this evening. You alone will be our guest for dinner. Afterward, we will talk."

"I'll return at sunset," he said. Then: "One more thing. I must see the Mistress."

"That's impossible."

"Tell her I asked. It is for her to decide." Again the woman nodded, and he turned, aware that the struggle had only begun.

The interior compound was far larger than when he had seen it last, with more shelters, although some of the original buildings still stood. The gardens to the west were in darkness, but the fading light showed the old laboratory and the animal pens as they had been. The largest building, a long, low structure of hewn logs, stood where the old, smaller dormitories had been. It had three large windows with panes of oiled sheepskin, and an ornately carved lintel above the wide doorway. The building was impossibly bigger than any new structure in the Capital, its window frames and neatly shingled roof as carefully wrought as if it had been constructed before the Change. Just behind and to the side was a more crudely made, tiny cabin with faint light shining behind worn, familiar shutters.

He looked away from the cabin and sucked in air, willing it to cool the bubble of nausea in his chest. He would remain calm; he would not allow these women to know how deeply he was affected by being here.

The door was opened by Katha herself. He was almost overwhelmed by the concentrated, humid smell of women and children. Conversation stopped as he entered, then a moment later a high-pitched buzz of voices began again. He felt as if he had entered a hive of alien insects, all darting about or hovering above wooden perches. He sat at a bench Katha indicated, and gratefully accepted a cup of warm brew, gulping at it to clear his head. The girl who had brought it was no more than sixteen, but she already had the hard, wary look of women who grew up in the Garden. A casual glance around the room showed more of the same: competent, tough, and deadly females. These were more capable than any before in history, the Principal was sure, even in the days before the Change, when women had been equal in numbers to men and, incredibly, had held leadership positions alongside them. Such a thing could never again be, of course, but he had to admit that the women of the Garden had proved they were at least capable of ruling themselves.

He held his cup for more brew, and Katha raised an eyebrow. "I see you like our brew. We make it from a new-grain we've developed recently."

The Principal forced his mind to remain steady against the irrational fear of new-plants and -animals, the terror of wild deenas personified in the nightmares of children. It was all nonsense, of course, but the Principal had always understood why so many of his population feared anything that smacked of science. Anyone who had seen a poison-bat or a new-goat could only shudder at the small, invisible monsters that created such deadly changes. No wonder two generations had incorporated fear of deenas into the ancient religions.

With the idea of contamination by deenas still in the back of his mind, the Principal made an effort to establish conversation. "I see things have changed very little," he said.

"We've grown in numbers," said Katha. "Most of the women you see here are the senior council. With younger women and children, and those who live outside the compound, we are one hundred twenty-six altogether. Of course, in the most important ways we haven't changed at all—as you will find out."

He looked carefully at her. Was she trying to provoke him?

Her face told him nothing. She went on, in the same calm tone: "I relayed your request to our Mistress. She always dines alone in her quarters, but she will see you after dinner."

The Principal nodded. At mention of the old woman his nausea had returned, and he fought an impulse to walk out, to return to the Capital and let the Garden and all around it be overrun by barbarians. He drained the second cup of brew.

"You must be very thirsty from your journey," said Katha. Again he looked at her sharply, but said nothing. Although none of the perhaps two dozen others had yet addressed him directly, he felt conspicuous, aware of the many eyes in the room examining him as if he were a specimen under one of their microscopes, no doubt hating him for what they had heard about him. He realized with a sudden shock that many of the women here—perhaps as many as half a dozen—were pregnant. That had been rare in the old days. There was something obscene about so many gravid women with no men around.

Just as Katha announced dinner, there was a commotion in the kitchen, and he heard a scrabbling, sliding sound, followed by high-pitched laughter. He watched in astonishment as a fat, furry animal came skittering out after a piece of sliced carrot, both of them colliding with the screen in front of the fire.

The Principal gaped. "Is that a fox-cat?"

"The first tame one we've ever seen," said Katha. "It was raised by one of our new members. Lisa, put Baby out."

The girl who had been serving brew set down her pitcher and approached the small animal, beckoning and clucking. The Principal watched in fascination. A tame fox-cat was important news, and that it had been accomplished here was all the more reason to move the women to safety. It soon became apparent that the little animal didn't want to go outside. Whenever Lisa got close to it, the fox-cat moved sideways or backward, always just out of reach. The other women were smiling, hiding laughter with their hands, as Lisa became ever more frustrated. Even the Principal was amused, although slightly uneasy whenever the animal came near to him. Lisa took a piece of cheese from a tray on the mantlepiece and held it enticingly to the fox-cat. It approached, sniffed at her outstretched fingers, then suddenly leaped into the air, turning completely around, and scampered under the massive wooden table at the far end of the room.

"Deenas take you, Baby!" said Lisa. "Evvy, come get your pet," she called to the kitchen.

After a moment another girl emerged from the kitchen and swiftly knelt on the floor just in front of the kitchen door, her dark hair hiding her face. The Principal turned to watch as the girl scooped the fox-cat up in her arms, then turned back to the kitchen.

Sorry that the diversion had ended, he held his cup for more brew, and then he felt something that made the hair on the back of his neck stand up. The sensation was so strong that he could not help but turn his head, and his eyes met those of the young girl. She was standing in the doorway to the kitchen, holding the fox-cat to her chest, and gazing at him with a frightening intensity. Her eyes were the color of plums and her face was so lovely it made the Principal dizzy. When she met his eyes it was with a look of recognition, and he knew that she knew him, but not how. She turned and slipped into the kitchen, but even when the door had shut, the Principal felt her presence in the room.

Katha gave him a curious look as she refilled his cup, but said nothing. His heart was racing as if he had just ridden at top speed. He thought of dozens of questions to ask, all casual, all seemingly innocent, and all brutally obvious. He said nothing.

He ate his dinner of roasted new-fowl, vegetable stew, and baked roots quickly, without tasting it. His metal cup was refilled more times than he could count with the sweetish flower wine he remembered, and there seemed to be much conversation and laughter throughout the meal, although he scarcely listened. Hilda, a pale, middle-aged woman who was the chief farmer, questioned him about growing conditions and new-plants and -animals near the Capital. He answered her automatically, scarcely registering the possible significance of the questions: his mind was fixed on the extraordinary young girl. No matter what the outcome of the council meeting tonight, no matter how he evacuated the women, be it voluntarily or through force, no matter if the fate of the entire District depended on it, the Principal was determined of one thing: he had to have that girl.

So focused were his thoughts that he had trouble bringing his mind to the business at hand when Katha rose and said, "I'll take you now to see the Mistress."

The old woman. He'd almost forgotten about her. The food in his stomach churned. This evening was as unsettling as a long night of dreams and nightmares. First, the beautiful young girl, and now the old woman. Perhaps a bargain could be worked out. . . . Even as the thought sprang to his mind, he knew that it was impossible, that the very last place on earth he could bargain for a girl was among the women of the Garden. He would have to take her some other way, by a trick, perhaps, or by force. But take her he would.

He filled his chest deeply with the chill night air as they approached the door of the old woman's cabin. Katha knocked and, in response to a quiet "Come in," opened the door.

"The Principal is here, Mistress," Katha said.

She was sitting on a chair by the fire, a blue-spined book in her hands. The Principal felt nothing when he saw her, only surprise that she was so old. None of the anticipated rage appeared, none of the hatred. He approached her slowly and inclined his head. 'Good evening, old woman," he said.

The Mistress looked up. "Welcome home, Will," she said.

Eight

It was almost as if he had never left. There was a sense of familiarity so total that it was displayed as formality. Whatever feelings they had once held for each other now lay buried beneath the conventions.

"I congratulate you," she said. "You've done everything you set out to do."

"Almost everything. The most important part of my plans still depends on your work." He glanced around the tiny, cluttered room. The shadows, the furnishings, the faint odor at once stale and faintly spicy—all were exactly as they had been nearly twenty years ago.

"I've been expecting this for some time," she said quietly. "But not you, personally."

"I wanted to accomplish the evacuation without force. I didn't think you would listen to anybody but me." He paused, then had to say it: "Zach is missing. Probably dead."

"I know," she said, without changing expression.

He started. How could she know? Plainly, she wasn't going to tell him, but the accusation in her eyes told him that she held him in some way responsible. The deenas take her.

"I've postponed this move as long as I could," he said. "These rebels—or whatever they are—are spreading. Refugees are beginning to come into the Capital, especially from this area. I can't leave you here, so close to the border."

"And the Garden will make you an impregnable fortress. You've only been waiting for an excuse to take it."

He shook his head in annoyance. "It's true that this place serves my purposes better as an army post. But that's not the point. Protecting your work is the important thing. Since I deposed the President, there's been no need for you to stay in such a remote area."

"What if we refuse to go?"

"I have an army of over two hundred men."

"Will you kill us all, then, and destroy our work?"

"You would never let that happen."

"It's not up to me," she said, her eyes flashing.

"I know better," he said. "I know that if you talk to the women and explain why they must go, they will do as you ask. And you know it too."

The old woman sat silently for several minutes. Finally, she spoke. "Two nights ago we fought off the most serious attack in decades. We are more capable than you imagine, but I'm beginning to fear we haven't the resources to be both scientists and warriors."

"You'll persuade the council?"

"I can't be sure all the women will agree. Katha, in particular, is not likely to give in easily. But I'll speak to them."

He relaxed. Thank the deenas it would not come to a fight. Up until this very moment he had not been certain how she would react. They sat in silence a moment. The old woman looked very tired. "How did you learn about Zach?" he asked.

"What I know and how I know it is no concern of yours," she said.

His face flushed with instant anger. He stood and walked to the other end of the room, breathing deeply. Aware of her eyes on him, he touched some of the articles on her laboratory table: an ancient microscope, a precious glass flask, some tiny, sharp metal knives. "I will stay and supervise the transition," he said, not looking at her. "Then I must return to the Capital. My men are camped in the clearing at the bottom of the hill." He paused a moment, not certain exactly what he was going to say next. "My men are well disciplined," he said then. "I'll instruct them to leave the women alone. But I can't be responsible for the actions of the women."

"Let me worry about the women," she said. "And be very sure about one thing. You will have none of them, ever. Do you understand?"

"My men will do as I say."

"I wasn't talking about your men." She flashed him a look so chilling that for a moment he was back in the Garden as he remembered it, a young boy in a prison run by strict women with breasts and abdomens like pillows, an unwanted slave, who would never be given the key to the mysteries locked in their rooms and bodies. The long-ago fear turned to a hatred so intense it brought him suddenly to himself.

"Have no fears, old woman," he said, returning her look. "Your little flowers are safe from me." *For as long as you live,* he thought. And from the look of you, that won't be long. And then . . . well, he was the Principal. He had all the resources of the District behind him, and within his own laws, nothing would prevent him from taking the girl with the plum-colored eyes.

The council was little changed from the meetings he had witnessed as a young boy, watching from behind windows or partly closed doors.

There were more women here now, but there was the same spirit of chaos, the high-pitched excitement and arguing of every view. The result was that it took hours to decide a matter that should have been settled by one bold decision. As the old woman had predicted, the strongest voice in opposition to the move was that of Katha: he could almost sympathize with her as she watched her rule slipping away.

It was foregone from the beginning that he would win, one way or the other; and the Principal sat silent, only answering questions, trying not to show his growing impatience. If there were only some way for men to reproduce without the help of women, he'd be more than happy to see the whole lot of them die out.

At last the vote was taken, and, inevitably, it was in favor of leaving quietly, without a fight. Throughout the tally Katha sat silent, her grim face reflecting what she must be feeling.

The council members were all elders, adult and middle-aged, though none so old as the Mistress. He had hoped for another glimpse of the girl, Evvy, but had not really expected to see her here.

The faces were sad, some tear-streaked, when the meeting broke up, and he felt awkward as he prepared to leave. Katha rose as he did, and he thought for a moment she would offer her hand, but she stood stiffly while he walked to the door. For the first time he saw that her bandaged arm was badly hurt and must be paining her.

"We can give you an escort to your camp," said the fat woman, Gunda.

"I know these woods well," he answered.

His sense of triumph was physical: he could feel it, expanding in his abdomen and chest like warm air. He ran carelessly down the sloping trail, feeling almost as if he could fly.

At last he had achieved his greatest conquest. From this time on, the women of the Garden and their work were under his rule absolutely.

The next morning the Principal gathered his troops and told them about the inhabitants of the Garden. At first the men were astonished and then excited at the prospect of guarding a compound full of women, but the Principal made it clear immediately that any man caught molesting any of the women would be executed at once.

The evacuation would take some time. Those soldiers who were to man the fortress would begin moving in as they helped the women to dismantle and load the many things which must be carried by the caravan of large wagons due to arrive from the Capital within a week. The women themselves were to carefully pack and hide all microscopes, books, and other equipment which would have identified their work as scientific.

The Mistress and Katha had both insisted that all men, including the Principal, be outside the compound by nightfall. They took care, too, to keep the younger girls strictly hidden from his soldiers. He had expected that, but even when he was busy with details, a part of him was excited by the thought that the astonishing young girl was nearby, perhaps looking at him secretly as she had that night in the lodge. It was difficult not to be impatient, but there would be time to think of how to take her after the evacuation was completed.

In any case, he would be very busy. While Red supervised the physical details of the move, the Principal directed a contingent of men in creating detailed maps of the entire surrounding countryside, up to and including the western border. This was not a formal border in any political sense, as was the border which separated his holdings from those of the Governor of the North; rather, it represented the extent of the area the Principal loosely controlled through patrols, taxation, and communications posts.

Now that he had the Garden, he could consolidate this part of the District and begin to move to the west, crushing as he did the Traders or any other tribe opposing the growth of his civilization.

The Principal had been in camp a week. He was completing the draft of a lengthy communique to Ralf, back in the Capital, explaining what had happened so far and giving instructions for further recruitment of troops, when Daniel and an older, grizzled soldier appeared at the opening of his tent.

"Pardon, sir," said Daniel. "Buck has found something. I thought you should hear his report immediately."

The Principal suppressed his annoyance. If it could wait, whatever it was, Daniel would not have interrupted.

Setting down his pen, he turned to the two men. "Report."

"I was with a party of six," said Buck, shifting from foot to foot. "We were doing what you instructed—mapping, looking for signs of Trader camps. We'd worked our way south along the lake into the swamps." He stopped, and then, as the Principal nodded impatiently, went on slowly. "This is a deserted part of the world, as you know, sir. We hadn't found much of anything. We were poking around in the marshes when I came upon a big pile of bones half-buried in the muck."

The Principal frowned. "Were there signs that these were the remains of Traders?"

Daniel stepped forward. "Buck asked me to come out, in accordance with your instructions to investigate everything. We pulled the bones out of the swamp. It took a good while. When we were through we saw that the skeletons had once belonged to a very large man and a mount."

The Principal felt suddenly cold. "There are many large men in the District," he said.

"That is true, sir," said Daniel. "But only one of them wore this ring."

Daniel opened his hand and gave the Principal a heavy gold ring. On its raised face was carved the profile of the Principal. There was not another ring like it in the world.

"I'm sorry," said Daniel.

The Principal nodded. He looked dumbly at the ring, which was still warm from Daniel's hand.

"Was there any indication of how he died?"

"The bones are old," said Daniel. "I'd say a year at least. The ribs are broken, but an animal could have done that after he died. We searched the area closely, but there was nothing else. Of course, loose weapons could have been taken by anyone." He paused, then went on. "We left the other men to guard the bones. We thought you'd want to give them a proper burial."

"Thank you," said the Principal. "Both of you. Give me a minute. We'll do it now."

Looking distressed and embarrassed, the men stepped outside. The Principal looked after them a moment, then down at the ring. There could be no doubt now that Zach was dead. The certainty of it did not seem as shocking as had the first news that Zach was missing. Perhaps he had already given Zach up those many months ago, and his mourning was complete. In its place was anger, hard and tight and hot. Whoever had been responsible for Zach's death—and it seemed likely now it must have been the Traders—would pay a thousand times over.

He opened his hand and looked at the ring again, then put it inside his personal pouch. Straightening, he stood and left for the burial.

Nine

From the first night the Principal arrived, Evvy had a picture of him always in her mind. Of course, he could have no way of knowing who she was or what she had done, but she couldn't shake an eerie feeling that he somehow knew her.

For days she had been studying him in secret: from behind corners, through breaches in the wall, past shutters and curtains. His face fascinated her. He was so handsome as to be almost beautiful, yet there were harsh, determined lines in his cheeks and above his eyes. The irises of his eyes were so dark that they appeared to be all pupil; once, the first night he came, those eyes had met hers, and she had felt pinned like an insect, unable to move, until he had looked away. His eyes retained their intensity whether he was giving orders, laughing, or shouting in anger, all of which he did frequently, shifting from one mood to another easily and quickly. She had a feeling his face was a mask, something he put on, like the yellow-trimmed cape he wore to set himself apart from his men.

Evvy longed to ask the Mistress more about him; she was aware that there was some tie between them and had heard rumors that the Principal himself had lived in the Garden as a boy; it must have been here, in fact, that he and Zach had become friends. Yet she was afraid to speak of him, as if mentioning his name would give him her secrets.

The truth was that whenever Evvy saw the Principal or thought of him, she thought of Zach. Zach had been the Principal's most trusted adviser and friend and had betrayed him because of her. The question was, *Why?* Katha and Gunda assumed that Zach had taken her because he wanted her for himself. But she knew that was not true, at least not in the sense they meant. Her feelings had been confirmed by the things the Mistress had told her about Zach's wife and child.

Perhaps someday she might have been able to persuade Zach to renounce his vow; now, of course, it was too late. Even if he returned for her, she was a Daughter of the Garden, and, though some Daughters left the Garden and even married, it was only with the full approval of all the elder women, and never to a man whose wife had died of the woman sickness. Though she still believed that Zach was alive somewhere, he was lost to her, and all she could do now was to protect his memory by seeing to it that the Principal never learned who she was or what Zach had done. The Mistress, Katha, and Gunda were the only women here who knew Evvy's true origin, and she was certain they would never reveal it.

The day before the march was to begin, the Principal invited all the women to attend a feast prepared by his men. To Evvy's surprise, the Mistress accepted for the Garden.

Having finished some last-minute packing of equipment in the animal pens, Evvy went to the women's wing to get her bathing things. She found Lucky there, sobbing into her pillow.

"Katha struck me," the younger girl said. There was a faint red mark on the side of her face.

Evvy put her arms around Lucky and held her a moment. She had noticed Katha's growing irritability. "What happened?" she asked.

"I don't know. I was loading a wagon with Jinny. I didn't even know Katha was there. All I said was I was glad we wouldn't have to stand guard anymore, and Katha g-grabbed me and slapped me on the face."

Evvy patted Lucky's shoulder. "The move is hard for her," she said. "I'm sure she didn't mean to hurt you."

Lucky wiped her eyes, then rolled over on her back. "Evvy?" she asked after a moment. "Are you going to the Principal's party tonight?"

"Of course," said Evvy. "Why not?"

"I don't know," said Lucky. "I heard Katha saying we shouldn't go, that it's a trick. I'm afraid, but I want to see what it's like."

"There's nothing to be afraid of," said Evvy. "We'll go together, and if we don't like it, we can leave."

Lucky smiled assent, her recent tears completely forgotten. Evvy herself was not as calm as she appeared; she felt pulled in two directions. Part of her was consumed with curiosity about the Principal and his men, while another part was terrified at the thought of spending an evening in his company. The fact that all of the women had been invited—and her curiosity—won the battle. At last she would be able to observe him closely, safely anonymous among the other women.

"The Garden is a state of mind as much as it is a location," the Principal was saying. "It is a place where ideas can live. Of all things in our society—more than buildings, more than laws, more than individual men and women—ideas determine our lives."

Most of the Garden's women and children were watching and listening attentively. Evvy, wrapped in a thick new-wool shawl, sat between the Mistress and Lucky. In front of them Baby lay curled, buzzing in contentment. On the other side of the large bonfire sat the soldiers. Most were bearded, like her first- and second-fathers; a few others were clean-faced like the Principal. All were silent and motionless, their eyes fixed on their leader. The firelight blinked shadows onto his face as he talked and was reflected back by his dark eyes. Evvy squeezed Lucky's hand, thrilled.

"The Garden has been here for two generations, ever since the Change," he went on. "It was started by a small group of learned men and women—by teachers and thinkers—who knew that disasters like the escape of the wild deenas could never happen again, because the Change itself had made such accidents impossible. But they also knew that comfort, freedom from disease and poverty, many of the good things from before the Change, could perhaps one day be restored. These brave men and women determined to preserve as much as they could of the learning of the past so that someday that learning can be used again to help mankind. The people of the Garden have devoted their lives all these years to saving and trying to increase knowledge, so that someday life will be more as it was before the Change."

He paused, and Evvy heard a murmur of voices. The Principal's men were whispering among themselves, some glancing at him with frowns. She heard one gruff voice say loudly, "Sounds like science to me," but the man was immediately silenced by his companions. The women were quiet, many of them looking surprised. The Mistress sat with her eyes closed, but Evvy knew that she was listening.

The Principal went on with a short history of how the compound had grown from a very few huts to the large townlike fortress it was today; how the inhabitants had given as much time and thought to self-sufficiency as they had to learning, from the beginning. "They saw that the Change caused so much misery because people had grown soft and ignorant, unable to care for themselves. So they began training children from an early age to do as much for themselves as possible, and to learn everything they could about the world. The first part of that philosophy, the need for self-sufficiency, has already spread through the District and helped to make our stability possible. The second, the vital importance of understanding the world,

I hope to spread. From the first day when I became a leader of men, I vowed that I would help to bring back civilization. Civilization is much more than law and order, and comfort. It is also learning, and creating new ideas, and art. The Garden is the seed of our new civilization, and it will continue to grow in its new home."

He paused again, and this time his audience remained silent, watching as he paced a few steps, then, with one hand raised, he concluded: "When it began, the Garden was made up of both men and women. Times and customs change, but I hope that soon both men and women can again work together for civilization."

The last part of the speech was delivered with such passion and conviction that Evvy found tears starting to her eyes. She realized that the Principal could not have achieved his power if he were not skilled at making speeches. Still, she was touched: it seemed obvious he had given this speech not only as an explanation to his men, but as a tribute to the women of the Garden. If he felt this way about the Garden and its objectives, what could be the source of enmity between him and the Garden's leaders?

There was silence when he had finished speaking, then again murmuring from both sides of the fire. Some of his men were looking suspiciously at him, while others nodded, or gazed at the women across the fire with narrowed eyes. The silence grew and with it a sense of tension. Then Evvy felt a movement at her side. The Mistress sat up straight and began to clap. Immediately other women joined her, and the applause spread across to where the men sat. After a moment, some of them stood and began cheering. The Principal smiled almost shyly and sat; Evvy was sure she could see relief on his face. He accepted a cup of brew from one of his men, then glanced toward the Mistress and nodded.

At a signal, the men who had prepared the feast began to set out dishes and pitchers, and conversations started and grew to a constant buzz.

"He seems to care about us," Lucky said, the firelight illuminating her freckled face. "Do you think he meant it?"

"I'm sure of it," said Evvy, still moved.

The old woman turned her head. "It's a struggle in him," she said. "There are still many things he doesn't understand, and never will."

Evvy was about to ask more when Baby did an astonishing thing. The little fox-cat had kept her ears pricked and given every evidence of paying attention to the speech. Now she suddenly got to her feet, stretched, and trotted around the fire straight to the Principal.

He was speaking and laughing with one of his aides, his teeth flashing white. As Evvy watched, the fox-cat sat on her haunches directly in front of the Principal, waiting to be noticed. After a moment, she gently touched his knee with a paw. Still the Principal did not react until the man he was speaking to laughed and pointed to the fox-cat. Evvy could not hear what the man said, but the Principal, looking surprised, spoke clearly and loudly.

"Why, hello, there," he said. He put out a hand and scratched the fox-cat between her ears. Baby stretched herself in the pleasure of being touched, then licked his hand. Evvy nudged the Mistress. "Look," she whispered. "Baby liked the speech too."

The old woman gazed across the fire and nodded. "I have learned to trust Baby's judgment," she said.

One of the women handed her a bowl of stew, and she turned to eat it without further comment. Evvy ate her own dinner and watched as the fox-cat curled up beside the Principal, who continued to talk, his hand lightly resting on the little animal's flank.

Evvy felt far more relaxed here than she could have imagined; she scarcely listened while Lucky kept up an excited stream of chatter next to her. "I never saw so many men," said Lucky. "They aren't so scary up close, are they? The man sitting next to the Principal looks kind, don't you think?" She giggled, then, when Evvy didn't answer, she went on: "What do you think of the Principal, Evvy?"

Evvy turned to her, startled. "I don't know," she said. She thought of the few things that Zach had said about him and remembered her terror the night he had first come. She also thought of his easy smile and the way his men looked at him and followed him. "I think he must be a very good leader," she said at last.

"He's awfully handsome," Lucky went on. "He looks like a picture in one of the Mistress's books. Katha says he's evil and cruel. He doesn't seem that way tonight, though."

The feasting continued for some time, and Evvy began to grow sleepy. Lucky too settled down, an occasional comment the only sign that she was awake. Some of the soldiers had begun to sing an old products ballad and were soon joined by a woman sitting not far from Evvy. Katha hissed at her to stop, but at almost the same time another high voice, and then another, joined in, and soon as many women were singing as men. It sounded wonderful to Evvy, who had heard very little music in her life except on the journey with Zach. Those who were not singing were talking and laughing loudly, men and women together, and Evvy suddenly realized, startled, that many of them were drunk. Never before had she seen anyone drunk act happy. Her second-father drank from time to time and always became morose, and sometimes mean, shouting and threatening to beat his wife and the children, although he never did.

"This is disgusting," Katha said loudly. "Can I be the only one who sees what he's trying to do?"

The Mistress, who had seemed to be dozing, opened her eyes. "Katha, please. Don't you know yet that it's not men who are our enemy?"

Katha seemed about to retort, but Gunda placed a gentle arm around her shoulder. She leaned over and whispered something in her ear. Katha shook her head angrily, but didn't speak.

The old woman's eyes closed again, and this time she truly did seem to be asleep. After a few minutes she slumped against the tree. At almost the same moment Lucky yawned loudly, then called to Katha and gestured at the old woman. Katha rose.

"It's time for bed," she said, in a commanding tone. "We've a long day tomorrow, and it's late."

Several women nodded and yawned, while others continued to sing and talk. Katha clapped her hands for attention, but before she could speak again the Principal looked up. "Those who wish, stay just a little longer," he said, smiling. "It's bad luck to break up a party too early."

"Superstitious fool," Katha muttered. With a poisonous look at the Principal, she knelt and, with Gunda's help, gently brought the Mistress to her feet. The old woman seemed still asleep—she had drunk a glass of brew, Evvy remembered.

"Aren't you coming, Evvy?" asked Lucky, her eyelids heavy.

Evvy considered. It was probably best to go now, but she was enjoying the singing, and, besides, Baby was not with her. She had become accustomed to going to sleep with the little fox-cat, although Baby generally left her late at night to hunt. "In a few minutes," she said. She glanced across the fire where Baby was playing tug-of-war with one of the Principal's men.

Lucky nodded. "Good night, then," she said and joined the other women and children who were walking through the gate and into the compound. There were more than a dozen women still present and perhaps four times that many men. Feeling quite grown up, Evvy settled herself a little closer to the fire and yawned. She would wait just till Katha returned. . . .

A hand was shaking her shoulder, a gentle voice speaking: "Has our singing put you to sleep?"

Evvy looked up to see the Principal's smiling face a few inches above her own. He was kneeling between her and the fire. She had fallen asleep against the tree.

"Oh!" she said, unable to think of any other response.

"I believe this is your fox-cat," he said.

Sleepily, and shyly, Evvy nodded. Baby rubbed against her, then abruptly turned and jumped at a large insect drawn to the fire. "Baby—" she cried and half rose, but the Principal blocked her way.

"Let her play for a few more minutes," he said. "You're not in such a hurry, are you?"

She wanted nothing more than to stay and talk to him but again could think of nothing to say.

"What's your name?" he asked.

She told him, stammering.

"Evvy, I'd like you to have a cup of brew with us. We've been enjoying your pet and would like to thank you."

His breath smelled of brew and new-smoke, but it was not unpleasant and reminded her of Zach.

"Thank you," she said. "I don't think I should—"

"For luck," he said. "Daniel, bring a cup of brew for my friend Evvy."

His aide crossed around to the women's side of the fire. He was a young, clean-shaven man with light brown hair, and Evvy thought he was nearly as handsome as the Principal. He moved unsteadily, but he was smiling. Perhaps, Evvy decided, the way people responded to drink depended on the circumstances. She accepted the cup, too shy even to say thank you, and sipped.

And spit it out. It was horribly bitter. The Principal and his friend laughed.

"A bit strong," said the Principal, "but you'll soon get used to it. You must never sip brew, but drink it down, like this." Draining his own cup, he demonstrated, then held it out to be refilled from the large flask Daniel carried.

Evvy tried again, taking a larger mouthful and forcing herself to swallow. It tasted no better, but felt warm and strangely pleasant. She could feel the path the liquid took down her throat and into her stomach. She paused a moment, then had another swallow.

"Better?" he asked. Again, she nodded. "Are you enjoying the party?"

She nodded yes.

"I'm glad you're having a good time, and I'm glad your sisters are too. I wanted the women of the Garden to know that I respect them; it's because of that I have to move you."

Evvy nodded again. She had understood this in his speech. She took another sip of brew while he again drained his cup. He had drunk more already than she had ever seen Marson drink, but he seemed steady; only his speech was beginning to slur.

"More brew," he said, holding his cup to Daniel. "And for Evvy."

She shook her head quickly, but he didn't seem to notice. Daniel returned to the other side of the fire to refill the flask. The Principal sat rather heavily at Evvy's side. He began to sing along to one of the songs, and for just a moment his voice sounded like Zach's. Startled, she looked at him, and he looked back, not quite focusing.

"Do you like music?" he asked.

She nodded, wishing that he would continue to sing and not question her.

"I haven't sung for a long time," he said. "Not since . . . well, never mind." He was silent a moment, gazing at the fire. "It wasn't an easy thing to decide," he said then.

For a moment Evvy didn't know what he was talking about, then realized he must mean the decision to evacuate the Garden. Without waiting for an answer, he went on: "There are pressures on a leader that other people can't understand. Terrible pressures."

"I suppose there are," Evvy said, beginning to feel uncomfortable.

The Principal's aide had returned, and both men continued to drink. The Principal turned again to Evvy: "You've hardly said a word to me, yet I feel that I know you. But I would remember if I had met you before. Did you ever have that feeling about someone?"

Evvy nodded; she had been thinking the same thing about the Principal himself. The cup of brew had made her very sleepy. She yawned, then got to her feet.

"Don't go yet," he said. He reached for her wrist, but stopped before touching her. "Please," he repeated. The way he said it made her think that he must be very lonely.

"I must," she said. "Thank you for the party."

"Before you go, tell me one thing."

She waited.

"Where are you from? I know you didn't grow up here."

Evvy started. How could he know that? Did he suspect the truth? She could think of no answer and stammered.

"She's a sensible girl," said Daniel laughing. "She's afraid of you."

"Don't be frightened," said the Principal. "I won't hurt you. I only want to get to know you. You are very lovely, do you know that?"

His face was still gentle and friendly, but his voice had

acquired a frightening gruffness. She continued to stand there, afraid to say more or to leave. She had begun to like him, in spite of everything, but now she remembered that he owned her, under the law. *If only Zach were here*, she thought suddenly.

And then she heard Katha's clear voice cut through the singing. "It's bedtime for all women of the Garden," she called. "The Mistress orders everyone inside."

Evvy straightened, relieved. She looked down at the Principal and was startled by the look he was sending in Katha's direction. Its intense hatred made Evvy's stomach turn over. The remaining women were stumbling to their feet now and moving toward the gate.

The Principal looked up and smiled tiredly. "It's been nice talking to you, Evvy," he said. "I hope we can do it again."

"Thank you," she said. She was not sure whether she dared to be so close to him again. He started to rise and stumbled, then laughed. He was, she could see, very drunk. If he was anything like Marson, he probably wouldn't even remember the conversation.

As she followed Katha and the remaining women through the gate, Evvy looked back. The soldiers were dispersing, those who hadn't simply fallen asleep by the fire. Only a very few, very drunk men were still singing. Among them were the Principal and Daniel. The Principal poured more brew from the flask, spilling it on his boots, and raised his cup in a toast. Despite the festivity of the gesture, Evvy thought that he was the loneliest, saddest person she had ever met.

Ten

The trek to the northeast would take several weeks. The weather held, but the number of men and women and supplies was vast: often streams must be followed several miles off route to find shallow spots for fording; each night elaborate camps had to be set up and then struck in the morning. As they had at the Garden, the Principal's men set up camp near, but strictly away from, the women's camp.

Evvy was traveling with the Mistress, in a large covered wagon pulled by mounts and containing most of the Garden's carefully packed and hidden scientific instruments: microscopes, glass tubes and slides, tiny sharp knives for drawing blood.

Evvy continued to study as they moved and found that her facility for reading and understanding increased as quickly as her fascination with the things she was learning. The Mistress insisted that Evvy spend more time on mathematics, but that did not interest her so much as history, and particularly the history of science as it had been before the Change.

She read about the Belgian monk, Mendel, and his experiments with beans, and about Darwin and his journey to the Galapagos. Quickly all that she had heard in the initiation rite became clear and real to her. No longer was DNA rampaging, invisible creatures—the "wild deenas"—but rather a part of the normal genetic makeup of all living beings. Until the Change, pairings of plants or animals always yielded predictable results; however, the experimental genetic material that had escaped during the Change behaved like viruses, entering the cells of plants and animals, becoming a part of their living genetic mechanism, and changing them in ways that could not be predicted. Evvy learned that these changed creatures, called mutations, were still being created, although not at so rapid a rate as just after the Change. She talked with Hilda about the problems of growing new-grain, which was wildly mutant and unstable. Because most natural wild-grain stocks had been allowed to die out in the time before the Change, it was difficult to create, with crosses, hardy, disease-resistant plants that would breed true.

The possibilities for scientific work seemed limitless, and Evvy could scarcely wait to arrive at the new Garden and begin. She thought she might try to mate Baby and raise tame fox-cats, crossing them for empathic ability. Or perhaps she would be allowed to work on the project to combat the woman sickness.

Without further urging, Evvy redoubled her efforts at learning mathematics, and was suddenly grateful for this long journey which gave her the leisure to read and learn for hours each day.

Because the caravan was so large, and because she was so busy with her studies, Evvy did not see the Principal again until they had been on the road for nearly two weeks.

She was sitting in the Mistress's wagon, looking out at the twilight, sleepy and full from a good meal of new-rabbit stew, when there was a knocking on the wooden side of the wagon, and the Principal stuck his head just inside.

"Hello? Is the Mistress in?"

Evvy gasped, startled. His pale face seemed to float in the darkness. He squinted, trying to see inside the wagon. Evvy wriggled farther back among the crates and barrels and murmured, "She isn't here now. She's gone to witness a birth."

"Who's there?" He frowned slightly, then smiled, in a sunny, wholehearted way. "It's Evvy, isn't it? I haven't seen you in quite a while. Don't by shy. Come out and talk to me."

Evvy crawled toward the front of the wagon and sat as far from him as she could.

"Don't be afraid," he said.

He lit a pipe of new-smoke and, leaning against the wagon, gazed at the fire. Just as at the party, Evvy couldn't think of anything to say, and wondered if he expected her to speak.

After a moment he spoke conversationally, as if they had been talking all day. "I know that most of my subjects are afraid of me; and it's right, they should be. A leader should be strong enough to command respect and obedience."

Evvy thought a moment, remembering her recent reading, then asked, "How did you get to be the Principal?"

He turned from the fire and looked at her. "That's a long, long story. I'll tell you about it sometime."

"Were you elected?"

He laughed. "No. Elections wouldn't work in the sort of world we have today, I'm afraid. Have you been studying history, then?"

She nodded, embarrassed. She felt hopelessly ignorant.

"Then you must know that the most important force in any society is its laws. Without laws, humans cannot live together. And without a strong authority to enforce those laws, they might as well not exist."

"Who makes the laws?"

"In the District, I do. I base them on the ideas that worked in the past and seeing what works in the present. That's the whole point—to make things work."

"Do you obey your own laws?"

He laughed again, without humor. "I think you've been listening to tales about me. Yes, I do obey the laws. Perhaps more strictly than anyone."

"Then why—" she began, then stopped.

"Why what? Go on, you can ask me. Pretend that I'm not the Principal for a moment." He smiled at her again, his face relaxed and boyish. She couldn't help smiling back. "Well?" he said when she still hadn't spoken.

"Why are the laws so harsh?" she finally said.

"These are harsh times," said the Principal. "You're thinking of the beating I gave one of my men yesterday, aren't you?"

Evvy nodded. It had been just after breakfast. The women were pulling up their tents and packing their possessions on mounts and in wagons when the morning silence had suddenly been shattered by a heart-stopping scream, followed by another. Then silence, and all had stopped work and looked at

one another in fear. After a moment, Katha had strode into the
center of the women's camp and announced with disgust that
the Principal was punishing one of his men for disobedience.
Remembering the anguish in that scream, Evvy again felt a
chill.

"That man had done something which could endanger all
of us," the Principal said. "The night before he had gotten
drunk and fell asleep on guard duty. He wasn't the only guard,
but the job was his responsibility, and he didn't do it. The
only way I can make my people understand how important
laws are is to deal severely with those who break them. I wish
that weren't so, but it seems it's been the problem of civili-
zations ever since the world began. I'm sorry it had to happen,"
he added, and Evvy believed him.

"Couldn't you just have taken away his pay?"

"That would not be visible enough. The idea was not so
much to make him suffer as to make sure the other men saw
him suffer, so they would think twice before doing such a
thing."

"But there was no harm done."

"That's true—this time. Listen to me. I'm responsible for
keeping all of you safe. As my guard, that man is an extension
of me. I must be able to trust him as I would myself. Those
who betray a trust are dealt with more harshly than those who
are just ignorant."

He spoke with such intensity that Evvy held her breath. No
wonder Zach had hesitated to cross this man. She wondered
what the Principal would have done to Zach if he had learned
of Zach's betrayal.

"Do you understand what I've been telling you?" the Principal asked.

"I suppose so," said Evvy. "But so many of your laws seem
unfair."

"Which laws?"

"I'm sorry. I think I've said enough."

"Remember, I invited you to speak. What sort of leader
would I be if I refused to listen to my people?"

Evvy knew from her readings in history that a great many
leaders in the past had indeed refused to listen to their subjects.

In some ways she was finding it as easy now to talk to the Principal as to the Mistress, or to Lucky, so she went on, "Why do you take such heavy taxes?"

"I wish I didn't have to, but there is limited wealth. I must pay the men who work for me—that is, who work for the people of the District. I pay the men who build roads, who patrol remote areas and fight outlaws. I pay the men in my army, and the judges. I must also pay for supplies, and food, to support all these men."

"But your tax men take so much. My second-father had to give up all his metal and nearly half his grain three years ago."

"That's wrong!" said the Principal suddenly. "No citizen should ever have to pay so much. Where was this?"

"It was—" Evvy suddenly stopped, realizing how much she had nearly given away.

His voice was cold with anger as he went on. "They must have been keeping some for themselves. Do you know these men's names? Can you describe them?"

"No," said Evvy quickly. "I was living with my grandfather then. I didn't see anyone, I just heard about it."

"Perhaps your father exaggerated?"

"I remember we nearly starved that winter."

"I thought you said you were living with your grand-father—." The Principal's eyes suddenly narrowed and he looked at her closely. "Where are you from, Evvy?"

He knew. Evvy was certain that he knew. But she had to answer. "From . . . near the Garden," she said. She added quickly, "I came to the Garden because my father couldn't afford to feed all of us."

"Why didn't you stay with your grandfather?"

"He died," she said. It was difficult to keep lying, and Evvy was afraid her voice would begin shaking.

"How did you hear of the Garden?"

"From my second-father. He . . . he used to trade with them."

"What does your second-father do?"

"He's a . . . trapper."

"I would like to speak to him or have my men speak to him. I must find out who those tax men are."

He was looking directly at her. Evvy knew that if she met

his eyes she would blurt the truth. All was now lost. The Principal knew who she was; he would claim her and take her away from the Garden. Worst of all, he would find out about Zach's betrayal. Her eyes filled with tears. After all this time, Zach's sacrifice had been for nothing. And then she had an inspiration. Turning to the Principal, no longer trying to fight the tears, she said, "He's dead."

"Who's dead?"

"My second-father. Outlaws killed him. They killed everyone. I buried him and my brothers and then ran away."

The Principal scrutinized her. She held her breath, praying he would believe her. He frowned and was about to speak again when the Mistress approached, leaning heavily on a cane. She looked tired and pleased. "Dori has had her baby," she said. "It was her third girl."

Neither Evvy nor the Principal answered, and the old woman looked puzzled. "Well? Her third girl?"

The Principal turned to her and spoke heartily, though his face was grim. "That's a real accomplishment, old woman. Congratulations."

"We're still not sure—" she trailed off, suddenly realizing how strained the mood was. "What are you doing here?" she asked him in a scolding tone.

"I need to speak to you. I've been whiling away the time with your friend Evvy."

The Mistress gave him a sharp look, then turned to Evvy. "Go in and sleep, child. I have business with the Principal."

"Yes, ma'am," said Evvy. She felt the Principal's eyes on her as she crept into the wagon. After a moment she peered through a slit in the side paneling. The Principal and the old woman had moved over by the fire, where they sat. While they busied themselves dipping herb tea from the steaming pot, Evvy slipped out the front of the wagon and circled to behind a tree where the two were sitting. She held very still and began to listen.

"I am leaving the caravan tomorrow to return to the Capital," the Principal was telling the Mistress. "General Daniel will be in charge. I've told him that he must discuss any major decisions with you."

"Katha is mayor of the Garden," said the Mistress.

"I'm aware of that. But as far as I'm concerned, you are the leader and always will be. Katha is a stubborn fool." He went on before she could comment. "I'll visit when you have reached the site of the new Garden. I hope to learn more about your work now that you will be nearby."

The Mistress nodded. "I or any of my scientists will tell you what you want to know."

They sipped at their tea, then the Principal said, almost sadly, "I miss it sometimes."

"You decided long ago that your destiny is elsewhere," said the Mistress.

"Yes . . . I suppose my life couldn't have been otherwise with the training I had," he said. "Don't think I'm not aware of that. Or not grateful for all I learned in the Garden."

"You have become a good leader, Will."

"Thank you," he said.

Evvy was astonished as she watched, holding her breath. It was evidently a moment of deep emotion for both; she could not even guess at what it meant. The Principal squeezed the old woman's frail hand for a moment, then awkwardly let it go and turned to watch the fire. The flames illuminated both faces, and Evvy realized how much they both reminded her of Zach: the old woman's light coloring and blue eyes, the Principal's sharp cheekbones and thin lips. Though he was a much smaller man, the resemblance was striking when you looked at it. Suddenly Evvy realized what she should have known before, that the Principal was Zach's brother, the Mistress's other son who had gone away twenty years ago and never came back.

Feeling ashamed of herself for intruding on their privacy, Evvy began to work her way back to the wagon. Then the Principal spoke again.

"Tell me something," he said casually. "The girl Evvy— where is she from?" Evvy stopped.

"Why do you want to know?"

"Curiosity, I suppose. She does not seem to be from this area."

"She's from near the Capital," said the old woman. "Her

fathers heard of us and brought her when they could no longer afford to keep her."

Evvy's stomach turned over. Her lie had been found out. The Principal continued in the same casual tone, "Are you sure of that?"

"Yes, I am. Now I've satisfied your curiosity and that's that."

"You've satisfied nothing," he said. "You're lying."

The Mistress pulled her arms to her chest. "It's no concern of yours where she came from," she said.

"It may be much more my concern than you can guess at," he said. And then his voice turned harsh. "Unless you already know." He paused, then went on. "I intend to find out the truth, old woman."

"Stay away from her," said the Mistress, her voice as harsh as his. "You cannot have her—ever. Not without risking everything. We will never let you take her, do you understand?"

"Suppose she comes to me willingly?"

The old woman smiled and looked straight at him. "That will never happen," she said. "Evvy has become a Daughter of the Garden."

The Principal spat, then abruptly stood. "You've won for now, old woman. I have urgent business and little time to think of the girl. But I tell you this. I have an idea who she is, and if I'm right, nothing on this earth—not the Garden and all its Daughters—will keep me from her." He rose, then bowed, in a sarcastic way. "Good night. I will see you at the new Garden."

He strode rapidly away, toward the men's camp. Evvy, her heart pounding furiously, scampered back to the wagon as quickly as she could.

For many hours she lay with her eyes open, listening to the sounds of the night. Over and over she saw the Principal's face, smiling openly, then contorted with rage. She heard his voice, his breath, his laugh. The images were so intense that she felt as if he were not in the men's camp but here, in the wagon, beside her.

PART THREE

The Garden

One

Most of the leaves had fallen, forming a thick, crisp carpet on the forest floor. The air was chilled and invigorating, and the Principal had to consciously guard against pushing his mount too fast. He was impatient and curious, wondering why he had suddenly been summoned to the new Garden.

He had not visited since the women had moved in, two years ago. Although he had been in frequent communication with them by writing, he had found excuses to avoid any contact, and, besides, in truth he had been busier these two years than ever before in his rule.

The Capital was now a thriving city, and he could no longer oversee the administration of all basic services. This meant training others to do the work for him. He had also started a school for teachers and healers, overseeing and in some cases creating the curricula himself. Even more time-consuming had been the constant training of new troops, some to man the increasingly important outlying fortresses, including the old Garden; others for police duty in the Capital, where they were charged with keeping order and arresting the growing number of Trader proselytizers.

He had also traveled a good bit in these two years: he had journeyed to the sparsely populated, bat-ridden northlands, where he reaffirmed his uneasy truce with the Governor of the North, an educated old man of little vision, who ran a feudallike system and who welcomed the Principal as an ally against the Traders, who had begun to move into the north too. Afterwards, for several months, he had led an expensive and fruitless expedition of exploration into the unmapped areas of the west where the Traders were believed to originate, finding nothing but ignorant, unkempt nomadic tribes, many of whom followed the new religion. Of organized structure or religious leaders there had been no trace, though the primitive peoples his troops encountered seemed more resistant to the ideas of civilization than even the people of the District had when he had first assumed control. The movement seemed to have sprung up everywhere at once like mushrooms after a rain, with no order or direction.

Unfortunately, the Traders' beliefs were taking hold in the Capital, and discouraging them consumed more energy every day. His subjects seemed eager at the least excuse to give up every vestige not only of civilization but of common sense. He had always had difficulty persuading the people of the Capital to bathe, to dispose of their waste in places other than the drinking-water supply, to attend the literacy classes which he encouraged by forgiving a part of taxes owed. There had been more resistance to all these since the Traders had come into the District with their doctrines equating cleanliness with godlessness, technology with the devil, and knowledge with damnation. It was as if all of mankind had suddenly chosen to return to the Dark Ages; but this was worse, because the knowledge existed, though it was no longer widely known, of the consequences of poor hygiene.

The Principal knew from his reading that it had taken hundreds of years for a few forward-looking scientists to persuade their peers to accept the theory of the bacterial spread of diseases, that as recently as two centuries ago people had died in great centers of healing, called hospitals, because doctors would not wash their hands. Today, the majority of the people in the District did not know the most elementary rules of hygiene, and those who had heard of them avoided them as evil mistakes of the past.

The theory of disease was well known to the Principal and Zach: as young boys in the Garden they had looked through ancient microscopes at the small creatures which lived in a drop of sweat or pus, and even in well water. At the time, both the Principal and Zach had been terrified of the small creatures, thinking them the personifications of wild deenas. It was only their systematic education in the Garden which had prevented the Principal and Zach from succumbing to the same superstitions and fears which made the lives of most citizens of the District more miserable than necessary.

In one respect only had the situation improved: after being repulsed several times by the soldiers at the old Garden, the Traders had given up armed attacks anywhere in the outlying parts of the District. The Principal liked to think that their militant arm had been defeated, but it seemed more likely they had simply changed tactics. Another western expedition would have to be mounted sooner or later to find the elusive heart of the Trader empire and cut it out.

At least he wouldn't hear Trader nonsense at the Garden. Perhaps this thought accounted for his strangely buoyant mood. Not one of his men shared his concerns and goals in the same way Zach had, not even Daniel, the best-educated of his generals. There was no one he could discuss these things with, really, except for the women of the Garden.

There was a sharp smell of woodsmoke, and his field headquarters, which guarded the neck of the peninsula, appeared. Leaving his escort, he rode the few remaining miles alone.

Again he tried to guess why the women might have summoned him so urgently. He realized he should long since have paid a courtesy call. Still, he doubted they expected courtesy of him, and on his part the thought of seeing the old woman again constricted his throat with remembered rage. He could still see her hateful, gloating face in the firelight the night she had informed him that Evvy had become a Daughter of the Garden.

The image of the girl, with her astonishing eyes, had appeared to him often in dreams and reverie. It was a neat trap: he owned her—he was certain of it—but he could never, without abandoning his greater concerns, have her.

He spat, as if to remove a bad taste. Well, two years had passed and no doubt she would now be too old for his needs. Seeing her again would be just the thing to rid him of his desire for her.

His compulsions, in any case, seemed to come upon him less and less. In the time since the move, he had had very few girls; none now for several months. In the mornings when he looked into the mirror, he saw gray strands in his hair; perhaps he was at last maturing, outgrowing the ruinous obsession that had controlled him for so long.

The new Garden had been transformed since he was last here. His men had repaired all cracks in the walls and the houses, and the women had planted and tended the gardens and orchards. Though the crops had long since been harvested and the ground was bare, save for stubble and brown leaves, there was a feeling of vitality and growth here.

The Principal stood by the gate, while the guard, a heavy, awkward girl with a sallow complexion, ran off to summon the mayor. The late fall breeze brought the fresh scent of fish and salt from the bay, and he breathed it deeply, remembering again the week that he and Zach had spent here, planning their final assault on the Capital, knowing that this time they would succeed or die. It was astonishing how memories of Zach continued to turn up unbidden, three years since his death. In spite of the finality of the burial, the Principal still found himself listening for Zach's quiet knock at the private door to his office, or for the haunting music of his feathered lyre. The Principal wondered if he would ever stop missing him.

He was brought to himself by the sound of a door slamming. A familiar figure crossed the wooden porch and strode along the carefully tended path.

"Good day to you," said Katha, her face carefully expressionless.

"And to you."

"The Mistress is anxious to speak with you. After you've cleaned up and rested, I'll take you to her."

Without another word she led him around the great stone house to a small wooden outbuilding.

The Mistress's room was in the basement of the main house. Like her old cabin, it was dark and stuffy, dimly lit by flickering fish-oil lamps.

The old woman was lying on a long wooden cot, bundled in blankets and propped up with pillows. She looked as if she had aged ten years in the two that she had been living here.

Her skin was yellowed and hung in folds; even her eyes seemed to have lost their fire. He was shocked and tried not to let his face show it.

"Good afternoon, Will," she said, as if she had last seen him just a day or so ago.

"Good afternoon," he said. "I'm sorry to see you're not well."

She snorted. "It's obvious that I'm dying, though I don't know how long it will take. It's some form of cancer, I think. They could probably have cured it before the Change, but I don't mind. I've lived far longer than I ever expected to."

He felt strangely moved by the news of her approaching death. At other times in his life he had wished for nothing so intensely, but now it hurt to see her so obviously weak and sick.

"This is why you summoned me," he said.

She shook her head impatiently. "I can die very well without your company."

He held in his anger, pity for her pain restraining him.

She continued, her voice surprisingly strong. "I called you here because we need your help. I must explain some things to you myself."

He relaxed. It was to be a matter of business, then. In other matters, except for brief moments, usually with Zach's intervention, they had never communicated except through a veil of mutual irritation.

Her face clenched then as a wave of pain passed over her, and he looked away until it had passed. This room was more cluttered even than the old one; from the dust on the instruments and books he guessed she had been too ill to work for some time.

"This new site has worked out well," she said, as if from a great distance. "At first, as you know, we objected to having your soldiers stationed so close by, but in the long run it has proved convenient in many ways."

"So I hear."

"You've heard that some of our women have mated with the soldiers, and that is true. It was most inconvenient for us to move when we did, and lose the services of the local men.

But your camp provides us with a far greater selection for our breeding experiments." She paused, then raised her head and moved it toward him. Automatically he leaned down, his eyes going to her thin lips to help him understand what she had to say next. "We believe that we have taken the first step in eradicating the woman sickness."

"What!"

She nodded several times, her lips smacking together between words as she continued. "We were working on it when you forced us to move. That was one reason for our opposition, though we could not tell you then. Do you remember the large number of women who were pregnant when you came to the Garden two years ago?"

"At the time it seemed unusual."

"We've long known that the illness is sex-linked, passed on by both parents but attacking only women. As you know, some women develop it early in life and some never do; and usually it kills a woman and her child upon the birth of her second daughter."

The Principal frowned. "As I remember it, the trait is believed to be carried on the female sex chromosome."

"Yes, the X chromosome. As nearly as we can tell, only those women who have received the trait on both their X chromosomes ever actually develop the disease."

"But those who have received the trait from just one parent could pass it on to their children?"

She nodded. "Since men have only one X chromosome, any man who carries the trait will pass it on to each of his daughters. A woman carrier's children will have a fifty-fifty chance of receiving it from her." She lay back and rested a moment, then went on, almost briskly. "All of this has been known—or assumed—for years. What we did not know was how the disease actually operated. About four years ago, old Alison got the idea that the disease was autoimmune, that somehow the women who became ill were reacting to something in femaleness itself. That the first affected girl-child would set up the sensitivity, and the second cause the illness to appear. Alison developed a serum from the blood of women who had died of the sickness, and we tested it on all the members of the Garden. Those who had more than one daughter did not show a reaction, but many with one daughter or no children or only sons developed a swelling at the site of the inoculation."

"Meaning that they carry the trait?"

"We can't be sure that the test shows carriers. But we are becoming quite certain that it indicates those women who have the trait on both X chromosomes." She raised herself on her elbows, her pale eyes glittering with excitement. "Will, since we began testing, we have allowed no women to mate except those who showed no reaction to the skin test. There have been thirty-six normal pregnancies in that time, half of them of girl-children, and no one has died of the sickness." She lay back, her face exhausted and triumphant.

The Principal caught her excitement. The details would have to be worked out, but clearly this work held the answer to the greatest threat ever to face humanity. Leaping into the future, his imagination saw that cooperation between him and the women of the Garden would indeed change the course of history, and that his name in future books would not be a footnote, but would be written large, as the savior of all mankind. So lost was he in this dream that he had to ask the old woman to repeat what she had just said in her feeble voice.

"This is only a beginning," she murmured. "We still need a method to discover which men are carriers—and why, indeed, the trait doesn't extinguish itself. At present we can only be certain of those few men who do not share a wife, where she has died of the sickness. Zach pointed the way first to that."

The Principal nodded. Although he had long since left the Garden when Zach's wife died, he knew that Zach had pored over the available information, finally abandoning all study and the Garden after satisfying himself that he was a carrier and that the death had, in truth, been his fault.

"For now, we are ready to begin testing the general population," she continued. "We'll need your help."

"All my resources are yours."

"My scientists have already drawn up plans. They'll explain everything to you in detail." She paused, then went on, speaking very distinctly. "I wanted to talk to you myself to get your pledge to fully protect any women who go into the Capital."

"Yes, of course."

"Protection in every way," she repeated. "And above all, from yourself."

He shook his head angrily. "No promises, old woman!"

"Listen to me," she said. "What's between us is in the past. I know I bear some responsibility for your hatred of women. But this is much more important than the way either of us feels. We are finally on the verge of an answer. Trouble between you and the Garden would destroy that. Katha is strong and a good leader, but she doesn't fully understand how important the work is. Don't do anything to jeopardize it. Promise me."

He had to stand. He walked to the window and parted the curtain, then looked out at the white November sky. He took three deep breaths, letting them out slowly, then returned to the old woman's bedside.

"I promise," he said. "There is no choice."

"I know you will keep your word," she said. She settled back into the pillows, as if completely exhausted. She seemed to slip into sleep, and he wondered what to do, when her eyes flicked open again. "You must meet with the women who will work in the Capital. All have volunteered, and all understand the possible dangers. They are irreplaceable, Will, as is their knowledge. Guard them well."

He nodded. "My men will protect your girls with their lives. Rest easy, old woman."

She laughed weakly. "Don't bury me too soon. I've some time left yet." Her eyes clouded. "I've been very lucky, to live to see the goal of my life nearly reached. If only . . . " She looked up at him, her face full of sorrow. "If only Zach could have lived to see it too."

He felt contaminated by the old woman and her stench of illness. Although he had intended to stay here the night, he could scarcely wait to return to the military compound, where he would sleep among men, in the clean air.

There remained only the meeting with the scientists who

would come to the Capital when he had worked out the details. All would, of course, be fanatical Daughters of the Garden, humorless and sexless. He followed Katha to the lab, cluttered as the old one had been with its odorous animal cages and strange instruments.

He opened his mouth to speak, then stopped. Waiting with the other two scientists, and looking more beautiful than she had as a very young girl, was Evvy. She had grown tall, and her woman's figure was evident even under the loose-fitting lab coat. She was a young woman now, nothing like the flat-chested, innocent girls he had always preferred.

It didn't make any difference. He wanted her so intensely that the feeling made him dizzy; and he understood at once why the treacherous old woman had extracted his promise at her sickbed.

Two

The Principal felt irritable as he approached the Capital. Although he had been away fewer than thirty-six hours, it seemed longer. The dirt, the noise, the stench, were over-whelming. As soon as he crossed the still-standing pre-Change bridge with its concrete pilings and rusting supports, he saw the heaps of refuse piled carelessly all along the riverbank. The crumbled pre-Change roadways were crowded with merchants and farmers taking their wares home on carts drawn by draft animals. Most of the men were dirty and shabby, drinking their home brew from flasks, shouting, arguing, relieving themselves in the street. At every crossroads ragged young boys solicited, selling themselves for the price of a meal or a cup of brew. Above them all stood the ancient buildings, crumbling and dingy, like crude caricatures of the shining marble structures shown in pictures from before the Change.

Three generations ago this had been a thriving metropolis, a center of the highest civilization mankind had ever achieved.

Now most living was clustered by the river and its tributaries, a stinking, concentrated mass of humanity with all its problems.

How could he hope to restore civilization when barbarism was so close to the surface? Was it even worth it to try to clean up and educate these dirty, wretched men and women with their rotten teeth and sallow complexions? Even as he thought of the difficulties that faced him, his mind was working on the immediate problem of establishing clinics for the testing of women and for the vast project on birth-control education that would follow. Automatically he reviewed government buildings that could be used. The scientists from the Garden would stay in the pre-Change mansion across from his own great House; they would be safe there, and he could keep an eye on them. At the thought of the women his anger rose again, sickening him. Evvy would be as close by as his stables; he might see her every day; and he had given his word to stay away from her.

As the Principal and his men turned off the broad avenue toward his House, their mounts were jostled by crowds leaving the closing markets on the mall. Some men recognized him and turned to wave or to call out, begging for a special favor or an audience. Usually he stopped and spoke to his people, but he was tired and irritable and wanted as little contact as possible with the unhappy subjects who were his chosen responsibility.

At the park just across from his House, a large crowd was gathered around a man standing on a crate. He was dressed in filthy leather garments but was clean-shaven, and spoke with obvious passion. Surprised at the size of the crowd, the Principal turned to watch a moment. Very quickly someone recognized him and called out his name. The man stopped speaking, then looked directly at him. For a moment their eyes met, and the Principal felt a chill go through him.

He paused in confusion, not certain what to do. History taught that freedom of speech was an important outlet in any society. Take away free speech and you guaranteed the spread of dissidence. But there was something frightening about this man, his look, his passion, and the attention of his listeners. The Principal turned to Daniel, intending to ask him to find out who this speaker was and what he was doing there, but suddenly the crate was empty, and the crowd was dispersing. The next instant the Principal heard shouts and a shrill whistle, across the street at the entrance to his House.

He turned and saw men running toward the porch. His heart thumping, he slapped his mount and quickly rode through the wrought-iron gates.

He jumped off his mount, handing the reins to a frightened-looking stable boy, and ran toward a bushy-bearded guard. "What's going on here?"

The man began to stammer. "The great library, sir. Someone has got into it with a fire—"

A fire! In the library! Will ran up the stairs and along the carpeted corridor to the library. There was a sharp smell of smoke, excited shouts, and the sounds of men running. Through the haze he saw several guards beating a struggling figure in the doorway.

At that moment Robin rushed up to him.

"Thank the deenas you're back!" the old secretary cried.

Will pushed past him into the library. The smoke was still choking. In the center of the room stood a large pile of ancient books, blackened and now sodden from the water that had been poured on them. The magnificent blue carpet had been ruined.

Glancing quickly at the shelves, he saw that the damaged books represented only a fraction of the many stored here, but his stomach still turned over at the thought of any damage to the irreplaceable knowledge of the past. He turned back to the door, where Odell, the housekeeper, was cowering. "Have someone clean these books and save what can be saved. Dry the pages that can still be read. Put as many men on it as necessary. Now!" Trembling, Odell set off to recruit workers.

The Principal turned his attention to the guards, their faces streaked with sweat and smoke. "Who is this man?"

"A new servant, sir," said Perry, the older of the guards. "Good thing Jason smelt smoke—the whole place would have gone up."

The man who had created the fire lay trembling in the corner, blood running from his nose and the corner of his mouth, his eyes wide and full of triumph. Or madness.

The Principal forced himself to look away from the wretch. He went to the windows and threw them open, then took three deep breaths, holding each before letting it out. When he had finished, he relaxed his fists and approached the man, keeping his breathing even. Slowly, he walked around the prisoner, whose foul, stale smell was remarkable even in a generally unwashed populace.

The prisoner looked up at him, curiosity flickering in his mad eyes, the bloodied mouth twisted in a demented grin.

"Who are you?" the Principal asked, meaning, *Why have you done this thing?*

The prisoner continued to look up at him, his face still split with the idiot grin. "Who are you?" the Principal repeated, his voice calm.

"His name's Jared, son of Martha," said Perry. "Least, that's what he told the housekeeper when he got hired."

Odell had returned and with a quavering voice was ordering servants to place the ruined books on slabs covered with cloth.

"How did you come to hire this man?" the Principal demanded.

Odell blinked. "We had a vacancy, and he showed he knew how to clean and polish. I didn't know he was crazy. I don't have time to check every—"

The Principal waved Odell silent and turned back to the prisoner. "Who sent you here?" Again, there was no response.

"I'll get the answers I want," the Principal continued. "I'm going to find out how this happened and who is responsible for it. I don't care how badly I damage you in finding out."

The Principal thought he saw a flicker of fear cross the man's face, but still he said nothing. "Who ordered you here?" When Jared still did not answer, the Principal kicked him in the belly hard enough to knock the wind from him. The prisoner grunted and twisted away. When he had recovered his breath, he gasped, "'Twas my own idea," he said. "I needed work."

"Who ordered you to destroy the books?"

A crafty look appeared on his face. "God," he said.

"What?"

"Almighty God. He orders all books and other science destroyed."

"Filthy Trader!" Perry put the point of his lance to the man's neck.

The Principal pushed Perry's arm aside. "Who is your leader?" he asked the man. "Who are you working with?"

"All men are my brothers," said Jared. "All men—but the godless scientists." He spat on the floor. Again Perry moved toward the man, and again the Principal restrained him.

The prisoner looked up at the Principal and grinned. "Our messiah will put an end to you and all your unholy ways. You can't stop us!"

"Who is this messiah? Name him!" But Jared curled into himself, again mute.

The Principal kicked him again, more gently, and turned away, disgusted at the man and at himself. He rarely employed torture, because it seemed to him both barbaric and an unreliable means of getting to the truth. But he would have this man tortured and then executed publicly, as a warning to any others who might think to bring their filthy Trader ideas into the Capital, and in the vain hope of obtaining some information, however slight.

Long after the prisoner had been dragged away, the Principal sat in the great library, at a carved oak table made long before the Change. On the ceiling were smudges from the oily smoke, and the ruined place in the carpet was now covered with a clean cloth laid by Odell's men. He looked from wall to wall, his eyes caressing the books, fewer than half of which he had read. He realized he would have to accelerate the program he had instituted in the first year of his rule of having books copied out and the duplicates stored in scattered repositories. He made a mental note to set up new training courses for copyists; this would help to absorb more of the unemployed young men still flocking into the Capital—those that weren't Traders, he reflected.

He could never hope to stop the Traders until he understood them more clearly, had some sense of their organization and codified beliefs. But the few prisoners he had questioned had seemed innocent of any theological system beyond an incoherent hatred of what they called science. Perhaps the religion had no structure. Perhaps the Traders were the forerunners of a race of new-people who did not think like ordinary men. This was an eventuality he and Zach had long been prepared for but had prayed would never come about. New-children were born every day, of course, but to his knowledge none had ever survived infancy, unlike such new-animals as mounts and poison-bats, which existed alongside and in many cases supplanted their genetic prototypes.

If only Zach were here, he thought, and stopped, surprised at himself. He had not thought of turning to Zach for help in quite a long time.

It had been over three years now since Zach had disappeared, three years since he had ceased to be the Principal's companion; and sometimes it seemed like only yesterday. The Principal closed his eyes and tried to visualize Zach's face, but all he could see was the ragged prisoner, blood and dirt streaking his lined face, his eyes gleaming with fanaticism.

Three

Walking quickly but carefully, Evvy picked her way along the broad Avenue, its surface paved with fine rock and strewn with animal and human wastes. On her left was the vast mall, sweeping from one end of the Capital to the other, its emerald grass cropped short by sheep and new-goats.

Just now the trees and weeds were whipping back and forth while merchants hurried to cover their wares ahead of the approaching storm. In the center of the mall, the Great Tower seemed to move too as dark clouds rolled past it. The sight of fresh produce reminded Evvy that she hadn't eaten. With a worried look at the clouds, she darted into the confusion of the market. In spite of the noise, the smells, the dangers, she felt completely at ease here.

She had been in the Capital half a year and was still thrilled with the city. As a very young girl she had lived in a town, but most of her life had been spent first in the barren northern hill country, and then in the Garden, with its quiet, strict ways. The city seemed to have no rules at all, not even the natural laws of rising and sleeping with the rhythm of the sun. Here there was activity at all of the hours of the day and night; and most of it concentrated on the mall, at once a marketplace, theater, and free home for those clever enough to avoid robbers and the Principal's soldiers.

At idle moments in the clinic Evvy liked to gaze out at the constantly changing scene, watching farmers, merchants, housewives, jugglers, pickpockets, children, acrobats, mount dealers, lovers, and brew salesmen all going about their business. Sometimes it seemed to her that in this one grassy area on a fine afternoon all possible human activity was occurring at once, in the open and among the trees. Once she had watched a yellow-clad poet kneel under a tree, singing and playing a feathered lyre. He was a thin, very young man with a homely face, and did not sing or play nearly so well as Zach, but when he had finished his songs, bowing and collecting the small contributions of his audience, Evvy's face was wet with sadness and longing.

The first day Evvy had arrived, along with Lucille and Lucky, the Principal had held a great rally on the mall just across from the clinic, an ancient building supported by marble pillars the size of trees, and sheltering a gigantic statue of a seated bearded man. The Principal had told them he had chosen this site because it was easily accessible from the mall, yet could be defended from all sides.

That night he had delivered a stirring speech to the assembled crowd. "Before the Change," he said, "there were more girl-children living than boy-children. Before the Change, mothers rejoiced at being with child, and seldom did they sicken or die. Before the Change there was one woman for every man, and families lived in happiness and plenty." He paused. "That time can come again."

As always when she heard him speak, Evvy was thrilled. She and Lucky were seated on a blanket on the grass. In a semicircle around them were four of the Principal's men, including Daniel, the handsome, clean-shaven young general, who was looking not at the Principal, but down at Lucky. Lucky was excited and couldn't seem to sit still or to keep quiet for a moment.

"Are there always so many people when the Principal gives a speech?" she asked Daniel; then, without waiting for an answer: "I love the way the buildings look in the torchlight, like ghosts of the past." She stopped a moment to listen, then continued, "He's so good at making speeches, Evvy, don't you think so?"

"Yes," said Evvy, laughing. "Shh."

The Principal was continuing, talking about his hope of curing the woman sickness one day soon. Without speaking directly of medical testing or birth control, he promised a piece of metal to any woman who would come with her husbands to the clinic and then return three days later. Evvy was startled by low, angry murmuring and looked into the crowd to see expressions of mistrust and puzzlement. She turned to Lucky, then Daniel, whose lips were set in a tight line. His hand, she saw, was lightly touching his sword. She shivered, then turned back and watched the Principal, who had seemed not to notice any negative reaction and was continuing to speak with passion, his face and body so animated that he looked as if he might suddenly rise into the air and fly out over the crowd.

When the speech was finished, there were cheers and applause, but beneath them was a deeper sound of suspicious murmuring. Still, despite the less than wholehearted acceptance of the Principal's project, Evvy was cheered to see looks of hope on the faces of many young women in the crowd.

As they walked home with the guards, Evvy noticed that Daniel and Lucky stayed a little apart, deep in conversation. She saw Daniel's hand brush Lucky's and then take it. Evvy smiled to herself, but at the same time she felt a pang and imagined for a moment that Zach was beside her, his big hand surrounding hers.

After that first day, Evvy saw very little of the Principal. She and the other women were busy with testing all during the day and evaluating the material till late into the night. The

Principal had appeared at the clinic briefly on the first morning of operation but had spoken to the women only perfunctorily, wishing them luck, then turning matters over to Daniel and his guards.

Evvy felt relieved and at the same time curiously disappointed. In spite of the terrible things he had told the Mistress that night on the journey to the new Garden, she was drawn to the Principal. It was almost as if he were two men—one visionary and charming, the other angry and unpredictable.

She knew that the angry Principal was capable of almost anything, even taking her from the Garden by force; but she also sensed that the other Principal would not allow anything to interfere with her work.

The routine never varied from day to day. Early in the morning the guards helped the women set up their tables, two to one side of the seated statue, where Evvy and Lucky conducted screening, and one on the statue's other side, where Lucille administered the test. When all was prepared, the guards stood back to allow women to enter one by one, followed in most cases by ragged dirty children and sullen, suspicious husbands. In spite of the guards and Lucky's reassuring giggles, Evvy felt safer with Baby there. The fox-cat seemed to sense that her presence would be frightening to the patients, and sat the whole day quietly, hidden by the table, at Evvy's feet.

At midday the clinic closed for a meal break, and then reopened for more testing or, twice a week, to give birth-control classes to the women who had proved susceptible to the woman sickness, or who simply did not want to bear more children. Evvy felt important and useful when she explained to exhausted and frightened women how to follow their own bodily cycles using colored pebbles and how to prepare abortifacient teas and fowl-gut barriers.

The first family that Evvy interviewed were typical of the hundreds that followed. The woman was young, scarcely older than Evvy herself, though her face was lined and anxious, and her body sagged from bad food and four pregnancies. She was dressed in a shapeless dark skirt and over-tunic, her hair neatly tied back with strands of blue wool. Her husbands were twins, both thin to the point of emaciation, with narrow, deep-set eyes.

Evvy smoothed the long, flat leaf-paper in front of her and dipped her pen into a pot of ink as if she were accustomed to doing this all the time. "Your names?" she asked, covering her nervousness with a businesslike manner.

"Gladyss, daughter of Gladyss," the woman answered. "These are my husbands, Walt and Wendell, sons of Maria."

"Occupations?"

"Fruit farmers," said Wendell, almost apologetically. "Me and Walt plant and gather, Gladyss tends to the trade."

Evvy recorded this information, then checked for her next question on the thin wooden board propped in front of her.

"How many brothers did you have?" she asked Gladyss.

"Four."

"Sisters?"

"I was the only girl. My mother died of the sickness when I was two."

Evvy nodded and recorded. "How many fathers did you have?"

"Three. Two brothers and my first-father."

"Did they take another wife?"

The woman shook her head and gave Evvy a look that indicated she hoped future questions would be more sensible. Now Evvy turned to Gladyss's husbands. "How many brothers in your family?"

At this point Wendell spoke up. "Ten altogether. But we're here to keep Gladyss from getting the sickness. And what about the piece of metal the Principal promised?"

"We'll get to all that," Evvy said calmly, surprised that her nervousness was gone and that she felt as authoritative as she sounded. "But we need some information first. How many sisters did you have?"

The interview continued, and Evvy learned with excitement that Walt and Wendell had three sisters and several girl cousins. This would be an interesting case to follow.

The line had been growing and now stretched down the long marble steps and into the street. Worried about the time, Evvy hurried Gladyss and her husbands to the table where Lucille would administer the scratch test. Evvy straightened her pile of leaf-papers before interviewing the next family and watched from the corner of her eye as Lucille scrubbed Gladyss's grimy arm clean with fire-berry disinfectant, then took a sharp glass pin and scratched the skin on the inside of her elbow. Gladyss cried out in surprise and drew her hand back angrily.

"Don't wash this arm today," Lucille said, "and come back in three days for your piece of metal."

Much to Evvy's disappointment, Gladyss and her husbands did not return. She was almost certain that the woman would show positive for the trait—and that her husbands were not carriers. This meant that any daughters Gladyss might have would have an even chance of being susceptible, and that Gladyss herself would probably never develop the woman sickness. What more it might mean, and how they could use the information, would depend on the results of hundreds of more tests over the coming months and years.

There were so many possible combinations that Evvy found herself growing impatient at the amount of time it took to thoroughly question each family that came in. And she was becoming increasingly angry at the large number—nearly half—who never returned for the results of the test and to receive their reward.

Even now, six months later, she could scarcely believe that anyone would refuse to accept free treatment that might save her life—or on a more practical level, than anything would prevent poor citizens of the District from following the instructions to win a piece of metal.

Pushing her way through the maze of stalls and display carts in the market, Evvy could smell the approaching storm. She was returning from taking Baby home; in the last few days the little animal had become restless, refusing to stay quietly hidden, and this morning she had emerged from beneath the table twice, growling and spitting, terrifying the patients. Evvy had been unable to calm her, and finally agreed to take her home at lunchtime. When she put Baby into the room she and Lucky shared in the mansion across from the Principal's House, the little animal would not stay quiet; she stationed herself by the doorway and began to howl loudly when Evvy tried to leave the room. Evvy sighed, then knelt and scratched her pet behind the ears. "I'll be back in just a few hours," she said soothingly. "Don't worry, Baby." At that the fox-cat mewled piteously, then took Evvy's skirt in her mouth, pulling toward the center of the room. Evvy gently pulled her hem free, then picked the little animal up and set her on the bed. "Now, stay here," she said. "I'm going, whether you like it or not." Baby remained on the bed, but she continued to howl. Evvy reluctantly left, feeling cruel as she shut the door on her pet's cries.

Baby's behavior worried her; perhaps, as Gunda had long warned, the little animal was finally reverting to her natural wild state. Or possibly she had simply been spooked by the approaching storm.

Just ahead of her Evvy saw a wooden cart heaped with purple and green fruits. The dispirited-looking woman who was trying to cover the cart and sell at the same time looked somehow familiar. Evvy peered at her while the woman counted out change. Her brown hair was tied back with blue yarn, and her torn and dirty tunic swelled over a soft bulge in her abdomen. Suddenly Evvy recognized her: "Gladyss!"

The woman looked up suspiciously, then a quick look of fear crossed her face.

"Do you remember me?" said Evvy. "From the clinic?"

"I don't know what you're talking about," the woman said. Clearly, she was shaken.

"I was sorry that you didn't come back," Evvy went on. "Do you remember the scratch we gave you? Did it ever start itching or turn red?"

"You'd better get out of here before my husbands come back," the woman said. "They won't like hearing your godless science talk."

Now Evvy noticed the double spiral, carved of wood, that the woman was wearing on a thong around her neck, and realized why she had not returned; somehow, between the time they had appeared at the clinic and the time they were to return, Gladyss and her husbands had become Traders.

As she sat munching a new-plum and watching people on the mall quickly taking cover from the gusty winds and pelting drops of the storm, Evvy wondered how many other test couples had been frightened by Trader beliefs. She would have to discuss this with Lucille and Lucky as soon as they returned from lunch; perhaps there was something they could do to persuade even Traders to return for the results of the test. In the meantime, she wanted to go back to the mall and shake some sense into Gladyss, but she realized that she herself could easily have become a Trader if Zach had not come and changed her life.

Zach. He had been gone four years, and still he appeared in her dreams almost nightly. He never changed, didn't grow older as she did. If he should return now, would he even recognize her?

"A bit wet out there, eh?" Evvy looked up, startled. Standing across the table from her, his yellow-bordered cape dripping on the marble floor, was the Principal. At the entranceway stood two of his men, looking like shadows in the dark light of the storm.

As always when she saw him, Evvy's heart seemed to stop beating. His soft woolen tunic was darkened from the rain, and glistening drops clung to his dark curly hair. At just that moment lightning struck a tree across the Avenue, lighting him in a way that made him look far taller than he was.

Evvy flinched at the thunder, covering her ears with her hands.

The Principal smiled. "If you can see it and hear it, it won't hurt you," he said. He sat on the table casually. "I see the rain has driven away your customers. Have you learned anything yet?"

Evvy smiled ruefully. "That people don't like to follow instructions."

The Principal nodded, looking more sober. "Perhaps I'll have to increase the reward," he said. "This is too important to leave to chance."

His voice sounded sad. She looked up, and at that moment there were several flashes of lightning in a row. The Principal seemed to flicker in and out of existence with each one. Evvy felt that a direct connection had formed between their eyes. The lightning stopped, and the Principal parted his lips as if to speak but said nothing. After a heartbeat, Evvy lowered her eyes.

They sat and watched the rain for a few more minutes. The black clouds were rolling quickly to the east, leaving a shining, eggshell-white sky behind them.

"Who would have thought you would come to the Capital?" the Principal said abruptly. "Who could have guessed your work would be so important?"

His voice was hoarse, and again Evvy was surprised at the sadness in it. But the next moment he leaped up and smiled. "I must get on about my business," he said. "Thank you for the shelter."

The summer heat was already turning the wet ground steamy as the Principal strode down the marble steps, flanked by his men. Almost immediately the lines began to re-form, and when Lucky and Lucille returned, the girls resumed their questioning.

"How many brothers do you have?" Evvy was asking a red-faced young woman. Her attention was so focused on recording the answers accurately that she didn't realize anything was wrong until she was suddenly seized from behind. The woman she had been interviewing screamed, and the patients scattered in terror.

Strong, thick arms gripped her tightly around the chest, pinning her own arms to her sides. Behind her, she could hear Lucky whimpering. All at once a clean-shaven man with curly blond hair leaped onto the table and began shouting to the crowd, who had been prevented from fleeing by armed men at the entrance.

Daniel and his men were fighting, but they seemed badly outnumbered. Over their yells, the blond man shouted: "Do you know where you are? This is a temple to science. These women are scientists. They are asking you to contaminate yourselves. They are asking you to join in their unholy crusade to spread the evils of the Change." Many of the clients stopped trying to escape and turned to look at him. Evvy heard murmurs of anger beginning to spread.

"Don't believe their lies!" the man shouted. "Tear up their notes! Destroy their instruments! Don't let them cause another Change!" He took the day's stack of filled-in questionnaires and ripped them into pieces, scattering them about the room.

"No!" cried Evvy. She struggled with her captor, trying to pull herself free. Now some of the members of the crowd, as if infected, had begun to tear the remaining notes and smash the wooden instruction boards and instruments. Lucky was sobbing, pleading with the man who held her.

"Don't listen to this man!" Evvy called out. "He is ignorant! This is your only chance for survival—" A rough hand was clapped over her mouth, cutting off her words. Now the crowd began to turn to her. She heard someone shout, "Godless scientist!"

For the first time since this had started, Evvy was afraid. She shrank back, seeing the hatred and madness on the faces of the men and women she had only recently been trying to help. She struggled desperately, but her captor only gripped her more tightly.

A fire was now flickering in front of the statue, the crowd feeding it scraps of leaf-paper and wood. "Kill the scientists!" came a cry. Two large, dirty men with crazed looks on their faces began walking toward her, and Evvy shut her eyes in terror. The next moment she was released, so suddenly that she pitched forward onto her hands and knees. She turned and saw the man who had captured her lying on his side, his head cut nearly from his neck. Above him stood the Principal, his face white as ash, his features twisted in rage. He was shouting orders to armed men who had appeared around him. Before Evvy could move or say anything, the Principal pulled her to her feet and pushed her toward another man. "Guard her with your life!" he cried, then turned and matched swords with an invader. The Principal's man held Evvy with one arm, the other hand on his sword. He pulled her close to a pillar, away from the fighting.

The Principal was shouting like a madman, his sword everywhere. As if in a dream, Evvy saw blood spurt from the chest of one man, the shoulder of another. The sharp sound of metal on metal mingled with screams of anger and fear. The man who was guarding her took a blow on his forearm and staggered a moment, but he did not let go of her; a moment later the Principal struck down the attacker. Nearly as suddenly as it had begun, the noise and confusion had disappeared, except for some distant shouts outside the building and the moans of injured lying on the slippery floor.

The Principal, his tunic splattered with blood, his face dark and coarsened, stood in the center of the clinic, sheathing his sword. Daniel, bleeding badly from wounds to his head and thigh, approached him, then opened his hands in a gesture of appeal. He was, Evvy saw, weeping. "It was men in my guard that let this happen," he said. "They must have been spies or converts."

"It was your responsibility," the Principal said, his voice as tight as his lips. "I can no longer trust you."

Daniel sank to his knees. "I resign my commission at once," he said.

The Principal struck him across the face, knocking him to the floor. "You haven't that right! I relieve you of it! You will be punished!"

Her guard had released her, and Evvy realized it was over. She stood dumbly looking at Daniel, who was slowly struggling to his feet, his face streaked with tears and blood. Then she remembered. "Lucky—" she said, starting to look around for her friend.

"She's dead," said the Principal. His voice had become very quiet. Evvy looked at him, not understanding at first. Then she heard a howl of mourning, and recognized Lucille's voice.

"They would have killed you too," the Principal said. "It was only luck that my mount went lame. I would have been outside the Capital when this happened."

Evvy stood a moment in shock. "Our notes—" she said.

"All destroyed. Instruments, notes, records—all gone. All that work for nothing."

Evvy felt cold. She looked at the floor, slippery with blood, and at the overturned table. The Principal's men had begun covering the bodies. She started to turn to where Lucky had been just before the attack. The Principal moved quickly and stopped her with a hand on her shoulder. She looked at him, the dark curls stuck to his forehead with sweat, and felt she had known him her whole life.

"You're a brave girl, Evvy," he said. The words pierced the cloak of shock she had pulled over herself, and she began to tremble. The Principal pulled her head to his chest and patted her shoulder while she sobbed into his tunic.

Four

The meeting room was smoky—the fire wasn't drawing properly—and the Principal repeatedly cleared his throat as he talked. The old woman—incredibly, still alive—lay in her room, too ill to be here. Katha was pacing the polished floor, irritation showing in every line of her face and every gesture.

"I say it's too dangerous," she repeated. "We've already lost one scientist. Are you trying to destroy us?"

The Principal looked just as annoyed as Katha, but spoke calmly. "It will be as safe as I can possibly make it," he said. "But the real work can't go ahead as long as the leader of the Traders is at large. He must be stopped."

"Let your own men stop him, then," said Katha. "I refuse to risk any more women."

The Principal took a deep breath, and then another. When he resumed, he spoke very distinctly, as if explaining something to a child. "I agree that the ultimate solution is to have my men do all the testing. But it will take time to train them— as you yourself pointed out. In the meantime, it's vital for the testing to resume—both to preserve the work already done, and to lay a trap."

Katha shook her head impatiently. She walked over to the fireplace, then squatted and peered into it, as if the answer to the dispute were responsible for clogging the flue.

Evvy, watching from a cushioned chair opposite the windows, sighed. She thought that the Principal and Katha were a great deal alike; neither seemed able to give in, even on a small point. In this case, though, the Principal was right: the screening must continue. Katha was a good leader, but she didn't fully understand the importance of the scientific work. She was far more interested in the logistics of running a community. She could probably, Evvy realized suddenly, lead the District every bit as well as the Principal.

Katha stood again and, her back to the smoking fire, began to speak. "You are the Principal. You control all the wealth and resources of the District. I can't believe that you are unable to capture the leader of the Traders."

"Nevertheless, I can't!" the Principal shouted, then again breathed deeply and went on. "My men arrest every Trader they find preaching openly. We have yet to gain usable information from any of them. We can't discover anything about this man. I've posted a reward for him. The man who catches the Trader leader will have more metal than I do. My men bring in Trader after Trader, some of them even claiming to be the messiah. But always—they're the wrong man."

"Perhaps your men are more in sympathy with the Traders than you suspect," Katha said.

"That's just it!" he said, now standing himself. "That's it exactly. Even my generals are beginning to think this man is somehow supernatural. It's gotten to the point where I can't be sure of anyone. The only way I'll slow the spread of this religion is to capture their messiah and prove he's just as human as the rest of us. And the only way I can capture him is to draw him into the open again—to the clinic."

"What you have just said proves your plan isn't safe. As you just admitted, you can't be certain who among your men is a Trader spy and who isn't."

The Principal looked weary. "That's not altogether true. I have a few close aides that I trust absolutely. And they will guard the clinic." He sat again, then went on. "Here is all I ask. Let me have two or three scientists, for just enough time to train a small group of my men in the testing procedures. Two days a week only we will operate the clinic. If the trap doesn't work after a few weeks, I'll abandon the idea."

Evvy thought Katha looked very confident as she shook her head, her long blond hair sweeping across her back. "I can't ask any of my women to take that risk," she said.

Evvy curled her hands into fists. Katha hadn't even listened. She was opposing the Principal just for the sake of opposition. It was as if winning her point were more important to her than saving the human race. Evvy closed her eyes a moment, remembering the screams, the slippery feel of blood on the floor, and the smell of death. She remembered Lucky, her enthusiasm and sparkling eyes, and remembered how she had looked in death, with all that energy stilled. She swallowed, then opened her eyes and stood.

"I'll do it," she said.

The Principal and Katha both turned and gaped at her. Gunda half rose. "Evvy, you don't have to—"

She continued, fighting to keep her voice calm. "I know I don't have to. But I know how important it is. And I've been to the Capital. I've already seen the worst thing that could happen. I think it would be easier for me than for anyone else."

There was a moment of silence, then Hilda stood. "I'll go too," she said. "Evvy can't train the men by herself." Two more women rose, including Lucille.

"Lucky belonged to all of us, as a Daughter of the Garden," she said quietly, "but to me she was, above all, my child. I know she would have wanted me to carry on the work, so her death will not be lost. I will go too." Lucille had lost weight since Lucky's death, and had become more taciturn than ever, but Evvy thought tonight she was beginning to look herself again, with a hint of Lucky's sparkling animation in her gaunt face.

"There are four volunteers," said Gunda into the silence. Katha stood in the center of the room, a frozen statue of fury, looking from one woman to another.

The Principal's face was unreadable. Evvy prayed that he would hold his temper now and keep his triumph hidden.

"I forbid this," said Katha.

"You can't do that," said Hilda. "And you know it. If it comes to a council vote, we will go. Don't split the Garden. You know what we've been working for all these years. It has to be done."

Katha stood still another moment, her entire body rigid. Evvy sensed that she would kill the Principal if she could, and that her feelings came from something more than the present dispute. But she wouldn't split the Garden. She crossed to the window and sat.

"Very well," she said. "But for safety, I insist that our own guards go along."

The Principal nodded. "That's an excellent idea. Your soldiers can be trusted completely, and I know they're well trained."

Evvy relaxed. The Principal was not going to provoke Katha further and was being generous besides. She felt a sense of exultation floating lightly above her fear. She looked at the Principal and saw gratitude in his eyes.

The three scientists and six soldiers from the Garden were given rooms in a wing of the Principal's own House. At the Principal's strict order they were not allowed beyond his walled yards and went outside only armed and under guard.

Evvy, Hilda, and Lucille began immediately to train seven of the Principal's men, most of whom had been recruited from among his literacy teachers and healers. An exception was Daniel, the former general, who had become subdued and sober since the Trader attack and seemed determined to atone for his tragic mistake.

Although all the men could read and write, none were trained in the mathematical skills they would need, and Evvy found that teaching them these skills consumed most of her time. She enjoyed the classes, which were conducted in a thickly carpeted parlor with polished wooden furniture and gently curving walls. The Principal's men were eager to learn, and good-natured, laughing more easily than did the women of the Garden. They treated the women kindly and with respect, and fussed a great deal over Baby, who generally observed the proceedings from atop the mantelpiece, her water-colored eyes alert and surprised-looking.

Daniel, in particular, was solicitous and took the first opportunity to beg forgiveness of both Lucille and Evvy, pledging that he would protect them with his life. He not only studied harder than the other men, he familiarized himself with all stages of the testing, from questioning to the follow-up statistical work. He had a better basic education than the other men and learned quickly. Evvy was glad that the Principal had forgiven him to the extent of allowing him to work on the project, though she understood that he was no longer allowed in the Principal's presence. After the attack, she had been afraid, seeing the Principal's face and remembering what he had once told her about men who betrayed a trust, that Daniel would be imprisoned or worse.

Evvy remembered the way that Daniel used to look at Lucky and wondered if he missed her the way she did Zach, if he was working on the project in dedication to Lucky's memory, as Evvy had become a Daughter of the Garden in dedication to Zach's.

While training proceeded, the Principal was having readers go about the Capital and into some of the nearby towns to announce that the testing and birth-control program would resume in some weeks, and posting the dates, the place, and the time. Evvy tried not to think about how soon it was, but concentrated instead on her teaching and on reading books taken from the thousands in the Principal's library.

Evvy loved the Principal's House, which more than any building she had seen seemed to reflect life before the Change. Although much was as shabby as anywhere in the District, still, the furnishings, hanging portraits, and carpets were well preserved and more carefully constructed than anything made since the Change. She had her own room here—an unimaginable luxury! It had a desk, bureau, bed, and two chairs, and—best of all—high windows made of glass, through which she gazed for hours, watching the teeming life in the streets.

She had assumed that, living in his House, she would see the Principal often, but in fact they scarcely met, and she only occasionally caught glimpses of him through her window as he strode impatiently about his grounds.

She felt that she knew him better than anyone else in her life, better even than Zach. Yet it was because of Zach, and her vow to protect his memory, that she could never feel completely comfortable with the Principal. Her fear of him had disappeared, but the secret of her origin and of Zach's betrayal would hang between them, always.

The day the trap was first to be set, Evvy woke before the sun. She sat up and looked out the window at the dawning light. At the foot of the bed Baby was whimpering and twitching in her sleep. The little fox-cat was pregnant for the third time in as many years, but had yet to deliver live kittens. Although Evvy would feel far safer having her pet with her at the clinic, she had decided not to subject her to the possible dangers there. At the thought of what might happen, she felt a tightening in her stomach and throat. At a final meeting the previous evening, the Principal had explained that he did not expect the attack to come on the first day, but that they must all be prepared for the possibility. The clinic would be heavily guarded by the soldiers from the Garden and the Principal's most trusted men. In addition, among the legitimate citizens coming for testing would be more of the Principal's men, posing as husbands to women for hire, who were to be well paid for their risk.

At the first sign of trouble, Evvy, Hilda, and Lucille were to crouch under the tables, where they would be guarded. When the meeting ended, the Principal had approached Evvy and taken her hand. "Don't be afraid," he told her. "I promise you will be safe."

She had returned to her room with her heart pounding, from fear and from his touch.

In the end it happened on the first day, and it happened very quickly. Evvy had become so busy with her work that she had forgotten the danger. The table shook, causing her to spoil a leaf-paper, and she looked up from her writing, annoyed, to see standing before her a handsome young man with curly yellow hair. He was bearded, and she was so surprised that all she could think at first was how familiar he looked; it was a moment before she recognized him as the leader of the fatal attack last year.

He smiled and looked directly into her eyes with an openness that reminded Evvy of the Principal. He pulled a short, sharp dagger from his sleeve and held it so she could see it, then said, "Don't say a word. Pick up your things and come with me."

From the corner of her eye, Evvy could see that the other women, including the guards, were too busy to notice anything, and the clinic had become so crowded that she was not sure where the nearest of the Principal's men was.

Her legs shaking, she stood, then gathered the papers in her hands and threw them at him. She saw him step back in surprise, and then she screamed.

Instantly the room filled with armed men and women; the party of Traders was so badly outnumbered that there was little fighting. The blond man, seeing that he had been trapped, stood where he was as the Principal's men surrounded him.

"That's him—that's the man!" Evvy repeated again and again, pointing. She was dizzy, and she thought for a moment she would be sick. "He's the one, the one who killed Lucky—"

Strong hands took hold of her shoulders and squeezed, then released her. She turned to see the Principal behind her. "It's over," he said. "We have him."

He approached the prisoner. "Are you the one they call the Trader messiah?"

The man nodded. "You've finally caught me," he said.

"Yosh, no!" cried one of his men, but the blond man shook his head and went on, calm and proud.

"I have always known that this would happen," he said. He looked at the Principal directly. "You will kill me, I know that. But you cannot kill my ideas. The truth will live."

"The truth is what you filthy Traders are poisoning," said the Principal.

The Trader shrugged. "The seeds have been planted in the

Capital. Nothing you do now can stop us." The man was as calm and certain as if he had peered through a window into the future.

The Principal had told Evvy and the others last night what would become of the Trader leader if he was captured. He would be questioned under torture, then bound to a machine body without food or water until he died. His body would stay there, at the base of the Great Tower, until it had turned to bones.

It was the most horrible death Evvy could imagine, but looking at the strangely intense face of the young leader, she was sure that he would face it calmly. The Principal was ordering his men to take the Traders to his prison, his voice sounding as strong and confident as that of the Trader messiah. But as he turned to look at his prisoner, Evvy thought she saw a flicker of uncertainty on his face, a tiny hint of fear.

Five

Though it was early morning, the Principal could already feel the sun hot on his neck as he stood outside the gate, waiting to be admitted to the new Garden. Nearly two years after she had told him she was sick, the old woman was at last dying.

He had set out immediately, as soon as he received her message, his own emotions so confused he didn't know quite what he felt. He could not imagine why she had summoned him—she had long since made it clear that he was no more welcome at her deathbed than in her life. Whatever her motive, it must be important to her, and therefore undoubtedly important to him and their shared concerns.

He felt certain that it must somehow have to do with his fight against the Traders. Although the women scientists had long since returned to the Garden, the men who were conducting the clinic were in constant communication with them. He himself avoided the clinic—and Daniel, who was now in charge of the project—as much as possible, but made it a point to keep informed about the testing, and he knew that the number of citizens seeking help had lessened, even though the reward for testing had been increased to two pieces of metal.

There had been no more incidents, but the Principal was coming to realize that he had made a terrible mistake in trying to stop the spread of the Traders by executing their leader. The huge rusted machine body where the man had died in agony was apparently becoming a shrine. Daily, bunches of fresh flowers appeared, despite the efforts of his guards to keep the area off-limits. The guards reported too that every day dozens of citizens approached, making the sign of the spiral as they passed the spot.

He had, the Principal now realized, made a martyr of the man, as the Jewish-Christian messiah had been martyred over two thousand years ago. But the deenas take it! What else could he have done? If the Trader leader had been executed in private or even been imprisoned, there would have been rumors about his reappearance, possibly attempts to help him escape. Yosh himself had seemed to understand this, and the Principal was beginning to suspect that he had, perhaps, deliberately sought martyrdom.

After the questioning, which had produced no information the Principal did not already have, Yosh and the four men who had been captured with him had been bound to the rusting metal sides of a great machine from before the Change that lay rotting at the base of the Great Tower. Not wheeled, like most machine bodies, the execution machine had once moved by means of metal treads; the remaining rusting links gave it an even more fantastical form than most machine bodies. Quite apart from the suffering involved, death on the machine was assumed by most residents of the Capital to involve an especially horrifying form of contamination by wild deenas. Though the Principal repeatedly and publicly denied that wild deenas or anything else inhabited the machine, privately he suspected that the superstition helped serve as a deterrent to capital crimes.

After three days, not certain why he did so, but drawn there—perhaps to show that he had no fear of the Traders—the Principal and two of his men had approached the crowd where the Traders lay dying in the hot sun. The Principal saw, among those who had come from curiosity or to jeer at a prisoner, many faces streaked with sorrow. He heard murmurs as the crowd parted before him, and then he was standing in front of the Trader leader. He was scarcely recognizable now: his face was darkened and cracked, his lips dry and blistered, the bruises from his capture and questioning showing blue and yellow beneath the parched skin. His eyes were filmed, yet a spark within them met the Principal's gaze. The Trader leader blinked, focusing, and looked at the Principal, waiting.

"What good do your Trader gods do you now?" the Principal said.

"There is one god only," said Yosh, his voice weak but surprisingly clear. "The god of nature. The god of truth."

"The god of lies, you mean," said Red angrily. The Principal waved him quiet.

"You're finished," said the Principal. "You're dying. Two of your men are already dead."

"We will live again . . . in truth," said Yosh.

The Principal was uncomfortably aware of the many faces and ears around him. He felt sweat beginning to dampen his tunic, and knew he should not debate with the man, should turn and walk away, but he could not help himself. He was drawn to the young leader, though he could not say why. He wanted to understand him, to convert him, as, perhaps, Yosh wanted to convert the Principal.

"I have no doubt that you are sincere in your beliefs," the Principal said. "But you are wrong, and your ideas are dangerous. I didn't want to do this. You left me no choice."

The Trader leader was silent for a moment, then he smiled grotesquely, a trickle of blood running from the corner of his mouth where the skin had cracked. "Are you asking my forgiveness?" he whispered.

"I ask nothing of you!" the Principal said. He was on the point of turning away, when the man spoke again, his voice weaker.

"Nevertheless, I do forgive you. You don't know any better. I could even thank you. You have done more to help us by this one act than we could have accomplished in a year of work in the District."

The Principal felt his anger subside, to be replaced by a prickle of unease in his belly. He knew that this was true.

The man to the right of Yosh moaned then, and muttered something. Yosh turned to him. "Have faith, Brother Martin. It will end soon." He shut his eyes, and for a moment the Principal thought he had lost consciousness, but the young leader's eyes opened again, to slits, and he began to speak, so softly and hoarsely that the Principal could scarcely hear him. "The seeds of evil have been planted in you," he said. "But I know that you are not yourself evil. I learned that from . . . Brother Zach."

The Principal started so violently that Red put his hand on his arm. "Are you all right, sir?"

"What did you say?" the Principal demanded, not certain that he had heard the man correctly. He could not have heard him correctly. "What did you say?"

He pulled away from Red and grasped the Trader leader's shoulders. The man groaned and opened his mouth, but his words were lost in a croak.

"Water!" the Principal shouted. Red handed him the water bag, and the Principal held it to the young man's mouth. Yosh turned his head away.

"Drink! You must tell me—"

"No," Yosh murmured. He sighed, then whispered, "Besides, if they see you give me water, they'll think you do it only to prolong my torment."

Recognizing that this too was true, the Principal turned and flung the waterskin to the ground, where it burst, the clear fluid disappearing into the sparse grass. The Trader leader seemed to be losing consciousness. In anger and fear the Principal strode across the grassy field back toward his House, Red and his guards scurrying to catch up. He heard, behind him, a shout: "Monster! Offer him water and then pour it out! May the deenas take you!"

He was so shaken he didn't even turn.

Standing at the gate to the Garden, he heard again the Trader leader's words. He could not have said *Zach*. Thinking it over a hundred times since, the Principal realized that his mind must have played a trick on him. No one else had heard anything.

"The Mistress wishes to see you now." The Principal looked up to see Gunda, the fat red-haired woman, standing before him. He took a deep breath, dreading the coming ordeal. He had had his fill of death and the dying.

The room was so darkened that it was difficult to see more than an arm's-length ahead. The old woman lay heavily covered, despite the late summer heat, her frail body nearly swallowed up by thick coverings.

The stench of sickness hung in the air like morning fog, and the Principal resisted an impulse to throw open the windows. The two women at the bedside stepped away, then left the room, and he approached her, feeling nauseated.

"I'm here, Mother," he said.

She opened her eyes and looked up at him, not quite focusing. He sat by the side of the bed. She was impossibly thin. He didn't know how she had managed to stay alive for so long. Possibly a wild deena was in her. Her hand rested on the coverlet beside her, so frail that it seemed to have no weight. For just a moment he had an impulse to cover her hand with his own.

"Will," she said, her voice only a whisper, "I asked you to come, because . . . you must think of the future."

"The future is assured now," he said. "Because of you and your work."

"Nothing is assured," she said.

He realized that she must be referring to his struggle with the Traders, and for a moment he thought of telling her all that had happened with the Trader leader, but she was speaking again.

"There's much to accomplish yet," she went on. "More, perhaps, than you will be able to do. I mean to say, you must provide for succession."

He stared at her, startled. How could she have known that

had been on his mind, ever since the first attack by the Trader spies? "I know it," he said.

She seemed not to hear him. "No matter what your personal feelings," she went on, "you must take a wife. One who is not susceptible to the sickness."

Again he nodded, astonished. At one time the old woman would have done anything in her power to keep him away from all women. Did she understand that he had changed? More likely the future of her project was more important to her even than her feelings about him.

"I will do it, old woman," he said.

"A wife," she said, with some intensity. "A companion, a helpmeet, someone who understands what must be done. Not . . . as you have done in the past."

He took a deep breath, and stood. "Is it your plan, then, to control my actions from the grave?"

She was silent a moment, then spoke, her weak voice full of disgust. "It has always been my hope," she said, "that you would learn to control your own actions."

Again he drew in air and held it. His anger was not lessened by the knowledge that she was right.

"Will," she said, when he did not speak again. "Sit down. Don't you think it's hard for me to say this? For a long time I believed that our work at the Garden was all that mattered. And in a sense it is. But I know now that it is meaningless without a structured society. Without your society. I don't want to see anything happen to it. The future of my work depends on the future of yours. And that depends on a stable succession."

He looked down at her, astonished. He knew what it had cost her to say these words. A flame of anger still licked at the corners of his mind, but it was mixed with the beginnings of respect. He let out a deep breath, then sat beside her again.

"I understand you," he said. "I have been thinking the same way for a long time now."

Her lips smacked together two or three times, then she gave a profound, exhausted sigh. "I wish," she said. He leaned closer to her, but then she began to cough, deeply and heavily. Her eyes rolled up until the whites showed. Alarmed, he opened the door and called for the women who had been attending her.

Several women rushed in and crowded around the bedside, their voices low and heavy with sobs. The Principal scarcely realized that Evvy was among them until his eyes met hers across the bed of the dying woman. She acknowledged him with a widening of her plum-colored eyes, then bent over the old woman, gripping her hand and stroking her hair. The Principal stood by the window, not wanting to be there, yet unable to leave. The Mistress looked once at him and seemed about to speak, then she closed her eyes and her breathing became more labored. After nearly an hour of struggle, during which she no longer seemed aware of anything, she again opened her eyes. She stared at the foot of the bed as if seeing something there. She lifted her head off the pillow, then murmured a word. Suddenly she became rigid, then fell back, her eyes open, at last gone.

The sobbing of the women in the room became louder now. The Principal lifted a corner of curtain. Outside the sky was bright with summer sun. He felt a tug at his sleeve. He turned to see Evvy, her face streaked with tears, her eyes red and swollen.

"I'm sorry," he said to her.

"I know you are," she said. "I know she was your mother."

The Principal looked at her in surprise. The old woman had never wanted that known, even among the women of the Garden. The other women were now doing the necessary things, all except Katha, who still sat at the side of the bed, her face dry, but rigid in mourning.

"Did you hear her last words?" asked Gunda, rubbing the back of her friend's neck.

"I heard," said Katha. "She said just one word." She looked up and caught the Principal's eye. She fixed him with a look of hatred so intense that he felt it to the soles of his feet, then said, "The word was *Zach*."

Six

The women and children of the Garden stood quietly at the grave while Gunda spoke of the Mistress's life and work. Evvy stood dreamily, tears silently sliding down her cheeks, while Katha was pale as a December sky, her feelings hidden.

The Principal himself felt numb. There was a feeling like sorrow in the pit of his stomach, but the only sense of loss he felt was for Zach, as if his mother's death had renewed his mourning for his brother. He felt regret too, that he and the old woman had not communicated more, particularly in these last years; but even at the end they had not been able to speak two words to each other without anger and misunderstanding arising. There was a great deal between them that would now remain forever buried.

He thought again of her last words to him. In many ways that conversation had been typical of her; despite her recognition of all that he had accomplished, there was no least hint of affection or forgiveness.

After the ceremony there was a simple breakfast. The Principal took part impatiently. He was staying only because Evvy had asked to talk to him. At last they went into the laboratory together. Despite her mourning, she looked lovely, her dark hair gathered at her neck and spilling down the back of her white lab coat.

"I have good news for you," she said without preamble. "We may have solved the major puzzle of the sickness . . . the reason the trait doesn't extinguish itself. Before she died, the Mistress examined our evidence and reasoning, and asked me to submit it to you."

He wondered if this were a form of posthumous flattery;

the old woman had never asked his opinion on scientific matters while she lived. He frowned, trying to remember the crux of the problem. "The difficulty," he said, "was that men who pass on the trait would in theory produce fewer offspring than those who do not. Is that right?"

Evvy nodded. "We have a great deal of statistical information from the testing in the District, and more from your soldiers in the field camp. We think the answer must be that the sperm that carry the trait are more mobile or in some other way more viable than normal sperm."

The Principal thought a moment. Of course. "And with polyandry the prevailing form of marriage . . ."

"Yes. Since each woman has at least two or three husbands, a carrier is more likely to father any children. What's exciting is that we should now be able to discover which men are carriers, once we've devised a test. If only we had more and better equipment. . . ."

"It's only a matter of time till you work it out," said the Principal.

"I think so too." She gestured, happy and enthusiastic. "Within a few years there will be no reason why any woman should ever die of the sickness. Once we have our test, that can be added to the work already being done at the clinic. And, of course, we'll have to open more clinics—and a training school for technicians."

The Principal had never seen her so animated. He caught her enthusiasm, envisioning a clean, well-fed, and literate population streaming in and out of the great centers of learning that would spring up around his clinics. Of course, the problem of the Traders would still have to be solved, but all at once he felt that nothing was beyond him. Evvy was speaking again, and he had to ask her to repeat what she had said.

"I have a present for you."

He laughed, startled and pleased. "What sort of a present?"

She rose, smiling oddly, as if she were trying to keep from laughing, and led him to the back of the long room, where he could hear the squeaking and scuffling sounds of caged animals. She stopped at a crate on the floor and knelt. "Come look," she said.

He knelt beside her and peered over the edge. Inside, Baby, Evvy's fox-cat, lay stretched on her side while three tiny replicas of her drank hungrily from her teats.

"Baby's babies," Evvy said proudly. "I want you to take one of them." Before he could protest that he had no time for a pet, she said quickly, "Listen to me. The day the Traders first attacked the clinic, Baby was agitated and wild. I finally had to take her home. I'm sure she knew what was going to happen. There have been other times when she acted to protect me. I think that if you keep a fox-cat near you, you'll be safer from Trader spies."

He looked at her quickly, then down at the animals. Two were identical in coloring to Baby's golden orange, while the third was lighter, with dark brown stripes streaking its flanks and limbs, and radiating from its eyes like a mask. The kittens' fringed, pointed ears were so large that they resembled wings. "Which one shall I take?" he asked, laughing.

"Whichever one pleases you," she said. "They're all males, and they're all healthy."

The striped fox-kitten rolled onto its back, then suddenly twisted and pounced on Baby's tail, which had been slowly twitching. Baby gently cuffed her child and shook the others off, then stood and stretched. She put her paws up on the edge of the box and yawned loudly before sniffing the Principal's outstretched hand.

"It's as if she knows what we're here for," he said.

"I think she does," said Evvy seriously, her voice full of pleasure.

"*Mowr?*" said Baby, jumping out of the box as if to give the Principal a better view. The striped kitten and one of its brothers had begun to wrestle with each other, rolling over and over, batting at one another with their tiny paws. The striped kitten fastened its teeth on the other's ear, and with a cry the golden baby pulled away. His brother followed for a moment, then abruptly turned and looked up at the Principal, its clear green eyes open in challenge.

"*Owr?*" it squeaked. "*Owr?*"

The Principal chuckled and tentatively reached his hand into the box. "Won't Baby be upset if I take one of her children?"

"I don't think so. She's been weaning them. I've watched her training them to hunt for small creatures. They're nearly as big as she was when I found her."

The striped kitten sniffed the Principal's hand, then suddenly turned and snapped at its own tail. The Principal withdrew his hand, startled. At that moment Baby leapt back into the box and held the striped kitten down with one paw, then began vigorously to wash it, her rough tongue moving over the kitten's face, back and tail. Her son squirmed and squealed in protest, but she didn't stop until its fur was damp and gleaming. She then looked quizzically up at the Principal and took the baby in her mouth by the back of its neck. With a gentle leap, she again left the box and set the baby at the Principal's feet. The little fox-cat shook itself, then stretched its legs up to the Principal's knees.

"I think," said Evvy, "that Baby and her son have chosen you."

The Principal put a tentative hand down toward the furry little creature at his knees. It took the tip of his thumb in its mouth and bit gently, then let go and began to buzz contentedly, rubbing against his legs.

"I name him Napoleon," said the Principal, smiling. "Thank you, Baby. And thank you, Evvy. I'm touched."

"I can't help worrying about your safety," Evvy said, rising. "And besides, you always seem so lonely."

The Principal felt his heart turn over. Suddenly he understood the old woman's last words to him. He took the baby fox-cat in his arms and followed Evvy to a nearby bench. "Come to the Capital with me," he said.

She nodded. "I want to help found a permanent school for technicians."

"I mean now," he said. "Today. Come with me."

Evvy looked at him. Her face was soft, and there was something more behind her eyes. Was it fear? She took a long time to answer. "I can't," she said.

"Why not?"

"My work is here."

"Bring it with you."

"I need a month or two more."

"Evvy, I want to marry you." He was almost as startled at his words as she appeared to be, but he realized he had been thinking of this for some time. Her dark eyes filled with tears, and she looked away, then shook her head.

The Principal glowered down at the hearth. On it lay two large pieces of marble and some chips, ruined forever. A chunk of splintered wood dangled from the carved ledge of the mantel. Lindy, the young serving boy, was cowering in a corner, while the baby fox-cat stood on the window ledge, growling in distress.

The Principal was ashamed of himself. His temper had again resulted in unnecessary destruction, but he couldn't stop it. "Send someone to clean this up!" he shouted at the boy. "And bring me another pitcher of brew."

He walked to the other end of the room, then back again. He had been unable to relax for a minute since leaving the Garden. He had left his men far behind, driving his mount so hard that she began to stumble, unable to catch her breath. But the faster he rode, the more clearly he could see the image of Evvy as she gazed at him with her troubled eyes and said:

"Thank you. But no."

At first he thought she had misunderstood him. Their lives had been entwined for so many years now, it seemed obvious that they were meant to be together. Never had he felt so comfortable with another person, never since Zach. He wanted to explain all this to her, to show her the reasoning. All he said was, "Why not?"

She frowned, then turned her head away. "I can't marry you. Please don't ask me to say more."

He thought a moment, then nodded. "You're a Daughter of the Garden," he said. "Your work is the most important thing to you. I understand that. But Evvy, Daughters can marry. My own brother was married to a Daughter of the Garden."

She turned back to him, looking frightened. "It isn't that," she whispered. "Please . . . forget me and let it be."

"You've heard stories about me," he said then. "About the way I've treated women."

"I don't believe them, it's not that."

"The stories are true," he said. Her eyes widened in surprise. "That is . . . they were true. For many years I bought and abused very young girls. I persuaded myself that it was my right—as Principal, to take release in any way I could."

Evvy said nothing, and he continued, "I could still do that," he said. "For that matter, I could reclaim any one of the girls—those that are still alive. Under the laws of the District they are still mine." Her expression did not change, though she had become pale. He felt again that she was the girl he had sent Zach to buy over five years ago.

"I'm telling you this so you'll know it's all in the past. So there won't be any secrets between us. I would never do anything to harm you. You must know that. I only want you with me. As Principal I can have a wife of my own, unshared."

She swallowed. "I'm sure many women would be honored to be your wife."

"I don't want any woman! I want you. I've wanted you for a very long time. You must have sensed it."

"I sensed something when I was younger. It frightened me then."

"You're not frightened now?"

"No."

"Then come with me."

She clasped her hands together and took a long breath. "I can't. I love another man."

"What other man?" he asked, shocked. He could feel his temper rising and took a deep breath before continuing. "It's Daniel, isn't it?"

She laughed without humor. "Daniel loved Lucky," she said. "He is my friend."

"Then one of my soldiers from the base camp. Name him—"

She shook her head. "The man I love is dead," she said. "And there will never be anyone else."

He looked at her as if through a fog, trying to understand what she was saying. Then, suddenly, with a certainty that froze him, he knew. The man she loved was Zach.

At that moment Katha strode into the lab. "Your men have asked me to tell you they are ready. And to remind you that you must start soon if you want to reach the Capital today."

He nodded impatiently, then turned back to Evvy. "Please come with me now. You don't have to promise anything. In time you may change your mind."

"Time won't change anything," she said.

"I can force you," he said then. "I am the Principal, and you are my subject." He clasped her wrist, hating himself for what he was doing, yet unable to stop. The baby fox-cat jumped off his lap, hissing, and Evvy pulled back, trying to free herself. Then suddenly her eyes widened and she looked behind him in alarm. He turned to see Katha, still in the doorway, both hands lifting her heavy, ornate sword.

"Let her go!" Katha cried.

"Katha, no!" Evvy wrenched herself away from the Principal and darted across the room. He saw what she was after a split second too late: his own sword, which, with his cloak and bag, had been lying by the entrance. She lifted the weapon and dropped it outside the open door. He watched in horror— was she trying to help Katha kill him? Could this somehow be a Trader plot? But Evvy was now standing between him and Katha, speaking urgently.

"Katha, I'm all right. Please go outside. The Principal is leaving. Don't provoke him."

And he realized that she had disposed of his weapon to save him from himself, to prevent open war between him and the Garden.

Katha's face was white with fury. "You have ten minutes to get out of here. Evvy, come outside with me."

Evvy cast a glance back at the Principal, then followed Katha.

For perhaps a full minute he sat there, trembling and breathing deeply. He felt a fool, disarmed by women, but he knew that Evvy had done the right thing. Nothing could be worse for his larger plans than blood between him and the leader of the Garden. He stepped outside, where his men, looking wary and with their hands on their weapons, stood ready. Katha too was poised for battle. Evvy stood between her and his soldiers, looking frightened and deeply unhappy.

The Principal took his sword from Red. "We'll leave now,"

he said, aware how harsh his voice sounded, "And I'll not be
back." He waited until his men were mounted, then climbed
on his own mount. From the corner of his eye he saw Evvy
give a small covered basket to Red, with a whispered word.
It was his fox-cat, he realized. Then she approached him.

He turned his mount away without another word and led
his men through the yard, then out the gate.

The Principal was pulled back to the present by hesitant
knocking. Lindy had returned with a pitcher of brew and an
assortment of foods. He watched while the boy bent to clean
up the ruined pieces of marble, then waved him away. He
poured a full cup of brew and drained it in one long swallow.

He sat at his desk, thinking to work, but his thoughts returned to the Garden. In disgust he pushed a heap of papers
onto the floor, again startling the baby fox-cat, which had just
curled up beneath his reading lantern. He had drunk so much
that he should have been dizzy, but he wasn't. The warm liquid
filled him, but did nothing to cure the complicated ache that
started in his belly and had spread through his whole body.

He could have anything else. He could—he would—prevail against the Traders. He would establish a great civilization
to rival those of the past. When history books were again
written, there would be whole chapters devoted to his works.
He would have everything except what he most wanted.

He brooded restlessly for a very long time. After midnight,
still unable to sleep or to anesthetize himself, he called for
Robin.

"Take this bag of metal," he said. "Get me a young girl."

Robin gaped at him. He had not served the Principal in this
way for years. "What sort of girl?" he asked.

"I don't care. All that matters is that she be young. Very
young. And she must have long dark hair. Pay whatever is
necessary."

After nearly two hours, Robin returned with a girl, younger
than Evvy but older than the children the Principal had preferred
in the past. The girl looked bewildered but pleased. He saw
from her ankle bracelet that she was from a house of women
for hire. She was pretty, and though she bore no resemblance

to Evvy despite her long dark hair, he decided she would do.

"You may go," he told Robin. "Instruct the guards not to let anyone in here, no matter what they hear."

"Yes, sir," said Robin. He looked terrified.

The Principal poured himself another cup of brew and offered one to the girl. She accepted it and began to sip, looking at him with interest.

"What is your name?" he asked her.

"Ania," she said with smile which revealed several missing teeth.

"Do you know who I am?"

"Of course," she said. "You're the Principal."

At that moment the baby fox-cat leaped onto the couch beside the girl. She drew back in surprise. "Is that a fox-cat?" she asked, sounding more curious than frightened.

"It's my pet," he said. "His name is Napoleon."

"Aren't you a pretty thing," she said, stretching out her hand to be sniffed. Napoleon licked her fingertips and crawled into her lap. She stroked his soft fur, looking like a delighted child. The Principal watched her for a moment, feeling strangely ill at ease.

"Where are you from, Ania?" he asked, his voice slightly hoarse.

"The west," she said, her face flushing.

"You're a refugee?"

"We were driven out by the Traders. My fathers had some old-style books on keeping bees. We used to raise new-honey. The Traders burned the books and all our things, and my fathers died trying to stop them."

Although she told the tale matter-of-factly, he could see the pain in her eyes. "How did you come to the Capital?"

"My little brothers and I hid till it was over. Then we walked for weeks. When we got here I sold myself. There was enough money to apprentice my brothers in a metal-working shop."

The Principal looked at her sadly. He felt no trace of his compulsion, nor even of desire. All he felt was admiration and pity. She was simply another person, like Robin. He realized now that for many years women had been not-real to him. In his dreams he could do whatever he wanted to young girls, because they did not really exist for him. He had learned too much now to make his dreams real ever again. With a start it came to him that he had truly changed. He was not suppressing his compulsion; it had ceased to exist.

After a moment Ania stood to refill the cups. Then she loosened the ties on her blouse. Almost shyly, she spoke. "I'm yours for as long as you want," she said. "What do you desire?"

"Just what we're doing," said the Principal. "Just talk. I wanted company."

The girl looked at him in astonishment, obviously only half believing him. Then, with a good-natured grin, she retied the neck of her blouse and sat down again. "That's fine with me," she said. "Because I've got so many things happened to me, I could talk for three days without stopping."

In fact, she talked for three more hours before the Principal finally fell asleep, soothed by her voice.

The next morning he let her go, with a generous bonus. He had no trouble sleeping that night, or the next.

Two weeks later Zach returned.

PART FOUR

Evvy

One

Zach awoke slowly, his eyes sticky with grime. He rubbed them gently and looked around at the four walls which he knew better now than his own face, which, in any case, he had not seen in the nearly five years he had been here. Five years of awakening to four damp walls of stone and mortar, with one small slit for a window; five years of filth, of meager food, of vermin which were now as familiar to him as the hairs on his body. He knew every chink in the stones which lined his cell, knew every nuance of the feeble sunlight which filtered in for a few hours each day, knew the footsteps of the guards individually as they paced outside his cell.

And knew also that today he would escape or die.

He sat up and stretched, then coughed for some minutes, awakening the pain in his chest that would be with him as long as he lived. Zach smoothed his coarse woolen blanket over the dried grass he had been lying on, then moved the scarcely three paces to the door where his breakfast was waiting.

He splashed his face with tepid water from the crude pottery bowl, then forced himself to down the hard dark bread and tasteless gruel; he would need his strength today and for many days yet to come. For just a moment he was almost overwhelmed with unaccustomed emotion: was it fear or anticipation? He took a deep breath and held it until the tightening in his belly subsided.

There was no time or energy now for anything but the thought of escape: all of his resources must be directed toward that alone. It might already be too late, of course; he knew nothing about affairs in the District beyond the bare fact that the Principal still ruled. He was certain, however, that

Will was engaged in a deadly struggle with foes who, for their own reasons, believed as passionately in their ideals as the Principal did in his, and he was equally certain that only one set of beliefs would survive.

This was why he must escape: to return to the District and tell the Principal everything he had learned about the enemy. Of course he would be executed afterward, Zach had no doubt of that, for his treachery five years before. The Principal might let any other man go, but never Zach, who had been closest to him of all men. The law must be obeyed—above all, by the Principal and his aides—or it had no force. No matter what other changes might have taken place in the District in these years, that one thing Zach was sure would remain.

For the sake of everything he believed in, he would succeed. He had endured more already than most men could. Perhaps a wild deena had made him strong, but more likely it was the almost magical skills of Jonna, who was now high priestess of the Trader Empire. Jonna, who had saved him from what had been certain death. It had been five years ago, but the memories were fresher than yesterday's. In imagination he could still remember the feeling of the knife between his ribs, the instant terror and rage, and yes, the sorrow, as he realized he would never again see Evvy.

Zach was in a twilight of shapes and shadows, sounds and whispers, a strange world where the only things familiar were the taste of blood and constant pain. With every breath it grew worse, and he tried to will his breath to stop, but the body, with a reason of its own, fought him and renewed the pain, again and again in an even rhythm.

He became aware that he was lying on a sled being pulled by a mount. Above spun a canopy of green and blue and brilliant sparkles of light. The sled moved steadily, but not smoothly, and each step the mount took added to his disorientation. After a while the canopy began to spin and then disappeared in a whirlpool.

He was alone on a vast beach. The ocean lay ahead, clear and welcoming. He tried to crawl to it, but the sand gave way, and the more he struggled, the deeper he sank. He was burning, his skin crackling and splitting, his lips turning black. Leya was standing over him, her golden hair a halo around her face. He tried to call to her, but his mouth was dry and she turned away without hearing him. Then a beautiful young girl with long dark hair appeared. She knelt and touched him with smooth, cool hands, and he could feel his pain and thirst slipping away. She held a large crystal vase full of pale green water, and it trickled into his mouth and down his throat, healing him as it went, making him strong everywhere it touched. Her eyes watched him, soft and large, the color of plums.

Gradually her eyes grew darker until they were searing points of black, and her face became cruel, with the sharp lines and glowing white teeth of the Principal. The crystal vase cracked with a sound which he felt rather than heard, and hot sand poured into his mouth and throat, choking him.

He could not breathe. He was drowning now, and every gasping breath brought pain so intense all he wished was to die.

"The outside wound is nothing; it is already healing. But if he doesn't heal on the inside he will die. Give me the herbs and a flame."

Zach felt the warmth of a nearby fire but could see nothing. There was a scent of smoke as sharp as the feeling of bare feet on wet grass.

Something touched his face, then his mouth.

"Breathe it in, breathe deeply. It will hurt at first, but then it will help."

The smoke streamed into his lungs. He choked, then quite suddenly coughed deeply. He felt everything within his body leave with the cough. When he had stopped the pain was so much less that his breathing came almost easily. He slept.

He was inside a large tent. Above him stood a hunched figure with a misshapen face: one blue eye and one brown eye squinting above a twisted and deformed mouth, the skin mottled red and white. The face was looking beyond him, and he became aware of a low, monotonous sound, as if many voices were chanting the same words over and over. The misshapen lips moved with the chanting and then fell still; the figure looked down at him and the strange eyes opened wide in surprise. Then the figure stood and walked quickly away, long white hair streaming behind.

The chanting continued and grew in intensity. Zach felt that it was a part of him, that it had entered him and had always been there.

Zach awoke. His eyes were filmed and each breath hurt, but he knew for certain that he was alive and that he was not dreaming. He was inside a round tent made of animal skins. A large wooden pole held up the center with smaller stakes at intervals along the sides. It was dark, but he could see the open mouth of the tent, beyond which all was green and light.

He was not alone. Behind him, voices were murmuring, but he could not hear what they were saying and didn't really care.

His mind worked through a fog of confusion. He could not hope to know where he was until he understood how he had come here; his clearest memories were of the dreams or hallucinations he had had in the night. Or was it more than one night?

He tried to sit up and the intense pain returned. He fell back, groaning.

"He's awake." It was a woman's voice, strangely familiar.

There was a sound of feet shuffling, then two faces appeared above him. One of them was the monstrous misshapen face from his dream; the other that of a very young, beautiful man with a sparse pale beard and tangled, curling yellow hair falling to his shoulders. Around his neck a carved wooden spiral hung from a leather thong. His eyes were pale green, and his face was calm and welcoming.

"How do you feel?" the young man asked.

"Better." Zach was not sure if the young man had heard him, but he smiled, revealing dimples, and turned his face. "Jonna, you've worked a miracle," he said.

"It was the herbs," said the monster, and Zach realized from her voice that it was a woman.

"Who are you?" said the young man.

"Don't tire him, Yosh," said the woman.

"Yes, of course," said the man. "We didn't think you'd live." His smile was open, his eyes so clear and intense that for a moment he reminded Zach of the Principal. With every bit of strength he could draw, Zach spoke again. "I am Zach . . . delegate of the Principal."

Again, he wasn't certain that he had been heard, but the man and woman looked at each other instantly. Zach knew that he had said too much or that he should say more, but his strength was gone, and again he slept.

The dreams returned, and the pain, but less biting. The young girl returned to him, with her crystal vase of water, and sometimes the Principal, his face a mask of hatred. Once the face that appeared was that of the misshapen woman, Jonna. He felt her hand on his face, and more than once scented the pungent smoke which brought relief.

The next time Zach was fully conscious could have been a few hours after the woman and man had first spoken to him, or days later. He saw clearly that he was still in the tent and that it was night. Beyond the tent flames danced and dark shapes moved about. A low murmur of chanting came from beyond the tent, but Zach could see no one from where he lay. He did not dare to turn his head for fear of reviving the pain. Presently he became aware of an intense need to cough, and fought it as long as possible, knowing the agony it would bring. When it did come, it was bearable, giving proof that he was indeed healing and that he would live. He could not remember why, but he knew that it was important for him to continue living, and with that one thought in mind, he closed his eyes, exhausted, and drifted back into the dreams that had kept him company for what seemed his whole life.

The voices were talking again. For a moment Zach imagined that he was back in the Capital, half dozing as the Principal and his generals argued policy.

"He said he was a delegate of the Principal—"

"Then where is his seal ring? He was so sick he didn't know what he was saying."

"We must find out what he knows."

"Give him time to heal, Galen."

"I tell you, Yosh, there have been patrols by the border. What was he doing there? The Principal knows something. I will question him when he next wakes up."

"No." The voice which Zach now recognized as belonging to the young blond man was firm. "There's no need for that. I will find out what we need to know."

"Yes, Yosh."

Zach opened his eyes to slits and looked in the direction of the voices. His eyes were met by the clear gaze of the young man. His face did not change expression, but Zach understood that Yosh had known he was awake and that he had been intended to overhear the conversation. After a moment Yosh turned back to the others and resumed talking, but Zach no longer listened: what he had overheard had brought back to him all that had happened, from the day he rode into the brewer's yard until the final fight with Ermil. He knew now that he had been stabbed in the chest by the little man's knife, that his lung had been pierced, and that it was a miracle he was alive. It was hard not to believe he was being kept alive for a purpose.

His heart thumped heavily as he remembered what his purpose had been: to deliver Evvy safely to the Garden. What had happened to her? No one had mentioned a young girl. And what about Orin? He had gone after Evvy, on the mount. . . . For a moment Zach thought he would be sick. There was nothing he could do for Evvy now, but as soon as he was able he would get away and find her, or avenge her if it came to that.

In the meantime, he must be cautious and discover who these people were who had saved his life. The young man, Yosh, seemed to wish him well, but there was something else going on beneath the surface. It seemed from the conversation that he was opposed somehow to the Principal. Surely he couldn't still be loyal to the President, who had been deposed many years ago? Zach had heard talk of a ragged empire in the west, but in all these years there had been no contact with any westerners but occasional nomadic traders.

He concentrated again on the murmuring voices, but before he could learn more, the need to cough overtook him. When he had finished he groaned weakly, and almost immediately a hand was on his forehead.

"I believe our guest is awake." The young man, Yosh, was smiling down at him. "Jonna, do you think he needs to breathe the smoking herbs again?"

"Perhaps," said the woman. "But he'll be very sleepy afterward."

"Then after we talk," said Yosh. "Do you think you can talk?"

Zach nodded. Then, with effort: "I owe you my life."

"The body, in its natural wisdom, heals," said the young man. "All we have done is help."

"Thank you nevertheless," said Zach. "Why . . ." He stopped. He had been about to ask why they had saved him, but wasn't sure he wanted to know.

"I'm sure you have many questions," said Yosh. "And so do we. We won't tire you. Only, tell us who you are and where you are from."

"My name is Zach, son of Ilona. I'm from the Capital. You've heard of it?"

"We've heard of the Capital," said Yosh. His face changed subtly.

"The Capital is a long way from here, friend," said the voice belonging to the man Yosh had called Galen. "What are you doing so far from home?"

The man approached, and Zach could see that his face held a look the opposite of Yosh's—guarded, unfriendly, and suspicious. Around his neck he wore a double spiral identical to those worn by Yosh and Jonna.

"I was on business," said Zach. He hadn't the strength to think of a lie.

"As we thought," said the man. "On business, perhaps, for the Principal?"

Zach groaned deliberately. The effort of talking had tired him, and he wanted to know more before he spoke again.

"Answer me!" said Galen.

Yosh put his hand on Galen's arm. "Wait," he said. "Zach

is exhausted, and sick. We'll talk with him later." Then, to
Zach: "I think it will be best if Jonna treats you now and you
sleep. Perhaps you will find answers to some of your own
questions in the morning, when we have our services."

Zach nodded, grateful. He sensed that there was danger
here, but for now he wanted only to rest.

Galen turned away, but not without an unguarded, hostile
glance, as if to say that he would get the information he wanted.
Then the woman came over, indifferently, and began to prepare
the burning herbs. Zach watched with interest as she mixed a
small bundle of green leaves in a bowl, added a pinch of some
dark powder, then crushed all together with a stone pestle.
There must be new-plants of some sort, that promoted healing.
He must find out what they were and deliver the information
to the Garden, so they could study it and perhaps learn to use
the plants to help all the people of the District.

The memory of the Garden stabbed through him like the
pain in his chest, reminding him again of Evvy, and of the old
woman, and the Principal, and all he had left undone. When
the woman had the herbs smoking and asked him to breathe,
he welcomed the sharp fumes, knowing they would soon blot
out his frustration and guilt.

After a few moments the woman left with Yosh and Galen.
Zach tried to think, but his mind was tired.

He fell asleep to the sound of many voices chanting.

Two

Crudely hewn logs and dried evergreen branches were piled
at the base of a large, flat rock on which Yosh stood. Surrounding him, sitting, kneeling, some standing, were perhaps

forty shabbily dressed people, the men bearded, the few women with long, loose, unkempt hair.

Zach lay propped on soft branches laid against the side of the tent, facing the rising sun behind the altar. The effort of being moved outside the tent had exhausted him, but he found his breathing was easier in this position, and that the air outside the tent was fresh and invigorating, as it had always been in this part of the country when he was a child.

Yosh was leading the group in a low, monotonous chant. The words were murmured, almost mumbled, and Zach found it difficult to understand what was being said. Something about sheep, pastures, and a valley, which sounded vaguely familiar. The words did not seem coherently arranged, and Zach soon lost interest. Instead he inspected the people who were gathered in this early morning ritual.

They called themselves Traders. Beyond this, Zach knew little. Religion, like almost all forms of civilization, had broken down after the Change and survived only in very small pockets of the old Christianity, Islam, and Judaism. Most citizens of the District used the forms of ancient rituals for marriage and burial, but there was little sense of religion as an underlying force in life. It was as if mankind had felt itself so let down by all of its leaders and gods that it had finally decided to rely on itself alone. There was a terrible void in most lives, Zach knew; and he and Will had both been expecting a revival of religious forms.

Perhaps it had finally happened, with these Traders. Perhaps a new religion would be good for the people of the District, adding a sense of stability to their precarious lives.

The chanting seemed endless. The Traders were more shabbily dressed than the general population of the District and much less kempt; this was understandable, however, given their obviously nomadic way of life.

Since he himself could never return to the Capital, Zach thought, perhaps someday he would be able to receive news of Will through the Traders, and perhaps too the kindly-seeming Yosh could help him discover what had happened to Evvy.

As the sun fully topped the mountain, the chanting abruptly stopped, and Zach turned back to watch. Now Yosh began to speak to his congregation in low, urgent tones. Most of what he said was lost in the cool morning breeze, but Zach was startled to hear the word *science* several times. A group of men near the front of the congregation stood together, then laid a colored box on the pile of branches and wood beneath Yosh's platform. Now Yosh stepped down and, taking a burning limb from Jonna, reverently held the fire to the branches. "In the name of God, I trade this artifact of science for the clean smoke of nature!" he shouted. "God's will be done!" replied the others. As the fire began to blaze up, Zach suddenly realized what this ceremony was about: the object which was beginning to char and then flame up on the pyre was a book.

Late that afternoon, after Jonna gave Zach his treatment, Yosh came in to sit with him.

"Jonna tells me that you are all but healed," he said. "Now it's just a matter of getting back your strength."

"Yes," said Zach. "I thank you again. Both of you. I would have died."

"You very nearly did."

"Tell me, Yosh. When you found me . . . was there anyone else nearby?"

"The body of a man we knew as Ermil."

That surprised Zach. He wondered what dealings Ermil could have had with the Traders. When Yosh didn't speak again, Zach continued, trying to sound casual. "Was there anyone else? A young girl, perhaps?"

Yosh frowned in puzzlement. "A girl? No. Why do you ask?"

"My daughter was traveling with me," Zach said. "When we encountered trouble, she ran off into the woods."

"We've had patrols in the area for weeks," said Yosh. "There has been no report of a girl traveling alone."

"When I'm stronger I must try to find her."

Yosh didn't answer for a moment, then abruptly he smiled. "You must be curious about the ritual you witnessed this morning," he said.

"It was most interesting."

"It is more than interesting," said Yosh. "It is nothing less than the beginning of salvation for mankind. And I'm happy that we've found you. We seldom get a chance to teach the truth to outsiders."

"Our sins began many thousands of years ago," Yosh was explaining earnestly. "When the first scientists chopped down the Tree of Knowledge to build an ark, they created the first Change. Men have been Changing the world ever since—and now we are paying for it."

"Some of those changes saved thousands of lives and reduced the suffering of millions," said Zach, exasperated. He had been talking to Yosh for only a few minutes, but it seemed to him that the conversation had gone on for many hours. Through his fatigue he felt a growing horror at everything Yosh had to say.

Yosh was nodding sympathetically. "You have been taught that, as have hundreds of generations. The truth, brother, is that those lives were not meant to be saved. Suffering exists only when we go against God's law. Men were not meant to live as they did before the Change, in cities with tall buildings, depending on machines and chemicals for life. We are meant to live in nature, as God intended. Every little Change is another step away from God. Only when the last traces of science are gone will He lift His curse and call back the wild deenas."

"You say all change is evil," said Zach, knowing even as he spoke that Yosh would not listen. "Yet you use manufactured weapons, and build tents, and eat with pottery implements like people everywhere."

Yosh didn't even look annoyed. "We construct nothing," he said. "We use what God puts in our path. And we only use those things that are helpful to us in spreading the truth. The rest, like the evil books, we destroy. When we have completed our work and science has been defeated, we will not need the other things."

"If it weren't for books," said Zach, "you would not know one thing about the history of mankind."

"We do not read books."

"Nevertheless, that is where all your knowledge of the past has come from."

"I know you can't help your beliefs," said Yosh sadly. "But eventually you will see the light. The truth is that all knowledge is within you, as it is within each of us." Yosh was speaking with such sincerity that Zach almost wished he could believe him. The young Trader sat back and smiled. "Enough talk of religion for now. It is your turn to speak for a while. I'd like you to tell me about the Capital. Is it true, for example, that the men living there are required to shave and to bathe every day?"

Yosh seemed as relaxed as if he and Zach were old friends. He was the only adult Zach had ever met who had no lines at all on his face. In some ways he seemed as artless as a child, but Zach knew there must be shrewdness and ambition behind the simplicity. Of course, he would tell Yosh as little as possible about the Capital. Perhaps the Traders were the harmless cultists they had seemed at first, but Zach was beginning to sense a growing danger—not just to the goals he and Will had worked for, but perhaps to the future of the race itself. He started to speak, but was not sure what to say. He did not know whether lies or the truth would be more harmful. After a moment Yosh spoke again:

"But I can see you're tired. Never mind. Rest now and we'll talk another time." With a reassuring hand on Zach's shoulder, Yosh rose to his feet and left the tent.

Zach watched him go. Through the tent flap he could see Trader men and women, content and purposeful, building fires, cooking, talking, ending the day like people everywhere in the District. But in his nostrils was still the scent of burning books.

Over the next several days, Zach continued to heal. When he could walk unassisted, he noticed that there were always one or two armed men just outside the tent. Although he had said nothing, Zach knew that Yosh must have saved him for a reason, and that the reason would become clear soon enough.

Meanwhile, Zach continued to witness the Trader services each morning, noting with helpless despair that every day another book was destroyed and lost to mankind forever. And daily he and Yosh continued their talks for an hour or two each afternoon.

Typically, Yosh would stroll into the tent, an open smile on his face, as if he were visiting a sick friend in the neighborhood. He would ask after Zach's health, then sit and begin talking to him of Trader beliefs.

"My first-father was a minister of the old religion," Yosh told Zach one day. "Of what is called Christianity. Religion had been the vocation of our family for generations, even before the Change. After the Change, it continued. We lived in a small town high in the western mountains. My father had a flock of ten families who would come to hear him read from a so-called holy book called the Bible. Science is so clever, you see, that it had clothed itself even in religion. Well, my father in his ignorance kept other books too and even raised fowl in a cage he had constructed from the body of a dead machine. We didn't know any better. We thought it was as good a life as could be expected.

"And then my mother died of the woman sickness. Her time had not even come, the pregnancy scarcely showed. Soon after, my younger brothers and sister all became ill from eating a stew made of new-plants. The child of our nearest neighbors was attacked by a fox-cat that same day, and he and all my brothers and my sister died on the next day, in terrible agony. That night my second-father killed himself by drinking fireberry poison.

"The day after, my first-father woke me early and made me watch while he destroyed everything inside the cabin. He threw plates and bowls to the floor, he pulled the wicks out of lamps and smashed their bodies against the stone fireplace, he ripped books in half and tore their pages into tiny pieces. He gathered the rubble, and all the manmade things from outside, and piled them in the center of the room. The last thing he put on the pile was the leather covering of his Bible, now torn into strips. He turned to me than and explained what he had done. He told me many of the things I have told you, and made me understand that I must work to undo the evils of the Change, to trade all things made by science for the natural ones provided by God in His love.

"When he had finished speaking, my father took a coal from the fireplace and set the pile of rubble afire. He picked me up and brought me outside the cabin. Then he turned and walked back into it. I will never forget his face. The look of suffering it had always held was gone. He was at peace. He didn't even cry out.

"I was young at the time, about nine years old. I remember looking into the flames and seeing all those ungodly things being consumed in the clean fire. I knew immediately that God had spoken to me through my father, and that He wanted me to begin my life as a Trader in His service. I have been teaching His truths ever since."

Zach had no answer. Yosh's story was not unusual, except for his mystical conversion. The conclusions he had reached would undoubtedly seem reasonable to most of the people of the District.

They sat in silence a moment, then Yosh turned the conversation to Zach. "And you, brother," he said, "you come from a part of the world where there are many things left from before the Change. Were your fathers too taken in by science?"

"I didn't grow up in a town," said Zach. "And I never had even a first-father."

Yosh raised his eyebrows. "But you have lived in the Capital," he said.

"Yes."

"You told us when we first found you that you are one of the Principal's men. I am very curious about him. We know that he has built an empire on the ruins of a pre-Change city. We know that all the area to the east belongs to him. And we know that most of his people are godless and are made miserable by the wild deenas."

"As are most men in the world today."

"But need not be, once they understand the truth. What sort of man is the Principal?"

"A good man," said Zach. "A dedicated leader."

"But misled by the devil," said Yosh. "Of course, I have not visited the District, except just across the border. I don't know what to expect in the Capital."

"You're planning to travel there?"

"Perhaps," said Yosh. "There is much to see and much to do in this world. Does the Principal guard his streets with soldiers?"

"Some streets," said Zach. "But truly, I have not been in the Capital for a very long time."

"Is he planning to extend the borders of the District?"

"I can't tell you that either. Only the Principal himself knows what his plans are."

Yosh shook his head and frowned. "I believe you know a great deal more than you are telling. And I wish for your own sake that you would tell me more."

Zach could not help liking Yosh. In spite of his beliefs, the young Trader leader was intellectually quick and instinctively warm and generous. There was no question that his desire to obliterate all traces of "science" was sincere and based on the highest motives. There was also no question now that Yosh represented a deadly threat to everything that Zach believed in. Daily, Zach was becoming stronger. He knew that he must watch for the right moment to escape and take his knowledge of the Traders to the Principal, no matter what the consequences.

Though he was carefully guarded, in some ways Zach felt himself a part of the Trader community. After services and the noontime meal, he and Yosh often sat together in the tent or under a tree, playing chess and talking. Yosh was quite a good chess player, and Zach suspected more than once that the younger man had let him win to save his pride. As they played, Jonna would often sit with them, kneading Yosh's back with her strong hands, her misshapen face partly hidden by a thin scarf. She seldom had much to say but seemed, as did most women here, content. At moments like this Zach too felt at peace, as if he had known these people all his life.

Beneath the contentment a more practical part of Zach knew that however much Yosh liked him, the Traders had not saved his life for the sake of friendship.

He was not entirely surprised when, after Yosh had gone on an extended trip into the heart of the Trader empire, Galen and two other men took him early one morning into the woods beyond sight or sound of the camp. There they tied him securely in such a way that twisting the ropes put unbearable pressure on the joints of his fingers and wrists.

As soon as Zach saw how the morning would go, he moved his center of consciousness into a quiet place deep within his mind, where he became a remote observer while Galen questioned him closely for several hours, asking the same questions under torture that Yosh had asked him in friendship.

In truth, there was very little Zach could tell them that they did not already know, and nothing that would prove immediately harmful to the Principal. What they wanted was simply confirmation that the Capital was, in fact, a repository of much that remained from the old technology; that there were vast caches of ancient weapons in the Principal's armory; that there was one great building and several lesser ones, called libraries, all heavily guarded and containing hundreds of thousands of those symbols of pre-Change evil, printed books.

It was only when Galen began questioning Zach about the Garden that he had to think carefully before answering. He was forced to admit that the Garden was indeed inhabited by women, and that they were under the informal protection of the Principal: these facts could be readily ascertained from any of the small number of people living near the border. He denied vigorously, again and again, the rumors that science was practiced in the Garden. Such rumors had understandably been prevalent in the area for years; never before had they assumed such sinister significance. At last Galen gave up, though Zach could tell he was not completely satisfied.

He was able to return to camp on his own feet, though he knew it would be some time before he could use his hands again. Jonna calmly attended to him, first putting a dislocated finger back into place, then setting three broken fingers on his right hand. She splinted each and wrapped them in wet leaves of a sort Zach had not seen, which shrunk as they dried, holding the splints in place. When she had finished, she applied soothing herb compresses to his swollen knuckles and wrists.

"Where did you learn the use of healing herbs?" he asked her while she worked, to distract his own mind.

She looked up, surprised. "It is something the women in my family have always known," she said.

He hesitated, then spoke again. "You have always seemed to me different from the other Traders. Are you a true believer?"

She shrugged. "What's important is that they treat me better than anyone did before. My husbands used to make fun of my face and beat me. Yosh says that my face doesn't matter. He says I have a beautiful soul."

Zach nodded thoughtfully. Yosh didn't, in fact, seem to notice that Jonna was different from other women. It must be terrible, he thought, to be a woman scorned in a world where women were a rarity.

"I haven't been with them very long," she went on. "But Yosh has ordered us to return to the Trader capital. He's told me I will receive true instructon there."

"When is this trip to take place?" Zach asked, suddenly alert.

"Tomorrow. Or so Galen tells us. We've been packing all day."

That night Zach lay awake long after everyone else in camp was asleep. His hands and wrists hurt badly, and he was not certain that he would be able to withstand more questioning, if, indeed, Galen didn't plan simply to kill him in the morning. He had hoped to be able to find out the location of the Trader capital, but saw now that he had already waited too long to make his move.

There was a guard outside his tent, he knew, and an unknown number of sentries at the perimeter of the camp. Raising his voice only as much as necessary, he called out for the guard.

After a moment, a young Trader entered, looking annoyed and sleepy. "What is it?"

"I can't sleep from the pain. Can you untie my hands just for a while?"

"I suppose it'll be all right," the young man said. "Brother Yosh left word that you were to be made comfortable." He stooped and loosened the bonds, freeing Zach's hands from the tent pole. Zach had thought to overpower him, but the risk of noise was too great unless he killed the man immediately, and he didn't want to do that. "Thank you," he said. He turned over and closed his eyes, then began to breathe slowly. He waited until the guard had come and gone twice, checking on him; then he got to his feet and quickly went to the back of the tent, where he awkwardly removed the stakes that held it to the ground. Then he wriggled out into the night. Not five feet away was one of the perimeter guards, sitting motionless in the dim moonlight. Moving as slowly and silently as he could, Zach crawled along the ground toward the nearest growth of bushes, then got to his feet and began to run.

He was disoriented in the dark, and had been away from the camp for only a few minutes when he heard shouts. He stopped and tried to decide which direction would most likely lead to safety. There was the sound of men crashing through the brush and the smoky glow of torchlight. He stopped thinking and simply ran, his breathing heavy and painful from the weeks of convalescence.

It was growing light when Zach suddenly came to a sheer rock face. He could hear the Traders behind him, drawing nearer. He looked up, knowing that it would be a difficult climb even with undamaged hands. Still, it was his only chance. He pulled off his tunic and wrapped it tightly around his right hand for protection, then, ignoring the pain, he forced his left hand to grip handholds as he began to inch upward. He had climbed perhaps one third of the way when he heard a shout.

"Stop right there!" Zach looked down. Galen and another man had bows trained on him. "I told Yosh not to trust you," Galen said.

The camp was noisy with the sounds of tents being struck and protesting animals being loaded. At midmorning Galen and his aide approached Zach where he sat bound securely to a tree. Zach supposed that they had come to question him again before killing him. In the hours since his capture he had given himself up to what seemed inevitable; he only hoped that he could maintain strength enough not to betray the Garden.

The two men untied Zach and guided him to where the

Trader caravan was waiting. Galen attached Zach's aching hands to the lead of one of the pack animals, and it was only when they began walking into the forest that Zach understood he was not to be executed; that, for whatever reason, the Traders were taking him with them to their base.

Three

The Trader capital was indistinguishable from any village in the District, though the level of construction of its few buildings was much more primitive than that found in even the most backward District areas. Crude cabins of roughly hewn logs, roofed with sod and bark, surrounded the village square, a grassy, parklike meadow. At the northern end of the square was an altar carved of stone and sheltered by three walls and a roof of boughs. At the southern end was a low, solid structure built in the ruins of a pre-Change building. Its small barred windows were nearly level with the ground, and its roof barely high enough to accommodate a man. This was the Trader prison.

Zach had only minutes to see these details; no sooner had the caravan arrived than Yosh, dressed in long, filthy robes, approached him, his face alight with his sunny, open smile.

"Brother Zach," he said, embracing him. "It's good to see you."

Zach just looked at him, bewildered. "What—" he started to say, his mind exploding with questions.

Yosh shook his head. "There's no time to talk now. This is where you will stay," he went on. "It's for your own protection. I'll visit when I can." Still smiling, he turned to greet other members of his camp, leaving Zach with Galen. Galen prodded him through the low door and down a narrow flight of stairs to a tiny dark room illuminated by a single fish-oil lamp.

The jailer, a stout man with a red face and tangled, deeply black beard, looked Zach up and down. "So this is the famous prisoner from the District," he muttered. "We know how to take care of scientists here!" He unlocked the door behind him, then led Zach through a narrow corridor and down another short flight of steps to what had evidently been the basement of the ancient building. The ceiling was so low that Zach's hair brushed it, and the only illumination came from flickering torches set in the wall at either end. The walls were of mortared stones, and four thick wooden doors faced each other, two on each side of the room. Each door was held shut by three massive metal bars secured in iron holders. There was a small peephole the size of a man's fist near the top of each door. Except for a faint moaning from behind one of the doors, the hall was as silent as it was dark and malodorous.

At the second door in from the stairway the jailer stopped and, his powerful muscles bunching, slid the three bars to one side. He swung the door open and told Zach to enter.

Zach hesitated a moment, trying to see into the dim cell beyond, then Galen jabbed his ribs with something sharp. "He says go in."

The door slammed shut and Zach listened to the bars being set into their holders while his eyes adjusted to the gloom. The cell was constructed of heavy blocks of stone, carefully mortared into place over the ruined ancient walls. Across from the door was a small barred window, just above the level of the ground, not quite the height of Zach's head, and perhaps the length of his forearm.

In width, the cell was only a few feet across, and its length was just enough for Zach to stretch out. Along the wall below the window was a pile of straw spread with a rough woolen blanket. To the right of the door was a small opening in the stone, slightly larger than the earthenware bowl set just inside it. The floor of pre-Change concrete was uneven and cracked, with scattered spots of mildew.

As soon as he heard the third of the bars slip into place, Zach inspected the cell closely, looking for some means of escape. The narrow window was out of the question; it was not large enough to put his head through, and even should he be able to enlarge it, it would take him weeks and would easily be observed from the outside.

The door was massive and immovable. Only the little opening for the chamber pot showed any hope of yielding, and, again, any work he did would be readily observed from the outside hall, where, he soon discovered, a guard patrolled regularly.

His only hope for escape would be somehow to break through the floor and tunnel outward and up like a mole. Not only would such work be risky, he realized that it would probably take him years to accomplish.

Feeling tired, and weak, and sick from the march after weeks of inactivity, he sat on the straw pallet, his back against the rough stone wall. It was late afternoon and the light filtering through the window was bright enough only to pick out shadows in the corners of the gloomy cell.

There would be no escape from this prison in the usual physical sense. He did not know how he could endure being so confined, away from fresh air and sky and trees. Execution would have been preferable.

Not, he told himself, that execution had been ruled out. He could not fathom why he had been brought here. Was there to be a public trial, in which he would be denounced as a scientist? Was he to be repeatedly questioned until every bit of information about the District was forced from him? Whatever would be, he hoped it would happen soon. He felt that he could not stay here for more than a very few days without losing his mind.

He was to be in the prison for nearly five years.

The first months of his confinement were the bitterest of Zach's life. Each day he hoped for word from Yosh, but his guards, who twice daily brought food and water and emptied the chamber pot, refused to answer questions or to engage in any conversation. His lone fellow inmate was, as nearly as he could tell, completely mad. He was given to periodic, maniacal shrieking and seemed to be too deaf to respond to any questioning. Zach quickly forgot about him, adding the weird noises to the background of constant discomfort.

He learned how poorly designed the prison was the first time it rained. Water dripped down the wall through the window, soaking his bed. Moving the straw to the center of the cell helped only a little. As the weather grew colder, snow drifted in and tiny icicles formed beneath the bars of his window. The food was monotonous and barely enough to sustain him, consisting of thin porridge with an occasional vegetable or bit of new-fowl, and hunks of dark, tasteless bread. At night the rats and insects which shared his cell ran about freely, brushing his arms and face as he tried to sleep. He slept poorly in any case; even his dreams were of the cell.

For the first few days he spent long hours gazing out the window, watching the poorly dressed, humorless Traders as they went about their business. Once he was startled as a small child's face peered into the window. Before he could say anything the boy's mother angrily called him away.

After several weeks of this he turned his back to the window and simply sat on the straw, resting against the wall. His hands were still swollen and the discomfort seemed to extend up his arms and into his whole being. His food, which he had eaten hungrily at first, he now left nearly untouched. He stopped asking the guards questions, stopped demanding to see Yosh.

No matter what the weather, he was always too cold, shivering under the blanket. Daily, he could feel his skin becoming slack as his muscles disappeared, and felt his eyesight was growing dim, as was his mind. He thought that he was slipping toward death or madness, either of which would bring welcome relief from the intolerable confinement.

Sometimes he thought of the Principal, and of Evvy, wondering if either was still alive. He began to spend more time in his memory, returning to the cell only when bodily needs forced him. His memories became waking dreams for him, more vivid and real than anything in this cell, this building, this town. Gradually, he moved farther and farther back in his mind, until he reached the time in his life of greatest happiness and greatest sorrow, the brief period of his marriage to Leya.

* * *

All he knew was that he wanted to mount Leya as often as possible, and to care for her in between, the way he had observed some animals taking care of their mates, licking them softly, curling beside them to give warmth, and protecting them from whatever came. He would bring her food, and skins to make clothing, and would build and keep for her a warm, snug cabin with a roof which kept out rain and snow, where they could be together in the evenings, talking in front of the fire.

All he expected from Leya was that she should be there and allow him to do these things for her, for as long as their lives together would be. He wanted from her far more but knew that she could not yet give it. For now, what he had was more than enough. Every week she smiled more often and sometimes laughed in her clear, high voice.

Her work kept her from the cabin sometimes for days at a time, but that was all right too, because she always came back. His work, tending the crops and animals, cutting wood, and guarding the surrounding woods, kept him busy and content. He knew that Leya and the Mistress wanted him back at the Garden, at least some of the time, but he was not gifted in scientific work and felt that what he could contribute here was far more important to his life and hers, as well as to the Garden. Another reason, which he kept to himself, was that he could no longer enter the Garden without remembering the night Will had left.

Sometimes he wondered what Leya felt when she returned to the Garden, but he never asked her. He had read enough of the history of the human race to know that he was as happy now as he could ever expect to be, and that there was no reason to think that this happiness would last.

It was at the end of a three-day period, when he knew she would be returning to him soon. He was surprised to hear a mount coming over the low hills through the shallow river, and when he saw that it was Leya, he knew immediately from the way she held herself that things had changed and that perhaps the happiness had ended.

* * *

"Are you sure?" Zach could not help asking the age-old question, but he knew the answer before she gave it, with a wan but frightened smile. His atavistic, unbidden feeings of joy won the fight with the worry, and he enfolded her. "I love you, Leya," he said. He held her so tightly that she could scarcely move. After a moment she spoke: "I know you do."

Week by week the baby grew, and finally it showed in Leya, in her figure and in the way she moved. Her moods changed even more quickly than usual, and he learned to be very patient with her, but it was not difficult, because he had always known that she was not like him, that her happinesses and sadnesses came and went quickly, without leaving the traces that his own sometimes did. The dangers they never talked about; the possibilities, the life they would build for the child, they discussed frequently.

Of course they both hoped and assumed that the child would be a male, and they picked out a name for him: Ilya, after his grandmother. Leya continued to work, but she went to the Garden less frequently and stayed for shorter periods of time and finally began to bring her work home with her, which Zach had long wished her to do. They had agreed that it would be most prudent for her to spend the final month at home; she returned from the Garden on this final journey in the company of two other women, on mounts laden with packs, containing small cages of the animals Leya was working with, and the few small tools of her trade that the Garden could spare her.

That night he had taken her into bed in his arms and held her closely, dreaming of making love to her, but knowing that she did not want it now and wouldn't again until after the baby was born.

He had sent for help as soon as Leya's contractions began, adding powdered color-root to turn his signal fire thick and red. As was customary for fathers, he was sent away from the area of the cabin until the outcome of the labor was known.

His wood stand was at a place equidistant between the cabin and the Garden. It was a cloudy summer day, not really hot,

but so humid with an impending rainstorm that the least exertion left him sweating and feeling tired. He positioned a log
on the chopping block, brought the axe up above and behind
his head, then swung it, *thunk*. He did this again and again,
the movements easy from long years of practice. Wood chips
flew around him, stinging his bare chest and arms. Cut wood
piled up around him, and his breathing grew heavy as his arms
began to tremble with the effort. He did not dare to stop, afraid
to lose the comforting sound of the axe blade biting into the
wood.

After a time, his muscles stopped responding, and he was
forced to rest for a moment. The sounds of the woods became
deafening. He heard birds calling their territorial limits to one
another; insects scuttling in the leaves; the warm breeze before
the storm, pushing the branches of trees. He shivered as the
wind took the sweat covering his skin. Sighing, he sat on a
log and examined the axe minutely. He had made it himself
from an old pre-Change axe blade, and a stout piece of hard-
wood he had carved himself, carefully fitting it to hold the
metal, and binding the two pieces together with strong new-
vine ropes. The ancient blade was as shiny as it must have
been when it was new: he took care to keep it clean with fish-
oil, and sharp on his whetstones. There were nicks and scores
in the metal, but it was probably, he thought, in nearly as good
condition as when it had been made, untold years ago. He ran
his fingers over the blade and looked for signs of wear on the
handle. This was the fourth handle he had made for the blade,
carefully carving and polishing during long nights in the cabin
while Leya read or worked on her projects from the Garden.

He stood, already feeling stiff, and began to gather the wood
he had cut into bundles of seven to ten each, tying them carefully with new-vine, and placing them to the side of his work
area, in a small shelter he had constructed. A squirrel suddenly
clambered down from a tree behind him. He turned, startled,
to see the little animal poised on its hind legs, its nose vibrating
with its breath, every nerve in its body stretched as it tried to
sense possible danger. It looked at him, its black eyes as shiny
as the axe blade, then just as abruptly it ran up the tree and
disappeared along a leafy limb.

Zach picked up the axe and began again to swing it, cutting the wood as if he could cut out everything else that was happening. Never had he worked so long and so hard. Soon there would be enough wood cut to last the Garden through the entire winter. And there was already more than enough for him and Leya. He became aware of another sound and realized that it was his own breath, rasping, wet, and too rapid. Still he did not stop, not even when the raindrops finally began to fall, washing away the dirt and sweat, then soaking him as a summer cloudburst developed. He could scarcely see what he was doing through the falling water, but still he swung the axe back and up, then down, splitting each precisely placed log as he did so, stopping only to move more wood into position.

"Zach!"

He turned, the axe half-raised, poised to split another log. Her head and shoulders covered with a dark shawl, the old woman stood looking at him. Her face was composed and without expression, and as soon as he saw it he knew the worst had happened. He turned back and finished splitting the log still on the block, and set the axe down; then, as an afterthought, he picked it up again, holding it below the top of the handle near the blade, and walked after the Mistress. They followed the trail side-by-side through the mud, neither saying a word, though once the old woman slipped on a wet rock and Zach took her elbow to steady her. In his other hand he still held the axe, gripping it so tightly that his short fingernails cut into his palm.

His reveries were so immediate that Zach felt again the hollow ache that the loss of Leya had created. It was so sharp and so like physical pain that the discomfort of his cold, damp cell seemed more a memory than a reality. No matter how he wished it, he could not stop his memories of Leya from ending in her death, just as he had been unable to prevent it in life.

Over and over he remembered his few brief months with Leya, then the busy, comradely time when he had fought with the Principal and his men to take over the District, and, again, his weeks with Evvy, when, for the first time since Leya had died, he had felt the warmth of caring for another person's needs. Day and night ceased to have distinctions, and he was sometimes surprised to open his eyes and find himself still in the Trader cell. Why, he asked himself at such times, had the Traders not simply put him to death? For what purpose could they be keeping him here?

He learned the answer only after he had been isolated and nearly starved for many months.

He had not been killed because Yosh wanted to save his soul.

Zach was sitting in his usual position, his back propped against the wall, lost in a summertime dream. Today he was riding through the forest with Evvy, then singing to her, as he once had to Leya, his fingers stroking the strings of his feathered lyre. Gradually he became aware of a noise, different from the sounds of vermin, or the pacing jailer, or the whimpers and scrabbling of his fellow prisoner.

It was the sound of a thick metal bar being withdrawn from the door. He blinked once, wondering if perhaps he were hallucinating, but then it was followed by another, and the solid *thunk* of a bar settling against the stop.

From the hall came the murmur of voices, one strangely familiar, and then the third bar was withdrawn. He looked at the door, dazed, not sure what was happening. The door swung open.

A man entered, but Zach could not make out his face, dark against the relatively bright light from the corridor.

The figure's head swung around, looked directly at Zach, then spoke: "Brother Zach. Don't you know me?"

Zach painfully shifted his body and squinted up at the man. A dim memory came back: "Yosh?"

And then Yosh was on his hands and knees before Zach, peering into his face with alarm. He put his hand to Zach's cheek. "Why, you're sick," he said. Angrily, he turned to the jailer beside him. "How did his happen?"

"He ain't been eating, sir," said the jailer.

"This is disgraceful! I ordered you to keep him well! Send for some good food—meat if you can find any. We mustn't allow this man to die."

Zach continued to look at Yosh. He had a dim sense that he should be angry, but all he felt was a fuzzy gratitude. That— and simple curiosity.

"Why didn't you have me killed?" he asked.

"Kill you? How could you think of such a thing? In another world you and I could have been friends—brothers. I want to teach you, Zach. To show you the way. I'm sorry this is the only place I can keep you safe—but I will see that conditions improve for you immediately. I've been away and I had no idea things had reached such a state. I never intended for you to suffer."

Once again he barked out orders, sounding strangely like the Principal. "Bring fresh straw," he called. "That's important to a man like our guest. And have someone clean out this filth—" Zach had long since stopped being fastidious in his use of the chamber pot.

The straw came almost immediately, and Yosh helped Zach to stand, then supported him while the cell was swept out. Looking through the open door, Zach knew he should try to escape, but his legs would scarcely hold him, and besides, it no longer seemed to matter.

For the next several days Yosh came every afternoon, bringing with him fresh fruit and vegetables. He gave Zach a warm cloak to replace the filthy, threadbare rag Zach had been covering himself with. Every day Yosh sat with Zach for an hour or two, encouraging him to eat and to drink a green herbal tea that Jonna had prepared to help him regain his strength. The brew tasted flowery, and when Zach drank it he felt warm, and safe, and grateful.

Once Yosh set up his chessmen, but when Zach tried to focus his eyes on them, they swam into multiple images. As he had at the Trader camp, Yosh talked about his own life and asked Zach about his. Scarcely aware of what he was saying, Zach told Yosh about his boyhood in the Garden and his marriage to Leya. He described how, after her death, he had cremated her and the dead child in their cabin, much as Yosh's father had created his own pyre. He went on to tell of his decision to join the Principal and fight for a world where women would no longer die of the sickness. Yosh listened, warm and sympathetic, never mentioning science or his own beliefs.

Zach continued to talk every day, reliving his years of fighting for the Principal, and his work for him since, overseeing the details of running the District. Yosh seemed especially interested in the customs of life in the Capital, and Zach told him all he could remember. He felt happy and comforted when Yosh was with him, and talked as long as he had strength, to keep him there.

One day, perhaps a week after Yosh had first appeared, Zach's head suddenly cleared. He awoke feeling almost himself.

The preceding days and months now seemed as unreal to him as a nightmare. He realized that he had been very close to madness, though he could not be certain how much of his confusion had come from his mind and how much from physical illness, or the potion that Jonna had prepared.

He also knew that he must not allow it to happen again. He was afraid that he had told Yosh far too much about the Garden, the Capital, and the Principal. He could not even remember what he had said, his recollection of their conversations blurring in his mind with his waking dreams of the previous months. He realized now that he must force himself to plan toward the only possible focus his future could take: escape.

He stood, shakily, and was appalled at how weak he had become. If the walls of his cell should suddenly dissolve in the next minute, giving him a clear path to freedom, he would not be able to walk more than a few steps before falling to the ground.

His first task, then, and the most important, was to begin to rebuild his body as well as he could in the confines of the cell. He walked the four paces from one end of the tiny room to the other, turned, and walked back. After repeating the short walk only twice, he had to sit down, his knees shaking and his breathing painful. But he knew from past experience that his condition would quickly improve, and soon he would be able to trot in place and to perform the arm- and back-strengthening exercises he and the Principal had practiced when they were boys.

It was a start, but an important one.

That afternoon, Zach had another visitor.

There was a thumping at the door and the jailer's voice came through the peephole. "You have a visitor, prisoner."

Zach stood back, expecting the thick bars to slide open, but instead a high-pitched voice called out, "Over here."

Astonished, Zach turned and looked toward the window. Filling it was the earnest, blemish-pocked face of a boy of fifteen or so.

"I'm Brother Billy," the boy said, smiling. "Brother Yosh has sent me to instruct you."

Four

And so began Zach's religious training. Billy never entered the cell but sat at the window, or in bad weather stood in the hall by the peephole, and spoke with Zach for hours each day. Since the Traders did not believe in books or in writing, all instruction and response were oral.

Zach at first tolerated these sessions, then began in some ways to look forward to them as a break in the monotony. He spent the rest of his time pacing in the cell, trotting in place, raising and lowering his body with his arms. He had no idea how he would escape, but intended to be ready when the time came.

In the meantime, his mind was occupied with the lessons in Trader theology. Billy made it clear that Zach was considered a kind of test case. If the instruction was able to reach one of the Principal's men, then anyone could be converted.

The lessons consisted for the most part of chants, to be learned by heart. Some of these simply retold the stories in the Bible from the Trader point of view, reflecting their belief that science and technology had been given to mankind by Satan. Rather than being an escape from the flood, Noah's Ark was seen as a cause of it; likewise, the story of Job's suffering was seen as a warning of the Change to come. In addition to the chanted stories, there were a number of Trader songs. These were, again, based on verses in the Bible and set to ancient folk and product melodies.

Billy explained earnestly that Zach must practice the songs and chants until he could perform them automatically and perfectly. It did not matter whether he believed the words or not; once he knew them by heart they would enter his consciousness and he would move closer to the truth. Zach enjoyed the opportunity to sing again and practiced the songs with enthusiasm.

The first time he let his voice soar during a lesson Billy's eyes widened. "If you weren't a scientist you could be a bishop," the boy said with awe. "Your voice is godly."

Zach was pleased and curious. "Your bishops are chosen from those who have the best singing voices?"

"Most of them," said Billy. "It's important that all the words and notes be right. That way the flock can follow. It is not an easy thing—the talent must be there, and the will. That is why we have so few bishops thus far. Brother Yosh intends to begin training children as soon as they are old enough to hold a note."

Zach was no longer listening. For the first time he began to see a way to escape. From that day forward he began to practice the chants and songs as seriously as he worked on his body, singing as he paced off the miles in his cell.

Billy's enthusiasm grew daily. Not knowing about the long hours of practice, he believed that Zach was able to get the songs perfectly right the first time he heard them.

Having now steeped himself in Trader theology, Zach had picked out what seemed to be its four basic tenets: Do unto others as you would have them do unto you, as long as they share your beliefs. Destroy all learning, science, technology, hygiene, and other practices and artifacts from before the Change. Destroy all people who believe in them and convert the rest. Finally, pray to God daily to kill the wild deenas.

The beliefs made a certain kind of simple sense, and Zach could easily understand their appeal. The only problem was that everything the Traders believed was dead wrong. If they were somehow able to prevail and set back or destroy the few advances that had been made in the Garden and the District, then peace, indeed, would reign on earth, because within another very few generations there would be no more human beings.

Because of his understanding of the beliefs and his ease in repeating them, Billy came to assume that Zach shared their sentiments. He was as proud of his pupil as a mother who has taught her child to speak a complete sentence.

One afternoon while Zach was waiting for Billy, the three iron bolts slid from the door and the door creaked open. Once again Yosh was standing before him.

For a moment Zach blinked to adjust his eyes to the light from the corridor. Something was different about Yosh, something he couldn't quite isolate, and then he realized: the young leader was clean-shaven, washed, and wearing fresh clothes. He did not look like a Trader.

"Do you like my disguise?" Yosh asked. "I'm off to the Capital. Will I pass for one of your Principal's loyal subjects?"

Zach felt a chill go through him. "Cleanliness is next to science," he said, quoting a well-known Trader credo.

Yosh laughed. "You've become a true Trader at last," he said. Then, as if to reassure Zach, he added, "It doesn't seem to cause illness, though I admit I felt weakened for several hours."

Zach nodded soberly. "You wouldn't want to do it very often."

"Just enough to blend in with the population."

"Then you go seeking converts?"

Yosh smiled. "We've had men there for two years, right under the Principal's nose. The population is ready for us, Brother Zach. Not all of them are so poisoned with learning as you were."

Zach was silent a moment, then said, casually, "You'll have to be very careful. The Principal's men are everywhere."

"Some of the Principal's men are converts. They keep us well informed."

"I meant," Zach went on, after he'd digested that last bit of chilling information, "that it's not easy to know all the ways of the Capital. If I were able to advise you . . ."

Yosh laughed again, then frowned abruptly. "Billy has told me of your remarkable progress, and I have no doubt that you see the truth. But the pull of the devil is strong in you, my friend. You were a scientist many more years than you've been a Trader."

Zach shrugged. He had not expected to be set free so easily.

"Well, I must be off. I wanted to say farewell. I'll visit you again when I return."

If you return, Zach thought. Now it was more important than ever to escape. If anyone could identify Trader spies, it was he.

Zach had long since mastered all the basic Trader chants and songs. One morning Billy pressed his face against the barred window, beaming and excited. "I've spoken to the First Bishop about you," he said. "He would like to hear you sing. He has given me permission to teach you the special songs."

"Special songs?"

"Everything you have learned was made from songs and stories before the Change. We have some new chants and a few songs that were made by Traders. One was even made by Brother Yosh. It is quite wonderful. Listen closely."

And he began to sing, in his high, wavering voice, the most primitive melody Zach had ever heard—more primitive even than a counting-rhyme from childhood. The words were worse: a garble about the death of scientists atop a prye of burning books.

Zach easily learned the song, pretending to be impressed. He knew that he could easily write a better song.

And why not? The next day, while pacing his cell and after practicing the new material, he began to make up a song of his own. He realized that to make it convincing he would have to imagine himself in the place of a true believer. He did so, remembering what Yosh had told him about his childhood and the catastrophes that had resulted in the death of his family. As he worked out the melody, he imagined how it would sound accompanied by the feathered lyre. When "The Madness of the Fathers" was as perfect as he could make it, he sang it for Billy. When he had finished, tears were rolling down Billy's homely cheeks.

"That is beautiful," he said. "The bishops must hear it."

In due course the three bishops visited outside Zach's cell. They looked exactly as Zach had imagined them: dour, elderly men, dressed in the ragged blue robes of the Trader clergy, and each with a remarkably long, tangled, and dirty beard. After introductions had been made, Zach sang his song for them, and two others he had since made up.

The bishops conferred together in whispers, then one approached the window. "This music is godly," he said. "You must teach us these songs for our services."

"It would be an honor," said Zach. He sang the verses again and again while the Bishops repeated and memorized them.

"Who would have thought a scientist could write such beautiful songs?" said the First Bishop before leaving.

"He is no longer a scientist," said Billy, blushing. "I've been working with him for over three years now. He is as much a Trader as you and I."

"Yes," said the First Bishop thoughtfully, "the proof is in the songs."

Zach thanked them humbly, hiding his excitement. His plan was working. He wanted to laugh at the thought of an escape which depended on the attempt to become a holy man in a strange religion.

When Billy came to Zach again he was brimming with excitement. "The Bishops are so pleased with the way I've trained you that they've picked me to go to the Capital."

"Congratulations," said Zach. "When will you be leaving?"

"In the next few weeks, when we receive word from Brother Yosh."

"I'll miss you and your instruction," said Zach, meaning it.

Billy trembled with pleasure, looking more than ever like a scrawny puppy. "I'm happy to have been able to serve you. And I'm grateful to you for the opportunity you've given me to convert other scientists."

"I've always thought," said Zach, "that a convert such as myself would be valuable working in the District. I know the Capital, and I know its ways."

"Maybe so," said Billy, "but they'll never let you out of here. I know that for a fact. Just before Brother Yosh left, he gave strict and irrevocable orders about you. You are never to be harmed, and you are never to leave this cell, ever."

Zach felt his stomach turn over. "Never?"

"Brother Yosh loves you too much to see you fall into scientific ways again."

In the end, though, it was Yosh himself who provided Zach with a chance to escape. He did this by dying a martyr on the machines in the Capital, a week after Zach's conversation with Billy.

Billy brought the news himself, his voice almost unintelligible through his sobs.

Zach was saddened; in spite of everything he felt a strong bond with the strange young Trader leader. But he instantly saw the opportunity which Yosh's untimely death offered him.

Late into the night, when the torches of all but the watchmen were dark, Zach worked in his cell, creating the most complex and beautiful song he had ever written. He visualized Yosh's open, gentle face, and put that into the melody; he remembered Yosh's passionate devotion to what he saw as the truth, and put it into the words. While he was writing the song he felt that he was a Trader. When he had finished, he had written a song at once heartbreaking, evoking the loss of a martyr, and at the same time inspiring, an anthem for the Traders. "The Death of Our Brother" might well become such an anthem, Zach realized, but it couldn't be helped.

He had Billy send for the bishops at the first opportunity. He sang the song for them and told them, humbly, that he wanted the opportunity to sing it once in front of the assembled congregation of Traders, to memorialize Yosh.

Zach had sung with feeling, and he knew they were moved. Billy began pleading for him: "The memorial will be soon. This is the most fitting tribute. No one else could sing it so well. . . ."

Zach saw, through the peephole in his door, that the First Bishop was nodding but still hesitant. "Brother Yosh himself gave orders that this prisoner is never to leave his cell," he said.

"It was to protect him from being corrupted again by science," said Billy. "But for the memorial—for an hour or two— under heavy guard, there won't be any danger." Billy was stuttering in his earnestness, and Zach felt moved, knowing how difficult it must be for the young preacher to stand up to his bishops. When Billy received no immediate answer, he added, "If Brother Yosh himself could have heard this beautiful song, I'm sure he would have been the first to relax the rules."

The First Bishop began to pace the corridor. "We'll see," he said at last. Inwardly, Zach relaxed. He knew that he had won.

When Billy and the bishops had left, he worked out long and hard, performing exercises and trotting in place until he was covered with sweat and every muscle in his body ached.

He was resting on his straw pallet when he heard the sound of the heavy bolts sliding back. For a moment he thought he had dozed and was dreaming. In all the time he had been here that door had opened only for Yosh. Perhaps they had divined his plan and had come to execute him?

A tall figure stepped inside, the face obscured by a hood. Immediately Zach recognized her: "Jonna!"

"Good afternoon, Brother Zach," she said. The woman had changed greatly in the years since he had last seen her: she was still ugly, that is, her features were still misshapen, but her face had become peaceful and calm, and now she moved with grace and assurance. Perhaps Yosh had been right: she had a beautiful soul, and had needed only love to let it shine through.

"You seem surprised to see me."

"I'm astounded."

"You may have heard that I am priestess in the Trader Church now."

"Yes, I had heard. I am terribly sorry about Yosh."

"He was a great man," she said, her features softening even more. "He showed me what goodness really is. It was because of him that I finally began to believe in the truth. He was of the Church, and it gave him power. It seems to me that power must have been sent from God. I only regret that I was not able to give him a child, to pass on his greatness."

"I think you gave him much happiness in the time you were together," said Zach sincerely and with perhaps a trace of envy.

"It's because of those years that I can go on without him. I'm devoting my life to the Church. To his memory. It's because of that I'm here."

Zach nodded.

"You must have wondered why you have not been killed. We have no need for male prisoners. The reason you have been spared is that Yosh loved you. He told me more than once that in a different world you would have been his closest friend."

"I always felt that too," said Zach.

"He cared for you too much to let you die a scientist. He knew that you could not help your background—although there are some Traders, I'm afraid a growing number, who feel the best way to convert a scientist is to kill him. Still, Yosh wanted to cleanse your soul, and that is why he had you brought here."

"That was good of him," said Zach, oddly moved. Like so many things about the Traders, this too made a kind of cock-eyed sense, and he knew that it had been meant in a loving spirit.

"As his widow, I have some power. Your young preacher has come to me and asked me to persuade the Bishops to let you introduce your song at the memorial service for Yosh. He feels that it would not break the spirit of Yosh's command to let you out, just the once, under guard, and to return you immediately. I have to agree that it seems right. Before I make a final decision, let me hear this song."

Feeling self-conscious and not a little dishonest, Zach stood and sang. When he had finished Jonna's eyes were shining with tears. "It brings him back," she whispered. "Thank you."

* * *

Two days later, Billy came rushing into the corridor, again stuttering in his excitement. On the special holy day set aside in Yosh's memory, one week from now, Zach would sing his remarkable song in the Trader high services.

Zach's joy at the news was not faked. This was, then, finally, his chance to escape. His only chance. If he were to fail in this attempt, he knew there would never be another.

Five

After he had finished his breakfast, there was nothing for Zach to do but wait. By late morning the sound of chanting began in the park outside. He went to the window and saw what appeared to be many dozens of Trader men, women, and children, gathering around the sheltered altar. In another hour or two he would be gone from here or dead. In either case, he would be a free man for the first time in five years.

Once it had been decided that he would sing at the memorial service, Zach had made no further plans. He had not been outdoors in years, and in any case was familiar only with the narrow slice of the town he could see from his window. He would use his wits once he was out, and seize whatever opportunities arose.

He had thought he might be given new clothing to replace his filthy rags, in honor of Yosh, but the Traders valued neatness no more than cleanliness.

The chanting grew louder, and Zach began to pace, not for exercise, but to relieve his tension. He was conscious that once again he was about to betray a trust. He had lied to Billy, whom he genuinely liked, and was perhaps even endangering him; he had lied to Jonna, who had saved his life; and he had written a song that was a tissue of lies. There was truth in the song too, and that was why it was so successful; but all the same it was a betrayal of Yosh, who had spared his life out of love.

Yet it must be done. The future of mankind might depend on his escaping and taking what he knew of the Traders back to the Principal. Once again, expediency won: the choosing of one commitment over another. He tried to look at it as a Trader would: as a "scientist," his mission was to save humanity, and therefore anything in that end was justified. He knew it was true, and he also knew it was wrong.

Billy and the First Bishop came for him just at noon. They stood by as three guards checked Zach for hidden weapons and securely bound his hands in front of him. Billy, grinning nervously, stood by, shifting his weight from one foot to the other. Zach was scarcely aware of the others; he was looking at every detail of the cell. He would never see it again. He had resolved that if he failed in his attempt to escape, he would not return here alive.

The escape proved far easier than he had expected. This was partly because of the beauty of the song itself. As Billy had earlier told the Bishop, "This was divinely inspired. He couldn't have written it if he weren't sincere."

And evidently everyone else believed that Zach was now a true Trader. Even the bishops apparently hadn't seriously considered that he might try to escape. His stirring tribute to Yosh seemed clear proof that Zach would follow Yosh's commands as scrupulously as any Trader.

For all of the Traders the will of Yosh was everything; Zach was sure that within another generation he would be elevated to the status of a god.

Trader women and children had attached hundreds of summer flowers to the three sides and roof of the shelter above the altar. Zach stumbled as the guards led him across the park. The beauty of the flowers, the grass, and the soft summer air had taken the strength from him.

Scores of congregants, some of whom, according to Billy,

had traveled hundreds of miles to be here, sat patiently on the grass, chanting and waiting for the service to begin. Most of them stared at Zach in frank curiosity; Billy had told him that the story of his song had spread quickly, making him famous throughout the Trader empire.

Zach sat on a low wooden bench with the First Bishop and Billy on either side of him, the guards standing at the back. They were armed with knives and swords but seemed as awed by the occasion as everyone else.

The service seemed to take hours, though in truth it probably lasted little longer than the noontime and evening services Zach had often heard from his cell. There were many familiar chants and songs, and the burning, for this special occasion, of three books. Finally Jonna stood to deliver a tribute to Yosh. She was dressed in a long blue hooded robe, and a pale veil partially covered her face. Zach had to admit that she looked almost beautiful as she spoke of her love for Yosh and his love for his people. When she had finished, the First Bishop spoke for a few minutes, retelling the story of Yosh's revelation and explaining how he had captured and converted Zach, a scientist who had been one of the Principal's own men. Then it was Zach's turn.

The silence became total when Zach stood. He stumbled as he got up, and put out his arms, then almost fell. Jonna motioned to the guards and they cut his bonds. Zach hid his relief. It would be easier this way. He did not have to fake the trembling of his knees as he mounted the altar. He looked out at the gathered congregation, opened his mouth, and sang.

When he had finished he could see tears on the faces of those sitting closest to him, including his guards. The First Bishop thanked him and signaled an end to the service, then Traders began to crowd around the altar. Men and women both came to Zach, wanting to touch him, to tell him how much the song had moved him. His guards stood back, while the bishops and Billy looked on, proud. Jonna even came to him and hugged him quickly, her eyes still wet with tears.

After the service a feast had been planned. Zach had assumed he was to be returned to the prison directly after the ceremony, but instead he stayed, continuing to talk to Traders and eating the morsels of food they brought him. After perhaps an hour of this, Zach told his guards that he needed to relieve himself.

They agreed readily, and the youngest of the three escorted Zach to the thick brush in the forest alongside the park. Zach hoped that the town was no bigger than the few buildings he could see. The guard apologized, embarrassed. "I hope you understand that I must stay here. It's orders."

"Of course," said Zach. Politely, the young man looked away while Zach fumbled with his trousers, so he didn't see the blow aimed at the back of his neck which, Zach hoped, had not killed him. Zach took the knife and sword, then simply walked away. He was certain he would not be missed for several minutes.

The town extended no farther than the length of the park, and in no time Zach was in deep forest. He did not know for certain where he was, only that he was somewhere in the uncharted western wilderness. It was late summer, and there would be a good bit of daylight yet for him to put as much distance as possible between himself and the Traders.

He could imagine the consternation when his deception had been discovered; Billy, he knew, would be heartbroken.

Zach looked at the sun, estimating the time of day and the direction, then began to trot east.

Six

After several weeks of slow traveling, constantly on the lookout for Trader patrols, Zach at last reached the western hills in the south of the District. He planned to go first to the Garden, to see the Mistress if she still lived, and to find out, if he could, what had become of Evvy. He tried not to have any expectations, aware that things must have changed a great deal in the time he had been in prison.

Still, what he found was a greater shock than he was prepared for.

Although he had tried to clean himself as soon as he was well away from the Trader settlement, the grime was too deeply embedded to come off with anything but repeated applications of soap and hot water; the parasites and stench would require a more civilized, or at least leisurely, approach. With his dirt, his unkempt hair and beard, and the rags he was wearing, the men now living in the Garden took him for a Trader.

Zach realized with relief that the Principal must have moved the women to the peninsula for protection; but the guards at the gate arrested him immediately and refused to answer any of his questions. He had hoped to find one of the Principal's generals in charge, or someone else who would recognize him, but there was no one here that he had ever seen before. He was questioned roughly several times, first by the guards, then their superior, and finally by the Commandant, a ruddy, big-boned man who looked at him with open suspicion as Zach began patiently to tell his story again.

"I am the Principal's brother," he said. "I have important information for the Principal. Please help me get to the Capital." He was standing in the old woman's cabin, now the Commandant's office, while the guards who had arrested him flanked him, their weapons ready. Although nothing of the old woman's remained, he remembered as if he could see them each table and chair, the rows of scientific equipment, and the dozens of shelves of books. The crude furniture and military equipment were jarringly out of place, as were the men, yet even his captors' distrustfulness couldn't stop him from feeling somehow at home.

The Commandant was picking his teeth and looking bored. "The Principal's brother has been dead for years," he said. "He has no other."

"I was captured by the Traders," Zach said with growing exasperation. "I've been their prisoner for five years."

"Traders don't take male prisoners," said the Commandant.

"Besides, if you're the Principal's brother, where's your seal ring?"

"I lost it," Zach said, aware how feeble his answer sounded. He spoke again quickly. "If I were really a Trader would I come to you this openly?"

"Who knows what a Trader would do?"

"He's a filthy Trader spy," said the Commandant's aide. "I say let's hang him right now."

The Commandant sighed. "Don't be too quick, Jerrod. Everyone knows how the Principal felt about his brother. Suppose what he says is somehow true?"

The younger man snorted. "Look at him. If that's the Principal's brother, I'm my own sister."

It was clear to Zach that the Commandant didn't believe him any more than his soldiers did, but the man seemed shrewd enough to realize that if by some chance the story were true, it would be prudent to let Zach reach the Principal. After several more days of verbal sparring, the Commandant sent Zach along with the weekly courier to the Capital.

He was tied securely to an aging mount and carefully watched by two young soldiers, both of whom treated him with contempt, referring to him as "filthy Trader."

Despite the circumstances of the journey, Zach's excitement grew as he approached familiar land. The road to the Capital was far better maintained now than it had been in the past; clearly the Principal had made changes, probably out of the necessity to improve communications with his new outpost in the west.

He had almost forgotten that he was probably riding to his death, nor did he think much about the information he would deliver to the Principal. One thing only filled his mind, making him feel like a child again: he was going home.

As they approached the Capital, Zach asked his guards for permission to bathe in the river, using soap. He couldn't help but think of Will's fastidiousness.

"A Trader? Wash? Why don't you just ask us to cut you loose and close our eyes while you run away?"

"You needn't untie me," said Zach. "Only help me to get some of the worst of it off."

The guard spat in disgust. "Sitting here is the closest I ever want to get to a filthy Trader," he said. Roughly, he shoved Zach to the ground. "Ask the Principal for a bath if he's such a good friend of yours."

"Maybe we oughtta clean him up," said the other guard. "Probably be the worst thing you can do to a Trader."

With that they both laughed loudly and passed another pipe of new-smoke.

In the end it was just that way—filthy, his hair matted and full of parasites, half-starved and in rags, his hands fettered in front and his legs shackled together—that Zach was brought to the House of the Principal.

As he and the couriers rode along the broad Avenue, ignoring the taunts of those who had spotted a prisoner, all he could think was that he was here. The Capital was noisier, and brighter, and far, far more beautiful than he had remembered it.

His guards told the same story at each of the security posts, beginning at the iron gate. "This crazy Trader claims he's the Principal's brother. The Commandant thought the Principal might want to question him."

At last he was taken to the office with rounded walls where the Principal conducted his public business. Zach saw very few familiar faces along the way. Undoubtedly all the generals were busy; from the improved condition of the roads, and the conversation of his guards, he gathered that the Principal was greatly expanding his army. In any case, it was doubtful if any of his old friends would recognize him now. Apart from the filth, Zach was sure he must appear aged by twenty more years than the five which had in reality passed.

Now, waiting in the wood-paneled hall, held against the wall by the museum-lance of the Principal's private guard, a man Zach had never seen before, he heard the couriers speaking to the Principal about the "crazy Trader," and then a bellow: "All right, you've come this far, bring him in!"

At the sound of that voice Zach felt as if a large hand had suddenly taken his body and were squeezing him in half. He was dragged into the familiar room. The Principal was standing behind his polished desk, his back to the light, his dark eyebrows pulled together in concentration as he peered into a book in his hands. Zach thought he saw gray hairs among the dark curls, then the Principal's face seemed to dissolve as everything that had happened in five years welled up and overflowed. Zach began to shake with sobs just as the guard pushed him into the center of the room. "Here he is, sir."

The Principal looked up, preoccupied and annoyed.

"Well?" he said. "I'm a busy man. Don't stand there blubbering. Tell your—" And then he stopped and stared. The small amount of color in his pale face drained away and he leaned on the desk for support as he continued to gaze at Zach. He mouthed the name "Zach" but made no sound.

"Are you all right, sir?" asked his guard, sounding frightened.

The Principal didn't move from where he was. Still leaning against the desk, he quietly said, "Unbind this man. Immediately."

Even more frightened, the couriers and guard began fumbling with the bonds, trying to untie knots that trembled with their own and Zach's shaking.

"Cut them, for the deena's sake!" Before the men could respond, the Principal himself strode across the room and cut through the ropes with his own knife. "All of you get out of here!" he cried, his face less than two inches from that of his private guard. "Tell my secretary to bring in food and drink! That's all!"

The men were very glad to go. Zach felt the Principal's strong arms around him, and he lifted his own arms, weak from having been tied, and embraced his brother, still unable to speak.

The Principal recovered first. He brushed a hand across his face and, in a voice still shaky, said, "You look terrible." He led Zach to the couch and helped him to sit. Zach's attack of weeping had ended. He wiped at his eyes and tried to catch his breath.

The Principal stepped back and looked at him, his face filled with joy and amazement. There was a knock at the door, and Robin came in with a large tray.

Will began speaking immediately. "No more visitors, no interruptions, I don't care what happens, I don't care if the lord of the Traders comes into the city to surrender—do you understand?"

"Yes, sir," said Robin uncertainly. He looked curiously at Zach, recoiling at the filth, then his face changed. "Great deena!" he said.

"Yes," said the Principal. "Zach has returned to us from the dead."

"But how . . . ?"

"I don't know. I don't care. We'll find out sooner or later, but all that matters now is that he is back."

"Yes, sir. Yes, sir. This is wonderful news. Welcome home, Zach." Impulsively the old man went to Zach, took his hand, then dropped it uncertainly and backed off.

Zach smiled. "Thank you, Robin," he started to say, but he still couldn't find his voice.

The Principal handed him a cup of warm brew. "Here. This will help you get a hold on yourself."

Zach eagerly accepted it. It had been a very long time since he had tasted brew, and it was even better than he remembered. As he took the liquid in short gulps, warming his throat and his stomach, a feeling of peace began to spread through his body. At last he had his breath. He looked up at the Principal, who was still standing before him, pacing from foot to foot in the quick nervous way he had, his face open with joy.

"I can't believe it's you," the Principal said. "I look at you, and I know you, and I don't believe you're here." Zach wanted to speak, but he had so much to say he didn't know where to begin.

"You must eat," said the Principal. He brought the tray to the couch and placed it beside Zach. There were sausages and bread and cheese, and Zach looked at the array hungrily. The Principal broke off a piece of sweet bread and Zach ate it in one bite, then washed it down with two large gulps of brew. He began to chew on a sausage, the rich taste seeming to explode in his mouth.

"I'll have a bath made up and call in the barbers," said the

Principal. "Or you can rest. I know you've been through a lot, I can't imagine what. Would you like to rest now?"

Zach shook his head.

The two men continued to eat and drink for some time. And still Zach found it difficult to begin talking. After he had eaten his fill for the first time in memory, and washed down the last of the sausage with brew, Zach at last said, "I have been a prisoner of the Traders for all these years."

"I guessed as much," said the Principal. "All this time I thought you were dead. My men found the place where you were attacked and brought me your things; later we recovered your seal ring from the remains of a skeleton. The man was so large we assumed it was you."

Zach's stomach turned over. The sausages had been far richer than the food he was used to, and for a moment he thought he would be sick. The dead man, whoever he was, could have gotten the seal ring from only one person, Evvy; she would not have given it up willingly, and that meant . . .

"Are you all right?" the Principal touched Zach's shoulder, his face very close and worried.

Zach nodded, and swallowed several times as the Principal continued: "When I saw that, I had to believe you were dead. It never occurred to me that the seal ring could have found itself on any finger but yours. I suppose I didn't think it was possible for you to be captured; and, of course, for a long time now the Traders have not taken male prisoners."

Zach nodded. He wanted to tell the Principal about Yosh, and the Trader plans for secret conversion, but he must explain a great deal more first. Part of that explanation would involve telling the Principal how he had betrayed him and why, and he could not bring himself to do that yet. He again fell silent, knowing that Will would attribute this to exhaustion. In his happiness the Principal seemed not even to notice Zach's silence. Zach basked in his brother's joy, unwilling to spoil it for now.

The Principal talked on and on. He told Zach of new developments in the District, of his struggle against the Traders, and Zach listened with growing misgiving. Will still saw the

Traders as crazed, ignorant fanatics, which, of course, they were; but clearly Will had no idea how dedicated and well organized they were. As always, Zach loved to watch the Principal talk, his face animated and expressive as he described the things which excited him. Even as a young boy he had never been able to sit quietly. Always his mind was working, making plans, dreaming dreams.

After a while Zach's head began to nod, and he fought his sleepiness, not wanting the evening to end. The Principal saw his exhaustion and called Robin, then ordered him to have the housekeeper prepare a bath. He put his strong arms under Zach's own and helped him rise from the couch, then walk through the long corridor and down the stairway to the large bathing-pool in the basement.

"You are so thin I can feel your bones," the Principal said.

The bathing-room was already hazy with steam as two servants poured kettles of hot water into the large blue-and-white tiled bath. Zach was suddenly, acutely embarrassed by his filth, his parasites, and the new scars crossing his scrawny body. The Principal seemed to sense his discomfort and instructed the attendants to leave after the bath was filled and thick towels laid out. He helped Zach peel off the filthy clothes, then eased him into the pool, disrobed, and joined him, lying back in the warm fragrant water.

After a few moments the warmth of the water had reached into every corner of Zach's being, and he felt that he could float here forever, never moving.

The Principal helped Zach to wash, with soap and a rough vegetable sponge, clucking at the amount of grime that had worked itself into all the pores and folds of his skin. This was the first time he had properly bathed in over five years, and Zach simply gave himself up to the pleasure of it, feeling the torments of the past years melt away with the dirt.

"We'll have to do something about your new friends," said the Principal distastefully. "You may have to finally shave that famous beard. Soon you'll be more like me than you ever imagined." He turned his head sideways. "Yes, you're beginning to look like Zach," he said. "How do you feel?"

In answer, Zach reached out and gripped his brother's hand,

slippery from soap. The Principal returned the grasp and smiled. "It's a start," he said.

Feeling more relaxed and at peace than he could recall ever having felt, Zach wrapped himself in a soft cloth robe, then followed the Principal to his old room, where he had not slept all these years.

"I kept the room for you," said the Principal. "I didn't want anyone else to sleep here. Some part of me must have known that you were still alive."

Zach lay down on the clean sheets, tightly spread over a mount-hair mattress, feeling as if his body had melted and were spreading into every corner of the room. He was very near sleep, and he looked up again at Will's confident smile. The last thing he saw as his eyes closed was his feathered lyre, hanging on the wall where he had always kept it.

Seven

When Zach awoke it was late afternoon; he had slept nearly round the clock. He lay without moving for a moment, savoring the feeling of peace and comfort. Through the open window he could see the top of the Great Tower and beyond it the trees bordering the river.

Slowly he stretched, working out the stiffness in his limbs. The feathered lyre gleamed on the wall in front of him, and he smiled, thinking of the Principal's sentimental dedication to his memory. He knew he should get up, but his body still ached with exhaustion. Despite the exercise he had taken in his cell, he was weak and out of shape. He could see that he would be unable to resume any of his duties until he had begun to rebuild his strength. And then he remembered that he would not in fact assume any duties, because he had committed treason and would be put to death. No matter how much Will loved him, Zach knew he would never be able to forgive his betrayal.

He sat up but still did not get out of the bed. He scratched his beard and hair, thinking of all he must do today.

"Good morning, sir," said a voice to his right.

Zach started and turned to see a boy slouched in a chair, gazing at him curiously. "I am Lindy," the boy said. "The Principal ordered me to watch and tell him as soon as you woke up. And to find out if you want anything."

"Nothing, thank you," said Zach, smiling. The boy bobbed his head and disappeared. Zach went to the wardrobe, where he knew he would find his old clothing untouched. He put on a soft gray tunic which had been one of his favorites. It hung from him as if from a cloak rack. The belt he used to fasten his dark trousers reached nearly twice around him. There was a small looking glass to the right of the bed. Although Zach had caught blurred glimpses of himself in water while traveling to the Garden, he had not yet had a clear look at the man he had become. He approached the mirror with curiosity and misgiving. Although he often teased the Principal for his vanity, Zach had always taken pride in his own appearance. The man who looked out from the mirror was a stranger. The hair was thin and matted, and more gray than blond; the face was gaunt and deeply lined, the eyes sunken and without a trace of humor. He looked, in fact, very much like most Traders. Perhaps the teachings had rubbed off on him in some deep and unknowable way.

There was a knock at the door, and the Principal let himself in. He was smiling and as full of energy as a puppy. Immediately he embraced Zach. "Good morning, brother," he said. "Although by now good evening would be more appropriate. I take it you slept well?"

"Better than I have in five years," said Zach.

The Principal stood back and examined him. "Quite a change from the wild-eyed Trader who came in yesterday, but we've got to fatten you up. And do something about that hair. Do you know, your hair was so dirty I didn't notice it last night, but you've gone quite gray."

"I was just noticing that myself," said Zach. "People will now take me for your father."

The Principal put his arm around Zach's shoulder. "Come along, then, old man. Let's get some food into you, and then off to the barbers."

The barber did not shave Zach's head but cut the hair bristly-short and applied herbal medicines to kill the remaining lice. His beard was shaved; this was the first time in his adult life that Zach had seen himself without it.

"Finally you look like a civilized man," said the Principal. He had been trying to get Zach to shave from their youth.

"I look like a stranger," said Zach. This new appearance was even more unsettling. The deep lines around his mouth and the mouth itself—straight and thin-lipped—reinforced the look of a man who was humorless and uncompromising. It was the face of a betrayer. Had he always looked like this?

"I've planned a feast for tonight," said the Principal. "A chance for all your old friends to see you again. I've been spreading the word all day. I'll tell you something, Zach, I feel like a boy again. It's as if I came back from the dead too. I did more business this one day than in the last two months." He looked closely at Zach and then frowned. "What is it? I thought you'd want to see everyone. If it's too much for you, we can postpone the celebration."

Zach saw the hurt in the Principal's eyes and quickly said, "No, of course not. It sounds like just what I need." But the longer he was with the Principal, the closer he came to resuming his old life, the more difficult it would be for Will when he finally learned the truth.

"I have to speak to you," Zach said after a moment.

"Yes, of course," said the Principal. "And there are a hundred questions I must ask you. But there's no rush."

"Some of what I have to tell you is urgent. More than you know. I've learned a great deal about the Traders and their ways."

The Principal nodded. "I executed their leader here last spring, but it doesn't seem to have stopped the spread of their ideas."

"They've made him a holy martyr," said Zach. "Stopping them is going to require all your resources. They have the power to destroy your civilization. I am deadly serious about this."

"I can see you are. And I know we'll have to do something about it soon. Great deena, I just hope we're not going to have a holy war on our hands."

"I'm afraid that's exactly what you have already."

The Principal looked worried, then he shook his head and smiled. "Together we can stop them," he said. "Together we can do anything, Zach. I've always known that. But there's plenty of time. Even if the Traders are converting half the city at this very moment, we can't do a thing about it tonight. So let's forget about business and concentrate on pleasure for a. while. When you've eaten and drunk enough to put ten more pounds on your bony frame, then we'll get to work."

Zach had to smile. The Principal was making things more difficult by the minute, but Zach couldn't help going along with him for the time being.

"You win," he said. "As always. But one thing: I know you have moved the Garden. I assume it's now at the peninsula retreat?"

The Principal nodded. "The neck of the peninsula is guarded by a training base. It couldn't be safer."

"How is the work going there?"

"Better than we could have expected. As a matter of fact, the problem of the woman sickness has been solved—"

"What!"

"Well, that is, there is now a way to test for susceptibility. We've had some difficulty getting the population to go along with it. I've sent for someone who can tell you all about it tomorrow."

There was one more question Zach had to ask. "One thing more, Will. Is the old woman . . . ?"

"She's dead. It happened a few weeks ago. She had been ill a long time." He squeezed Zach's shoulder.

"If only I had come back in time."

"She believed you dead, Zach. If you had returned, the shock might have killed her sooner."

Zach was astonished. He was saddened by the news of his mother's death but not really surprised; she had been very old. What stunned him was that Will seemed to share some measure of sorrow. "Had you grown closer, then, toward the end?"

The Principal laughed shortly. "Not really," he said. "There was never any love between the old woman and me. It's just that we both came to understand we've been working for the same thing all along."

Zach smiled. "All my life I tried to convince you of that. Both of you."

"I guess we were too much alike to listen to you," the Principal said. He frowned, then went on. "At the end, she called me to her deathbed. It turned out she wanted to put forth another of your old projects. The gist of it was that it's time for me to settle down and produce an heir."

Zach stared at Will. Things must have changed more than he could imagine. The old woman he had known would rather have seen Will's empire crumble than have him marry. And Will himself—

But Will was on his feet. "It's getting late," he said. "There's all the time in the world to talk about this. For now, we have a great deal of serious eating and drinking ahead of us. So no more business, and no more questions. Agreed?"

"Agreed."

"By the way," the Principal added, stopping so suddenly that Zach nearly bumped into him. "I have questions too, brother. And I'm expecting the answer to one of them tomorrow."

For an eerie moment Zach had the feeling that Will already knew everything, but the Principal's face immediately relaxed into a smile of anticipation as they approached the banquet hall.

Zach awoke the next morning with a taste in his mouth like poison-bat wings and a fierce throbbing headache. For a moment he thought he was back in prison and opened his eyes expecting to see damp stone walls. Instead he saw curved wooden panels and glass-paned windows framing an overcast sky. He couldn't think where he was, then realized that he was lying on a couch in the Principal's office, where he dimly remembered coming after the banquet. The Principal himself was sprawled across his desk, snoring loudly. Curled against his ankles, its face buried in its paws, was the striped fox-cat baby the Principal called Napoleon. When Will had first shown him the animal, Zach had been astounded—both at the thought of a fox-cat living tamely indoors and at the idea of Will taking on the care of a pet. At the feast last night, though, he could see that Napoleon suited Will's playful side as it scampered about the room, chasing stray morsels of food and attacking unguarded ankles. Watching Will with the animal, Zach again had the feeling that Will had changed in ways beyond his understanding.

It had been a wonderful party, taking Zach back in memory to the early days of Will's rule, when optimism and youthful exuberance had made every victory a cause for excitement and celebration. In those days Will had given banquets often, sparing no expense in honoring an achievement in battle or the consolidation of some new service for the growing District, like the first founding of a school for literacy. Though Zach had never been as gregarious as Will, he had always enjoyed the chance to talk, joke, and sing with Will's generals, soldiers, healers, and teachers. The formal occasions for banquets had grown fewer over the years, but Will had never lost his delight in playing the host, laughing and drinking with his men as if he were one of them, and not the Principal.

The banquet was held in the large dining hall that the Principal used for festive occasions. Its faded blue walls and carpet were illuminated by dozens of fish-oil lamps hanging from brass fixtures on the walls. Two long, beautiful, polished pre-Change tables were covered with embroidered cotton cloth and set with bowls of flowers, dining implements, and pitchers of wine and brew. Women for hire and serving boys circulated with trays of cheese, bread, fruits, and meats, while a musician played product ballads on a piano that was said to be hundreds of years old. At first Zach had felt shy and somewhat intimidated by the crowd of noisy, boisterous men, many of whom he had never before seen; but after the Principal had pressed on him several cups of new-grape wine, he had begun to relax and then to enjoy himself. Ralf, Red, and a dozen others had repeatedly taken his hand or embraced him, some of them sentimental from drink, and all genuinely glad to see him. He had never considered how many people had missed him—and how much he had missed them. He had taken a great deal of ribbing about his clean-shaven face and short gray hair. There had been much drunken laughter and song; in fact, they had all behaved and felt like small children, which, of course, was the point. Last night the Principal had seemed happier and less driven than Zach had ever seen him.

That happiness would have to end soon. Today. Zach couldn't put it off any longer.

He pulled himself to his feet and stretched, thinking that he desperately needed some water. Then he noticed that someone, probably the ever-thoughtful Robin, had placed a tray containing a large pitcher of water, and another of fruit juice, just inside the door.

The baby fox-cat opened its eyes and stretched, then jumped off the desk to rub at Zach's ankles, asking to be let out with a plaintive *"Mowr?"* Smiling, Zach quietly opened the door, then picked up the tray.

He heard a groan as he finished his second cup of juice, so he poured another and brought it to the Principal.

"Great deena," said the Principal. "I feel as if I've been dead for a week."

"You look it too," said Zach. He handed him the juice.

The Principal drank it in one long swallow, then hopped up and began to gulp from the water pitcher. When he had finished, he upended the pitcher and poured the remaining water over his head.

He shook his head like a wet mount, then smiled sheepishly. "A little better," he said. "Some party, eh?"

"Thank you," said Zach.

"No thanks required. Loosen up a little, like you did last night. I never heard you sing so well—or so loudly. Did the Traders teach you to warble like that?"

"As a matter of fact, in a way they did," said Zach.

"You could have a new career as a minstrel. Though I have no intention of letting you leave my side again. Perhaps we'll just invite selected patrons to hear you and fatten the tax rolls—" He stopped as there was a knock at the door. "Ah," he said. "Yes?"

Robin stuck his head in. "Good morning. The women from the Garden are here, sir."

"Good. Make them comfortable. Zach and I are going to my private quarters to bathe and change. Have breakfast sent to us there." He turned to Zach and added, "If your stomach feels anything like mine, breakfast isn't an appealing thought. But I insist on it. We'll get some meat back on you yet. Then afterwards, there's someone I want you to meet."

As Zach waited in the Principal's office for the Principal to return with the emissary from the Garden, he tried to puzzle out Will's strange manner. He had hinted more than once that he wanted to question Zach about matters that were obviously troubling him; he knew that Zach had a great deal to tell him about the Traders; yet he was taking as the first order of business a meeting with a representative of the Garden. Most likely, Zach decided, this was simply a courtesy. The Principal knew how deeply interested Zach had always been in the Garden's work, and perhaps too he wanted to show off the latest developments.

He heard the Principal's voice in the hall. "I'm sorry if I alarmed you. I wouldn't have sent for you if it weren't very important. I'll explain everything later. But now I want you to meet someone."

The Principal preceded his guest into the room, then turned, watching as she walked in. His face was expressionless. Zach followed his eyes to the door.

Zach knew her immediately, although she was a grown woman now, and taller. But the same grace and beauty, the same astonishing plum-colored eyes, gave Evvy the charismatic presence she had possessed as a young girl. His mind swirled with a hundred thoughts: surprise, shock that she was here with the Principal, and joy at seeing her alive and unharmed. He half rose from the couch, holding his breath.

It took Evvy a moment longer to recognize Zach, and at

first she looked simply puzzled. She glanced quizzically at the Principal, whose face was now fixed on Zach, then again at Zach, and suddenly she became absolutely motionless. Her mouth parted and the color drained from her face. "Zach," she whispered.

She took two uncertain steps toward him, then abruptly sat in the nearby armchair, staring at him.

"Evvy," said the Principal, "this is my brother Zach. Zach—"

Zach sat back. "I know her," he said.

The Principal leaned against his desk, his arms crossed carelessly in front of him. "Yes," he said, "I can see you do. And I suspected as much."

Zach sank into the cushions and forced himself to look at his brother. The rage he had been expecting was absent; in its place was a look of bewilderment, and something else. Zach realized it was sadness, which colored Will's voice when he spoke again: "Very well," he said. "Now it's time for me to ask questions. I've long suspected that you were captured while you were defending her. But now I want to know how it happened. How did Evvy get to the Garden, and why did she never tell me who she was? What really happened five years ago?"

Eight

As he lay awake that night, Zach reflected that it had been the most painful afternoon of his life. Never would he forget the puzzled, trusting look on the Principal's face when he had to answer: "I was not defending Evvy when I was captured. I was taking her to the Garden."

"Zach, no—" said Evvy, but he went on.

"I betrayed you, Will. This is what I have been trying to tell you."

"Betrayed me?" The Principal looked bewildered. "What are you taking about?"

For a moment Zach thought he might yet take back his words, but it was too late. The Principal's face began to change with understanding, and Zach continued. "I did not intend to bring Evvy to you," he said. "Not then and not ever."

The Principal continued to look at Zach, not moving. Then he swallowed and turned away. He walked to the window and stood with his back to the room, looking out at the clouded sky. Zach watched him helplessly, then turned to meet Evvy's gaze, but she too turned away and he felt suddenly alone in the room. He was dizzy, as if he were imagining or dreaming everything that was happening. The Principal continued to stand with his back to them, and Zach could see his shoulders move as he took deep, slow breaths. He had done this since he was a child whenever he was hurt or challenged; he had once told Zach that it calmed him and gave him time to decide what action to take.

"You have done more harm than you know," said the Principal at last. He turned back, his face set in tight lines, and addressed Evvy. "It's him, isn't it?" he said. "He's the one you love?"

Evvy nodded.

"I've known it all these years."

"Will," said Evvy, "for a long time I've suspected that you knew, but—"

"Be quiet!" said the Principal. Evvy sat back as if she had been slapped. Zach could only stare at the two of them. Something beyond his understanding had happened between them, and was happening still.

Now the Principal turned to Zach, and Zach could see the famous rage building beneath the composed surface, waiting to explode. But when he spoke, his voice was calm. "I never would have believed it," he said. "I've thought many things, I've known for a long time who Evvy was, and yet I never suspected, never dreamed..." He broke off. "Anyone else," he said finally. "Anyone but you."

"It didn't happen the way you're thinking," said Zach.

"And how am I thinking?"

"That I and Evvy... that Evvy and I..."

"The girl's in love with you. She's told me so often enough, she just never mentioned a name."

"Will, please," said Evvy. "Zach is telling the truth. He never touched me, he never knew that I loved him, and he never loved me."

Zach listened without understanding. The news that Evvy had loved him all these years was as bewildering as the fact that she was here now.

"The deenas take it," said the Principal suddenly. He sat heavily at his desk.

Evvy rose and approached him. "It happened over five years ago," she said. "It's ancient history now."

"Sit down," said the Principal. He turned to Zach. "Tell me what happened."

"What happened was this. Evvy saved my life. I came to know her and realized that I could not turn her over to you."

"Knowing that your refusal meant you could not return to the Capital?"

"Yes."

"Knowing that I depended on you? That you were turning your back on everything we had worked for together?"

Zach swallowed. "There was no choice."

"You left the feathered lyre and those other things as a decoy, then, so that I would think you had been captured or killed."

"Yes."

"Didn't you consider how it would affect me to hear of your death?"

Zach didn't answer. Nothing he could say would make the Principal less bitter. The Principal looked at him again, then at Evvy, and back at Zach. His eyes still held more puzzlement than anger. He spread out his hands.

"Couldn't you simply have returned her to her family and

come back without her? It wouldn't have been the first time you refused to carry out an order."

"I considered that. But I felt she would have a better life among the women of the Garden. Her family was poor and nearly starving, and, besides, they had sold her."

Evvy was looking at the floor, tears silently slipping down her cheeks.

"That raises another point," said the Principal. "Evvy, do you know that legally I still own you? I paid a lot of metal to your parents for you."

"I've always known it," said Evvy.

"Then Evvy is not—" Zach started to speak, then fell silent, not sure what to say, not knowing if he wanted an answer.

The Principal understood him. "There is nothing between me and Evvy," he said. His tone was flat and final. After a moment, he spoke again. "Ah, Zach. If only you'd thought to trust me, as I always trusted you. Didn't you know that if you cared so much for Evvy's well-being, I would never have harmed her?"

"The compulsion was always stronger than you. You would not have been able to stop yourself—"

"No, Zach!"

At last the anger was there in his face and in his voice. The Principal rose and leaned with both palms outstretched on the desk, his arms trembling as he faced Zach. "It wasn't what I might do to Evvy that concerned you, brother. It was what you yourself might do. You were in love with her but couldn't admit it. That's why you betrayed me. And that's why you conceived the romantic notion of taking her to the Garden. You didn't have the courage to take her for yourself, so you delivered her to the one place where no other man could ever have her!"

The words stung Zach, and he couldn't think of an answer, because there was none.

"What had you planned to do once you had taken Evvy to the Garden?"

"I didn't know," said Zach. "I hadn't thought it out. I thought I might go west and find out what sort of people lived there."

"Well, you did that after all," said the Principal. "And Evvy made her way to the Garden and prospered there, and I—" he stopped and began to pace. "This is a fine mess we have," he said. "I don't know what to do. Deenas take it, I don't know what to do."

"I didn't want to hurt you," Zach said. "But I knew I must tell the truth. I knew this even as I was planning my escape and making my way back here. I knew I had to tell you everything I knew about the Traders, and I also knew returning would mean my death."

"Your death? What are you talking about?"

"My betrayal was an act of treason," he said. "Under your law as written. And the penalty for treason is death. I have been aware of that all along."

Evvy gasped. "Is this true?"

"It's true," said the Principal wearily. "Although the question of treason is open to interpretation. But suppose Evvy had not reached the Garden. Suppose everything happened just as it did, except that when you came here you did not meet Evvy. What would you have done then?"

"I would have done the same. I would have told you the truth. I tried to do so yesterday."

"There would have been no need for you to say anything. I would never have known the difference. Why couldn't you let it be?"

Zach waited a moment, then answered. "I couldn't put more dishonesty between us."

"What's between us now is far worse," said the Principal. He sat again at his desk and shut his eyes as if by that act he could erase everything that had happened in the last hour. When he opened his eyes, Zach and Evvy were still sitting before him, quiet and unhappy.

"I can't think," he said. "I must be alone for a while. I don't care where you go or what you do, but I insist on one thing. I don't want the two of you to be together, alone or with other people. I will trust you to carry out my wishes. No one else must know anything about this until I have decided what to do."

"I'll remain in my room," said Zach.

"Will," said Evvy, standing. "May I say something?"

"No. There has been enough talking. Now go, both of you!"

Zach and Evvy left the office side by side without saying a word. When they reached the end of the short entrance hall, Zach turned right toward his room and Evvy continued straight ahead.

"This is what I have decided," said the Principal. It was the next morning, and Zach knew that none of them had been able to sleep; that Evvy had been thinking of him, as he had been thinking of her, and that both of them had thought most about the Principal, who was again standing behind his desk, looking as if he had been in battle.

"What you did, Zach, was not treason," he said. "It was not treason because I choose not to interpret it so. In any case, there is no question of my having you put to death."

"Those close to the Principal must obey his laws more strictly than common citizens," said Zach, quoting from one of the Principal's pronouncements from his first days of attaining power.

"You sound as if you *want* to be put to death," said the Principal. "But you must know I could never harm you, no matter what you have done." He paused, then went on in the same detached tone. "Nevertheless, I can no longer trust you. And I can't have you near me without trust. What I have decided is to send you into exile. You will be given clothing, and metal, and a good mount fast enough to take you across the border in a week. You will never return. Do you understand?"

"I understand," said Zach, his throat aching.

The Principal turned to Evvy. "As for you, Evvy, I don't know what to do about you. I can't stop wanting you. I suppose I could force you to stay with me, but every time I look at you, I'll know that you love Zach and not me. I offer you the chance to go into exile with him, if that is what you want."

Evvy and Zach looked at one another, then back at the Principal.

"What about my work?" she said.

"You are not the only scientist at the Garden. But stay if you wish. If you do I will not see you again. It will be best that way for both of us."

"Stay, Evvy," said Zach. "And don't let him keep you away forever. He is a good man and you will come to love him."

"But I do love him!" she said.

Both men looked at her in astonishment.

"That is what I wanted to say to you yesterday, Will," she went on. "Before you made this horrifying decision. That I have come to love you and realized it only at the moment I saw Zach. You are so alike, the two of you, and yet so different. You are like two sides of the same metal coin, and I love the whole metal, not just one part of it." She took a deep breath and continued before either man could speak. "Now you're asking me to choose between you and I can't do it."

"You must stay with Will," Zach repeated, his voice sounding strange in his ears. "I cannot take a wife, Evvy. Years ago—"

"Yes, yes, I heard all about your vow from your mother," she said. "Well, what if you are a carrier of the woman sickness? So, probably, is Will. But it doesn't matter, I'm not susceptible, so you can't hurt me. Doesn't either of you see the answer? It's so simple. We will all be married. Marriages between two brothers and one woman are the most common type."

"But I betrayed—" said Zach.

"I can no longer trust—" said the Principal.

Both had started speaking at once, and when they stopped, Evvy went on, giving them no chance to continue.

"Don't you see what you're doing? Yes, Zach, you betrayed him, a very long time ago. But you wouldn't do it again. You wouldn't do anything to harm the Principal, ever. Would you?"

Zach shook his head, afraid to speak.

"Yet now you're preparing to commit an even greater betrayal. You're turning your back forever on everything you've worked for and everyone who loves you." She turned to the Principal. "And you, Will. You've talked to me so many times about your dreams for the District, about your intention to solve the woman sickness, to extend civilization for the benefit of the whole human race. Don't you care about these things any longer?"

"Of course I care about them!"

"Then why are you sending away the scientist who is the closest to achieving your goals? Why are you sending away the man who is your best hope for overcoming the Traders? Why are you sending away the two people who most love you and whom you most love? Will . . . Zach . . . is your pride really more important to you than everything else?"

She stopped and looked from one man to the other. Zach felt as if there were a bubble in his chest, expanding to the point of bursting. He wanted nothing more than to put out his arms and embrace Evvy and Will together, but he knew, even before Will spoke, that it was too late.

"No, Evvy," said Will. His voice was quiet and heavy with sadness. "It's not that easy. Too much has happened. You draw a lovely dream, but even a dream must be based on truth and on trust. No," he said again. He turned his back to them and walked to the window. "My decision is final."

Nine

For a long time after Zach and Evvy left the office, the Principal remained standing by the window, looking out at the wet weather. He told himself that it was over, that a chapter in the book of his life had been finished. Now he must turn his mind to other things.

As yesterday, when he had first learned the news of Zach's betrayal, he was unable to think. He felt the need for physical action, for movement and purpose, to uncloud his mind. He thought at first to go hunting, but it was raining intermittently, and besides, he wanted, above all, to be alone. The thought of explaining Zach's absence to anyone was more than he could bear at the moment.

He became aware of a low muttering sound, then felt a tug at his trouser leg. He looked down to see Napoleon, his little fox-cat, growling softly, its tail twitching in invitation to play. The dark stripes of its fur reminded him of the color of Evvy's hair, and for a moment he wanted to throw the animal out, never to have to be reminded of her again.

The baby fox-cat rolled over on its back and looked up at him with its clear green eyes. *"Mowr!"* it said, sounding exasperated. He smiled in spite of himself and knelt, then stroked the small creature on its stomach. It promptly stopped growling and licked his fingers, then began to buzz in contentment.

With a sigh, he picked up his pet and called for Robin.

"I'm going walking in the northern park," he told him. The northern park was one of several sections of the District that technically belonged to the Principal and that he often used for hunting and exercise. It was patrolled by his men and was off-limits to poachers and squatters. He could walk there, safe and alone, without fear of being disturbed by anyone.

Robin had clearly divined that something was very wrong, but he did not ask questions. "Yes, sir," he said, his eyes narrowed in a worried frown.

The Principal accepted an escort to the park; but once arrived, he left the men with his mount and set the fox-cat on the ground. It followed while he wandered, looking at the late-summer foliage, stepping close to a tree for shelter when the rain became heavy.

As he walked, he thought, though not in a logical, linear fashion. He had hoped to be able to make his mind blank, allowing his subconscious to help him sort out his difficulties and decide what he must do next; the work of the District must, after all, go on. But however hard he tried, he could not clear his head of random thoughts; even counting his breaths failed to prevent vivid scenes from coming into his memory. He remembered the day that Zach had joined his band of fighters outside the Capital in the days before they had taken control of the District; how he and five of his men, including Daniel,

then a boy, had saved Zach from as many of the President's
men, who had taken Zach for a spy and came close to beating
the life out of him. He remembered how, gradually, he and
Zach had regained the mutual trust they had always had as
boys, and how more and more he had grown to depend on
Zach and his counsel; how they had finally toppled the President in one bloody battle lasting two days; and the heady
weeks that followed, freeing the people that the President had
imprisoned, lifting the burden of confiscatory taxes, beginning
to build the foundations of a true government.

He remembered, as if it had just happened, his sense of
loss when he had heard that Zach was missing, and the anguish
when he had thought him at last buried. And remembered again
the betrayal. As he walked, the fox-cat scampered alongside
him, occasionally pouncing into the brush after some scuffling
noise, then always returning, with its concerned *"Mowr?"*
There was a break in the clouds, and the sun shone on the
vapor, creating a rainbow. The Principal sat on a fallen tree
and watched it, his hand absently stroking his pet, which had
jumped up beside him.

"It's you and me now, eh, Napoleon?" he said. In answer,
the fox-cat pressed its wet nose into his palm and began buzzing.

For five years now he had thought Zach dead. He had
accepted the loss as final; and he could accept it again. It had
been five years since he had turned to Zach for counsel; five
years since he had relaxed late in the evenings, listening to the
soothing sounds of the feathered lyre. Nothing had really
changed; he had only to accept the thought once again: that
Zach was dead to him.

The changing quality of the light told the Principal that it
was getting late. The walk had restored him, and he felt almost
himself again. He turned back to the area where he had left
his mount with the guards.

Suddenly the baby fox-cat began to emit a strange, high-
pitched howl he had not heard before. Its little tail began to
quiver and he saw, startled, that its fur was standing out all
over its body, making it appear far larger than it was.

"What is it, little one?" he asked, and then he stopped. Just ahead of him on the path stood a wiry disheveled man with a filthy twisted beard. In his hands was a thick staff. The man appeared at once menacing and uncertain.

The Principal started, involuntarily stepping back, then he moved forward again and held his ground. "Who are you?" he asked, more annoyed than angry. "What are you doing here?"

"We be doing no harm," said the man.

"Stand aside," said the Principal. "No one is allowed in this preserve. Where are the others?"

The man moved tentatively, raising his staff as if to strike the Principal, but Will's sword was in his hand. "I said stand aside."

The man lowered his staff and moved quickly. "It's soldiers!" he called, and the Principal heard murmuring and the sounds of people moving. He followed the stranger and saw a party of five: a woman, with two young boy-children; and two other men, one old and apparently blind, the other little more than a boy.

"Who are you?" he repeated. "What are you doing here?"

The man holding the staff turned and again brandished it menacingly, then the woman shrieked, "Great deena—'tis a fox-cat! The devil himself is among us!" With one hand she gathered the two small boys to herself, with the other she began rapidly to make the sign of the double spiral, over and over.

With dismay rather than anger, the Principal realized that this must be a band of Traders. Their poverty and ignorance made him feel ill. "You've no right to be on this land," he said. "How did you come here?"

"All land is God's land," said the youth, his face white with fear and defiance.

"We was sent here," said the blind man in a feeble voice. "The time of judgment is come on the Capital and all its people."

"Trader beliefs are against the law," the Principal said. He thought of calling for his men, but they would probably not hear him at this distance. Clearly, he had nothing to fear from such a frightened, ill-organized band of refugees. "Get off this land now. I won't arrest you if you go peaceably."

Still making the sign of the spiral, the woman looked to the older men for guidance. The Principal turned to look too, wondering what to do, wondering if he should have these wretched immigrants arrested, and then he was startled by a sudden shriek as if truly the devil himself had suddenly appeared in the clearing. He whirled to see the youth brandishing a knife. But clinging to the young man's arm was Napoleon, his sharp, tiny teeth locked on the boy's wrist. At almost the same moment there was a crashing in the brush, and beside him suddenly stood the two guards who had accompanied him to the preserve.

One guard quickly subdued the young man, who had thrown the fox-cat to the ground, and was moaning and holding his wrist. The other had disarmed the older man, who now looked bewildered and frightened.

"Filthy Traders," muttered Perry, the younger of the guards.

The Principal took a deep breath and let it out. "You were ordered to stand at the perimeter!" he shouted, aware that his anger was not really for the guards. "Why are you here?"

"Sorry, sir. Captain Robin ordered us to keep close behind you, sir, no matter what your orders."

Again the Principal took a deep breath. Of course Robin had done the right thing; he had sensed the mood the Principal was in. Although he had never really been in danger from these Traders, he realized that in other circumstances he might well have acted too rashly for his own safety.

He suddenly remembered the little fox-cat and turned. Napoleon was sitting in the clearing, mewling softly, licking his left forepaw, which seemed bent at an unnatural angle. He knelt and stroked the small furry head, then picked the animal up, trying not to touch the injured limb.

"Arrest these Traders," he said, fighting the incongruous feeling that he was giving the wrong order. "When we return to the Capital, see that they are questioned. Now it's getting late. Let's go."

As soon as he returned to his House, the Principal had his personal physician tend to Napoleon, whose paw had been dislocated. Then he took food and drink and shut himself away in his office, the one place in the world where he felt most comfortable. He told himself that he had only to get through this one night; then Zach and Evvy would be gone and everything would be as it was before.

It was late and the Principal had been drinking since early evening. Tomorrow he would call a meeting of his generals to discuss the war with the Traders. Tomorrow he was to make an address, now twice put off, to a gathering of young boys just taken into his service. Tomorrow Zach would go into exile, probably with Evvy, and he would never see either of them again.

On his desk lay writing leaves, thickly scrawled over with his plans. His empire. The empire that was to save the world from certain destruction. In a room fifty feet down the hall, guarded by men that he knew were not needed, Zach slept, or lay awake, preparing for his journey. And in Evvy's room . . .

The matters that had preoccupied him his whole life were far more important than anything that had happened in this office, yet all he could think about was the events of the last days, and the look on Zach's face, and on Evvy's, as he had announced what must be.

Alexander, they said, had died from drink. It was the curse and the solace of a leader, of the man who took responsibility for others. He poured more brew but didn't touch it. He should try to sleep but was reluctant to close his eyes on this, the last night that Zach and Evvy lay sleeping in rooms so near that he could call out their names and they would hear. In a round basket beside his desk the fox-cat mewled softly in its sleep, its bandaged leg resting on a cushion.

There was a sudden sound in the far corner of the room.

He started and his eyes traveled to his sword, lying sheathed beside the desk. "What is it?" he called, knowing the answer already: in that corner was the door which had not been used regularly in over five years, the door which led through a hidden corridor directly to Zach's room and was used only by Zach when he wanted private access to the Principal.

His hands clenched into fists as he watched the narrow door creak open, then Zach stood before him. His throat constricted as it had three days ago when the couriers had brought their

Trader prisoner to his office. There Zach stood now—as then— alive, his brother, the person the Principal had known the longest in his life and had loved the most, and who had betrayed him.

Zach was holding a sheaf of papers, and once again the Principal noticed how pale and gaunt he was, how sickly-looking, and wanted to go to him, to embrace him, but Zach had made that impossible. At the same time the Principal wanted to have Zach thrown into prison, to watch him suffer on the machines. "I said that I would not see you again," he said. "What are you doing here?"

"I'm not here to ask pardon," Zach said. "I know there can be none. But I must talk to you. I've been drawing up notes and making a map. Only listen to me, as if I were one of your generals, and let me tell you what I know of the Traders. If I can't do that, all of this has been for nothing."

The Principal took one deep breath and let it out. "Sit, then," he said. "And report."

When Zach had finished, it was very late. The Principal's head ached from the details. The biggest difficulty in trying to fight the Traders had been their apparent lack of formal structure, and now he had the key to their organization. The town where Zach had been held seemed to be the center of the empire, and with the aid of the map, it should be possible to find it and destroy it. Overcoming the enemy would not be easy, but with this new information he would able, at least, to start.

"This is everything I know," said Zach. "If I find out anything else that may be of help, I will try to send word to you."

"You're not returning to the Trader empire?"

Zach shook his head. "I don't know. I will go where I must and do what I can to help you fight them. It's our shared purpose, and it's what's left." He sighed, then rose. He seemed about to turn away, but still stood there. "Will," he said finally, "I want you to know I am sorry. When it happened, I felt I had no more choice than you have now. I would not change what I did, but I . . . might have done it differently. When I was making my way back here, I was not thinking of the Traders, I was not thinking of Evvy, I was thinking of you. It may be hard for you to hear this, and impossible to understand it, but it is the truth. I know it doesn't change anything."

The Principal looked up at Zach, meeting his eyes for the first time since this discussion had begun. He wanted to offer him something to eat, something to drink, but knew that he did not dare. "Get some sleep, brother," he said. "You'll need your strength tomorrow." He rose then and grasped Zach's hand as he would any of the general's. "Good night."

Ten

Zach looked at the bundles he had packed. On the Principal's orders Robin had given him a leather vest and breeches, piles of soft cotton tunics and trousers, and a thick cloak made of new-wool. There were blankets and drinking skins, enough metal for a family to live a year in the Capital, a bow and arrows, a short sword from the museum collections, and a sharp, well-balanced knife. He glanced about the room, not wanting to leave it, aware that he would never see it again, and his eyes came to rest on the feathered lyre, still hanging on the wall. He was hesitant to take it; he felt that it now belonged to the Principal, given to him forever on the day Zach had left it by the ruined campsite.

Of course, Will couldn't play, and probably wouldn't even want it, as a painful reminder of what had happened. He slipped it off its peg, then sat in the chair by the bed and began awkwardly to attach and tune a set of strings. His hands were no longer as flexible as they had once been; in spite of Jonna's arts, the broken fingers had not set quite properly, and he had been out of practice for many years. He began to pluck the strings, playing a song that had been a favorite of his and Will's. He had first learned it in the days just before the final assault on the Capital when Will, Zach, and a handful of the Principal's men had been hiding out in the long underground tunnels that radiated from the Capital like the anchoring strands on a spider's web. At first he could not make the strings respond the way he wanted them to, but his fingers soon remembered what to do. The melancholy tone filled the room and seemed to fill Zach's body too, with an aching sadness and regret for all that had been and all that would never be.

In a very few hours it would be dawn, and time to go. After leaving the Principal he had bathed and dressed for the journey, knowing that sleep would be impossible for what remained of the night. The flickering shadows cast by a single fish-oil lamp seemed to move in rhythm to the music.

He was startled by a sound and looked up, his hands still on the strings. His guard put his head just inside the door, blinking sleepily. "You have a visitor," he said.

Zach straightened in the chair. No doubt Will had last-minute questions about the Traders. The door swung open, and Evvy entered.

"I couldn't sleep," she said. "And then I heard you playing. Please don't stop."

Zach stared at her. His fingers still moved over the strings, but his hands were suddenly shaking so violently that he produced a jumbled discord.

"You mustn't come in here," he said.

She didn't answer. He saw that she too was trembling. She remained just inside the doorway. The guard shrugged and left, closing the door.

He set the lyre on the bed. For what seemed many minutes, but was probably only a moment or two, they continued to look at each other. She was wearing the same light blue tunic and trousers she had worn that morning, and her hair was pulled into a knot on the back of her head, making her appear very much a grown woman; yet somehow this new maturity made Zach realize how very young she was still. Her face was as pale as he remembered it that first day at her parents' house all these years ago, and he felt as if her eyes were piercing his heart. At last he looked away. "Ah, Evvy," he said. He heard her soft footsteps approaching.

"Zach, we must talk," she said.

He couldn't think what to say. He looked up to see her standing before him, looking as frightened as he felt. "You're making a terrible mistake," she said. "Both of you."

"There is no choice for either of us."

Evvy sat at the end of the bed and looked down at her feet. Her right hand was turning a dilapidated bracelet on her left wrist, and he realized with a jolt that it was the feather bracelet he had once made for her. At last she spoke. "I know him, Zach. He doesn't really want to send you away. You mustn't let him do it."

"It is his decision," Zach said. "He is the Principal." He sat a moment more in silence, then stood and walked to the window. It had begun to rain, and he could see nothing beyond the glass but blurred points of light.

"During all these years I've thought of you," she said then. "I've remembered everything that happened when we were together, and wondered what caused you to do what you did."

"You know the Principal's reputation," said Zach.

"He told me himself," she said. "But you knew it too, before you took me from my family. Zach . . . when we were together you used to protect me, by keeping the truth to yourself. There's no need to do that now."

Zach sighed. "Ah, Evvy. When Will sent me to fetch you, I had never done such a thing for him before. I had always hated his dealings with young girls. It was the only important thing we ever disagreed on. He asked me to do it, just that once, because I was the only person he could trust. I refused for several weeks. Finally he promised that if I agreed, it would be the last time. The last time he would ask me such a thing, the last time he would buy a girl. I shouldn't have, but I finally agreed. Then, when I came to know you, it seemed that all that mattered was to see you safe. I couldn't bear the thought of what might happen if I took you to him."

She was silent for several seconds. When she spoke again her voice shook. "This has always been between you."

"Since we were boys." said Zach.

"And it was the cause of the trouble between him and the Mistress, wasn't it? I've wondered about that so often. I always

assumed it was because of something he did in the Garden
before he went away, that he must have taken one of the women
or girls, without obeying the laws for mate selection. Was that
it?"

"That's what he thinks," said Zach. "That's what she let
him think."

"Then what was it?" Evvy rose from the bed and came over
to the window. She put her hand on Zach's arm. He started
and drew back, wondering how much more to tell her.

"He was . . . was and is . . . the most brilliant child the Garden had ever produced," Zach finally said. "He was able to
read almost before he could walk. He was the ultimate product
of what our mother had tried to do. His father was selected
very carefully, much more so than mine. She loved my father,
but he died soon after they coupled." He paused, aware that
his words were wandering. He thought a moment before continuing, wanting to be certain that Evvy understood. "He was
raised as carefully as he was bred, to maximize his gifts. His
lessons were different from the rest of us, broader, more in-
tensive. It was my mother's plan that he would be the greatest
scientist the Garden had ever produced. It was her plan that
he would do in one lifetime what it might take the Garden
generations to achieve."

"But he didn't want to follow someone else's plan," said
Evvy.

Zach began to pace about the room. "He was always more
interested in the forces of history than in the work going on
in the Garden. He saw what we did there as a tool, as something
that could help to build a new world. But he wanted to be the
one to build that world." He shrugged. "I always understood
that. Our mother never did. And she never forgave him."

"I think she came to," said Evvy thoughtfully.

"Perhaps," said Zach. "In any case, what happened when
Will left was just the excuse for a final break. It had been
coming a long time. He knew it and she knew it."

"But everything he has done since has been based on the
philosophy of the Garden," she said.

"Yes," said Zach. "That's why I joined him after I too left
the Garden. That's why I've fought for him all these years,

done what he asked me without question, and . . . forgiven his dark side."

"But you have never forgiven it," said Evvy.

"What?" Zach looked up.

"You have not forgiven him, Zach. If you had, you wouldn't have taken me to the Garden five years ago, no matter how much you cared about me. Will was right about that. And you wouldn't be preparing now to turn away from everything you both believe in, unless you are still holding on to your anger at him."

Zach thought a moment, then sighed. "I don't know," he said. "You may be right. But it doesn't have any bearing on what is between us now. Evvy, you must know how important loyalty is to him. I betrayed that loyalty. It is time I kept a promise to him." He looked at the bundles he had packed, lying in a heap beside the door. Evvy continued to stand at the window, her eyes dark pools in the flickering light. "What will you do?" he asked.

"I'm not returning to the Garden," she said. "I've sent for my things."

"You can't go with me. You know that."

"I never thought to go with you," she said. She sounded angry. She raised her head and he could see tears shining in her eyes. "No matter how much I might want to, even if you wanted me, I couldn't go, because it's more important to stay here and fight. And you must stay too. How long will it be till the Traders decide to make Will a target? Zach, stay and help us fight them. You know how they think. You can recognize their leaders."

He didn't answer. He knew that she was right, as she had been the day before.

"I've come to understand something," she said then. "Something that you understand too, but have forgotten, or that your pride won't let you see. Zach, what happens to the Principal is much more important than what happens to any of us. His life is more important than pride, or love, or promises. If he should die or something should happen to him, who among his generals is strong enough to lead? And even if one of them takes over, how committed will he be to the testing project?

Only those who grew up in the Garden truly understand it."
Her face twisted in the effort not to cry, and Zach wanted to
go to her and hold her, as he had when she was a child. But
he had no comfort for her.

"Even if I felt it was right to stay, the Principal wouldn't
permit it," he said at last.

"Don't you want to stay?"

For several breaths Zach could not answer. Then he muttered, "What I want doesn't matter."

She nodded. "You and Will. I thought I knew you so well,
yet I never expected such . . . stupidity from both of you. But
I'm not going to let you do this—either of you. I'm going to
talk to him. I think I know how to make him listen to me."

Zach felt his heart turn over. "He's angry now, Evvy. When
he's in this sort of mood, he's unpredictable."

"I'm not afraid of him," she said. After a moment she added,
"I only wish you felt differently." She took a handkerchief and
wiped her eyes, then looked at him, her face achingly lovely.
"Zach," she whispered. She took a step toward the door, hesitated a moment, then approached him and took his hands.
"Since we parted five years ago, there has not been a day that
I haven't thought of you and missed you," she said. "You
opened up the world for me, you gave me a new life. No matter
what happens, I want you to know that I am grateful . . . and
that I love you."

He continued to look down at her a moment, trying to find
the words to answer, then he simply pulled her toward him.
As he held her, all the complex feelings that had begun five
years ago returned. He pressed his face to the top of her head
and wished that he could stand here forever, holding her tightly,
smelling her fragrant hair. Then he kissed her, on her forehead
and cheek, and let her go. "Good-bye, Evvy," he said.

She seemed about to speak again, then she abruptly turned
and slipped out into the corridor. Zach stood thinking a moment. He did not know what she planned, but he was certain
that whatever she said, Will would not change his mind. He
checked once again the things he had packed. When all was
ready, he walked to the window and looked out at the town

beginning to come to sleepy life. The ache of sadness and regret that had been with him since yesterday was a weight as heavy as the door which had sealed his Trader prison. He shut his eyes and remembered Evvy, soft within his arms. Then he remembered Will, talking, gesturing, scowling, laughing. No matter what he might face in exile, he was certain it would not be as painful as the knowledge that he would never see either of them again.

Eleven

The Principal sat behind his desk staring at the discolored rectangular spot on the wall where Zach's portrait had hung until early this evening, when he had pulled it down and thrown it into the fireplace. One of his hands rested on the flank of his pet fox-cat. The other was buried in his hair, pressing against the throbbing pain in his head.

He knew that he should go to his quarters and prepare for bed, but he also knew he couldn't sleep. The things that Zach had told him chased one another in his mind. He was certain that Zach had not exaggerated the fanaticism and degree of organization of the Traders, and if he were right. . . . For the first time the Principal was beginning to feel a hint of unease that perhaps he would not prevail over the Traders after all. It was true that the testing project was succeeding on a small scale, but the world was a big place, and his Capital and District only a small part of it. If he could not instill his own beliefs into this well-organized empire, what hope had the rest of the world?

He remembered again the band of Traders he had encountered that afternoon: ordinary people, like any of his own subjects, who found wild deenas and the personification of the devil easier to accept than teachings about birth control and hygiene.

He was aware that there were other enclaves like the Garden hidden elsewhere in this vast continent, and perhaps around the world. But were there other leaders like him, who had grown up knowing the truth? Had other scientists found the secret of transmission of the woman sickness? Once he had hoped that as the District grew and prospered he would be able to establish communication with other such communities; someday perhaps even to build great ships and renew links with the rest of the world. Now he hoped only to hold what he had and find some way of countering the Traders and their poisonous doctrines. He felt a sudden, intense desire to call Zach in and discuss these matters with him, then in the next instant his anger arose again, nearly choking him. On the desk the baby fox-cat shifted and turned over, emitting a sleepy growl.

Perhaps he should reconsider his decision. He knew well his own tendency to act from the anger of the moment, without giving sufficient thought to the best plan. Zach's counsel had always calmed and stabilized him, giving him time to reflect. Yet it was Zach's admission of betrayal that had brought him to this anger, more intense than any he had ever known. Still, nearly everything that Evvy had said had contained at least a germ of truth: he did not truly want to continue to rule without Zach beside him; and Zach would certainly never again betray him. He had made that clear by returning from the Trader prison, thinking that his return meant certain death. He had confirmed it by accepting the sentence of exile.

Of course, Evvy had been wrong about the most important thing, that the three of them should marry, for it was clear that Evvy and Zach loved each other. A normal triad marriage under the circumstances was out of the question: he knew his own jealousy too well. But why could he not give in to the inevitable and simply give them his blessing? That way, they would both be near and the three of them could work together on the problem which, he was beginning to realize, was beyond his powers to solve alone.

The question of succession would even be solved. Should

he die, there could be no better leader than Zach, who was well known and well liked, both among the population and among the Principal's men. Likewise, any offspring of Zach's and Evvy's would be the natural inheritor of all that he had built.

The only thing wrong with this plan was that the Principal knew he could not tolerate it, no matter how right it might be. Even the thought of Evvy going away with Zach made his stomach turn over; if she stayed it would be worse, because he would know that she was nearby, and that he could not have her.

His thoughts were interrupted by a sharp knock at the door. His immediate reaction was alarm. It was well past midnight and Robin knew better than to disturb him tonight, when he had left instructions not to be called but for the most serious emergency. He rose, taking his sword from its sheath. "Come in," he said.

The door pushed open and a slight figure stood framed in the doorway. He blinked, not believing his eyes. It was Evvy.

His mind would not work. What was she doing here? First Zach, and now her. He had given strictest orders that he would not see either of them again, under any circumstances. How had she slipped past the guards?

"Will, you must listen to me," she said, her plum-colored eyes wide, her face at once vulnerable and determined.

"Go away," he said. "Nothing you say will change my mind." He turned his back, aware that the gesture was childish. He heard the door shut and turned back. She had come into the room like a ghost. She was dressed in a pale, cream-colored blouse and skirt, in the southern fashion, and her long hair hung loose about her shoulders. Her hands trembled slightly, and he could see her chest move beneath the soft folds of her clothing as she breathed.

She looked directly at him for a moment, then sank into the armchair where she had sat yesterday, and smoothed her skirt in front of her. "I have been talking to Zach," she said. "He is as stubborn as you. Both of you know that the most important thing is to continue the work we are doing, and to defeat the Traders. And both of you are putting your quarrel first."

"It's more than a quarrel," said Will. He felt awkward, at a disadvantage. Clearly Evvy was going to have her say, unless he had her physically removed from the room. He replaced his sword in its sheath and sighed, then sat behind the desk. "I know what you feel for Zach," he said. "Don't ask me to keep him here. Go with him if you like!"

"You sound like an angry child, trying to hurt others by hurting yourself. Where is Will the Principal? The great leader whose mission is to restore civilization? If that were your true concern, you would not be sending Zach away, no matter what he had done."

He felt very tired, and a little ashamed. "What you're asking is impossible," he said. "Evvy, go. Go with Zach."

She was silent, then she took a deep breath and spoke. "He doesn't want me."

"He doesn't feel it's right to take you," he said irritably.

"He doesn't want me," she repeated, with some intensity. "He has never wanted me, not five years ago, not now. He cares about me—yes, he loves me—but as a daughter. That's all I have ever been to him or ever will be. He has never loved any woman but his wife who died all those years ago."

"Did he tell you that?"

"No, but it's true. I suppose I have known it deep down all along. The Mistress told me as much when I first came to the Garden, but I chose not to listen to her." Evvy stretched out her hands to the baby fox-cat, which had awakened and was sitting on the edge of the desk, licking its wounded paw. She took the animal and placed it in her lap, where it curled into a ball. She started to speak again, then stopped. "May I have a cup of brew?" she asked abruptly.

"Of course," he said, surprised. The things that Evvy was saying, and her manner, were bewildering. Never had she seemed so familiar with him, so sure of herself. It was as if she had been used to counseling him for years, like Zach. He poured a cup for her, and one for himself. She sipped hers, grimacing at the bitterness, and he remembered again the young girl he had talked to across a campfire all those years ago. His desire for her began to rise and he looked away.

Evvy set the cup down and sighed. "When Zach took me

from my family, I was a child. He was the first man I had ever known besides my fathers. He was kind to me in ways that my fathers were never able to be. My feelings for him grew on the trip. I think he sensed them and tried to discourage me. But I was young, and alone in the world except for him, and he became everything to me. I think that in time I would have realized that my feelings were just a child's obsession. But then he disappeared, and everything else happened."

"I saw how you looked at him when you recognized him yesterday."

"When I walked into your office and saw him there, I thought my heart had stopped. It was like seeing a dream, or a ghost come to life. But it was only that, a dream, don't you understand?"

"Are you denying that you still love him?"

"Of course not. I'll always love him. He was my first love. But Will, my feelings for him were based on a child's fantasy. They aren't the love of a women for a man. They aren't like the feelings I have for you."

Will shut his eyes tightly and took a deep breath. He could feel his anger returning. "If all this is true," he said, his eyes still closed, "then why did you turn down my proposal? Why have you never, in all these years, told me the truth?"

"At first it was because I was afraid of you. But then . . . I kept quiet because I wanted to protect Zach. I saw how you are, how unforgiving. I saw what you did to the guard at your camp, and to Daniel. I didn't want that to happen to Zach, or to his memory." She paused, took another sip of brew, then continued. "I turned down your proposal for the same reason. To protect Zach. I've wanted to be near you, close to you, so many times, but I've always been afraid that I would give away the truth."

He looked at her face for a hint that she was lying, but her eyes were as open and clear as ever. "You're not going with him, then."

"Haven't you heard anything I've said? Will, I want to be with you."

He was bewildered. "Are you saying that you want to marry me?"

She nodded. "When I proposed a triad marriage, it was because I was frightened of losing either of you. I thought it was the only way we could stay together. I realize now that it wouldn't work. And I realize now . . . as I realized for the first time yesterday, that I want to be your wife."

"Alone."

"Yes. We belong together."

"And what about Zach? Where does he belong?"

"At your side, where he has always been, where you want him to be."

He stood and began to pace. The anger had settled in and he felt it, like a pressure, building in his chest and behind his eyes. He stopped and stood a moment at the far corner of the room, wanting to get away from her, knowing that when he turned she would be sitting there still. "What you are saying," he said, his voice steady, "is that you would marry me to preserve the work in the Garden. To save Zach."

"In part yes," she said. "But most of all because I love you. As a woman loves a man."

He wanted to believe her, but the anger would not let him. The slow, deep breaths he was taking seemed only to intensify his rage.

When he didn't answer, she lowered her eyes and stroked the baby fox-cat. Then she picked it up and gently set it on the desk. She rose from the chair and came toward him, her hands open in appeal. "Will, I love you. Don't you want me now?"

He took another deep breath and held it, but it did no good. He was so angry he was almost dizzy. And he was frightened too, as the ghost of something he had thought was long buried began to stir in him. "Don't do this," he said. "Leave me, Evvy. Go away now."

She didn't answer. Her hands were still stretched out before her. His jealousy and anger filled his heart, his mind, until there was no room for any other thought or consideration. He took her wrists and gripped them tightly, till she cried out. Then he took her by the shoulders and began to shake her, hating her, hating himself, unable to stop. She twisted and tried to pull away, but he held her tighter. "I know how you feel about him!" he said. "How can I believe you? What are you trying to do to me?"

"I'm trying to show you the truth!" she shouted. "Stop it, Will! Stop what you're doing and look at me! Look into your own feelings!"

He continued to shake her. He wanted to throw her across the room. Through the sound of blood pounding in his ears, he heard the high-pitched howl of a distressed fox-cat, and nearly stumbled as Napoleon bit into his trouser leg and began to pull. Evvy suddenly pulled one hand free and struck him across the face. "Stop it!" she cried.

Without thought he slapped her once, hard, then suddenly came to himself and let her go, feeling weak and ashamed. She stumbled, her face paler than before, but she didn't move away from him. He didn't know what to think, what to do. "Leave me, Evvy," he said. "Too much has happened. Too much harm has been done already."

"Then it's time to stop it. Now. Tonight."

He wiped his forehead with the back of his hand and took a deep breath. "What about Zach?"

"He feels he has to go, to atone for his betrayal. No matter how you feel, for the sake of the future, you mustn't let him do it. He is the only man who truly understands the Traders. Suppose their leaders come into the Capital? Who would know them but Zach? Please . . . even if you send me away, you must keep him here."

"If I don't? Do you still want me?"

She looked at the floor and hugged her arms around her. He held his breath, waiting for her answer. At last she looked up, her eyes rimmed with tears. "I love you," she said. "I think I have for a very long time. You have always stirred something in me that I've never felt with anyone else, not even Zach, not even today. I want you to touch me, but in love, not anger."

A part of him wanted to turn away, but another part wanted her more than anything he had wanted in his life. All the feelings of the past years welled up in him, the anguish at losing Zach, the hurt, the anger at the betrayal, and most of all his desire for Evvy.

She reached out her hand and touched his.

A pale hint of dawn showed outside the window, though smoking fish-oil lamps still cast shadows throughout the room. He opened his eyes and turned to see her lying beside him on the couch. Her eyes were open, and she looked sleepy and peaceful. Her pupils were so wide they almost obscured the startling color of her eyes. He stroked her back, her warm skin smooth under his fingers. Never in his life had he felt so close to another person.

He wanted to speak, but didn't know where to begin. She put a finger to his lips and said, "Shh. This is the truth, Will. The only truth."

He looked at her in wonder. "Why weren't you afraid of me?"

"Because I know you love me. Because we are meant to be together."

"What about the Garden?"

"Daughters of the Garden can marry, as you know. I think that Katha will not approve, but I can persuade the other elder women to agree. It will, in a way, be seen as a triumph for the Garden, for us to be united. It will be a formal declaration that our interests are the same."

"Ah, Evvy," he said. "It has always been so hard for me to know the right thing to do. How could I ever have ruled without Zach? How could I continue without both of you?" He stretched and yawned, then looked at the light beginning to stream in through the window. He stroked her shoulder, then sat up and pulled his clothes from the tangled pile at the foot of the couch where Napoleon was sleeping. When he had dressed, he leaned down and kissed her, on the forehead, the eyes, the lips. She grasped his hand and smiled.

He stood looking at her, scarcely believing that she was here. "I think," he said, "that if Zach had brought you to me five years ago, I would not have seen you as who you are. You would have been just another of the young girls I thought

I needed." He squeezed her hand and smiled sheepishly. "It appears now that my brother did the right thing after all."

Then he turned and without another word walked to the corner of his office and through the narrow door that led to Zach's room.

MORE FROM QUESTAR®...
THE BEST IN SCIENCE FICTION AND FANTASY

___**FORBIDDEN WORLD** *(E20-017, $2.95, U.S.A.)*
by David R. Bischoff and Ted White *(E20-018, $3.75, Canada)*
This is a novel about a distant world designed as a social experiment. Forbidden World recreates regency London, Rome in the time of the Caesars, and a matriarchal agrarian community in a distant part of space—with devastating results!

___**THE HELMSMAN** *(E20-027, $2.95, U.S.A.)*
by Merl Baldwin *(E20-026, $3.75, Canada)*
A first novel that traces the rise of Wilf Brim, a brash young starship cadet and son of poor miners, as he tries to break the ranks of the aristocratic officers who make up the Imperial Fleet—and avenge the Cloud League's slaughter of his family.

___**THE HAMMER AND THE HORN** *(E20-028, $2.95, U.S.A.)*
by Michael Jan Friedman *(E20-029, $3.75, Canada)*
Taking its inspiration from Norse mythology, this first novel tells the story of Vidar, who fled Asgard for Earth after Ragnarok, but who now must return to battle in order to save both worlds from destruction.

In Outer Space!

___**WHEN WORLDS COLLIDE**
*by Philip Wylie
and Edwin Balmer* (E30-539, $2.75)
When the extinction of Earth is near, scientists build rocket ships to evacuate a chosen few to a new planet. But the secret leaks out and touches off a savage struggle among the world's most powerful men for the million-to-one-chance of survival.

___**AFTER WORLDS COLLIDE**
*by Philip Wylie
and Edwin Balmer* (E30-383, $2.75)
When the group of survivors from Earth landed on Bronson Beta, they expected absolute desolation. But the Earth people found a breathtakingly beautiful city encased in a huge metal bubble, filled with food for a lifetime but with no trace either of life—or death. Then the humans learned that they were not alone on Bronson Beta . . .